SECRET OF THE SINISTER SIX

AVAILABLE NOW

X-Men/Doctor Doom: The Chaos Engine Book 1
X-Men/Magneto: The Chaos Engine Book 2
X-Men/The Red Skull: The Chaos Engine Book 3
By Steven A. Roman

The Science of the X-Men
By Link Yaco and Karen Haber

X-Men: Shadows of the Past
By Michael Jan Friedman

X-Men: The Legacy Quest Book 1
X-Men: The Legacy Quest Book 2
X-Men: The Legacy Quest Book 3
By Steve Lyons

SPIDER-MAN

SECRET OF THE SINISTER SIX

by
ADAM-TROY CASTRO

INTERIOR ILLUSTRATIONS BY
MIKE ZECK

MARVEL

ibooks
new york
www.ibooksinc.net

bp books inc
New York

If you purchased this book without a cover you should be aware that this book is stolen property. It was reported as "unsold and destroyed" to the publisher and neither the author nor the publisher has received any payment for this "stripped book."

Special thanks to Mike Thomas, Mike Stewart, Bob Greenberger,
and Bobbie Chase

SPIDER-MAN: SECRET OF THE SINISTER SIX

A BP Books, Inc. Book
An ibooks, inc. Book

PRINTING HISTORY
BP Books, Inc. hard cover edition / March 2002
BP Books, Inc. mass market edition / March 2003

All rights reserved.
Copyright © 2002 Marvel Characters, Inc.
Edited by Dwight Jon Zimmerman.
Cover art by Mike Zeck
Cover design by Mike Rivilis

This book may not be reproduced in whole or in part,
by mimeograph or any other means, without permission.
For information, please write: BP Books, Inc.
24 West 25th Street, New York, New York 10010

The BP Books World Wide Website is
http://www.ibooksinc.com

ISBN 0-7434-5832-X

PRINTED IN THE UNITED STATES OF AMERICA

10 9 8 7 6 5 4 3 2 1

To Joe Siclari and Edie Stern

AUTHOR'S NOTE

The lag between the writing of this novel, and its publication, has led to tremendous differences between the status of Peter Parker's life as depicted in this novel and the current state of affairs as it appears in the regularly-published comic books.

Therefore, those of you who like to keep track of continuity should keep in mind that this book, and its predecessors, take place in the short period between the death of Peter's clone Ben Reilly, and Norman Osborn's villainous takeover of the *Daily Bugle*. During this blip in Marvel history, Peter's Aunt May was still believed dead. Mary Jane Watson-Parker was a sporadically-employed model and actress best known for her parts in soap operas and B-Movies. Spider-Man may have been distrusted by the authorities, but he still enjoyed something close to public acceptance on his better days. He was still a reserve member of the super hero team known as the Avengers. So was his former (and, alas for those who believe in super-villain rehabilitation, future) enemy, the Sandman. The relations between Dr. Octopus and the rest of the Sinister Six were strained, but not yet plagued by the open vendetta they would someday share. Quentin Beck, aka Mysterio, had not yet been diagnosed with his brain tumor, nor had he begun the deadly vendetta against Daredevil that closed out his criminal career. His suicide, and the Chameleon's, were still in the future. Alert readers will no doubt notice other telltales, which may have changed drastically in the issues that followed. Who knows? By the time this advisory is printed, they might even have changed back.

Either way, I hope you enjoy this look into the not-so-distant past.

Adam-Troy Castro

PROLOGUE

The Casbah

To some, its very name bespoke mystery, intrigue, and romantic foreign adventure.

To the tall, silver-haired predator who arrived that particular night, whose shoes alone cost more than some of this place's denizens could earn in entire years of piteous begging, it was one with Mankind's other cities: an open cesspool.

Granted, in Tangiers, where not everybody had access to indoor plumbing, that may have been a more literal appraisal than most. But the tall silver-haired man saw the comparison on a philosophical level. He registered the heat that gripped the city's streets, locking in the smells as if they were creatures too rare and too precious to be permitted escape; he noted the rats scurrying out of darkened passageways; he observed the crushing poverty of the wretches huddled in the doorways, and he saw nothing romantic or exotic about this place.

He saw a sewer for people.

Another man, a philantropist perhaps, might have been disillusioned or horrified or moved to immediate political activism.

This one merely saw his treasured prejudices affirmed.

As far as Gustav Fiers was concerned, the vast majority of human beings (with but a few notable exceptions, himself included), were slope-browed, mouth-breathing vermin, with about as much intelligence, or meaningful input into their own destinies, as cattle being driven up the ramp to the slaughterhouse. He believed that most men and women lived and died leaving the world neither richer nor poorer for their passage—and that if their existences had any meaning at all, it was to provide raw materials, and occasional cannon fodder, for those like himself superior enough to rise above the common herd. Places like the Casbah pleased him by providing such a vivid illustration of these principles.

Next to that, the unpleasant smells, and the puddles of filth that ruined his thousand-dollar shoes, were minor annoyances at worst.

Gustav walked briskly, ignoring the beggars who wanted alms and the entrepreneurs who wished to offer their services. He took no notice of anybody until they pressed too close, and he was forced to raise his wolf's-head cane in warning. They always backed off. This pleased him too. Gustav was a spry and healthy septuagenarian, who had been treated with exceptional kindness by the ravages of time. Another man his age might have been beaten and robbed in some of the places he now wandered, but he had never experienced any such difficulty. The common herd instinctively knew better. He had a predator's bearing, in a world filled with sheep.

He followed a circuitous route through increasingly narrow streets and alleyways until he took a sudden right turn into a recessed little alcove he knew. There was a boy there, sitting cross-legged on a ragged piece of burlap, his filthy hands tapping a chipped wooden bowl. The youngster's eyes were white and clouded, his clothes filthy, his mouth an illustration of inadequate alternatives to twentieth-century dentistry. But he was not cattle; the smile that spread across his face, as he recognized the silver-haired man, both proved that he was not blind and showed a level of streetwise understanding that many in this dungheap of a city would have done well to emulate. He said: "The American."

"Please," Gustav sniffed in distaste. "I am no American."

"Your brother says you were born in America. He says that your parents both enjoyed American citizenship. He says that your family made its fortune in America. He says that you are an American no matter how hard you try to deny it, and that your pretensions toward a past in the European aristocracy demonstate a pathetic need to justify unwarranted feelings of superiority."

Gustav cocked his head in amusement. "Isn't my brother the same man who always says we can choose our own countries?"

"Your brother says he chooses his own borders. This is not the same thing."

"Ahhhh. And assuming I do not wish to spend the rest of this lovely evening parsing my brother's addlepated political philosophies with a penniless ragamuffin whose future has already been gnawed to the bone by circumstance, where may I find the man himself?"

"He is across the street," the boy said. "His crosshairs have written death on the back of your head."

That caused Gustav no alarm whatsoever. He simply sighed with bemused affection, and said: "The poor boy always tries so hard to impress me.—Does he truly think I'll credit his willingness to pull the trigger on me, his own brother?"

The boy said: "He said to tell you that he would do just that, without hesitation, if your purpose here is to harm or exploit his master."

It galled the old man to imagine any member of his monied and aristocratic family ever willingly calling another man master. But he shook his head, and said: "Not at all. I have information his master will find most useful."

"Then turn around."

No sooner had the boy spoken the words than Gustav felt a presence filling the empty space behind him. It was not a common sensation for him; he had lived this long in large part because he was not the kind of man other men could sneak up on easily. The awareness that this time somebody had succeeded was by itself enough to put a name and a face to the culprit. But he smiled, turned, and faced his brother anyway.

It was, as always, like facing his mirror image. The two men were not twins, but they looked so alike it scarcely mattered. Both were tall and slender, with gentlemanly bearing, high foreheads, flared eyebrows, and eyes that contained ice instead of warmth. Advancing age had also granted them both matching silver hair and sunken cheekbones. They also shared expensive, if conservative, tastes in clothing; their suits were as impeccably tailored as military dress uniforms, their ties as precisely knotted as sutures. They even both affected canes with silver wolf's-head handles. Gustav's brother had only one pretentious affection that Gustav himself did not: a trenchcoat worn loose around the shoulders, like a cape. Gustav had always considered this gauche, but had never deigned to mention it.

SECRET OF THE SINISTER SIX

They were brothers, separated by some piddling difference in age, and personal philosophies so much at odds that only the ties of blood prevented them from becoming deadly enemies. Gustav Fiers was a businessman; admittedly a criminal businessman whose various enterprises had turned spilled blood to spun gold on five continents, but a businessman nevertheless. He was motivated by the accumulation of wealth for its own sake, and he measured his position in life by the growth of a personal fortune already far too great to be spent in a dozen lifetimes. He considered anybody without the ability or the ambition to accumulate similar riches a nonentity who deserved scorn for failure to master the rules of the game.

Family pride required him to make an exception of his brother, who had chosen a different path. Karl Fiers had no interest in wealth. Indeed, he disdained it. He embraced anarchy, and fought for the bloody destruction of all of Mankind's institutions, including Money, just as a matter of principle. He had spent decades assassinating kings, blowing up banks, and fomenting revolutions, in order to keep the fires of chaos building. But unlike Gustav, who had often wreaked similar havoc as an investment tactic, Karl planted his seeds just because he liked the chaos that grew from such fertile earth. He worked for any cause that would indulge him in these passions, and had spent the last several years as the loyal chief assassin of the world-famous monster that Gustav had just travelled to Tangiers to see.

It was fair to say that each brother considered the other totally misdirected. It was also fair to say that, for two men otherwise totally incapable of love, they still took pride in each others' varied accomplishments. Why not? Even monsters bow before the tug of family.

The two men clasped each others' shoulders, a gesture

that was the closest they ever came to an all-out embrace.

Karl said: "So how many corrupt millions did you make this month?"

Gustav replied, "Five."

"Ha! You're slowing down."

"Not at all. This was a time to start new projects, not reap the harvest of old ones. How many men did you kill this month?"

"Twelve. Five specified targets, seven bystanders claimed by collateral damage."

Though impressed, and to a degree proud, Gustav still pretended boredom. "I should be permitted to deduct points for your sloppiness."

"I don't see why," Karl said, reasonably enough. "That would give me a score of minus two—which cannot be achieved in the assassination game unless you also save some lives, or spawn children to count as positives. I have done neither. Besides, as you very well know, there are no innocents in war."

"Or in capitalism," Gustav replied, a fond reference to a certain African village he'd recently ordered exterminated as the easiest route toward local mineral rights. "It is good to see you, brother. Will you dine with me later?"

"If my master doesn't order your death, I would be pleased to. I have just the place in mind, too."

"Make reservations. You always have such excellent judgment. Meanwhile . . . Malik?"

And Karl's eyes darkened, just enough to show the murderous impulses that always roiled beneath. "I warn you, brother . . . do not call him that to his face. Not if you wish to live. He has forever rejected the name Alfred Malik. Formerly, henceforth and forever, he is only the Red Skull."

* * *

Granted the degree of his brother's somewhat excessive loyalty to the colorful terrorist in question, Gustav Fiers refrained from saying the first thing that came to mind, which was: Oh, please.

The genuine Red Skull had been a common busboy by the name of Johann Schmidt, chosen randomly by Adolf Hitler himself to be reinvented as the human embodiment of the terror that his regime was intent on inflicting upon all conquered nations. Fitted with a realistic death's-head mask that he was never seen without, Schmidt had proven even more formidable than his mad sponsor had dreamed, gaining in power, influence, and ambition until he became one of the most feared figures of the Second World War.

Gustav Fiers, an investor in several illegal (and indeed, for an expatriate American, downright treasonous) business ventures that had proven invaluable for the Skull's worldwide spy network, had enjoyed an amicable working relationship with the fellow. He had provided the Skull with weaponry, intelligence, and even transportation and discreet medical services on a number of occasions. He had aided the Skull in the elimination of several human nuisances. He hadn't shared the Skull's abhorrent political or racial philosophies enough to act on them himself. He had more than his own share of prejudices, but he also believed that moral principles of any kind were a barrier to the needs of profit. Even so, he had developed a strong respect for the man, which the Skull had, in his own common way, reciprocated.

The Red Skull born Johann Schmidt had vanished at war's end. Nobody had known whether he was alive or dead, still active or in hiding.

That had been decades ago.

The world espionage community, which should have

known better, had unaccountably accepted this newly emergent Red Skull, this pretender born Alfred Malik, to be the same man. But he wasn't. He was just a second-rate communist agitator with a lookalike mask who was intent on riding the original Skull's fearsome reputation to a similar position of power. Oh, he was still a dangerous man, and one too formidable to risk underestimating. But the depth of his vision was best measured by the fact that he'd stolen an identity forged on the political extreme completely opposed to his own. That, alone should have spoiled the disguise for Malik with anybody intelligent enough to pay basic attention. But then, Gustav supposed, the world espionage community was too entrenched in its own game of musical backstabbing to reject comrades incapable of remaining loyal to their own causes. In any event, Gustav was one of the few people outside Malik's organization who knew this new Red Skull to be the fraud that he was.

Facing this new Red Skull in the man's tastelessly appointed office—a nightmare tapestry of ferns, oriental rugs, incense, and arched doorways with bead curtains—Gustav could only think: I knew the Red Skull. I worked with the Red Skull. The Red Skull was a valued business associate of mine. And you, my dear Malik, are no Red Skull.

Gustav did not express his scorn out loud, but contented himself instead with perfecting the bored quality of his gaze. He sat in the appallingly uncomfortable armchair the faux-Skull reserved for guests and supplicants and simply stared at the man, saying nothing until Karl had finished obsequiously backing from the room. He then suffered another unconscionable delay as the faux-Skull attempted to intimidate him with the ruthlessness of the commands he barked into his desk phone. The faux-Skull fitted a French cigarette into a tapered holder, took a deep drag, and said: "You are looking healthy, my old friend. Someday I must ask you the secret you and your brother share, for so ably bearing the weight of your years."

"It is called superior breeding, Malik. A trait you must find as foreign as originality."

If the faux-Skull took offense at the reminder that his disguise had been originated by another, he hid his annoyance well. "Your brother says that your parents are both still alive. Given your own advanced age, I am impressed."

"You should be." Both elder Fiers were indeed still alive, several years into their second century. However, endangered by the activities of their sons, they now lived under assumed names in a heavily armed compound somewhere in Thailand. There was little hardship involved. Extraordinarily wealthy themselves, and still actively investing, they lived in sybaritic luxury, unknowingly functioning as living savings accounts, ripe for assassination the second Karl or Gustav decided they needed to inherit. Gustav made a mental note to check today's stock listings to determine whether now would be the most profitable time, and then changed the subject. "I say, the explosives I helped you obtain for your Capetown operation were satisfactory, were they not?"

"Yes." The faux-Skull exhaled a cloud of smoke. "And the Soviet military aircraft, and the Israeli reactor plans. You have always provided most worthwhile merchandise, at a fair price. And your brother Karl has always proved just as reliable in his services as assassin. Did I tell you that I now affectionately call him the Finisher? He—"

Gustav broke in before the pretender could launch into some favorite terrorism anecdote. "I did not come here to engage in your puerile version of small talk. This was a business visit."

"Oh? Is my account not up-to-date?"

"Your payments have always arrived on time, and in the proper denominations. No, it is not that."

"Then why inquire about my satisfaction? Can you truly believe our relationship permits you to call in favors?"

Gustav was rapidly running out of patience. "We do not do favors, you and I. Not for each other, and not for anybody else. No. I asked because I wish to remind you that I offer trustworthy goods—and I am here to render a valuable service indeed."

"Tell me what it is," the faux-Skull demanded, "and I will tell you whether the Red Skull deigns to buy."

It was the word "deigns" that finally aroused Gustav's anger. He rose to his feet, and declared: "Let me make one thing clear to you . . . Malik. I have no respect for you. I believe you are operating way out of your league. I believe that you have little future in this line of endeavor. I also believe that if you somehow manage to continue avoiding the authorities you bait with this ridiculous, impudent masquerade of yours, you will still come to a bad end . . . because your predecessor, the genuine Red Skull, shall not take kindly to your imposture when he returns."

The faux-Skull's grin was like an unhealed wound. "If he returns. I doubt I have much to worry about, there. He is as dead as Cain."

"If you truly place your faith in that," Gustav sneered, "then you are not only a fool, but a damned fool."

The faux-Skull placed his gloved palms against his desk and slowly, imperiously, rose to his feet. "I should order your death at the hands of your beloved brother."

"Oh?"

"He would do it if I commanded him. Without hesitation."

"Indeed he would," Gustav conceded. "Utterly without

hesitation. But without resentment, as well? Would even you actually be short-sighted enough to plant a simmering need for vengeance in the heart of your most deadly assassin?"

The two men were now facing each other nose to nose across the mahogany desktop—or at least (Gustav reflected later) as close to that condition as they could get, as the faux-Skull wore only a noseless death's-head mask.

The silence between them was pregnant with hatred, scorn, and murder.

The real Red Skull, faced with such insults, would have struck Gustav dead with his own hands, damning the consequences in lieu of the immediate satisfaction his rage demanded. The faux-Skull, perhaps intimidated and perhaps merely keeping his options open, sat back down and spoke in a diplomatic voice that betrayed no sign of his previous anger: "We fence over imagined slights when there's still mutual benefit in our association. It is counter-productive. So tell me, my friend: why did you come here? What is it you're proposing to sell?"

Gustav did not sit. He reached into his jacket pocket, removed a cigar, bit off the tip, spat it out, then lit the tip and puffed away for several seconds, both calming himself and re-establishing his own control of this situation. After several seconds he spoke in a voice that, like the faux-Skull's, betrayed no sign of their strong mutual emnity. "You have recently recruited some new field agents; a married American couple who go by the names of Richard and Mary Parker."

The faux-Skull blinked in surprise. "Yes. A truly appalling pair of traitors. They hate each other with a delightfully murderous passion. The work they do for me displaces the aggression they would otherwise almost certainly channel toward killing each other."

"And they have already shown their capabilities by performing certain small tasks for you, am I correct?"

"Courier work," the faux-Skull said dismissively. "Minor intelligence gathering. Nothing critical. Nothing involving wetwork. But all well accomplished. If they continue to work out, I intend to promote them to positions of higher authority at the earliest appropriate opportunity."

Gustav blew a smoke ring. "I had the same opinion of them, once."

"Oh? You know them?"

"I thought I did. When they worked for me, on my Croesus operation."

The faux-Skull leaned forward, sudden suspicion in his eyes. "But your Croesus operation failed."

"Indeed. It did."

"Were they less than fully efficient?"

"They were very efficient indeed . . . at being undercover agents of the United States of America."

"No!" the faux-Skull grimaced.

"Yes," Gustav said. "Together with the rest of their team, recruited from several western powers, they destroyed Croesus, seized my profits, and came dangerously close to apprehending me as well. I saw enough of their affection at that time to know that this mutual hatred they now pretend to feel for each other is absolutely as counterfeit as their past pretended loyalty to me, or their current pretended allegiance to you. They are not traitors to their country at all. They love it unconditionally, much as they love each other. And if you do not take immediate steps to eliminate them now, preferably in some manner that would cast serious aspersions on their integrity, and therefore give their superiors in Washington reason to disbelieve any information that they might have already gathered . . . well. In that case, Malik, I can promise that your inevitable downfall will come sooner rather than later."

The faux-Skull was on his feet again, that small percentage of his normal skin color which showed at his collar-line now almost as scarlet as his mask. "I will kill them. I will kill them and then I will kill everybody in their families."

Gustav held up a finger. "Excuse me," he said. "I provided this information for a price. You may kill the Parkers. You may disgrace them. You may do anything you wish with them. Indeed, I would be very pleased if you tasked my dear brother with the job."

"I intend to."

"But as partial payment for providing this crucial information, I do require you to limit your vengeance to Richard and Mary alone. I myself reserve exclusive right to plan future vengeance against their loved ones. Specifically, any extant offspring."

The faux-Skull cocked his grotesquely-masked head, and regarded Gustav more closely. "Why?"

"Because I do not war on children."

"Scruples, Gustav? For one such as you?"

"Hardly," Gustav said. "Standards. I have always played the glorious game of Revenge at my own pace. When striking against the families of my enemies, I am more than willing to wait a few years for their offspring to reach the age of maturity. That way, when I ruin their lives, they can fully appreciate the magnitude of my revenge. Even resist, insofar as they can. I find the hunt far more sporting that way."

The faux-Skull was incredulous. "But you are already a man in your seventies. Can you truly be so certain that you'll live long enough to pursue a vendetta against enemies who are only children now?"

"As I said: superior breeding. You worry about killing the senior Parkers. Leave the next generation to me."

The faux-Skull drummed his fingers against the desktop, brooding. "Very well. I suppose I can sacrifice that particular pleasure.—But you had said 'partial' payment. What else do you request?"

"To illustrate graphically just how much I value their lives," Gustav Fiers said, "the princely sum of one American dollar."

The faux-Skull spent exactly one second digesting that. Then the grotesque smile spread across his face again—and he threw back his head and laughed. He was a terrorist, and a mass-murderer, and a monster in the shape of a man. He was a human obscenity who profaned the earth with every step. But he did absolutely appreciate a good jest. And Gustav Fiers had just provided him with one of the best he had ever heard.

He even provided his own follow-up line: "Do you have change for a five?"

Several days later, Richard and Mary Parker died in a plane crash arranged by Karl Fiers, in his role as the Finisher. They were found surrounded by manufactured evidence that seemed to implicate them in the genuine theft of United States classified documents. Malik made sure that the news was leaked to the papers, rendering them posthumously infamous as the worst alleged traitors since Ethel and Julius Rosenberg.

That much happened a little more than twenty years ago.

In the next few years, the following important things also took place.

Gustav Fiers, investor in chaos, continued to make obscene profits investing in chaos throughout the world. His various enterprises contributed to wars, revolutions, biological and ecological catastrophes, and human suffering in dozens of countries. He remained free despite the best efforts of international law-enforcement agencies to bring him to justice. Well into his eighties now, he even picked up a brand-new alias that perfectly communicated his image of himself: the Gentleman.

He also acquired, and began to train, a silent, diminutive young girl named Pity, who had been born with certain gifts that would render her invaluable as an assassin. Using the most advanced mind-controlled techniques extant, the Gentleman conditioned her from early childhood to obey his every word. This left her little will of her own, and an intact conscience so she could be forever tormented by the atrocities she was made to commit at his command.

Peter Parker, son of the disgraced Richard and Mary, grew up in Forest Hills, Queens, raised by his kindly Uncle Ben and Aunt May. None of them suspected that the daily doings of their lives were regularly reported to the Gentleman, in preparation for the day when they would all be punished for what Peter's mother and father had done.

The unseen threat hung over Peter's entire life like a death sentence.

He never would have known he was doomed to an early death, until the moment it came to claim him.

Then everything changed.

When Peter was 15, the Gentleman received word that something astounding had happened. The boy had been bitten by, of all things, a radioactive spider. This had not killed him. Instead, through some bizarre, one-in-a-billion miracle of biological alchemy, it transformed him into a superstrong, fantastically agile, wall-crawling marvel of nature who called himself Spider-Man. Supplementing his powers with a home-brewed web fluid, and learning from bitter experience that with great power comes great responsibility, he became a part-time super hero, fighting evil men with names like Doctor Octopus, Mysterio, the Vulture, Electro, and the Chameleon.

The Gentleman, who found this fascinating as well as pathetic—surely an adequate mind would have found far more profitable ways to employ such a gift—decided to let the situation develop. He had ordered the observers who'd brought him this information executed to keep the secret safe. And he continued to watch, taking deep pleasure in the many ironies that began to overtake the young man's life.

That turned out to be a mistake.

It was evening, in the quiet book-lined study where Gustav Fiers sometimes retired to contemplate the many accomplishments of his life.

The room was a treasure-trove, filled with forgotten folios, one-of-a-kind first editions, and volumes so rare that even the world's greatest savants had no clue they existed. They included lost plays by Aristophanes, the long-lost director's cut of the silent movie classic known as *Greed*, the journal of certain shocking explorations undertaken and later suppressed by Sir Richard Burton, and a slightly singed manuscript for the presumed-destroyed first draft of Stephenson's *Dr. Jekyll and Mr. Hyde*. He even had the manuscript a young Ernest Hemingway had flung into the ocean, in the vainglorious belief that all writers should burn their earliest offspring; it was a masterpiece that easily dwarfed anything else that worthy savant had produced. A scholar could have spent lifetimes in this room, just cataloguing the solutions to great historical and scientific mysteries. Fiers, though erudite, was no scholar. Someday, he might sell a few: if whim dictated, he might burn them instead. It mattered not. He was The Gentleman. And a Gentleman, by definition, owns.

One of his many servants, a now very aged oily little man by the name of Ugarte, who the Gentleman had commanded since rescuing him from police authorities in wartime Casablanca, entered through a hidden doorway. "Forgive me, sir. I thought you might want to know."

"What?" the Gentleman asked irritably.

"It is about your brother."

"Karl?"

"Yes. He has . . . left the world of the living. Violently."

The Gentleman sat up a little straighter. He did not feel shock. Karl had been, after all, by that point a man in his eighties, working a very dangerous profession. Though time had slowed him down and forced him to rely on technological solutions for most of his assassinations, the risks would have had to catch up with him eventually. No, he was not shocked; but the news still hit him hard. After all, now that their sister had finally succumbed to the encephalitis that had kept her bedridden all these years, and their parents had been . . . well, turned in for their cash value, for lack of a better phrase . . . Karl had been the only person on the face of the planet for whom Gustav felt any emotion even approaching love. He felt the void. "How?"

Ugarte swallowed. "He had been . . . tasked to eliminate somebody who was harassing his long-time employer. He used the guided missile array in the back of his limousine."

The Gentleman nodded. As the Finisher, Karl had enjoyed a number of successes with such devices. "And?"

"The target doubled back, leading the guided missile back to its source."

"Impossible!"

Ugarte shrugged apologetically. "It happened. Karl was mortally wounded in the explosion."

The Gentleman still couldn't understand. "But... who could possibly outmanuever one of Karl's missiles?"

Ugarte didn't want to say the next part. He averted his eyes. He licked his lips. He avoided the Gentleman's gaze. And then he said it: "Spider-Man."

The Gentleman almost shouted: *Parker?* But Ugarte had not been trusted with that particular secret. He merely fell back and repeated: "Spider-Man? The American crimefighter?"

"As near as I can reconstruct," Ugarte said, helplessly, "he came to Tangiers to investigate the murder of the Parkers. I do not know how he got involved... but he blew up Karl and defeated the false Skull and obtained the evidence he needed to prove their innocence. It's only a matter of time before the U.S. intelligence community revises its verdict. He's... won. I'm sorry."

The blood roared in the Gentleman's ears. He felt a colossal emptiness in his belly, and an unfamiliar sick sense of loss that it took him several seconds to identify as the emotion lesser human beings experience far more frequently as grief. *How... interesting,* he thought distantly. *I actually loved somebody. I never suspected. I wonder if he felt the same way?*

Then he closed his eyes and fought his way back to rational thought. Karl. His brother and only peer. Dead. Young Parker. Who he had left alive, for the moment, on the theory that vengeance against him might be more sporting that way. Whose emergence as a self-styled crime fighter the Gentleman had observed with amusement. Whose continued existence, new abilities and all, the Gentleman had allowed. Who had, somehow, unknowingly and unwittingly, crossed an ocean to draw first blood in a war he could not even suspect.

"Karl . . . "

The irony of it was almost delicious.

But Karl was still dead.

The Gentleman grimaced, considering what he would have to do. He could, if he wished, complete his vengeance easily. Now. He could send assassins to this Spider-Man's home, to this place called Forest Hills, and he could have them eliminate not only Parker, but also his aunt, his friends, his employers, and everybody he knew. He could excise this cancer, and all the tissue surrounding it. And he could sleep well knowing that his duty had been done.

Yes. That would satisfy the needs of Blood.

But Blood was not enough, now.

The Gentleman needed Parker—Spider-Man—damned to a living hell before he died.

He needed Parker to torment himself with guilt for the loss of somebody he loved. He needed Spider-Man to condemn himself for a failure great enough to counter-balance all the petty successes of his career. He needed to destroy Peter Parker, and he needed to destroy Spider-Man, and he needed to strike a fatal blow against the city that Spider-Man called home. He needed Spider-Man to know the name of the man who had destroyed him. And he needed to make a profit doing so, not just because it was the way the Gentleman had always operated, but because the all-encompassing nature of such a victory would only torment the wall-crawler further.

An opportunity that met all of these requirements might take years to arrange.

But that was all right.

As the Chinese like to say, revenge is a dish best served cold.

And the Gentleman knew how to be very cold indeed. . . .

* * *

The Parkers were cleared. The false Skull was, as predicted, assassinated by the true one. Spider-Man continued to fight for the city of New York, honestly (if naively) believing that the murder of his parents was a closed book. He had no reason to believe otherwise. After all, Karl Fiers and Albert Malik were now both dead; as far as he knew, nobody else had ever been involved. As for the Gentleman, he bided his time, and collected his data.

More years passed.

The past seemed to recede.

Until that unbearably cold winter month that the Gentleman arrived in New York, his fresh-faced assassin Pity in tow. He was about to resume his deadly vendettas against both Peter Parker and his alter ego Spider-Man, armed with the delicious, hard-won knowledge that they were one and the same...

CHAPTER ONE

Winter in Manhattan.

The sky was the color of asphalt. A cold, bitter wind whistled down the avenues, whipping the coats of the miserable pedestrians hugging themselves as they rushed toward places of shelter. The filthy remains of the most recent snow sat piled on street corners, like islands connected by the black slush oceans that accumulated at every slight depression. Wind chill ruled the streets; even folks who preferred the cold walked facing the ground, their lips chapped, their cheeks flushed, their expressions contorted into the grimaces of people who could feel the very air around them transform into a creature with frigid, gnawing teeth.

It was an exceptionally harsh New York winter, after several mild enough to exacerbate fears of global warming. Nobody was ready for it. The streets were a mosaic of hacking coughs and runny noses and stares of pure misery. Homeless people who usually preferred the parks to the city's notoriously dangerous shelters fought each other for beds, warm alcoves, and heating grates. Tenements burned one after another from fires caused by faulty space heaters. Coffee and tea were consumed by the bucket. And weathermen kept a constant look at the skies, warning of fronts poised to turn all of this into a winter storm capable of dropping not inches but feet of snow on the city streets.

Max Dillon, strolling down 3rd Avenue on this most beautiful of all days, felt positively balmy.

He was balmy, of course—in the psychological sense. Some would have called him insane. But he was also balmy in the meteorological sense. Had be been any more balmy, he would have been giving off steam. Warmed from within, he'd dressed for weather thirty or forty degrees warmer than the actual temperature dictated: dungarees, sneakers, a long-sleeved shirt, with nothing but a light trenchcoat to function as his sole concession to the expectations of everybody required to feel the cold. Some who saw his goofy, daydreaming smile imagined that it must have been his mood alone that warmed him. And they weren't entirely wrong, but his mood enjoyed substantial support from his own version of central heating.

Dillon was a dull-looking crewcut man of average height and moderate build, possessed of the kind of face that one would assume to have been specifically designed for frustrated scowling. But today his eyes were bright; downright electric, in fact. Together with his smile, which betrayed a warmth normally alien to his personality, they made him look downright likeable—a quality he had not possessed since the accident that had befallen him on his very last day of his job as a power company lineman. That accident had somehow turned him into a human dynamo, able to harness and project the power of electricity. Since then, in his career as the super-criminal known as Electro, he'd been so very far from likeable that he actually qualified as frightening. But today people smiled at him as he passed by, as if the very sight of him warmed the heart of anybody lucky enough to pass within his sphere of radiant happiness.

It was almost enough to make him empathize with this "life is beautiful" nonsense he sometimes heard.

By the time he entered Vukcevich Florists on West 83rd, he was whistling.

He entered the normal way, through the door, which was genuinely unusual for him in regards to retail establishments. Usually, he blasted his way through the walls. The novelty felt strange, but pleasantly so. He especially appreciated the little bells that jingled to signal his arrival. They were cute. Festive, he thought.

"Be right with you," said the florist, a fortyish moustached man who resembled a gene-splice between Mark Twain and the goggle-eyed silent movie comedian named Ben Turpin. Humming, he wrapped a bouquet of long-stemmed roses for his current customer, a pudgy young man in his early twenties who seemed genuinely embarrassed to be seen making this purchase. He ran the guy's credit card, gravely wished him luck, then turned to Dillon as the pudgy young man left. "And hello to you, sir. I do hope you're enjoying this gorgeously beautiful day."

Dillon glanced out the window, at the skies the color of slate. "Beautiful?"

"But certainly, sir. It is always beautiful in my shop." The florist gestured at the multicolored bounty of nature that surrounded him on all sides.

On most other days, Dillon might have sneered. Today, he smiled in appreciation. "Good point."

"And you, my friend, are positively glowing."

"I am?" Damn, he'd been meaning to watch that.

"Of course. You are clearly a man in love."

Oh. That. Dillon's grin turned goofy. "Yeah."

"I knew it. It's like you're wearing a sign. Will it be roses? A dozen, perhaps?"

Dillon felt his cheeks burning. "Yeah. Fine."

"Two dozen would be even better, you know."

"Then three dozen," said Dillon, who was positively scarlet now.

"Do you want to fill out your card while you're waiting?"

Dillon nodded, and took the proferred pen.

Alas, he didn't have any words. It wasn't that he had no experience with women: hell, he'd even been married once, until she'd divorced him for his lack of ambition and he'd been forced to move back in with Mom. But physical affection had been difficult since the accident which had led him to his new career; there tended to be, well, too much of a spark these days. Lethally so, in some cases. And while he'd been working on his self-control in recent years, the lady he wanted to woo now, Pity, presented special problems of her very own. She was totally mute, totally withdrawn, and totally under the thumb of the creepy old man she worked for. She would have qualified as a shrinking violet if she wasn't also a superpowered ruthless international assassin. Dillon was sure he could bring her out of her shell if he could only come up with the right things to say. But he was also sure that the wrong words would drive her further away.

It was so unfair. They had so much in common, after all. They were both outsiders. They were both unappreciated. They were both sensitive. They had both spent their lives being knocked around by fate and by super heroes. If they could just get past this psychological conditioning she'd been subjected to since early childhood, and free her to act upon her heart, as Dillon was free to act upon his heart, then love, marriage, and even a couple of kids could not be far behind. Dillon was certain she'd had the same thoughts. He'd always been able to read women that way. What could he say? It was a gift he had, or imagined he had.

But he still had no idea what he was going to write.

He considered: SOME LOVELY FLOWERS FOR MY LOVELY FLOWER. He considered: FOR THE ROSE IN MY LIFE. He even considered: I WILL KILL THAT OLD CREEP FOR YOU. That would have been most romantic of all.

He settled on FROM MAX.

(Did she even know his name was Max? He wasn't sure. He'd have to subtly work it into a conversation, somehow.)

The florist returned with a double bouquet. Dillon handed the man a hundred dollar bill from his recently inflated bankroll and wondered just how long it had been since he had done something so mundane. Imagine. Paying the man. With money. He hadn't made a simple cash transaction in months—most of the time, he either stole what he wanted or had it provided to him at whatever maximum security holding cells the feds managed to stick him in. It occurred to him, briefly, to wonder why he devoted so much time and (ha, ha) energy to stealing cash when his powers had always largely freed him of the need to use it.

"Keep the change," he said.

"My," the florist chuckled. "You do have a case, don't you?—I will warn you to get these lovelies inside quickly. It's bitter cold out there."

"I'll keep them warm," Dillon promised.

This, of course, was actually what he did once he got out onto the street—generating a low-level electrical field around himself that raised the ambient temperature a good thirty degrees. He moved through the Manhattan crowds so quietly that nobody he passed had the chance to register anything but the most fleeting moment of relief.

It was midway to his destination that Dillon experienced a truly horrible thought. There were, after all, four other adult men among his current business associates. What if any of them liked Pity the same way he did? What if one of them made a move before he could?

Well, he'd incinerate whoever it was, of course. But was it a possibility?

He concentrated furiously. Okay. Forget Toomes right off. He was a zillion years old and he looked like an old Wild West hanging judge; his days as a ladies' man had probably gone out with the first incarnation of the hula hoop. Beck was also totally out of the picture. He was dashing enough, but he'd also been oddly, completely oblivious to women for as long as Dillon had known him. (Dillon had always wanted to ask him about that.) Smerdyakov, on the other hand, was a potential problem: the guy's whole shtick was looking like anybody he wanted to, which meant that being Cary Grant or Gary Cooper or Tom Cruise or any of those other pretty boys was far from beyond his capabilities. Dillon would be right to worry about Smerdyakov. But really, Octavius was the real problem. The Doc may have had the haircut of Moe from the Three Stooges, the physique of a little boy statue holding up a hamburger outside a fast-food restaurant, and the personality of the most pretentious chef ever to hold a job in Paris, but he'd also demonstrated a baffling personal magnetism that had prompted at least two women to become murderous super-villains just as a way of staying close to him. If Octavius truly intended to make a play for Pity, the competition would be fierce.

He thought about what he'd have to do, if this came down to open hostilities between himself and Octavius.

Despite his protective cocoon of warmth, he shuddered.

SECRET OF THE SINISTER SIX

Even super-villains can know fear.

There was something about this latest version of the Sinister Six that gnawed at him. Actually, that something was a someone. Pity's mysterious and very wealthy guardian, if that was the right word for it, known only as the Gentlemen. The Gentleman had brought together four members of the original team—Adrian Toomes, the high-flying Vulture, Quentin Beck, the genius of special effects known as Mysterio, Anatoly Smerdyakov, the master of disguise known as the Chameleon, Otto Octavius, who thanks to his life-like and ultra-powerful adamantium tentacles was aptly named Dr. Octopus, and himself, Electro, the master of electricity. Together with Pity and himself, the Gentleman stated that his reason for this latest grouping of the Sinister Six was to destroy Spider-Man. The Gentleman also said that if everyone followed his orders to the letter, not only would Spider-Man be destroyed, but the four super-villains would also become incredibly wealthy. So far the Gentleman had been as good as his word. Toomes, Beck, Smerdyakov, Octavius, and he had been more than amply paid for their attacks against Spider-Man.

But that didn't mean things were going smoothly within the ranks of the Sinister Six. Octavius and already threatened to kill the Gentleman. Dillon was amazed that he hadn't carried out that threat. Dillon also felt that the Gentleman wasn't telling them the whole story.

Dillon hoped that the answers wouldn't result in him losing everything and landing behind bars.

A few blocks downtown, Dillon descended to a subway station. He purchased a token—another banal transaction that brought a bemused smile to his lips—then waited until the next uptown train left the station, carrying with it the handful of commuters who had been sharing his platform.

After a quick glance at the opposite track, to determine that it was deserted as well, he leaped off the platform and onto the third rail.

For Dillon, the sensation was a lot like dipping his toes into a heated pool: warm and invigorating. He said, "Ahhhhh."

And then, still balanced on the rail but not wavering at all, he harnessed the current the same way an electric motor would and used its energy to start propelling him forward. Slowly at first, but with increasingly accelerating speed, he rode the rail into the darkened tunnel before him. He gained speed faster than the subway train had, and without the sense of resistance that anything that large conveys as is overcomes its own tendency to stay put. His passage made no sound at all but for the soft whoosh of stale air parting to allow him through.

It occured to him that he could easily catch the train that had just left and utterly destroy it, as well as everybody aboard, before it reached sanctuary at the next station only a few blocks up.

Extortion against the subway system. Interesting. A possible future project.

But not now. Now he had flowers to deliver.

Dillon surfed the rail until he spotted the signpost, an innocuous-looking patch of flourescent paint glowing against the tunnel wall. He hopped down to the tracks. A tunnel rat hissed at him; he pointed a finger at it. The air suddenly had the tang of ozone as crackling electric energy built up in Dillon's hand. Then a bolt of lightning shot out of his fingertip and hit the rat, reducing it to a mound of blackened meat. Then he walked the four steps to an alcove that required only a slight shove in the right place before it became an open doorway, leading into a narrower tunnel lit by halogen lamps.

Dillon smiled and entered.

The headquarters his employer, a nasty old guy called the Gentleman, had provided Dillon and his associates was a spacious townhouse in the upper eighties. It was luxurious, equipped with every conceivable amenity, and so carefully chosen for privacy that the Gentleman had also rented the townhouses on either side just for the sake of keeping them vacant. It even came equipped with this tunnel, a secret passage that snaked a hundred yards beneath the city streets to connect the basement to this section of subway line. The small army of illegal off-the-books workers who had labored for weeks on end just to provide Dillon and his friends with this convenience were now all dead and buried in unmarked graves. Nobody, least of all Dillon, could deny that they'd done a very good job.

Dillon passed through the long tunnel into the townhouse basement, which (despite an impressive wine cellar) was not much of an improvement over the subway track. Rather than ascend to the house proper, he climbed the steps to the enclosed rear courtyard, closing the cellar door behind him.

The fresh air invigorated him, as the main problem with secret passages to subway tunnels, however well-built, was that they tended to stink something awful.

But that was not why he took an extra-deep breath now; instead, he just needed to gather up his nerve for the next step.

Speaking his heart.

He rose off the ground and flew to a certain window on the third floor of the townhouse.

Pity's room.

The window was ajar a crack. Dillon had left it that way. He slipped the fingers of one hand beneath the window, pulled it open, and clambered inside, careful to avoid brushing his double bouquet. It was dark in the room. Not unnaturally pitch-black, as things tended to be whenever Pity was around, but a dim, oppressive dark, ruled by shadows. Dillon hesitated, then gently placed the flowers atop her made bed, making certain that the card was prominently placed.

Then somebody said: "Flowers? For me? You shouldn't have."

It was not the voice Dillon had imagined hearing from the silent Pity.

It was not even a woman's voice.

It was instead a soft and papery voice, that spoke in cultured accents—yet seemed to have been dipped in venom.

Max Dillon narrowed his eyes, turned, and took in the sight of the hated figure seated in the easy chair on the opposite end of the bedroom. The mysterious benefactor known as the Gentleman had been sitting so still that Dillon's cursory glances had utterly failed to register his presence there. That was odd, as presence was one thing that the Gentleman possessed in abundance. His face may have been as craggy and as worn as any other man in his mid-nineties, but they still bore the stamp of the handsome figure he must have been decades ago: he was tall, robust, tireless, and possessed of a pair of cruel black eyes sharp enough to pierce an enemy's heart. The most hateful thing about him was his smile, which projected the self-satisfied superiority of any man capable of reducing other human beings to catalogues of their faults and inadequacies. It was impossible for anybody to become the recepient of that smile and not feel primally violated. Dillon, who would have found that sufficient reason to despise the man, hated him all the more for the knowledge that Pity had lived her life enduring an endless series of smiles just like it.

There was something odd about the Gentleman this time. He was not dressed in his trademark tailored suit, as he'd been every other time Dillon had ever seen him. He was in a black silk bathrobe, covering pinstripe pajamas so perfectly shaped to his frame that he might have been able to get away with wearing them in public as a suit.

"What are you doing here?" Dillon snarled. "Waiting for me?"

"Not at all," the Gentleman said, with infuriating politeness. "I was resting from a long day. This is my room, after all."

"This is Pity's room."

"Not at all. With the authorities now aware that I'm in town, I have judged it unwise to remain in my prior accomodations at the Plaza."

"And where will Pity sleep?" Dillon asked, his anger rising. "In here, with you?"

"Not at all. I have toyed with the idea of telling her to take a flannel blanket down to our subway access tunnel. After all, we shouldn't leave such a potentially valuable entranceway unguarded."

The thought of Pity forced to spend long nights in that dank, freezing passageway, with only rats and cockroaches for company, was enough to make Dillon snarl again. "Do you always have to be so cruel to her? Can't you just leave her in peace for five minutes?"

The Gentleman removed a cigar from his bathrobe pocket, and sniffed it with evident pleasure, but did not light it. "She was the daughter of my enemies. And I have sworn that she will never know a moment's peace, as long as she is under my control. Of course, I have already pledged to give her to you once all the phases of this operation are completed. You may then provide her with more dignified accomodations, if you desire. But you will never succeed in freeing her soul. I promise you that."

Dillon's eyes flashed lightning. He advanced upon the old man, his face a mask of energized hatred. "I am going to kill you as soon as our business is over. You know that."

The Gentleman chuckled, betraying absolutely no fear at all. "Take a number. Rest assured that Pity shall receive your lovely gift, for all the good that will do either of you. And go tell the others that I shall be ready to brief them on the next phase in a few minutes."

Dillon didn't return downstairs until he went to his own room, removed his civvies, and donned the costume that had made him infamous: a skintight green suit with a yellow lightning-bolt pattern that formed an inverted V across his chest. He didn't particularly expect trouble, but with his previous bouyant mood now turned as bitter as a shattered dream, he felt better dressed for carnage.

Stomping downstairs, he remembered what the atmosphere in this townhouse had been like only ten days earlier, before the Gentleman arrived with Pity in tow to present the terms of his proposed operation. The guys had all been irritable and impatient and bored waiting for their proposed sponsor to show up. They had, however, also enjoyed a certain casual familiarity that manifested itself in their willingness to spend their enforced down time shooting bull, playing cards, and (in Beck's case) rotting his mind with hour after hour of cheesy sci-fi on cable. They had dressed casually and, with the possible exception of Octavius, whose major leisure-time activity seemed to be ranting to himself about his genius, lazed about like any other bunch of buddies on their day off. They may have complained about it at the time, but they'd enjoyed themselves.

Not now. Because they all still bore the bruises recently inflicted by their battle with Spider-Man, they were frustrated by the Gentleman's continued refusal to describe his master plan more than one step at a time. They knew it had to be something big, worth waiting for if they had to, but the old guy had turned out to be an arrogant, insufferable prig even by the standards of their line of work. The waiting had turned to brooding, and the boredom had turned to seething anticipation. Toomes and Beck now wore their work costumes all their waking hours—an affectation that reduced Toomes to just a grumpy old man in a bird suit and Beck to a grumbling, silent presence in an opaque goldfish-bowl helmet. As for Octavius, he had stopped removing his mightily-tentacled adamantium harness, even to sleep. He paced back and forth, muttering to himself, his metallic tentacles undulating around him like an honor guard of cobras.

Dillon himself had donned street clothes only because he'd judged it more romantic to buy Pity her roses rather than steal them. But he sympathized with the frustration the others felt. He wanted to blow up something. Anything. If not the Gentleman, then perhaps a wall-crawling busybody in a stocking mask.

As Dillon reached the bottom of the stairs, Leonardo DiCaprio edged by him, with a comment that had something to do with being the king of the world.

Dillon ignored him. "The Gentleman says he'll be right down."

The monster movie on the TV cut away to a commercial for the Frank T.J. Mackey seminar. Beck turned down the volume. The artificial light rendered his complexion, a road map of past acne scars, especially pale this week. He was never a happy man, but he looked more than ever like a man whose stomach was choosing this moment to rebel at whatever he'd had for lunch. He cleared his throat—a delightfully rheumy noise he'd been making every ten minutes this week—and rumbled: "Joy."

Toomes just look old and sour. "Reason to celebrate."

"Says he's ready to brief us on the next phase."

"That's nice of him," said Toomes. "Isn't that nice of him, Quentin?"

"Positively princelike," Beck muttered.

Rodney Dangerfield wandered by, tugging at his tie, and declaring that he got no respect, no respect at all.

The men in the room had all developed identical opinions of the Gentleman. He had pockets deep enough to pay handsomely for their services, but he was also the human equivalent of a fish left to rot beneath the passenger seat of your car. He did not improve with familiarity.

Beck had once grumpily asked the Gentleman, during one of their strategy sessions, why he went so far out of his way to be so unpleasant all the time.

The Gentleman had grinned and said, "Because it suits me."

Dillon, who had been stealing, kidnapping, murdering, and blowing things up for almost a decade now, thought that kind of attitude just plain wrong.

Pity wandered in, as always half-woman and half-wounded pout. In her usual day-to-day outfit of black tights and puffy white blouse, she looked less like a deadly international assassin than anybody Dillon had ever met; she was only a hair over five feet tall, was baby-faced enough to pass for a teenager although she was several years into her twenties, and sported a hairdo that she might have deliberately copied from the young Princess Di. She also maintained an air of emotional fragility so palpable that was next to impossible to say anything to her without worrying that it was going to make her cry. The vertical scars she bore on each cheek seemed less a memento of past battles than a reminder of abuse survived. As always, Dillon gave her his best warm smile. As always, she failed to acknowledge it; she just passed him by. This time she went to the easy chair where Toomes sat glowering at the fire, and quietly handed him a cup of Earl Grey.

Toomes, startled, flashed one of his rare unmalicious smiles. "Thank you, my dear. That was very sweet."

Dillon wanted to spew. Pity had been doting on Toomes all week long, bringing him tea, doing him favors, even listening with rapt attention as Toomes told pointless and interminable anecdotes about his misspent youth. Since Toomes hadn't ever done anything even remotely interesting with his life until turning to crime in his old age, she was probably the only person on the entire planet willing to listen to him. Dillon had originally pegged this as simple compassion on her part, until he realized that she deferred to Toomes simply because he was so old.

The Gentleman had described the hold he had on her as state-of-the-art psychological conditioning, instilled since early childhood; he had bragged that while she clearly hated him, and clearly loathed the atrocities she was forced to commit at his command, she would still rather die than consider disappointing him in any way. She had obviously seized on the elderly Toomes as a substitute authority figure, worthy of her obedience whenever her true master the Gentleman was absent.

This only deepened Dillon's hatred of the Gentleman. And gave him cause to wonder whether Toomes might be the key to freeing Pity from the man's poisonous influence.

But how to turn that key? Did Dillon dare tip Toomes to the power he held over her?

Pity exited, this time passing by Stephen King, who was busily scribbling a new story in the corner. Octavius, who was standing nearby, glared at her with obvious resentment and said: "We shouldn't discuss the Gentleman in front of her. She's his creature. She probably tells him everything we say."

"I hope she does," Dillon said. "The nasty, pucker-faced old geezer."

"I don't like that reprobate any more than you do," said the annoyed Toomes, "but I honestly wish you'd retire that word geezer. Some of us do belong to his generation, you know."

"Toomie," Dillon said, "you may be a crotchety old coot, but I would never dream of calling you a geezer."

Toomes considered that, and displayed a graveyard of unevenly-spaced teeth. "Wise of you . . . Max."

There. Toomes had called him Max. With any luck, Pity had heard.

Singer Michael Bolton ambled by, butchering a classic Beatles tune. Everybody ignored him, just as they had ignored Adam Sandler and Dan Quayle and Harlan Ellison and Tom Hanks and every other inappropriate celebrity who had passed through the room in the last few minutes.

"This is our opportunity to renegotiate," said Octavius, whose tentacles were bobbing about like frantic puppies competing for their master's attention. "If the hateful old fool is indeed finally ready to tell us the nature of the madness he's planning, then we have to present him with a united front. We have to remind him that we're more than just mindless lackeys. We have to take the control he wishes to deny us!"

"I have no problem with that," Beck said, from beneath his fishbowl helmet.

"Me neither," said Toomes. "Except that—"

Jim Carrey wandered by, performing a very theatrical double-take. Everybody ignored him except for Dillon, who had taken all he could stand of this. "What's up with Smerdyakov?"

Beck coughed. "He's been morphing faces all day. His equivalent of fidgeting, I suppose."

"He's still upset about the way his part of the plan went down last week?"

"Wouldn't you be? Defeated by a civilian?"

Dillon, who had once been defeated by a dorky physics student at Empire State University, empathized. He hopped over the back of the couch and landed in a seated position. "Well, maybe he'll feel better when we get our next installment. I—"

Pity rushed out of the kitchen, moving right past the still-glowering Octavius to a vantage point at the foot of the stairs. Her expression was as blank as ever, but her posture was alert, even apprehensive—the look of a woman always prepared for immediate action, because delays of even a second had never been tolerated. The subsequent sound of the Gentleman descending the stairs, his leisurely pace less a function of his advanced age than his imperious refusal to be seen hurrying for any reason, was almost redundant in context. The other men in the room could all see from her demeanor that she knew her master was arriving.

It was another reason to hate him, out of an ever-expanding catalogue.

When the Gentleman appeared at the bottom of the stairs, Dillon saw that he'd dressed for the meeting. He'd donned his usual elegantly-tailored black suit, and he carried his wolf's-head walking stick, clicking it against the tiled floor with every step. His smile was, as ever, venomous. "Ah! I see that you're all gathered. I trust Max told you to expect me."

"He did," Beck said drily, "but we stuck around anyway."

The Gentleman acknowledged the jest with a nod. "Then let us gather around to outline the next phase of your employment. There are profits to make. Pity, fetch me a brandy, and hurry back. You'll want to hear this too."

As the Gentleman moved to the center of the living room, and Beck used the remote to silence the TV, Octavius advanced menacingly, brandishing his tentacles like clubs. "Not just the next phase," he growled. "The entire plan."

The Gentleman was neither surprised nor intimidated. "Oh. Doctor. Do we truly need to have this tiresome discussion again? —As I stated when first presenting the terms of your employment, the plan is what I bring to this partnership. Premature disclosure leaves you free to kill me and continue on your own."

Beck removed his helmet, revealing an impatient scowl on an acne-scarred, thuglike countenance. "Maybe we ought to kill you anyway, old man. Because your plan doesn't seem to be working all that well so far."

The Gentleman chuckled at that. "You refer to the apparent failure of the Day of Terror you declared against Spider-Man? But that was not a failure at all, dear boy! You may not have killed the wall-crawler, or succeeded in ruining what little reputation he has, but those were only secondary goals, minor indeed next to the city-wide distraction that permitted Pity and Electro to steal the cannister we really wanted. Indeed, I thought you all performed your chores admirably—with the extreme exception of Anatoly, the only one of our merry band who permitted himself a humiliating defeat by a civilian."

That was a low blow; Smerdyakov had in fact had his butt royally kicked... by an actress-slash-model named Mary Jane Watson-Parker. The fact that she was evidently an unusually formidable actress-slash-model, and that she'd also been a major player in the defeat of one of Beck's recent schemes less than one week previous, scarcely mattered. Among people who fight super heroes on a daily basis, being defeated by a civilian, let alone a civilian woman, was just about the most humiliating thing that could possibly happen. It had left Smerdyakov in such a volatile mood that his teammates had been tip-toeing around the subject all week long. Even Octavius, hardly the most sensitive man on the planet, had held his tongue out of simple respect for Smerdyakov's feelings.

Now the Gentleman had gone and brought it up. Apparently, just to ratchet up the unpleasantness a notch.

Smerdyakov's latest disguise—a cadaverous-looking Marilyn Manson—faded, replaced by a featureless white mask that failed to hide the extreme anger of the man hidden beneath. "She got in a lucky shot!"

"Since I've seen your bruises, I daresay she got in a couple dozen." The Gentleman tapped his silver-handled walking stick against the floor twice for emphasis. "But no matter. Your incompetence was not enough to prevent the acquisition of the cannister."

Smerdyakov stepped forward, his mask contorting into enraged caricatures, to match the anger of the man. "You did not think me incompetent when you required me to free several of these people from the most closely guarded maximum security facilities in the country. You did not think me incompetent when you required me to obtain information none of your other operatives could. You did not think me incompetent when I pulled you out of Somalia that time.

You have always come to me for results, and you have always treated me like a dog. Well, no longer! I have damn well earned your respect, old man, and if you even think you can talk to me the same way you talk to everybody else—"

The Gentleman dismissed him with a gesture. "Very well. I withdraw the comment."

"If you think that halfhearted retreat is anywhere near enough—"

"As I said," the Gentleman continued, raising his voice to outpower the Chameleon's anger, "we will interpret your loss to the third-rate actress as a momentary lapse. And, as I said, at least we have the cannister. That was the important thing."

Toomes stirred at this second mention of the cannister. It had been kept in a state-of-the-art secure facility on Governor's Island, and the Gentleman had been willing to throw Manhattan into absolute chaos to obtain it, but he had not yet divulged the nature of its contents. "What's in it, anyway? Nerve gas?"

The Gentleman accepted his brandy from Pity. "Nothing so mundane."

"Plague virus?" Beck ventured, perhaps seizing on that as a possible explanation for the headaches that had been plaguing him all week long.

The Gentleman shook his head. "Please. Unlike some of you, I have never been malicious for the sake of being malicious. Only when it suits me. Profit has always been my primary motive."

"Yeah, but if you were into blackmailing the city—"

"I am not. Large-scale terrorism as a means of extortion never works, in my experience. There are just too many risks involved with collecting the payment. For what it's worth, the contents of the cannister are totally harmless to living things. I could break the seal in this room without any of you ever noticing—at least, not in terms of your continued robust health, physical and (as far as it goes) psychological. You would soon witness other effects, of course."

"What, then?" Toomes asked.

The Gentleman removed a cigar from his jacket pocket, clipped off the tip, lit it, and took the first deep puff. "That is still classified."

At that point, Octavius evidently decided he had taken more than enough. Moving with a speed that made the act itself almost invisible, the Doctor's adamantium arms lifted him to waist height and flew him across the room like a missile. Pincers a thousand times harder than the hardest diamond closed on the Gentleman's lapels and lifted the old man off the ground, pulling him close to Octavius until only inches separated the two scowling faces. "I will not tolerate any more of this infernal secrecy of yours!" Octavius shouted.

Darkness licked at the corners of the room. Pity leaped to the ceiling and adhered there, anger marking her usually forlorn face. Everybody else in the room froze, prepared for the free-for-all that seemed about to happen.

The Gentleman, unconcerned, glanced at Pity. "Excellent reaction time, my dear. But unnecessary. I will take care of this. You may back down. The same goes for the rest of you." His gaze flickered back toward Octavius. "You have a concern?"

"Yes! We are not your lackeys! We are your partners!"

Still unconcerned, despite his obvious discomfort, the Gentleman said: "You are my employees."

"We are more than that! You are helpless without us!"

Astonishingly, the Gentleman chuckled. "Say that again when you have managed to avoid incarceration for as many decades as myself. Or indeed, even for a few months at a time."

Octavius snarled. "You mock me?"

"No. I state a simple fact."

"If we wanted to force you to talk—"

"You would still learn nothing," the Gentleman said. "I am an old man, with not much time left on this Earth. There is little in this life still capable of frightening me. Least of all you."

The faces of Octavius and the Gentleman were practically touching now. Octavius spoke in his most dangerous tone: "You are a fool."

"Clearly not. Telling you the plan in advance would mark me as a fool." Still dangling from the Doctor's tentacles, the Gentleman raised his right hand to his lips and took another drag from his cigar. His subsequent words were all accompanied by puffs of smoke that detonated like bombs against the Doctor's face. "I understand that some of you might not approve of this condition. If you wish, you might leave my employ now, taking the five million apiece already paid and sacrificing the five million apiece I promised on completion. There is certainly no way I could stop you; ours is, after all, not the kind of contract that can be enforced in a court of law. But you would also be sacrificing the even greater riches at stake. That," the Gentleman said, "is entirely your choice."

For a moment, nobody in the room (except possibly the Gentleman, whose confidence never wavered), knew what Octavius was going to do.

Then Octavius directed his tentacles to lower the other man back to his feet. The tentacles withdrew only a few inches before hesitating, then returned to straighten out the Gentleman's rumpled lapels. If that seemed to imply an apology, the Doctor's next words proved otherwise: "If you do not live up to your promises, old man... you will wish I'd killed you tonight."

The Gentleman smiled his hateful smile. "If you attempt such a coup again, my dear Octavius... then so will you."

There was no doubt in anybody's mind that both men were capable of making good on their threats.

The Gentleman gestured for everybody to sit down. The still-grimacing Octavius obliged by taking a seat on one of the couches. Dillon, hating the Gentleman as much as Octavius did, but seeing that the confrontation had been postponed for now, chose an easy chair. Smerdyakov, still nursing a grudge of his own, picked a seat beside Octavius, his eyes brimming with resentment. Toomes and Beck shared the other couch, their own expressions impassive. As for Pity, she simply dropped from the ceiling and took her place beside the Gentleman, her features once more only a wan and lonely mask.

The Gentleman enjoyed several contemplative puffs of his cigar, perhaps hiding just how much his showdown with Octavius had shaken him, perhaps forcing the Six to wait out of sheer principle. But at long last he looked up, rubbed the spot beneath his right eye, and began. "Now that we have re-established the chain of command, I suppose there's no harm in giving you some idea just how much of this operation remains uncompleted. Essentially, there are three additional steps. The next one will be to obtain another vital piece of equipment; that should only take a few hours, and may be done at your leisure sometime tomorrow afternoon. Pity will not be with you for that phase, as I shall have need of her services myself all day long, but you should not expect any extraordinary difficulties without her. Once that task is accomplished, I shall immediately provide the next installment of your wages and brief you on the most critical part of the operation. At this point, I promise you, you will all enjoy a much clearer view of our mutual goal."

"Will we be done then?" Beck asked.

"No. To keep myself indispensable, and therefore free of your capacity for betrayal, I shall hold back one vital step even at that point. Taking care of that one primary detail, at the same time you're fulfilling your group assignment, shall be my own personal responsibility. If you kill me before then I shall not be able to do my part, and you shall experience only limited success on the operation. If you leave me alive... well..."

The Gentleman's smile spread across his aged features like a cancer metastasizing across flesh.

He puffed his cigar, waved away the smoke, and grinned at a room filled with murderers with reason to hate him.

"... then the scholars," he said, "shall need to labor overtime to produce a newly adequate definition of wealth..."

CHAPTER TWO

Consider, now, the phenomenon of Truly Bad Ideas.

Great ideas may come along only once in a lifetime. When the right individual is blessed with the right combination of perfect opportunity and perfect inspiration at the perfect time, the result can be a world-shaking inspiration that nobody else could have had.

Bad Ideas are significantly more common.

Indeed, it's not unusual for entire hordes of people, who may be worlds apart in background and temperament and personal resources, who have nothing in common except for opportunity, to all come up with essentially the same Bad Idea. They will all be tremendously proud of themselves. They will all leap headfirst into action, armed with the utter conviction that they just came up with a Bright One. And they'll all believe—or act like they believe—that Nobody Else has ever walked into a brick wall by coming up with this very same Bad Idea before them.

There was one particular Bad Idea that had occurred to a large number of people over the past few years. It was a very

Bad Idea, but it was growing more popular all the time.

Today, it was Mitchell Silverman's brainstorm.

There's not much that needs to be said about Mitchell except that he was twenty-seven years old, built like an anorexic lampost, severely nearsighted, tremendously talented in electronics and totally clueless about everything else. Mitchell, who worked in the backroom of a VCR repair shop in Queens, didn't get out much. What made him truly dangerous to himself and to others was that he didn't pay much attention to the rest of the planet. He never read the papers, never watched TV, never discussed current events or the state of the world, and immediately forgot any news stories he happened to pick up by osmosis. This state of affairs had led to him overlooking, that is completely missing, that is never once taking note of, such minor trivialities as the OJ trial, the Monica Lewinsky scandal, the war in Kosovo, and the frequent near-destruction of the planet Earth by various aliens, megalomaniacs, and madmen.

This helps to explain his total lack of awareness that many, many, many, MANY people, over the past few years, had come up with the very same Bad Idea he now believed belonged to himself alone.

That idea was to build himself a bright, colorful costume equipped with all sorts of offensive weaponry, and venture out into the city streets to commit robberies.

He honestly thought he was the first guy ever to do this.

He wasn't even the first guy this week.

Designing a costume that was essentially a blue bodysuit with a mask exposing only the bottom half of his face, he studded it with the dozens of differently-colored flat disks that he had designed as weapons. Some of the disks were grenades, others guided missiles; some fired lasers; some delivered electric shocks; and some spun like buzzsaws and sliced pretty round tunnels in walls. Two of them, clamped to the soles of his bright yellow boots, provided enough vertical lift to permit flight. He had to be extra-careful with those, since they had a tendency to fly in opposite directions and leave him dangling upside-down in the abyss between them. But a couple of hours of practice in the elevator shaft had rendered him reasonably competent in their use. There were even some disks that did nothing, an innovation he called a brilliant strategy to keep the cops off guard, but which was actually due to his inability to come up with enough gimmicks to cover every square inch of costume.

He called himself the Disk Jockey.

He meant the name to inspire fear.

He looked like a guy covered with polkadots.

Clearly, as folks with bad ideas go, he was really going to town in a big way.

And things did seem to go pretty well in the beginning. On his first day over Manhattan, he spotted an armored car, swooped down, blew a hole in the roof and flew away with two big bags of loot.

It was so easy he wondered why nobody had ever thought of this before.

Then he encountered one major reason why what he'd done was a Truly Bad Idea.

It was a sound, immediately above him.

Thwip.

The Disk Jockey looked up and saw something that made no sense at all: a masked man in a red-and-blue body stocking, somersaulting through mid-air in a position that would have put most professional contortionists to shame. The masked man held the end of a long twisted cable in one hand. He shouted something about the Disk Jockey being a "bunkie" (whatever that was) and made a disparaging remark about the Disk Jockey's costume (like he was in a position to criticize), before hurling a punch that had a lot in common with some express trains.

The impact hurled the Disk Jockey the equivalent of half a city block before his gyroscope disks compensated and set him on course again. "Ow!" he shouted, as he flew down a narrow crosstown street. "What the dickens did you do that for?"

The man in the red and blue costume kept pace right behind him, leaping from one rooftop to another in dizzying tangles of contorting arms and legs. "Dickens?" he repeated. "Dickens?"

"Yes, *dickens*! Do you have a problem with my vocabulary?"

"Dickens," the man in the red and blue costume mused. He did something too fast for normal human eyes to register (something that involved that thwip sound again) and dropped into the Disk Jockey's path, this time dangling from a knotted cable of some kind. "Forgive me, but that's not usual super-villain banter."

The Disk Jockey changed course to avoid him. "What's a super-villain?"

The man in red and blue made the thwip sound again, and kept up. "Aren't you the guy who just robbed that armored car?"

"That's right! And who are you, that you should care?"

"You don't recognize me?"

The Disk Jockey, now seriously annoyed at the antics of this pest, hurled a rotating-buzzsaw disk. "Should I?"

The man in red and blue easily dodged the deadly missile. "All right. You're beginning to scare me now. Tell me you really don't know."

"I don't know, I don't know! This just struck me as a good

way to make a few extra bucks! But you will regret the day your path crossed that of—the Disk Jockey!"

The man in red-and-blue did fall behind then, but only because he was too convulsed by uncontrollable laughter.

The Disk Jockey, coming in low over the rooftops, experienced the first inklings of a ghost of a shadow of a suspicion that this new career move might have been insufficiently researched.

He took a sudden left turn into a narrow air shaft between tenements, dropped four stories in less than a second, zipped through an open window, scared the devil out of a family of four having lunch, smashed through another window on the other side, then rocketed straight up, cleared the rooftop, and drained power from all other systems to provide himself an extra added burst of speed.

Then the man in red and blue popped into view beside him, easily keeping pace with a series of grasshopper leaps. "Lemme give you a clue."

"I don't want your clue!"

"Does the term friendly neighborhood super hero mean anything to you?"

"I don't even know what a super hero is! Now leave me alone!" The Disk Jockey hurled a grenade disk, which burst against a tenement wall in an explosion of brick and plaster dust. The pest disappeared inside the cloud, but the Disk Jockey couldn't make himself believe that this was permanent. He needed to do something else, something drastic, something that would permit him to escape and analyze precisely where this idea of his had gone so disastrously wrong.

Like many people victimized by their own Truly Bad Ideas, the Disk Jockey then attempted to compensate with a tactic that made his first brainstorm look like genius.

He swooped down and took a hostage.

Specifically, a skinny old man in a blue gortex coat, who he'd spotted puttering around a pigeon coop on the rooftop. The old man, who seemed to be in his early seventies, was as an opponent more in line with the Disk Jockey's skill level: he was totally taken by surprise when the Disk Jockey landed beside him, whipped out another buzzsaw-disk, and held it to his throat. "Don't move!" the Disk Jockey shouted. "This thing can take your head clean off!"

The old man froze and dropped his sack of pigeon feed. "Oy. Don't hurt me. Don't."

"I'm serious here!"

"So who's arguing?" The old man spoke with the slightest trace of a German accent, leavened with years of Bronx influence, and his tone was not so much terrified as resigned. He wore what appeared to be a soft knitted disk over his bald spot. The Disk Jockey's cluelessness is best measured by the way he interpreted this item: not as the yarmulke it was, but as an offensive-weaponry disk not unlike one of his own. "So what is it you want from me, maybe?"

"You're my hostage!"

"So it was a stupid question, already. Forgive me for living."

The pest in the red-and-blue body stocking dropped down onto the edge of the rooftop, keeping his distance in a manner utterly at odds with his previous nonchalant approach to danger. His voice had also taken on a new level of seriousness: "Don't you dare hurt him, bunkie. I promise, you won't like my attitude shift if you do." His masked head moved imperceptibly. "Don't worry, Mr. Rabinowitz. I'll take care of this, just as I did last time."

The old guy said: "I'm not worried, Spider-Man. But this is the kind of habit I can do without, if you don't mind me saying."

The Disk Jockey did not know what to react to first—his

pursuer's name, or the revelation that he'd just picked a hostage his pursuer knew. His mouth fell open as he tried to formulate a sufficiently frightening threat of his own.

Spider-Man turned his attention back to the Disk Jockey. "Some thugs tried a protection scam on Chaim's newsstand a couple of years back. I took care of them."

"Wasn't even my first time getting rescued by a super hero," Rabinowitz said self-deprecatingly, as conversational with his captor as he was with his potential rescuer. "My platoon got saved by Captain America and Bucky during the war. Such nice boys.—So what are you going to do with this guy, webslinger?"

"Something I do all too rarely with guys like him. I'm going to talk."

"Nu," Rabinowitz shrugged. "You're the expert."

Despite being the ruthless kidnapper who had his blade to the throat of a potential victim, the Disk Jockey was beginning to feel a serious loss of control. His voice quavered: "Stay back! I mean it!"

Spider-Man held up both palms in a placating gesture and approached only enough to sit down on the edge of a waist-high stone chimney. "Relax. I'm serious when I said I think a talk could settle this. —Mr. Rabinowitz, am I fair in saying that as a man who, before his recent well-deserved retirement, ran a busy newsstand for forty years, you've had a chance to read more newspapers and magazines than the average person? And that you've always been pretty up on what's going on in this city?"

"I'm informed, if that's what you mean. That mayor, he—"

"Please. Let's stay focused." Spider-Man turned his head. "And you, Mr. Disk Jockey—"

Rabinowitz made the sound of strangled laughter deep in his throat.

"—is it true that before today you somehow never encountered the concept of a super hero or a super-villain?"

"How many times do I have to keep saying it?" The Disk Jockey cried, with increasing defensiveness.

"Forgive me," Spider-Man said. "I'm only, like, the front page of the *Daily Bugle* two or three times a week. You mean to tell me that you have never heard of Captain America? Thor? The Fantastic Four? The X-Men? The Avengers?" He stopped, dumbstruck by the Disk Jockey's continued incomprehension. "Razorback?"

"No, no, no, no, and no."

"Not even Razorback?"

"I said no."

Spider-Man seemed to have difficulty absorbing that. "Are you new in town?"

"Lived here all my life."

"And yet—" (here the man in red-and-blue seemed to have difficulty keeping his voice down to a normal volume) "—you somehow completely missed the occupation by the hordes of Atlantis, the invasion of the Asgardian fire demons, the rampage of Count Nefaria, the insurrection by Magneto and his band, the attack of the Living Monolith, the war against Onslaught in Central Park, and half a dozen separate visitations from a planet-eating demigod in the form of a sixty-foot white guy with a purple W on his head? Do you really expect me to believe that?"

The Disk Jockey had a sensation that would have been familiar to anybody unaware that his pants had fallen down at a formal dinner party—i.e. he knew that he'd just made a colossal fool of himself in some manner, but was at a loss to determine precisely how. "Do you really expect me to believe that part about the guy with the purple W?"

Never frightened, Chaim Rabinowitz now seemed perversely fascinated by this. "*Gott in Himmel.* This guy should only buy a townhouse in Chelm."

Unsure what that meant, the Disk Jockey said, "I—don't really follow current events..."

"Current—"

"It doesn't matter!" The Disk Jockey shouted. He moved his buzzsaw-blade a little closer to the old man's throat. "Because if you don't let me go, I'll cut this old fool's head off! I promise I will!"

Spider-Man simply made that placating gesture again. "That's the second time you've made that particularly threat, and I really oughta go back to my usual strategy, which is spending the fifteen minutes bouncing you all over this rooftop. If nothing else, it'll keep us all warm. But given what we've just found out about you, for once in my life I'm gonna show some mercy. Can we just, like, postpone your brilliant escape until after I explain some basic facts of life to you?"

The Disk Jockey didn't waver. "It's a trick."

"No, it isn't. I promise you, kiddo, that when Spider-Man says he'd rather talk than beat you up, it's a good idea to say yes. If you still wanna fight me after I'm done, then I'll be happy to oblige you. But in the meantime, can you give me just a couple of minutes here?"

"As long as you understand that the old guy dies the first time you try something funny."

"Third time you said that," Spider-Man noted. He addressed his next words to Chaim Rabinowitz: "Don't worry. Nothing's going to happen."

Rabinowitz said, "I already figured that out."

Spider-Man turned his attention back to the Disk Jockey. "Since Mr. Rabinowitz follows current events, I'll let him back me up here. There's this bunch of criminals I know who call themselves the Sinister Six—"

"I already have trouble believing you," the Disk Jockey sneered. "I mean, even if they are criminals, why would they call themselves sinister? Who's proud of a thing like that?"

"Hey. Don't ask me. There's also a group out there called the Masters of Evil, and another one called The Brotherhood of Evil Mutants. They're proud of it. If we're gonna continue having this conversation, you're gonna have to accept that much, at least."

"It's true," Rabinowitz testified.

The Disk Jockey grumbled a bit, then conceded. "Go ahead."

"All right. Let me tell you a little bit about these guys. The Sinister Six, I mean. Most of them have been around for years and years, causing trouble all over the place—robbing, killing, blowing up things, trying to take over the world, what have you. You know. The usual stuff. As a freelance crimefighter, I'm not too fond of any of them.

"One of them is this ugly snaggletoothed old guy, Adrian Toomes, he's got to be in his seventies or even eighties by now. He calls himself The Vulture, because he has this green bird suit that he wears, complete with wings. And he may look like some deluded nutjob you find taking the express elevator up to the eightieth floor balcony, but he really can fly, and he's fast and agile enough to dodge rifle fire and outmanuever SWAT team helicopters. Not that bullets can penetrate his armor, anyway. The wings are pretty dangerous all by themselves; he keeps the metal tips sharpened to a razor's edge, and uses them to slice through armored cars, bank vaults, things like that. His favorite trick, when he's feeling mean, is to snatch up people on the street and hold them hostage on rooftops. With his speed, he can collect dozens of prisoners faster than they can get away, and he has absolutely no problem with dropping people from great heights whenever he feels like it. You want a capsule summary of his personality, just think of him as a guy who's profoundly disappointed with everything that's ever happened to him since the day he was born, and who wants to take it out on the general public, and who happens to be powerful enough to make it happen.

"That's one.

"The second guy I'm talking about is a Russian fella by the name of Anatoly Smerdyakov, who calls himself the Chameleon. Now, he's not much of a fighter, this guy, and once it finally comes down to me and him and our respective fists the battle is pretty much a dead issue, but that's not what makes him dangerous. You see, he has this gimmicked-up suit that gives him the power to disguise himself as anybody he wants to be at a moment's notice. He can be a policeman, an army officer, the President of the United States, your best friend, even a homeless guy on the street; and he can go anywhere and do anything and get away before anybody realizes anything's wrong. He can turn himself into the person you trust most and stab you in the back; he can turn himself into you and ruin your life by committing crimes in your name. He's pretty ruthless. I've lost track of the number of people he's known to have killed.

"That's two.

"The third guy I'm talking about is a washed-up Hollywood stuntman by the name of Quentin Beck, who calls himself Mysterio. Now, unlike Smerdyakov, Beck happens to be a world-class fighter; he's agile, and well-trained, and able to swallow an impossible amount of physical abuse before he even starts to consider falling down. He has a kick, just for starters, capable of taking your head off. But that's not what makes him so dangerous. You see, he's also one of the world's leading masters of special effects. He has so many ways of fooling you that he can make you think you're seeing miracles. He can float on a pillar of smoke. He can appear and disappear at whim. He can pass through solid walls. He can make you run screaming in terror from people trying to help you, then trick you into seeing a solid floor where there's really a fifty-story drop. Heck, if I wanted to stand here all day, I could tell you all of his gimmicks. But let's just give you an idea by saying that not so long ago, he spent a full year terrorizing this one poor guy with hallucinations, driving the fella insane just to prove he could. Not a nice man, this Mysterio. You with me so far?"

The Disk Jockey didn't at all appreciate where this was going. "Y-yes."

"Okay, now. Where was I? That was number three, right?"

"Right," said Mr. Rabinowitz, who, hostage or not, seemed to be having the time of his life.

"Okay," Spider-Man said. "Now, none of those guys are exactly poster children for mental health, but the fourth guy is probably the wackiest of the group. His name is Max Dillon, and he calls himself Electro, the Human Power Battery. Now, I don't have the time to go into how, but somewhere along the line, he got charged up with enough raw electricity to light up a city. He never runs out of it, either. He can release more lightning than a medium-sized thunderstorm and still have enough left to totally incinerate a city block or two. Try to shoot him and the bullets explode before they get close. Try to throw him in the river and he'll vaporize thousands of gallons of water without getting wet. He can fly, hurl ball lightning, blow up cars and buildings by pointing at them, give you seizures by disrupting the flow of the nerve impulses in your brain, and completely drain the power from any machine you might build to fight him. Now, you figure, a guy like this, he'd just make millions the honest way by getting a job driving turbines for the power company—but no, he prefers levelling neighborhoods and laughing at anybody who tries to stop him.

"That's four. You getting the trend here?"

The Disk Jockey's heart was pounding. "G-go on. You're not scaring me."

"Glad to hear it. The next guy I want to talk about is actually a woman. Her name's Pity. And I . . . " For the first time, Spider-Man hesitated, and a genuine note of pain entered his voice. "She's new. I don't know all that much about her, yet. I don't really think she really belongs with the others. I think she's being forced . . . and I intend to work on freeing her. But she's still pretty dangerous. In addition to being able to walk on walls, and jump three stories straight up, and fight about as well as anybody I've ever met, she has this little trick she does with darkness; she can summon it up in the middle of an otherwise sunshiny day, and swallow up entire buildings in a blackness no known light can penetrate. Flashlights won't work. Neither will sonar or infrared or any night-vision goggles you can buy. She can see perfectly well in it, though—and she'll break your neck with a kick while you're still stumbling over the furniture on your way to the light switch.

"That's five.

"And as if all of that wasn't bad enough, I have considerately saved the worst for last. Dr. Otto Octavius, who goes by the name Dr. Octopus. Here's a guy, I can't even begin to tell you what's dangerous about him. Just to start with, he's one of the ten most brilliant scientists on the planet—an expert in the electromagnetic spectrum, who knows more about the effects of radiation than anybody else alive. Combine this with the fact that he's also a totally murderous psychopathic terrorist, who only one year ago (just picking one example at random, you understand) tried to kill about a billion people with nuclear weapons planted in several dozen major cities worldwide. Not a nice guy, and that's not the least of it, because I haven't even mentioned this special harness he wears that comes equipped with four flexible metal tentacles which move fast enough to deflect gunfire and are strong enough to swing subway trains like baseball bats. I'll note that the harness and the tentacles are made out of adamantium, an artificial alloy that once forged is indestructible enough to survive ground-zero nuclear explosions without a scratch. Next to that, anything else you might throw at it is just a bad joke.

"So. Let's summarize, kiddies. The Vulture. The Chameleon. Electro. Mysterio. Pity. And Doctor Octopus. All together, known as the Sinister Six.

"As I said, six of the deadliest human beings ever to walk the face of this planet.

"And the point I've been leading up to, all this time, is this —

"Just one week ago, all of those charming people got together and came after me on the same day. First one at a time. Then all at once. They took hundreds of hostages all over the city, threatening to kill as many as they could, and daring me to stop them. They called this their Day of Terror.

"It began early in the morning.

"I not only saved every single hostage, but I also sent all of those aforementioned lunatics running for their lives by mid-afternoon.

"I went home and had time to take a nap before dinner.

"And now you want to fight me alone."

Spider-Man looked at the hostage. "Mr. Rabinowitz. As a guy who keeps track of current events—was all of that accurate?"

"Well, I don't know about the nap part," Mr. Rabinowitz said, "but aside from that, yah, pretty much so, near as I could tell."

Spider-Man nodded. "Right." He turned toward the Disk Jockey and said: "So go ahead. Take your best shot."

The Disk Jockey opened his mouth. Closed it. Made a noise like a woodchuck brushing against an electrified fence. Closed his eyes. And showed that, spectacularly uninformed or not, he still had more good sense than most other people in the career he'd chosen for himself.

He fell to his knees and whimpered: "Please don't hurt me."

Several minutes later, as Spider-Man braved the frigid winds above midtown, he reflected that half-truth could be a powerful weapon.

He hadn't mentioned that while he'd defeated the various members of the Sinister Six by mid-afternoon, as stated, he had not actually succeeded in capturing them—and that his victory had been such a near thing he'd limped back home carrying a catalogue of serious wounds.

He hadn't mentioned that this time out, the Sinister Six were working for Gustav Fiers, a ninetyish, self-proclaimed "investor in chaos" who called himself the Gentleman—and who had been one of the most wanted international criminals in the world for much of the century just past.

He hadn't mentioned that if the Gentleman was involved, then the Sinister Six were after far more than mere revenge—and that they were expected to return any minute to finish what they'd started.

He hadn't mentioned that the Gentleman's presence in New York had turned this latest return of the Sinister Six into an intensely personal war for Spider-Man. Not long ago, the man behind Spider-Man's mask, Peter Parker, had discovered photographic evidence that seemed to indicate that his parents had had another child, a daughter, sometime before his own birth. He had furthermore discovered that Fiers was the man responsible for betraying those parents to the Red Skull ... an act which had led to their deaths. And that Fiers might have also stolen their daughter, christened Carla May Mendelsohn, training her throughout a cold childhood of mind control and psychological indoctrination to become the wan, silent, tormented, but no less deadly, personal assassin he had christened Pity.

Spider-Man had spent the last week not knowing whether to hope this wasn't true—or that it was. If Pity was his sister, the last remnant of the family Fiers had destroyed, Spider-Man needed to know for sure. But even if she wasn't, Spider-Man had seen and heard enough to believe that she was an innocent corrupted against her will, committing her crimes under extraordinary duress. Either way, he ached for what she'd been through. Either way, he had vowed to free her.

Losers like the Disk Jockey (or three other half-baked super-villains called the Hypno-Hustler, the Big Wheel, and the Monocle, who had each chosen the last couple of days to make their long-belated reappearances, and who had each provided less than five minutes of distraction apiece before going down for the count), weren't doing much to take that vow off his mind. Not just because of Pity. But because whatever the Gentleman had in mind for the Sinister Six could only be disastrous news for the city of New York.

Bereft of any other ideas, Spider-Man swung down to a telephone kiosk on Broadway and, ignoring the slack-jawed stares of passersby, charged a call with an anonymous long-distance calling card his alter ego Peter Parker had purchased at a convenience store in Queens.

SECRET OF THE SINISTER SIX

A few seconds later a receptionist answered. "SAFE here."

"Hello," Spider-Man said. "I'm trying to reach Agent Doug Deeley."

"Are you a super hero, sir, or is this a personal call?"

Ah, the eternal unflappability of receptionists! Spider-Man was willing to bet cash money that this was not some temp hired for the day. "Tell him it's Spider-Man."

"Hold on, Mr. Man."

Spider-Man, put on hold, mused that the world of espionage had reached a sad state of affairs when even super-secret spy agencies used Barry Manilow for Hold music.

SAFE, an acronym for Strategic Action For Emergencies, was a federal agency coordinating armed response to extraordinary crises like terrorist attacks, super-villain assaults, and supernatural visitations. Their leader was a no-nonsense career officer named Colonel Sean Morgan, and their headquarters was a massive hovercarrier maintaining constant watch from a thousand feet over the East River. Doug Deeley, a tall, affable black man in his mid-thirties, was SAFE's official liason to the super-heroic community. Deeley, who had already established good relations with the Avengers and the Fantastic Four, had worked closely with Spider-Man during the Day of Terror crisis. Spider-Man trusted Deeley only as much as he trusted anybody in authority (namely, on a moment-by-moment basis), but he still instinctively liked the man, and had at Colonel Morgan's suggestion called him an average of three times a day throughout the past week, just to touch bases as they waited for the Six to drop the other shoe. Spider-Man could only hope that the Feds had somehow managed to apprehend the Six on their own; it was freezing out here, and he was beginning to catch a cold.

Barry Manilow clicked off in mid-tribute to the songs

that make young girls cry, and a deep voice rumbled: "Deeley here."

"What's the matter with you, Doug? Aren't you paramilitary types always supposed to end all your transmissions with 'over'?"

Deeley's tone betrayed his amusement. "Only during tactical field communication, webslinger. Not on the telephone. I don't suppose you're calling from home."

"Nope. Not that naive. I know all your incoming calls are traced. I'm using a pay phone and a calling card."

Deeley tsked. "I am so glad I don't have a secret identity. Must be a real pain. Remind me never to have an origin."

"Consider yourself reminded."

"I don't suppose you've managed to find and defeat the Sinister Six since the last time you checked in."

"Damn. You blew my surprise."

"Really?"

"No, I'm kidding," Spider-Man said, rolling his eyes at the thought of the Disk Jockey. "How's the Brain Trust? They making any progress?"

"Brain Trust" was a reference to the special task force Colonel Morgan had convened to coordinate intelligence gathering and strategic planning for the ongoing Sinister Six situation. It was currently composed of Special Agent Clyde Fury, Strategic Analyst Vince Palminetti, Crisis Counsellor and Psychological Consultant Troy Saberstein, and the group's wild card, a 90-year-old, long-retired treasury agent named Dr. George Williams. They had spent the past week poring through the voluminous backlog of FBI, Justice Department, and Interpol files regarding Fiers and the Six. Deeley said: "What do you expect? They're driving each other crazy with theories."

"Can't be an easy job."

"It isn't. The Six are tough enough, but they're not one-tenth as elusive as their new boss."

"Well," Spider-Man said, "it can't be easy tracking down somebody who's stayed ahead of the law since the 1920s."

"It's an impossible job, web-slinger. The dossier on Fiers may have a lot of hard data, but there's also a lot of guesswork and speculation and inconclusive evidence. And they go back so far in the history of so many law-enforcement agencies all over the world that they contradict each other more than a stadium filled with JFK conspiracy theorists—or, for that matter, Oliver Stone in a room by himself. Williams is the only one who seems to be able to make sense of it all ... and no wonder, given how much time he's spent on the job. Sharp as a tack for a guy that old ... and fairly obsessed, too."

That was putting it mildly. Williams had been doggedly tracking Gustav Fiers for more than sixty years, since first missing him at the site of the *Hindenburg* disaster. His quest had continued through three decades of nominal retirement and hadn't stopped even when most world governments declared Fiers probably dead of old age. Though partially disabled by a stroke, Williams remained as driven a stalker as any man Spider-Man had seen this side of the Punisher. "I don't blame him," Spider-Man said. "At his age, he's got to be aware that he's racing the clock. Don't they have anything at all?"

"Nothing substantial," Deeley said. "One little thing. There's been an unconfirmed Gentleman sighting on the part of a retired treasury agent, old protegé of Williams working security detail at some art auction downtown. He says he saw somebody fitting the Gentleman's description paying about a million dollars in cash for an original Andrew Wyeth."

"Why wouldn't he have reported something like that at once?"

"In the first place, because he figured he had to be wrong. Gustav Fiers would have to be pushing a hundred years by now, and our man figured him to be probably long dead. He contacted Williams through a mutual friend only because it kept bugging him, and he was pretty flabbergasted to hear that the hunt for this dirtbag's gone active."

Spider-Man grunted. "Do you believe it was the Gentleman?"

"Could have been. Probably was. But I have trouble understanding why a self-proclaimed investor in chaos would be buying fancy art in a city where he's the target of a federal manhunt."

"Unless," Spider-Man said, "he was trying to save it from whatever he thinks is about to happen."

"That's a nasty thought. Whatever's up, I hope your wounds are healing, because I sure get the feeling that we're going to need you working at your peak whenever the other shoe drops."

Spider-Man, who had taken a real beating during his last day-long battle with the Six, winced beneath his mask. "Yeah. Me, too."

Later. Forest Hills, Queens. A quiet residential neighborhood of tree-lined streets, aging but well-maintained clapboard homes, retirees living on their savings and young families just starting out in life. The community had the added benefit of being old enough to predate the postwar construction boom of the late forties and early fifties, which meant that it also predated the days of cookie-cutter development—a vintage ensuring that not every house looked like every other house. These homes had personalities, reflecting the personalities of the people who lived there.

One of the oldest houses in the neighborhood was a

modest Victorian split-level, zealously guarded by a battalion of protective trees. It was a three-story home, with a spacious attic and enough rooms to have once served as a rooming house for senior citizens. Nobody would have had to step inside to know that the stairs would creak and the furnace would be unpredictable and that the walls would resonate with the laughter and the heartbreak of the generations who had played out their daily dramas here. Few would have considered it a luxurious place to live. But few could have looked at the freshly painted walls and the neatly trimmed yard and not known that there were people who would always picture this unassuming little structure as the center of their world.

Peter Parker, who had grown up here and now shared this house with his wife Mary Jane, had lived any number of places: from cluttered chelsea apartments to luxury duplexes. But this house would always be home.

As he emerged from the attic, wearing a freshly-laundered pair of civvies, and wondering just how long it had been since he'd entered or left this house the normal way, through the front door, he couldn't help feeling a little safer and a whole lot warmer just for being here.

He brushed down his "hood hair," descended the stairs, and entered the living room, where Mary Jane Watson-Parker, sometime supermodel, sometime action-movie actress, sometime soap-opera queen, always gorgeous redhead and (for the last couple of years) beloved wife sat in her pink terrycloth bathrobe, sniffling like the martyr she rarely permitted herself to be. Poor Mary Jane, who was normally as healthy as a stableful of horses, and who was almost as resistant to colds and fevers as her super-resilient hubby, now nursed a particularly nasty bug. The hacking cough was already gone, but her nostrils were still red and irritated, and her emerald eyes puffy and bloodshot. This, in Peter's estimation, lowered Mary Jane's rating all the way from 10 to 9.999; if anything, she managed to make viral misery look downright cute.

As he approached, she waved him away. "No! Dod't! You dod't wadt what I hab!"

There were about three different ways to interpret that sentence, two of them piggish. Peter chose the one intended. "I'll risk it, Red." He kissed her, then hopped over the back of the couch to plop down beside her. "How are you feeling?"

"Bedder now, Tiger." She blew her nose. "Annnnh. I dod't usually get dese, but when I do dey hit like one of the guys you fight."

"You should stay at home another day or two."

"Wish I could. But I godt a meeting with the dean tomorrow." Mary Jane had just been hired by Empire State University to teach an evening acting workshop, two nights a week, starting with the upcoming semester. With her last acting job an absolute disaster, through no fault of her own, the job would provide some badly needed extra income that wouldn't interfere with days spent going to auditions. She sniffed. "An' Jill Stacy's been abter me to spend a night wid her . . . I mide take her up on it some day soon. Whad aboud you, hero? Sabe the world today?"

It was the kind of question that might have been rank sarcasm in another marriage, but merely natural curiosity in theirs.

"Naah," he said. "Just dealt with a clueless jerk who thought being a super-villain was a good career move."

"Whad's so unusual about dat?"

"I talked him out of it."

That surprised her. She honked into a tissue and emerged with her cold-voice substantially improved. "Talked?"

"Uh huh. Talked."

"As in using your powers of persuasion rather than your fists?"

"Essentially," Peter said.

She shook her head in disbelief. "Maybe the world's getting more sane."

"Or the bad guys are getting more lame."

"Too bad you can't just do that all the time. So this isn't gonna be one of those guys who keeps coming back on a monthly basis—"

"No chance. This guy was definitely a one-timer."

"Must have been," Mary Jane said, without asking for details. "No sign of the Six, then?"

"Nope. Wish I could say that was good news, but —"

She spoke with genuine feeling. "Nothing connected with those maniacs is good news."

"Except putting them in prison again," Peter said, "which, given how often they escape, is a temporary solution at best. Right now I'd be willing to settle for that."

She shuddered. "I'll settle for another draw and you coming home alive."

"As long as I have your gorgeous smile waiting for me, no problem. I've cleaned their clocks before and I'll do it again. I'm only taking this one so hard because Pity might be—" He cut himself off in mid-sentence, unwilling to complete the thought.

Mary Jane placed a concerned hand on his knee. "She might not be. Remember that. Remember that you've been fooled by this kind of thing before. And with the Chameleon involved again—"

The Chameleon had once attempted to uncover Peter Parker's connection to Spider-Man with a complicated scam involving a pair of imposters posing as a "miraculously survived" Richard and Mary Parker. Peter had already entertained the theory that the supposed existence of a previously unsuspected older sister was more of the same. He sighed. "I know, I know. Sometimes it seems like I've made a career of having my entire past rewritten every time I sneeze. But this time . . . ah, well. I'm all talked out on the subject. Aside from your shnozz, what kind of day did you have?"

Mary Jane rolled her eyes and indicated the pile of movie scripts on the coffee table. It was horribly ironic; after almost a full year of struggling without success to find a new acting part, she was suddenly hot again. That status was due less to her considerable beauty and respectable acting talent than to the headlines she'd recently earned for her heroism during two separate crises involving first Mysterio and then the Chameleon. She did deserve credit for her help preventing Mysterio from murdering everybody on the set of the Direct-To-Video quickie *Fatal Action IV*, and for overcoming a hostage situation at Empire State University to give the Chameleon the beating of his life. The fact that these two incidents had taken place only a week apart had cemented Mary Jane's sudden massive surge in popularity. But her status as flavor of the month had only led to more offers, not better ones. Against her will, she had achieved the wrong kind of temporary fame. She now attracted the kind of producer who wanted to cast her as a gimmick, not because she might be good in a part. As she put it, with a grimace, "The more notoriety I receive from getting caught up in the middle of these lunatic super-villain slugfests of yours, the stupider these movie offers become. If I take any of these, it'll probably ruin me permanently."

"That bad?" Peter said.

"Worse."

"What are they? More catfights-in-women's prison pictures?"

"I wish." Mary Jane rolled her eyes. "Get this. The worst one I got today was about a ballet dancer trying to communicate with giant marionettes on an alien planet."

Peter winced. "A ballet dancer? Really?"

"Yup."

"Who writes this crap?"

"I dunno. But I don't want any part of it.—I still have the contract to appear in *Fatal Action IV*, which looks like it will resume shooting in a few months, but it's probably best to hold out and remain off the big screen for a while. Fortunately, the acting workshop's a go. —Meanwhile, I'm taking a few quiet days at home. And nights, too, if you're wondering. Been awful lonely around here, with you searching for your sister and your old sparring partners at the same time. Think you can stand to forego the web-slinging through sub-freezing temperatures for just a couple of hours, in favor of activities that might actually keep your poor suffering wifey warm?"

Peter scratched his head. "I dunno, Red. Checkers?"

"Too slow-moving."

"Monopoly?"

"Too Republican."

"Rock 'Em Sock 'Em Robots?"

"Too reminiscent of your favorite hobby."

"Well, Gee," Peter rubbed his head theatrically. "What else can a guy do when it's cold outside and he's stuck indoors with his gorgeous and extremely affectionate wife?"

"I dunno, Tiger," Mary Jane said. "Why don't you take a stab in the dark?"

And he did.

For Peter Parker, it was the last peaceful night before the coming of the storm.

And if he was not entirely able to forget his troubles this night... if his danger-detecting spider-sense did maintain a low-level subliminal buzz that kept him staring restlessly at the ceiling instead of enjoying the well-deserved sleep that might have increased his chances of surviving the hours and days to come... then he attributed the feeling only to his apprehension over whatever the Sinister Six had planned.

Nothing he felt was enough to alert him that the danger was even closer than he suspected.

But had he acted on his feelings, and followed them to a certain tree-shrouded alcove on the rooftop of a house across the street, he would have learned that the war was about to strike a lot closer to home.

He would have seen a patch of darkness more impenetrable than any of the shadows that surrounded it.

Pity.

Following orders, and waiting for her opportunity.

CHAPTER THREE

11:36 A.M. The next morning. Sometime before the many deaths that would soon drench the day in blood.

Although the cold and overcast weather was the same as yesterday's, the ambience of the city streets had changed. Now it was more than the simple animal need for warmth that hurried New Yorkers from one place to another; it was also apprehension. The massive storm system that had dumped feet of snow on Chicago and caused emergency conditions throughout much of the upper midwest may have still been at least a day away from these concrete canyons, but it was already being joined by another storm system coming in from the north. Nobody caught outside today needed the three-day forecasts on TV to feel the lid of that atmospheric box starting to close shut. Something extreme was going to happen. Everybody could feel it. And nobody was looking forward to it.

The Gentleman, who enjoyed snow only when he could peer through a hotel room window and chortle at the sight of the lowborn miserably trudging through slush, allowed himself the slightest frisson of concern as Pity, now returned from her mission at the Parkers', escorted him through the streets of the Diamond District.

Not worry. He was adamant about that much. He never worried. Worry is the emotion of the powerless. Aristocrats like the Gentleman showed concern. On his face it registered as nothing more than a slight narrowing of the eyes. The confidence in his bearing was still there. That was important. He was a wealthy man. He was superior. He exuded his superiority. He would not show fear before those who were less than wealthy, and were therefore less than human.

He allowed Pity to guide him past a patch of foul-looking slush, and said, "Thank you, my dear."

She said nothing. Of course. She simply remained by his side, holding tight to the alligator skin suitcase in her right hand.

It was not his legal status that caused him concern. In another country, the Gentleman might have resisted showing himself in public so soon after orchestrating a major terrorist attack like last week's Day of Terror. But not here. Here both Pity and the Gentleman wore the most laughable of disguises; he had adopted a pair of tinted sunglasses, and she wore a colorful knit cap that accentuated her innocence and youth. Aside from that, they both dressed the same way they had the day they'd made themselves known to Octavius and the others—the Gentleman in his conservative suit and camelhair coat, Pity in her tight black pants, white patent-leather boots, and puffy snow-white goosedown jacket. They were wanted felons. In a proper police state, they would have been spotted with ease. But this was America, land of the TV-addicted blind. Anybody who noticed them at all saw a kindly old man and his attentive granddaughter. Most people probably considered them cute.

No, the Gentleman had no concerns about the law.

But the weather was definitely reason for concern. After all, a major snowstorm arriving before the completion of this matter could complicate things. It could force him to delay until weather patterns were willing to cooperate, and by so doing exacerbate the already significant tensions between himself and his employees. The Gentleman enjoyed playing them for the fools that they were, and he took deep pleasure in the sport of using their greed to keep their growing hatred of him at bay... but he also believed he knew precisely how far he could push them, and waltzing that fine line would be difficult if the weather decided to hurl him, unwilling, into the riskier territory beyond. He wasn't absolutely certain he could maintain his authority if circumstances required a delay even as brief as an additional 48 or 72 hours.

He supposed he could handle it. After all, he'd cut it this close before: in Casablanca, in Hue, in Waco, and in Sarajevo. But the sporting factor was definitely beginning to lose its... safety margin.

Meanwhile, he was going ahead as planned.

He stopped before a storefront labelled YEGANEH TREASURES AND PRECIOUS STONES. The establishment inside appeared to be a flourishing but otherwise unremarkable jewelry emporium, with the usual assortment of engagement rings and pearl necklaces glittering in glass showcases. Two of the three customers were matronly middle-aged women in furs; the third was a pudgy young man who appeared terrified by the commitment he was about to make. The sales representatives hovered above with the oversolicitousness of nurses afraid that their ailing patients were not quite strong enough to stand on their own. The Gentleman supposed that the store probably offered sufficient service for the common trade, but it was not quite his destination. He located a locked door to the left of the store itself, with gold lettering etched into the glass: YEGANEH WHOLESALERS AND APPRAISERS. AVAILABLE BY APPOINTMENT ONLY. UPSTAIRS.

The Gentleman used his wolf's-head walking stick to press the intercom button. One appallingly discordant buzz later, a muffled voice said: "Can I help you?"

"Yes." The Gentleman used the name of a long-deceased operative, who had acquired many valuable treasures for him in the years before the Second World War, only to die when a treasure obtained for another client proved more than he could handle: "I am Mr. Belloque, here with my grandniece Michelle."

"Ahhhh, yes, sir. We were worried about you. Step inside. The elevator will be down momentarily."

The door clicked. The Gentleman entered first, allowing Pity to trail behind. The short narrow hallway inside was brightly lit and conspicuous with surveillance cameras; a sign advised anybody stupid enough to need the additional explanation that all visitors were taped. A patch of darkness, cast by Pity, passed over the Gentleman's face long enough to prevent those cameras from acquiring a clear view. He escorted her into the dingy little elevator at the end of the hallway, then endured the ride up to Yeganeh's importing offices.

The individual who opened the accordian-gate on the second floor was a round-shouldered man in his early sixties, with moist skin, a self-deprecating cast to his eyes, and an impressively drooping nose. Dressed in charcoal-gray slacks and a patterned sweater-vest over a light blue button-down shirt, he smelled vaguely of peppermints. When he spoke, the Gentleman detected in his accent distant traces of

Poland overlaid with what must have been several decades in Israel. "Good morning, good morning. I'm Sabi Yeganeh. — We spoke on the phone?"

The Gentleman controlled his considerable distaste long enough to clasp the other man's hand. "Jean-Claude Belloque. And this is Michelle. She does not speak."

"Ahh," Yeganeh said, his eyes warming with instant, and disgustingly sincere, empathy. "It's a joy to meet you, dear."

Pity said nothing. Of course. She simply held eye contact for a moment, then dropped it.

Yeganeh was uncomfortable enough to turn his attention back to the man he thought was Belloque. "Come, come, sit down, take a load off. Cold like today's, it's not so easy for people our age, eh?"

The Gentleman had, of course, already been entering middle-age when this pretentious fool was entering his first classroom, but he didn't voice his objections to being placed in the same facile category. "Thank you. That's very kind." He clutched his walking stick as if he really needed it, and allowed Pity to escort him to a stool beside the central display case.

Yeganeh's upper offices were not geared toward the general public, which meant that the gilt facade of the main store downstairs could be eschewed in favor of an austere, utilitarian decor that communicated the total absence of nonsense by abandoning any attempt to be fancy. The walls were wooden panelling, the floor tile, the space clean but unadorned; even Yeganeh and his folksy demeanor seemed a deliberate step down from the smartly-dressed young men the Gentleman had seen serving the customers down below. Yeganeh did not address business matters immediately, but instead served both Pity and the Gentleman tea, assured the Gentleman that he had permission to light up his cigar

("What? We should stand on ceremonies here?"), and remarked that he had been worried about Mr. Belloque, who had been expected an hour ago.

The Gentleman humored these stabs at conversation with polite charm. He did not enjoy dealing with Jews any more than he liked dealing with Blacks or Chinese or People Who Worked In Menial Occupations. They all deserved prominent positions on his personal list of human beings who barely deserved that classification. His list of human beings who did deserve to be considered such was so short that at times he seemed alone there. He was a demanding soul, but he maintained his standards.

At long last, Yeganeh seemed to realize that Mr. Belloque had next to no interest in being sociable. "So. Shall we begin?"

"Gratefully," the Gentleman sniffed. "You have received the transfer?"

"It cleared three days ago. Ten million dollars." Yeganeh shrugged as if to indicate that he found the amount trivial. "Not exactly the kind of advance payment we are used to receiving from a new customer."

The Gentleman merely chuckled. "I was assured you could fill my order."

"Oh, we can, we can. It's just unusual, is all I was saying."

In other words, the Gentleman thought with disdain, *it's not common, like the rest of your clientele.* "I have done most of my business on the Continent, dealing directly with my suppliers in South Africa. I am here, tolerating your significantly-higher prices, because of a temporary shortfall that should be rectified soon."

"One hell of a shortfall," Yeganeh said.

Under normal circumstances, the Gentleman would not have bothered to pay this pitiful nonentity any heed at all;

he would have ordered Pity to kill the man and his employees and flee from here carrying all the treasures she could hold. She certainly had more than enough power, even though smash-and-grab tactics like that were more problematic in this city clogged with super heroes than they were anywhere else. But using that kind of technique once made it more difficult to get away with doing it a second time—and the Gentleman's Want List had required him to complete many transactions this size with dozens of jewelers, auction houses, and rare art dealers all over Manhattan. The purchases he had made so far, some through trusted intermediaries, had totalled more than a quarter of a billion dollars. These, together with various other expenses he'd incurred in New York, including the monies budgeted for his dealings with the Sinister Six and the losses of several major bank accounts raided by international law enforcement authorities, had recently brought his hard currency levels dangerously close to Zero.

He was risking everything on this one. Everything.

But he was an old man with nothing to lose.

And he did, after all, have his delicious revenge to console him.

"Yes," he echoed. "It was, as you say, one hell of a shortfall."

Yeganeh tsked. "Ah, well. One man's shortfall is another man's opportunity, right? Of course right. You sit there and I'll be right back."

As Yeganeh turned to open the safe, the Gentleman brooded about all the time this was taking. His dealings with Yeganeh, taking place as they did after the Gentleman's presence in this city had been revealed to the authorities, were particularly risky. He had wanted to complete this transaction earlier this morning, but he refused to carry such valuables around this cesspool of a city without Pity as bodyguard. He had also been forced to wait for her when her deadly assignment of the night before had kept her out in Forest Hills a couple of hours longer than anticipated. He hadn't even enjoyed the satisfaction of being able to punish her for a failure he could legitimately construe as her fault. The Parkers, man and wife, hadn't left their doomed tinderbox of a home until 9:15 this morning. The package Pity had been tasked to deliver had kept her occupied in their living room until almost 10:15 A.M. The delay may have been annoying, and possibly dangerous, but given Peter Parker's talent for sensing immediate danger, it had also been absolutely necessary.

Yeganeh began to bring out diamonds on trays. The Gentleman began his inspections. He made occasional soft noises of approval or disapproval as he selected the largest and most valuable, utterly ignoring Yeganeh's various stabs at commentary. All nonsense aside, he did not have to reject many; he was less than halfway through his task when he gave one of his exceedingly rare compliments. "You do offer quality goods, sir."

"Thank you," Sabi Yeganeh said.

The tray occupied by the stones the Gentleman had declared definites filled up quickly. He was prudent to select a variety of sizes, from the small and easily saleable to the multi-carat monsters with greater value but more limited marketability.

When the Gentleman finally completed his transactions, Yeganeh performed his calculations. "You are two hundred thousand over. Do you want to arrange another wire transfer?"

"No need. Michelle is carrying sufficient cash."

Yeganeh colored. "That's pretty dangerous, in this town."

"She is a responsible young lady. I trust her."

"No doubt," Yeganah colored, "but I'm afraid we cannot accomodate transactions this large in cash. I'm not saying that you would be a risk for this sort of thing, but the chances of counterfeiting..."

"Understood," the Gentleman said. "Would you take the difference if I added another hundred thousand in cash for your personal use? That would not have to be reported as income by the business?"

"That would be illegal and unethical, sir."

"Oh, spare me. I am not a representative of any law-enforcement agency. I am a businessman in a bind, operating on a strict deadline. I will even have my bank in Zurich guarantee the transaction against any problems with the cash; the personal payment to yourself will just be an inducement to expedite the process."

Yeganeh considered it, then said, "All right. If Zurich offers those guarantees."

The Gentleman provided him with the necessary information, and smiled pleasantly as Yeganeh retreated to the telephone.

When he turned to Pity to retrieve the cash from the briefcase she was not by his side.

He was not surprised he'd failed to notice—after all, she'd been trained to move with the stealth of an errant thought. But she was supposed to be more obedient than that. His cold eyes swept the room, half-expecting to find her hidden within one of her protective zones of darkness. But she was in plain sight, her back to him as she studied a glass case mounted on the wall.

He should have known. Her childhood may have been stolen, but she retained a certain degree of annoying innocence: notably, her attraction to bright and shiny things.

The Gentleman approached to see what it was, determined to chastise her if it was anything that should have been beneath her notice.

It was not.

Rather, it was a golden necklace, suitable for a queen. The chain links, inset with diamonds and pearls and one huge emerald, dangled a thick curtain of finer chains with sparkling smaller gems interspersed as generously as the costume general they most assuredly were not. The centerpiece, designed to be worn at the base of the wearer's throat, was the solid gold bloom of a rose, its craftsmanship so exquisite that even the Gentleman, a man notorious for his resistance to awe, shivered from the conviction that a touch would reveal living flower and not cold precious metal.

He was so very impressed that he rewarded Pity with a moment of praise. "Good girl."

Behind them, Sabi Yeganeh chuckled. "A real beauty, eh?"

The Gentleman did not turn to acknowledge him. "A treasure."

"It is the most beautiful item in my store."

"Also, I daresay, the most precious."

"Easily," Yeganeh said. "It's an historical heirloom."

"Given its level of craftsmanship, I would be stunned indeed to find that it was not. These days, this country is incapable of creating such a genuine masterwork."

Yeganeh hesitated before continuing. "It dates back to the days of the Czar, over in Russia . . ."

"I know who the Czar was," the Gentleman murmured. He certainly did; it had, indeed, been his behind-the-scenes machinations that had prevented the last survivor of the royal line, one Anna Anderson, from claiming the riches he had already so profitably looted.

"The combined worth of the gold and the stones price at a little over a million. But the piece itself, the artistry, its historical significance, is more than enough to double that amount. It's more a museum showpiece than an item meant to be worn. I've considered auctioning it at Sotheby's, but frankly, I value it far too much to ever—"

"Three million," the Gentleman said, still without turning around.

"Excuse me?" Yeganeh said. "Sir, I hope you don't think I was trying to—"

The Gentleman whirled. "You were displaying a treasure that gave you source for pride. I crave the same pleasure. Three million."

"I thank you, but it's really not for—"

"Three million five," the Gentleman said. "If not, I shall cancel all of today's other purchases and take my business elsewhere."

He was prepared to order Pity to kill the man if there was any further resistance. That's how much he wanted this necklace for his own.

It was a personal good-luck ritual he had practiced in many of his past business ventures: the salvaging of one major treasure from every city he needed to vacate before the arrival of some major calamity in which he harbored financial interest. It had served him well in Nanking before the Japanese invasion, in Dresden before the firebombing, and in Hue before the Tet Offensive. The necklace would be an excellent trophy of New York in its last days as one of the financial capitals of the world. If this foolish, strutting man would only agree to relinquish it.

Yeganeh hesitated . . .

Nothing, to Peter Parker's mind, defined the indefatigibility of New York and its people more than the continued existence of the *Daily Bugle*.

The tabloid was like the city it represented. It was stubborn, infuriating, rude, and often wrongheaded enough to make you cry. It had teetered on the edge of bankrupcy, fought its way back, eagerly compromised its integrity at some times and stubbornly refused to give up an inch at others. It survived direct assaults devastating enough to destroy small countries. It kept going even when nobody would have blamed it for having the good sense to roll over and die. It was easy to hate, just as easy to love, and impossible to reconcile even for those who harbored both reactions simultaneously. Like the city, it also had a disconcerting knack of earning back years of lost faith just when you needed something to believe in. Peter Parker, who in his guise as Spider-Man had endured the paper's scurrilous assaults on his reputation for years, could not have been blamed for wanting to wash his hands of the place forever. But he considered it home, almost as much as he considered the house in Forest Hills home. It was part of him. It was like the city that way, too.

If nothing else, he had to admire its resiliency. Just one week ago, the climactic battle of the Sinister Six's Day of Terror had left much of the lower floors a gutted shell. Any more damage and the building might have been shut down or condemned outright. Certainly, many of the office workers in the lower floors had needed to be relocated to temporary space at WorldWide Business Centers, many blocks uptown. The massive reconstruction that would allow them to return to work here wouldn't be completed for weeks. The City Room, which he entered now, had been wrecked almost as badly. There was still a freezing draft from the crater Doctor Octopus had made of publisher J. Jonah Jameson's office. But with all that, the *Bugle* had not missed a single day of publication. It was still hitting the streets with its peculiar blend of low-class sleazy innuendo and higher-end investigative reporting, giving equal weight to the brilliant work of Vreni Byrne, Charlie Show, Ben Urich, and Betty Brant, and the frequently incomprehensible antics of the perpetually irate Jameson.

Peter had often wondered if the main reason so many people gave credence to Jameson's ridiculously invective-laden publishorials was the compensating high quality of the news coverage that appeared on every other page. It was possible, he supposed. Certainly, it provided one possible explanation why Jameson was not laughed out of town for blaming Spider-Man for everything from transit strikes to Mad Cow Disease.

As Peter stepped off the one working elevator (the other four down since the Sinister Six invasion), he spotted several of his friends and co-workers braving the clammy, sometimes fitfully-heated air of the damaged building in the spirit of dedicated journalism. Most people were dressed in sweaters and jackets; some had on mufflers or hats with earflaps. Secretary Glory Grant, dressed for winter in Antarctica, rushed by, saying hi and bye in the same breath. Betty Brant nodded from the desk where she sat arguing over the phone while performing her drum solo with pencil tip and coffee cup. Charlie Snow, trapped on another phone call, rolled his eyes and said, "Oy-Flipping Vey." The bristly-haired, paintbrush-moustached publisher himself stood in a corner of the newsroom arguing loudly with a representative of the repair crew from Damage Control, Incorporated—Jameson taking the position that as an establishment so frequently trashed by super-villains, the *Bugle* really ought to be entitled to a frequent customer discount.

Giving Jonah a wide berth, Peter glanced at Auntie Esther Friesner, the *Bugle*'s embittered and downright frightening Advice Columnist, who as always nearly bit her perpetually dangling cigarette in two when she read the first two lines of the next letter on her daily stack of correspondence from the terminally dysfunctional. A mother-in-law question, Peter supposed. Auntie Esther hated mother-in-law questions with a passion bordering on the insane—she hated every piece of mail she had ever received, but mother-in-law questions added an extra electrified jolt to the perpetual knot of tension that roiled at the base of her spine. One day she'd received a hundred mother-in-law questions and started setting fire to things. Peter, who like everybody else at the *Bugle* (including Jameson himself), couldn't help being a little afraid of her, moved a little more hastily as he passed her desk.

The man he wanted to see was the paper's best investigative reporter, a fortyish, sandy-haired, chain-smoking bundle of bronchial spasms by the name of Ben Urich. Urich, whose hacking cough was sometimes so bad it confounded witnesses who doubted his ability to remain standing, was no walking advertisement for physical fitness, but he was a bottomless pit of energy when it came to tracking down a story. This was the major reason Peter had been so happy to secure Urich's aid on the ongoing investigation into the background of his parents. The other major reason was the man's strong sense of ethics. Many reporters acted like getting the story overrode all other considerations, but Urich was rumored to be sitting on half a dozen major headlines only because he saw them as simply nobody's business.

Peter found the notoriously cipherphobic Urich tapping away at the ancient Olivetti he preferred to the *Bugle*'s word processing system. "Hey. Ben."

Urich didn't take his eyes off his typing. "Hey yourself. Grab me a coffee, willya, kid? I'll be with you in a minute."

Aware that in a second or two Urich wouldn't even remember making the request, Peter went to the break room and secured the man's favorite blend of pure caffeine and petroleum-byproduct sweetener. Despite his own serious coffee jones, he hesitated several seconds before securing a second cup for himself. He liked to consider himself an afficianado of the beverage, and considered what the *Bugle*'s percolator did to the humble coffee bean a serious supervillain-level crime. (He also seriously resented the sign on the wall behind the coffeemaker: THE BUGLE PAYS FOR THIS COFFEE. DRINK IT AT YOUR DESK WHILE CONTINUING TO WORK.) But he relented, got a cup for himself, and made his way across the bullpen to Urich's cubicle.

He put the coffees down, flipped an unused chair around backwards, and sat again, resting his chin on the backrest. "Hey again."

"Hey yourself," the still-typing Urich said, without any obvious sense of deja-vu. A second later, he registered the smell of coffee. "Did I ask you to get that?"

"Yes, you did."

"Huh. Damned if I can remember."

Peter chuckled as Urich took the cup. "That must be one hell of a story you're working on."

"I don't work on any dull ones, kid." Urich took a sip, expressed distaste, then returned to the typewriter. "Be with you in a sec. Meanwhile, you might wanna take a gander at the green file folder, there."

Peter obliged, expecting more information about his parents. What he found, to his dismay, was his own morgue file. The clippings went back almost a decade, and ranged from a tiny squib about his Uncle Ben's murder to longer stories where he appeared as "innocent bystander" witnessing various crises at the *Bugle*, Empire State University, and elsewhere around the city. Most, but not all, of the stories were related to Spider-Man. The wealth of material was dizzying. Peter's head spun by the time he looked up and met Urich's appraising eye.

"Background," Urich said. "I had the idea I couldn't know the parents without first refreshing myself on everything I knew about the son."

Peter didn't know what to say. "B-ben, I..."

Urich's eyes turned dreamy. "I've got to tell you, Peter—for a nice college kid from Forest Hills, you've certainly led an interesting life. I almost forgot some of this stuff. I mean, framed and tried as a serial killer that time, fortunately cleared of that; attacked by dinosaurs in Antarctica, of all places; a high school girlfriend with a super-villain brother; a college roommate turned costumed terrorist loon; a movie-star wife who beats up on super-villains as a hobby; a career photographing super heroes for this paper; a pair of murdered secret agent parents. And now, it seems, the possibility of a missing older sister you never knew you had."

Peter could only come up with a lame, "Well, if you take all of that out of context..."

But Urich wasn't finished. "Who's writing your days and nights, kid? And how can I have him drug-tested?"

Urich had a point, even if he couldn't know that he was only seeing the tip of that particular iceberg. What would he say if he knew that Peter had also time-travelled back to the Salem Witch Trials, fought demons in otherworldly dimensions, and been instrumental in helping to prevent a lovesick alien demi-god from blowing up the solar system as an offering to his girlfriend? What would he say if he knew that Peter had met—actually met, and fought—both Dracula and the Frankenstein Monster? What would he say if he had known that Peter had once said hi to a pretty girl on the street, and been faced down by the woman's boyfriend, a humanoid duck named Howard? Heck, what would he say if he knew about the time the Beyonder, an omnipotent being from another plane of reality, had wandered into Peter's apartment and asked to use his bathroom—an incident which Peter wasn't even sure qualifed among his life's ten most surreal moments? Peter decided not to mention it. Instead, he said, "Yeah, well," which served as a good, generic response. "Whoever it is, sometimes he seems to make more sense than other times."

"I'd give the fella a slap in the puss, is what I'd give him."

"He probably deserves it," Peter agreed, with feeling.

"Anyway," Urich sipped his coffee, "Regarding your Mom and Dad, I reached out to some colleagues who work UPI out of Prague. They made some inquiries about this Felix and Lisa Mendelsohn of yours."

Peter leaned forward. "Yes?"

"Well, this much is certain. An American couple using those names and fitting your parents' general description did live in that city during the time period in question. There are too many corroborating testimonies to doubt that. They had a small flat in a median-income neighborhood. Folks who still live there remember them as the stereotypical nice quiet couple who kept to themselves and minded their own business. The husband was supposed to be in some kind of security work, and the wife was a full-time stay-at-home Mom. The neighbors do remember a baby girl named Carla May. They also all say that the Mendelsohns moved away suddenly, leaving no forwarding address." Urich coughed at length into his fist. "All of which seems to confirm the information you found in your parents' NSA file, which indicates that they were living there under those names during the period in question."

"You say that almost as if you don't believe it yourself."

"Wherever spies and spooks are concerned, it doesn't pay to be sure about anything. Besides, there's something about this whole setup that seems awfully neat. Almost as if it's more what we're meant to see than what we'd actually see if we knew where to look."

Peter nodded. He had learned to respect Ben Urich's instincts over the years; the man wasn't always right, but he did have a talent for knowing something was wrong. "What are you saying? That the neighbors are lying?"

"Not even a remote possibility, kid. A couple of dozen separate witnesses, of varying ages and occupations, can't all come up with identical lies about a couple they knew two decades ago. I refuse to believe a conspiracy that large still holding together after this long—not when history teaches us that it's impossible to put three plotters in a room without one of them immediately wanting to sell out the other two. So the Mendelsohns were real. And so was their daughter." Urich hacked into his fist again, then met Peter's gaze. "No, I can't tell you what bothers me precisely—but it's activated all of my bull hockey detectors. Either we've missed something, or we're being played."

"But how?" Peter asked.

"I have absolutely no idea. I'm only toying with the idea that maybe the Mendelsohns weren't your parents."

"But how is that possible? The NSA file—"

Urich, who had never been the warmest of all men, placed a fatherly hand on Peter's shoulder. "Understand, kid. They almost certainly were your parents. There's every reason in the world to believe that they were. And if they were your parents, then Carla May, wherever she is now, is by definition your sister. But we are talking about two people who moved out more than twenty years ago, after months of living under aliases and avoiding any close attachments. They didn't do anything to make themselves memorable. Under such circumstances, eyewitness testimony of any kind is suspect at best—especially when it's so unanimous."

"So you don't think it was them."

"Let's just say I believe the jury's still out." Urich stubbed out his cigarette, mourned its loss, then moved on: "I'm already far deeper into this investigation than I want to be, given its absolute uselessness as *Bugle* fodder, but the mystery's still got my nose up. Soon as I finish this piece, and do a little work on another I have brewing, I'm going to continue making calls and let you know what I find."

"Thanks, Ben. I owe you one."

"You owe me twenty, after this," Urich said, in a tone that signified his intention to collect. The man operated by Favor Bank, and kept very accurate books. "Now leave me alone. I've got to get this done so I can make my two o'clock."

Peter nodded, thanked him again, and stood up, momentarily at a loss over what to do next. He'd submitted his Disk Jockey photos the day before, to less-than-enthused reception. He'd already checked in with Deeley and found out that nothing was happening on the Sinister Six front. He'd dropped off Mary Jane at ESU, where she was having another meeting with Dean Farnswell of the Theatre Arts Department. He was between work assignments. As much as he wanted to make the Gentleman pay for arranging the deaths of Richard and Mary Parker, let alone wring from the old man the truth about Pity's identity, he had spent so much time in costume lately that he didn't relish the prospect of immediately courting chillblains at forty stories. What he needed, badly needed, was a good old-fashioned human moment. He wondered if he could corral Betty Brant Leeds for lunch.

Unfortunately (and typically), the costumed part of his life chose that moment to intrude—in the form of Editor in Chief Joe Robertson, who came barrelling out of the conference room that, since the destruction of his own office by the Sinister Six, had been drafted as his new temporary workstation.

Robertson was a soft-spoken, modestly built black man in his early fifties, whose cottony gray hair and gentle demeanor belied a personal force of will that had long served him well as the *Bugle*'s resident conscience. Jameson had hired him years before, initially as City Editor, with the express understanding that his responsibilites included providing the voice of moderation that Jameson knew he needed to keep his own excesses (both managerial and journalistic) in check. Auntie Esther had explained it best: "Remember that book and movie, *The Horse Whisperer*? About the guy who knew how to handle horses? Well, Robbie's a Crackpot Whisperer. He keeps Jameson from breaking down the gate of his corral." Whatever terms you used, Robertson's avuncular presence was undeniably one of the elements that made the *Bugle* not only a place of business, but also a second home for so many of the people who worked there.

At the moment, Robertson wore the urgent look of a news editor who desperately needed a warm body for a breaking story. His eyes scanned the city room, initially finding no likely suspects, then narrowing when he spotted Peter. He half-walked, half-ran between the rows of desks, charting a course that precisely matched Peter's move to meet him halfway. "Peter! Emergency assignment!"

Peter was already checking his camera bag for spare film. "Why? What's up?"

"There's some kind of crisis in progress over at the Diamond District. Fatal shooting in the street. Early word's that this Pity character was at the scene."

"Pity?" Peter's crest fell. *Please. Don't tell me she's killed someone.*

"That's right." Robbie continued the briefing while rushing Peter to the stairwell. "It's the first sighting of a Sinister Sixer since their Day of Terror, so this may be big. I've already paged Billy Walters and Ken Ellis, telling them to drop their own assignments so they can get over there and find out what's happened, but we need art if we can get it, and you've always been the best we have at getting across town in a hurry."

Peter really hated when Robertson said things like that. The man had always possessed a spooky talent for Not-Quite-Hinting he knew who Spider-Man was. Comments like that had kept Peter guessing for years.

He stopped at the stairwell, grateful that the current condition of the *Bugle*'s elevators relieved him of the pretense of waiting for a ride. "How current's the report?"

"Two minutes, no more. It's still a hot situation. They say she's already fled the scene and started moving uptown at rooftop level. There are cop cars pursuing her from the street, and a helicopter closing in on her from west of her position. If Spider-Man or Daredevil or the Fantastic Four or somebody else in that line of work doesn't become part of this mess before long, then we all woke up in the wrong city without knowing it this morning. We need you over there—now. You have what you need?"

Robertson was referring to cameras and film, but Peter was calculating just how much web-fluid he had left. "Yeah, I'm set. I just hope it's not all over before I get there."

"I wouldn't worry about that too much, son!" Robertson called, as Peter bolted into the stairwell. "After all, nick of time is what you're famous for!"

Already four flights down, and exiting the stairwell on one of the wrecked lower floors, so he could change to Spider-Man, Peter grimaced.

He hated when Robbie said things like that.

He really did . . .

CHAPTER FOUR

Rand-Meachum International, a conglomerate specializing in the development of cutting-edge technology, has offices in twenty American cities and six foreign countries. Its assets at any time number in the low billions. Even so, it cannot be said to exist on quite the same plane as such colossal entities as Roxxon, Microsoft, and Stark-Fujikawa. If they are Corporate Gods, then Rand-Meachum is merely a very, very powerful corporate titan, large enough to have survived the merger mania of the eighties and nineties and ambitious enough to be edging toward its own place at the very top.

One of its smaller research facilities is a four-story, windowless structure in an industrial park in New Jersey, some sixty miles from Manhattan. The building occupies the equivalent of six city blocks and sits on a fenced-in perimeter providing a two-hundred yard grassy lawn on all sides. Nobody gains admission without first stopping at the front gate, where armed representatives of the cutting-edge security firm Silver Sable Limited check each visitor against a master list of authorized employees and visitors. The loading dock, accessible from another guarded entrance, is manned by Silver Sable representatives who carefully inspect all trucks before any cargo is offloaded.

The last serious problem here was a demonstration just outside the main gate by Animal Rights advocates who, a couple of years earlier, had somehow gotten (false) information that the facility housed a genetics lab performing unnatural experiments on rhesus monkeys. There were no rhesus monkeys, or for that matter, lab animals of any kind inside the building. The closest thing they found was a guppy tank that decorated a reception area on the second floor. As Rand-Meachum considered the work actually being done here strictly proprietary, persuading the Animal Rights advocates that they'd screwed up had taken far more time than any of the computer programmers, metallurgists and particle physicists on staff would have believed. But that situation was long over and done with, and life at the Facility had resumed its previous routine—which was, if you listened to chief researchers Warren Gold and Philip Askegren, the single greatest technological leap since Wilbur and Orville Wright.

At about the same time blood was spilled in the Diamond District, Gold and Askegren were performing some final calibrations in a shielded control room overlooking the massive four-story silo they had christened The Birthing Chamber. It was a pretentious name, of course, but one they considered compensation, for they themselves had been nicknamed Abbott and Costello way back in grad school. They didn't really look anything like that old-time comedy duo, but the figures they cut whenever they stood side by side just happened to invite that comparison. Askegren ("Abbott") was tall and thin, with receding sandy hair and a complexion similar to Corrasable Bond typing paper; Gold ("Costello") was stockier and a full head shorter, with greasy black hair and a complexion veering toward the excessively pink.

Gold had cultivated a moustache to discourage the comparison, but it wasn't a very good one; it refused to connect beneath his nose. He tended to rub the hairless spot with his index finger whenever sufficiently deep in concentration; he rubbed it now as he studied a fresh anomaly on his console readout. "We have a spike in the gain. Four point five three."

"Compensating," said Askegren, rolling from one monitor to another on a stool equipped with casters. He had the annoying habit of wearing his white coat draped around his shoulders, so it flapped like a cape whenever he moved with sufficient suddenness. It was so transparent an attempt to invest his sedentary job with a swashbuckling flair that only his pre-eminence in his field prevented the quirk from qualifying as pathetic. He typed a few lines of code in workstation five and said: "Spike descending. Three point two seven. Two point six. Levelling off. I have stability to fourteen decimal places."

"Are we free to go? Resins free of noise from the data spike?"

"Noise levelling off," Askegren reported. "Inert readings. Inputs all clean of signal degradation."

"And the Oltion Field?"

"Optimal to fourteen places. First systems check Triple A. Second systems check initializing." Askegren took a deep breath, and spoke in a more conversational tone: "Pamela Sue Anderson again?"

"Naaah. Bosses monitoring this time. Cheesecake's no good for posterity."

"Then what?"

"Use the Silver Surfer."

"Cool. Silver Surfer it is." Askegren loaded a file from a

database that now contained over one hundred three-dimensional images, from celebrities to creatures out of myth and legend. The glamorous women were the most frequently consulted, but the others had all been used once or twice as well. "Three minutes to test. Let the world know we're ready to rock."

The two partners grinned at each other, as genuinely excited as they always were whenever their work seemed to be taking another giant leap toward fruition. In their minds the Nobel Prize was not only a given but an Understatement. If what they had in mind worked, they might conceivably be canonized. And their enthusiasm was catching—when Gold got on the intercom to confirm that all of the projects' other support teams were greenline, the excitement in each individual project leader's voice was downright palpable.

The isolation lock beeped twice just as Gold got off the horn with Doctors Goodman and Monella from Team Plaid. The beep was a formality; fun as cloak-and-dagger security requirements might sometimes be, it could get awfully lonely locked in here, and anybody capable of getting this far was authorized to visit anyway. The door wasn't ever locked unless the Birthing Chamber was in use, and required so much work to set up that this rarely happened more than once a month or so.

The vestibule revolved, and Joey Green limped in. He was a paunchy, freckled, redheaded security guard in his early thirties; the kind of guy who was always inordinately impressed with everything, and not at all shy about letting you know. He was so much a part of the facility that he'd been retained even after most of the security staff had been replaced with Silver Sable's crack team of mercenaries. The limp was courtesy of a case of gout that had been afflicting Joey's right foot for the better part of six months now. He grinned and waved at Askegren: "Hey, brainiac. Still messing around with the Star Trek stuff?"

Green's customary greeting hadn't been funny the first two hundred times he'd used it, but it had developed an uncanny zen-like resonance. Askegren had actually missed the daily repetition the last time he'd taken a long weekend. "It's not Star Trek stuff, Joey. It's Buck Rogers stuff. I thought we had that settled."

"Yeah, well, right, whatever. Beam me up, Scotty, right?"

"Right," Gold said. Like Askegreen, he loved these content-free conversations; after a morning spent swapping numerical readouts to the multi-decimal, Green's determined vapidity was better than a coffee break. "Anything we can do you for, Joey?"

"Well, I'm really sorry about this, guys, but I have been asked to remind you about updating the parking stickers on your respective chariots. The money men know who you are, of course—hell, they'd be stupid not to, since you're the whole reason this place exists—but jeez, they really would prefer it if you apply the new stickers by the end of the week. Would that be a problem?"

Askegren, whose very job description included bending the laws of physics, smiled at a scrolling screen of numerals. "Not in the grand scheme of things, Joey."

"That's just swell," said Green. Then he hesitated, and glanced out the plexiglass shield at the Birthing Chamber, where a bell-shaped Oltion Field Generator dangled over a vat of adamantium resins. "Say, you guys running a test today?"

"In about twenty minutes. Why? Do you want to watch again? We're not doing Pamela Sue, I'm afraid."

"That's all right," Green said. "I want you to power down the generator, de-activate the shields, disengage all the energy locks, cut all the data feeds to the Manhattan office, and turn all the variables down to zero point zero."

Askegren started. "Why?"

"Because," Green said, producing a revolver and speaking in an accented voice that neither of the two scientists knew, "I will shoot you both very dead if you don't."

For Askegren, the sight of the weapon was like a cold spear through the base of his spine: it silenced and paralyzed him utterly.

Gold's reaction was significantly more unfortunate. He shouted an obscenity and leaped for the red call button on the nearest workstation. By the time he got there the top half of his head had been reduced to bloody shrapnel radiating from the bullet's point of impact like a sine wave. He collapsed across his workstation, then slid downward, leaving parts of himself on his keyboard and monitors.

Askegren stared at the man who had been both his best friend and his partner in pushing the boundaries of man's knowledge. His entire eulogy was, "You," followed almost a full second later by, "But—"

Joey Green marched across the room, levelling his revolver at Askegren's forehead. With every step he took, his demeanor and appearance changed. His limp disappeared. His nose flattened. His lips smoothed out. His red hair faded to nothingness, and the skin of his familiar face became instead a featureless white mask, marked only by the vertical seam than ran from his scalp to his chin and the narrow slits that accomodated both his eyes and his mouth. The eyes behind the slits were as cold as anything Askegren had ever seen. The bottom half of the mask curved to reflect the cold smile of the murderer whose features it hid. "Greetings. I am the Chameleon. I am only one member of an unstoppable force about to assault this building. You are now faced with an opportunity many of your co-workers won't share: the chance to decide whether you will still be alive at day's end. Do what I say and I shall let you live. Act as foolishly as your friend and you will soon be an outline drawn in masking tape. You have precisely ten seconds to decide."

The cold steel of the barrel was a burning O on Askegren's sweaty forehead. "P-please...I have a baby daughter..."

"And generous death benefits sufficient to provide for her. You now have five seconds."

"Wh-what do you want?"

"I want you to power down the generator, de-activate the shields, disengage all the energy locks, cut all the data feeds to the Manhattan office, and turn all the variables down to zero point zero. If it takes more than ten minutes for you to accomplish all that, I will mail your widow a memorial ballpoint pen to complete her benefits claim. Start...now."

Askegren's mouth worked noiselessly for the first ten seconds. Then the Chameleon repositioned the barrel of his weapon so it faced the trembling scientist's right eye. The barrel seemed unnaturally black, but it was still possible to see a short distance into that narrow little tunnel, and speculate on just what lurked at its opposite end...

Askegren said: "I'll do it. J-just give me some space to work, okay?"

"With the understanding that you'll join your friend in death the instant you try to betray me. You now have about nine and a half minutes."

His heart thumping in his chest, Askegren began to work.

Lew Awsten, the Project Administrator at this facilty, was a balding, egg-shaped man in his early fifties, marked by his remarkable talent for locating the ugliest eyeglass frames any man could wear without instantly reducing himself to total social pariah. His current pair were thick, jet-black monstrosities that made his head look like a construction site surrounded by scaffolding. He looked like the standard cliché image of the nerdy scientist, but though he had a Ph.D. in electrical engineering, he hadn't participated in any of the research being done here. His chief talent was running the day-to-day support operations of this facility, making sure everything ran so smoothly that the brain boys truly in charge of this cutting-edge research were never bothered with minor details like dealing with Maintenance or Security.

He was, in short, that peculiar specimen unique to modern corporate life: the Boss whose job required him to not really be in charge.

Even so, he did possess a certain proprietary interest in the work being done here. He did try to keep abreast of its progress, even when he didn't completely understand it. And when Dr. Askegren sent down word that today's operation was being scrubbed at the last minute, he couldn't help feeling a little disappointed.

He decided to visit Abbott and Costello later, to see if there were any needs he could expedite.

But first he'd call the Tokyo office to tell the travelling CEO, Mr. Rand, that the test was scrubbed. That was, after all, the other half of his job: dealing with the big boss so the two geniuses didn't have to.

He reached for his desk phone.

It became a cobra and reared up at him.

He said, "What the—"

Then his office capsized. Gravity turned over on its side, leaving Awsten and his desk clinging to the side of a sheer vertical drop. Awsten gasped and clutched his desk, knowing that this couldn't be happening, not really, wondering if this was some symptom of the stroke his doctor kept promising if he didn't lay off the saturated fats. He reached for the phone, which had become a phone again, but which was now tumbling away from him, moving in slow motion it seemed, taking forever to fall away from him, cruelly taunting him with the reminder that help could no longer be summoned that easily.

He heard an explosion in the outer office, the sound of walls suddenly reduced to rubble. His secretary, Melanie, screamed, her voice cutting off in mid-syllable.

Then something slammed into his ribs and hurled him to the floor-no-longer-a-floor-but-a-wall. Pain and vertigo assaulted him. The far wall of his office receded, now hundreds of feet down, now thousands. Transformed against his will from fat executive to stranded rock-climber, he clutched the narrow threads of carpeting beneath his fingers with the desperation of a man who needed them to be thick cables capable of supporting his weight.

A man's voice purred: "No, you didn't really want to make a report to Mr. Rand, did you? You just want to hang here, holding on to dear life. You want to hang here until somebody comes to rescue you."

Awsten managed to turn his head, and caught a glimpse of a bizarre caped figure floating in mid-air at an angle that simply made no sense no matter whether floor or ceiling or wall was accepted as officially Down. The figure was tall and athletic, wearing a checkered green costume notable both for its ornate gauntlets and for the opaque goldfish-bowl helmet the man appeared to have instead of a visible head. The cape billowed out behind him in ways that suggested a roaring wind, even though the air currents in Awsten's office were as still as only the best climate control could manage.

Awsten remembered something from the recent news. Something about a movie star murdered to make a point. He managed, "M-mysterio?"

The caped man swooped near, chuckling behind his unwieldy helmet as he pulled the pin from a pineapple grenade. "I do so love the opportunity to get out and meet my public."

Awsten did not live long enough to beg for mercy.

Bill Wilson, who ran the front desk at this Rand-Meachum facility, was a show guard as opposed to the real guards provided by Silver Sable. Sitting behind a curved desk greeting all the guys and gals as they came in from the parking lot, watching them sternly as they lowered their eyes to the optical reader, was his idea of a perfect job—certainly a vast improvement from the one he'd held before a brief foray into disability and retirement bored him silly. That one, sitting at the front desk of the Emergency Psychiatric Unit at Midtown Hospital, had seemed relatively work-free too, until the day one loon broke in to kill another loon, and Bill's heroic resourcefulness had been required to save the day. (That wasn't actually the way it had happened, but it was the way Bill remembered it; even more than most people, he'd always been the star of his own personal movie.)

Anyway, what with one thing or another, this job was much better than the last one. Here, the only loons he needed to deal with were scientists, and all he needed to do to shut out that lunacy was not pay attention to whatever they were saying. With the real security being performed by the Silver Sable guys, he was just a receptionist with a badge. Talk about stress-free assignments.

At least until now, when the parking lot outside the building rang out with the sounds of smashing metal and shattering glass. It sounded like a demolition derby out there. Bill looked up from his book of half-completed *TV Guide Crosswords* and saw the damndest thing; it looked like a pudgy man on stilts, bobbing up and down over the cars, actually flinging some of them skyward as he approached Bill's vestibule at dizzying speed. It wasn't until the front entrance erupted in an explosion of glass, and a pair of sinuous adamantium tentacles snaked in to snatch the helpless Bill from his station, that Bill (who did occasionally read the papers, whenever he found a discarded one he could claim for free), felt the first suspicion that he knew who was behind this.

Bill knew he was right when a pudgy man supported by another pair of flailing tentacles bobbed into the lobby at near-ceiling height, his rounded face twisted into a hateful sneer. By then, the tentacle that had grabbed Bill had wrapped itself around his body three times, squeezing him with a force that wrested agony from compressed ribs.

Bill croaked out the name of the man who was about to murder him. "Doctor . . . Octopus . . . ! Why . . . ?"

The pudgy man grimaced. "Why? You dare to question me?"

Bill couldn't breathe. His mouth moved soundlessly.

Octopus sighed. "I really don't enjoy senseless killing. And under different circumstances, I might have allowed you to live. But I am working for an employer I despise, under conditions that severely compromise my dignity, and I am in no mood to show mercy to nonenties who have the temerity to question my motives. Therefore . . . "

The tentacle grasping Bill coiled so tightly that the loops all but disappeared. There was no longer any room for anything alive inside the spiral it had become. Or for that matter, anything intact. The remains of Bill Wilson hit the floor in pieces.

Doctor Octopus moved deeper into the building, smashing down walls as he went.

He smiled.

He'd lied about not enjoying it.

By this point, despite the delay Mysterio had arranged by taking out Awsten and the rest of the administration staff, a general alert had sounded all over the facility. Every control room, from Team Orange to Team Plaid, received directives for evacuation. Coded distress signals, pre-programmed into the site's alarm system, went out to local and state police, as well as Silver Sable's main office at the Symkarian Embassy in Manhattan. All around the building security personnel grabbed their pulse rifles and took up position. At their various assigned battle stations, determined to protect the Birthing Chamber at the heart of the building. Those lab technicians and support personnel who could make it out of their respective sections, to emergency stairwells and other shelters, fled to safety at all possible speed. Some made it. Others did not. The invaders were not interested in taking detours just because helpless civilians happened to be in their way.

Two of the Silver Sable operatives who hurried to join their embattled comrades on the front lines were Carlos Perez and Christina Santiago. They had been standing guard at the perimeter fence, and had witnessed Dr. Octopus's assault on the front entrance from a distance of fifty yards. Although Octopus had hurled several of the cars in the parking lot their way, Perez and Santiago wasted no time worrying about their own safety; they just made a silent joint decision and pursued him anyway. Airborn vehicles thudded into the grass on all sides as the two agents zigzagged through the line of fire, their weapons charged and ready. Perez shouted into his communicator as he ran: "We have a

P-1 Situation! Repeat P-1! Multiple Paranormals in Full Assault! Multiple Para—"

A shadow loomed over him. He thought it was one of tha automobiles Dr. Octopus had thrown. He hurled himself to his immediate left, confident in his ability to escape; after all, even two-ton missiles cannot alter direction in mid-fall, and even the most unaerodynamic car ever constructed was still subject to the laws of physics.

But the shadow changed direction, and followed him.

Perez looked up just in time to see the razor-sharp green wing, designed to look feathered but as metallic as any knife, descend with a force that sliced him in half.

Twenty feet away, Christina Santiago saw everything. She saw the grimacing, snaggle-toothed old man in the winged costume cut down her partner, the most capable Symkarian soldier she'd ever known, with an ease so extreme it suggested boredom. She did not scream. She did her job. Even before the two halves of her partner and friend hit the ground, she took aim and fired everything she had at the bird-man now turning his homicidal attentions toward her.

Christina Santiago was one of the foremost sharpshooters in her squad. She excelled particularly in taking down flying objects; in training, she'd scored one hundred percent taking down flying robot drones designed for evasive action.

Her best shots never even got close.

She expected to be cut in half, too, but instead, she was grabbed under the arms by two gnarled hands. The jolt as she was yanked off her feet almost dislocated her shoulders. Her neck whipped back, her pulse-rifle tumbled out of her grip, and she cried out as she saw the wreckage-strewn campus, the research facility, and the surrounding patchwork quilt of houses and roads and patches of gray and white all recede beneath her feet.

They were easily a thousand feet up before the old man (who didn't seem to actually need to flap those wings of his, and therefore suffered no difficulties carrying her), levelled off.

Santiago shouted: "Who are you? And where are you taking me?"

The old man chuckled. "My name should be obvious, my dear. I am the Vulture. As for where I'm taking you—you wound me. I am not taking you anywhere. In fact, now that I've treated you to this magnificent view, I intend to let you go . . ."

She screamed.

He followed her all the way down, his cold, dead eyes betraying no sympathy at all.

Elsewhere: Doctor Cynthia Monella ("Team Plaid"), assigned to support duty at one of the auxiliary control rooms, listened to the ubiquitous screams and explosions and sounds of destruction, and knew that the assault would soon arrive at her location.

She heard pulse-rifles being fired; that would be the Silver Sable people, defending the Birthing Chamber from the invaders. The rifles were first-class ordinance, powerful enough to drill neat holes in armored divisions. They needed to be, with terrorist loons like Hydra and A.I.M. itching for a chance to seize all advanced technological research for their very own. Unfortunately, from what she could hear the Silver Sable troops shouting in the hallway, the enemy wasn't even being slowed down.

Monella, a petite (5'4") brunette in her early thirties, had picked up most of her technical education in the Marines, and she knew her way around combat. She'd personally experienced only one firefight—that one a dustup in the

Saudi Arabian desert—but she knew what they were like; she had taken her medical discharge hoping never to see one again. Strictly speaking, she and her Number Two, Judi Goodman, were supposed to stay low in the event of any crisis... but strictly speaking, the sounds of combat were approaching so quickly that she didn't think the Team Plaid control room would be a safe place to stay any longer. Thinking quickly, she made a command decision she was not officially authorized to make. "Purge the memory."

Judi shuddered at the muffled sound of a nearby electrical explosion. "B-but... today's data..."

"Purge it. We can't let those bastards, whoever they are, get their filthy hands on whatever we have."

"Will we have time?"

"Not to see it through. But we can start the purge before thinking of escape. I'll take full responsibility."

Typing furiously, wincing at every shout or distant explosion, the tall and gawky Judi pulled down the Emergency Procedures Menu and selected the prompt for System Purge. This ordered the computer to scramble the site database and wipe out all data acquired since the last backup was messengered to the Main Office in Manhattan. That was only a twenty-four hour loss, but given how much this research cost on a daily basis, it was still going to hurt. Monella might have worried about it being taken out of her pay were there any chance of her ever making that much money in all the remaining years—or, given the situation, minutes—of her life. Monella pulled Judi out of her chair, typed the first emergency password, then the second, then the third. The computer began the purge.

The next explosion, just outside, was close enough to knock the data binders from their places on the reference shelves. Outside, pulse rifles blasted, and somebody emitted a high, bubbling, and clearly very final scream. Monella made out the words of a shout, clearly meant for any civilians still capable of hearing it: "Fall back! Fall back! They're killing everybody!"

Judi had turned white. "I don't think I can do this..."

Monella reached up and grabbed the much taller woman by the shoulders. "Don't think about it. Just stay low and aim for the emergency stairwell across the corridor. It's only a few feet away, and it's a push door, so you won't even have to turn the knob. Just lower your head and go. We'll be across in two seconds."

"And then what?"

Monella had absolutely no idea, but half the secret of survival was staying alive long enough to improvise. "Just follow me."

She led Judi to the security-locked door, taking a deep breath, surrendering to fear just long enough to tremble at the sounds of battle emanating from the hallway. It occured to her that this escape attempt might actually be more dangerous than just sitting tight and waiting for the carnage to pass; it was a terrible risk even for somebody like herself, who had been trained for battle situations, and much worse for somebody like Judi, who had never experienced anything worse than bumper-to-bumper traffic on I-95. She wondered if she should just leave Judi behind with a promise to send help if possible. And for a moment, she came close to doing just that.

But then the choice was taken out of her hands—

—the eastern wall of the control room exploding in a cloud of dust and other debris—

—a bespectacled fat man carried by four writhing tentacles coughing as he emerged through the shattered opening—

—the tentacles whipping about like questing worms, seizing electrical consoles and ripping them from the walls in burst of sputtering flame—

—Judi gasping, "It's D-doc—"

—Monella recognizing the figure too, knowing from his reputation that remaining here meant certain death—

—hearing another explosion, somewhere, not too far away—

—Monella propelling her stunned partner through the revolving lock—

—praying even as she did that any horrors ahead of them were not quite as deadly as the infamous monster she was now forced to flee.

But what they found ahead of them was hell on earth.

The hallway was redolent with acrid haze. Half a dozen security people in skintight armor raced by, pulse rifles at the ready. One, a man with a bushy walrus moustache, turned to shout at Monella, his words obliterated by a deafening explosion from further down the corridor. Two others took up positions at either side of him, levelling their weapons at an unseen enemy further up the corridor. A whitecoated man, more dead than alive, only barely recognizable as Team Scarlet Coordinator Peter Rawlik, lay hideously disfigured at their feet. The air smelled of blood and ozone and overcooked meat. One thunderclap and brilliant flash of light later, the man with the walrus moustache completely vanished, the air misting scarlet with all that remained of his existence on Earth. The two Silver Sable operatives with bazookas held their positions anyway, firing round after round at the human monster approaching from the other end of the embattleed corridor.

The murderer in skintight green strode toward them in an oval of sizzling light, his eyes bursting with corruscating energy, his arms rippling cauldrons of living lightning. It was impossible to guess at his features; he glowed far too brightly for Monella to discern anything but a dorky crew-cut. He was like a star, come to earth in the form of a malicious child, and though he took out one defender after another with bolts of energy that fried them where they stood, he gave the impression that he regarded this outing as a real hoot. His stride reminded Monella of the male lead in a romantic musical, just before he breaks into song. Certainly he had no worries on his shoulders: the pulse bolts fired by the weapons of the Silver Sable agencies detonated into bursts of harmless light long before they touched him.

Judi froze. "Cynthia, I can't—"

A gleaming adamantium tentacle smashed through the revolving lock behind them, its pincers clutching hungrily at empty air.

Doctor Octopus.

Monella snapped out of her paralysis. She yanked Judi out of the way of the slashing tentacles and behind the Silver Sable agents who were still bravely holding their ground, still firing shot after shot in the vain hope that one of their plasma bolts might possibly get through. One of the agents heard the tentacle smash through the wall behind her and whirled to face the new attack.

He was clubbed dead by that tentacle before he had the time to face it. Meanwhile, the glowing man at the end of the corridor shouted something about wanting people to remember his name.

Electro.

It seemed too comical a name to befit this evil force of nature.

But Monella wasn't laughing. With two impossibly powerful super-villains converging on her position, she only had eyes for the door to the emergency stairwell. She leaped at it, felt her heart skip as the door blessedly swung open at her touch, and darted inside, turning only when she realized that the panicked Judi had torn free of her grip; the silly girl had instinctively darted back toward Team Plaid Control, in search of a safe haven that no longer existed.

Monella whirled just in time to see one of Electro's stray lightning bolts strike Judi.

The effect was instantaneous; were it not for the unfortunate literal meaning of the word, Monella would have been tempted to think of it as "electric." Judi convulsed violently, her limbs thrashing with an abandon that suggested wild dancing. She emitted a sound that might have been a scream, but which was crippled by the fresh limitations of the lungs reduced to ash in her chest. She charred and exhaled a cloud of ash and finally fell, twitching uncontrollably in the manner of a corpse still animated by the forces that had torn the life from her. Even before the next lightning bolt struck, incinerating her utterly, her now-blackened clothing was already spouting tongues of angry flame.

Monella wanted to leap back into the corridor, grab one of the fallen pulse rifles, and fire hot plasma at Electro. Who knew? She might have gotten in a lucky shot. She might have given him what he deserved.

But it was far more likely the fast track to suicide.

She whirled again and retreated further into the relative safety of the stairwell, barely ahead of a massive explosion that sent fistfuls of gravel slamming into her flesh. Her eyes burned. *What's going through their heads?* she wondered. *What can such murdering bastards possibly be thinking?*

Nodding at Dr. Octopus, who had directed him to stay on this level mopping up any more security forces he might encounter, Electro reflected that he really couldn't stop thinking of Pity. It was too bad she couldn't make it today. He missed her. He had no way of knowing that sixty miles away, the latest battle between Pity and Spider-Man had just reached a most unfortunate conclusion...

Outside, a squadron of state troopers converging on the embattled building ran off the road when they thought they saw another dozen automobiles, barrelling down the road at high speed, about to smash into them head-on. Two of the cop cars rolled in the massive pile-up; one officer was killed, four others critically injured, one disabled for life. As those who'd survived the multiple accidents relatively intact stumbled from their vehicles, moaning and cursing, Mysterio flew above their heads, cackling madly. Several of the officers got their heads together enough to fire shots at him. Mysterio, still laughing, simply disappeared in a puff of white smoke. He was replaced by the hurtling form of the Vulture, wearing the snaggle-toothed grin of a man who was only beginning to enjoy his fun.

Considering himself damned, not knowing how lucky he was to still be alive and unhurt, Askegren watched through the specially shielded glass as the new arrival, Doctor Octopus, invaded the deactivated Birthing Chamber itself. After hesitating at the now-inert mixed resin vat, Octopus used his tentacles to climb to the top of the Chamber and attack the Oltion Generator itself. That was the bell-shaped connection-studded device affixed to the Chamber ceiling. From the efficient sense of purpose Octopus demonstrated by immediately attacking the bolts that held the twenty-ton device in place, it was impossible for Askegren to avoid the realization that this had been the target of the invasion all along.

Askegren, who had endured most of this nightmare meekly accepting the presence of the revolver the Chameleon held to his head, cried out, "What do you think you're doing?"

To his horror, Octavius heard him. The pudgy man in the soupbowl haircut stopped what he was doing and turned toward the Chameleon. His own voice sounded tinnily through the control room speakers: "As I informed that other slug at the front desk, I am not in the mood for impertinent questions. Kill him, Anatoly."

Askegren shouted fast enough to outrace the Chameleon's trigger finger. "N-no! Wait! I'm not trying to stop you! I know I can't—but don't you understand? The Generator's useless to you!"

Octavius froze in mid-operation. "Interesting. You may continue."

"It's not the Process! It's just a component of the Process! It's just one cog in a network of machines extensive enough to fill this building to five sub-basements! It can't make the Process work by itself! Hell, we can only make the Process work for thirty seconds at a time as it is!"

Octopus made a gesture that stayed the Chameleon's hand. "Most intriguing. And since I see from the resin vats below that this Process of yours has something to do with the manufacture of adamantium—a metal I always find useful—I might be back someday soon, to learn just what you were doing here."

"You . . . don't know? You're not here for the Process? Just for the Oltion Generator? I don't understand . . ."

"You're not being asked to understand," Octopus said with a peremptory wave of one hand. "But you have given me food for thought, today. You will be permitted to survive so you may complete the researches I will one day claim for my own use.—Anatoly? Please silence this fool. Temporarily."

Askegren did not see the butt of the revolver slamming against his head, not once but repeatedly. The brain swelling he suffered from the concussion did not quite kill him. It kept him on the critical list long enough to miss not only what remained of the siege, but also the funerals of all the friends and co-workers who had died today. He would not wake up until days after the world found out why the Sinister Six had needed to come here—and by then, it would be too late to change a damn thing.

Maybe, he'd think then, that was one definition of being lucky.

There was not much left after that. With the goal all but achieved the bloodshed was already winding down. Elsewhere in the building Electro continued to hunt down and wipe out security forces, but there weren't many of those left, and he was just human enough to show mercy to those with enough common sense to beg for their lives. Up in the air the Vulture used a scavenged pulse rifle to force a police helicopter to keep its distance. He did not shoot it down, even though that would have been easy. Down at ground level Mysterio used his powers of illusion to keep the civilians and security personnel from fleeing various nightmares of his own design—but he now limited his activities to terror alone, having accomplished more than enough killing for one day. As for the Chameleon, he simply relaxed and guarded the unconscious Askegren with a care that practically qualified as protective.

Five minutes after breaking into the Birthing Chamber, Dr. Octopus succeeded in detaching the Oltion Generator.

Showing no strain as he held its massive bulk in two of his tentacles, he shouted: "Ha! I've got it! Coming?"

The Chameleon shook his head. "No. I'll signal Electro to join you, but I'll make my own way out. I have personal business to attend to."

This did not make Dr. Octopus happy. He had frequently expressed his feelings toward colleagues who quit jobs while they were still halfway done. But since there was no immediate need for the Chameleon's services he acquiesed, leaving the building through the great gaping hole he had torn in the roof for that purpose. He rendezvoused with Mysterio, the Vulture, and the simultaneously-exiting Electro outside, where they made their escape in full view of the dozens of survivors trembling and weeping at the horror they'd been forced to endure. Police helicopters tracked the escape of the four murderous super-villains until the criminals hit the outskirts of Newark, at which point the surveillance equipment finally established that it had been tracking a group of holograms Mysterio had designed to cover the actual route.

The *Daily Bugle*, showing its usual sense of consistency, would soon blast Spider-Man, whose vigilante activities it condemned every other day of the year, for not doing anything to stop the massacre. This was despite the fact, as documented elsewhere in the paper, that Spider-Man had been busy enough risking his life somewhere else.

Nobody seemed to notice that the Chameleon had not accompanied his partners on his way out of the building. Nor would they notice as he used a series of persuasive disguises to escape the building and make his way back to the city.

And he had special arrangements to make that were not on the official agenda . . .

CHAPTER FIVE

The carnage at Rand-Meachum was still several minutes away when the Gentleman exited Yeganeh Jewelers, his slave Pity in tow.

The old man's expression was half self-satisfaction, half distaste: the self-satisfaction derived from successfully negotiating the purchase of the Czarina's necklace, the distaste a reaction to once again encountering the same dull, common faces he had been forced to confront every day since his return to this misbegotten country. One sweep of his eyes and he could see an array of homeless people, messengers, business people, wealthy indolents, and mumbling eccentrics, none of whom betrayed even the slightest glimmer of the commanding personal light he usually considered the bare minimum for anybody who wished to be considered truly human. He felt soiled just to be standing on the same city street with these people.

It was possible, he supposed, that some of them might actually be elevated to a higher form of life in the face of the extreme chaos he intended to rain down upon their lives.

Swords tempered in fire, and all that. Considered that way, this enterprise might actually be considered a charitable act.

The Gentleman shuddered. He considered the charitable impulse both base and decadent. His distaste for it was so extreme that he avoided all investments, however profitable, that promised beneficial results for anybody other than himself. He avoided trickle-down economics. It was a sign of wasted investment opportunity.

In any event, he felt relieved that his errand in the diamond district—one of many similar shopping trips he'd conducted since his arrival in America—had been concluded with such a blessed minimum of complication. He had feared a replay of the ignoble calamity that had befallen his old diamond smuggling partner, Dr. Christian Szell,. The one and only time Szell had ventured here from his usual haunts in South America, to consolidate his assets, he had been forced to commit a murder or two just to protect his investment. He'd been abducted, robbed, and shot by a commoner gradstudent with a grudge, after decades of successfully evading the elite manhunters of the world. The Gentleman, who was human enough to mourn his few true friends, wiped a single tear from the corner of his eye and moved on.

Traffic on the narrow crosstown street was moving at a glacial pace, thanks to an excess of taxicabs and delivery vans competing to pass through the one-lane space between the parked cars on either side. This, however, rebounded to the Gentleman's benefit, as so many things in this life did—it prevented him from needing to hurry to meet the stretch limousine he'd summoned from Sabi Yeganeh's showroom. The Gentleman knew it was his limo because he'd recognized the driver, one Ivan Rastokov, whose skills behind the wheel had served both himself and the Chameleon on several occasions. Ivan had always been dull, stolid, unimaginative, and common—all the things that the Gentleman ranked along with poverty as the signifiers of the barely human—but he'd also always shown a remarkable degree of discretion, which made him invaluable to an entrepreneur of the Gentleman's ilk.

"There," the Gentleman said, pointing his wolf's-head walking stick at the limo. "Come along, dear."

Moving with an agility that belied his advanced years, the Gentleman darted through a narrow space between parked automobiles and leaned over the driver's side window to provide Ivan with his destination. He did not get in the limo himself, but he gallantly held the door open for Pity as she slid into the back seat and placed the treasure-laden suitcase on the seat beside her.

She made room for him, but he shook his head. "No, I believe I'll take a walk around Manhattan today; there is, after all, no telling when I'll have my next chance. You know what to do. Secure today's purchases in the usual place, and then return to the townhouse as soon as that's accomplished. You may not—"

The cretin driving the pale green monstrosity immediately behind the limousine, who no doubt considered his own stupid errands of world-shaking importance, leaned on his horn to punish the doddering old man who was taking so long to say goodbye.

The Gentleman took his time giving Pity the last of her instructions. "I know that you have not yet eaten, or had anything to drink, today, but you may not partake of any refreshment until these treasures are safely with the others. If you wish, you may have an apple and a cup of warm water when you return to the townhouse. But not before. Is that clear?"

Pity said nothing. Of course. But her understanding was implicit.

The Gentleman slammed the door, and signalled Ivan that it was all right to go. The limousine moved slowly down the street, barely accelerating at all in light of the stop signal glowing red at the next intersection.

The idiot in the pale green monstrosity, a doughy individual with skin that resembled a tactical map at some Pentagon war room, pulled up just enough to lean out the window and snarl: "Who the hell do you think you are, Pops? Blocking traffic like that?"

The Gentleman regarded the subhuman fool with the dispassionate remove of a naturalist watching birds migrate south. And then, with one smooth, confident movement, as deftly executed as any swordthrust by any master fencer, he lifted his walking stick and jabbed the offensive creature in the neck right above the Adam's Apple.

He did not draw blood or cause permanent injury. But the idiot in the pale green monstrosity immediately doubled over and gagged. The idiot in the bright pink monstrosity immediately behind him began to blare his own horn in protest.

Rolling his eyes at the stupidity of it all, doubly certain that the subhumans of this city deserved everything that was about to happen to them, the Gentleman turned on his heels and strolled away, humming a happy aria. He moved quickly to avoid any complications that might have been caused by the impromptu etiquette lesson.

As a result, he completely missed the catastrophe that befell Pity and her driver even before their limousine managed to pass the first intersection.

Stopped at the red light, the wanly beautiful young woman named Pity sat in silence, her expression as blank as any canvas yet to enjoy its first stroke of the brush. She might have been a porcelain doll or a helpless catatonic, or just an unhappy human being lost in thoughts that she'd never been permitted to share. But she revealed nothing. Her training required no less.

The driver, Ivan, glanced at her in the rear-view mirror. "To hell with the old man, dear. If you're thirsty, there's plenty of juice in the bar. Take something. I won't tell."

Pity said nothing. Of course.

Ivan said, "I mean it."

She licked her lips, but made no move to accept his offer. She knew the man who owned her. He'd be able to tell.

Ivan muttered a disgusted curse under his breath.

And then, catastrophe.

The driver's side window shattered, spraying him with broken glass. He gasped, and turned reflexively toward the source of the disturbance, already reaching beneath his uniform for the Glock in his shoulder holster. Before he could reach it, a leather-gloved hand at the end of a leather-jacketed arm reached in through the shattered window and grabbed hold of his wrist.

With her speed and reaction time, Pity would have already made it to the front seat to defend him were it not for the need to counter a secondary attack being aimed at her. She had spotted it immediately. A hulking, burly figure of a man, wearing a long rain slicker over what appeared to be several layers of indifferently-laundered gray sweatshirts was winding up to assault the passenger door window with a sledgehammer still dropping from concealment into his hands. The man, whose scalp had recently been shaved with far more care than his spottily bristled jawline, had the kind of physique that testified to many years of obsessive training in prison exercise yards. He shouted something obscene as he raised the sledgehammer high above his head and brought it hurtling downward toward Pity's window.

Pity fell back against the seat and kicked the door with both feet. For the door, it was a lot like being hit by a speeding Mack truck that had somehow, impossibly, materialized inside the car. It snapped its hinges and slammed into the man with the sledgehammer with an impact that dwarfed anything his chosen weapon might have done. It flung the sledgehammer from his grasp, lifted him off his feet, and slammed him against a nearby parked car with a force that must have left him with splinters instead of ribs.

Pity would have gone to Ivan's aid then, but that's when the tertiary attack shattered the rear window. A shooter, somewhere behind her. The car was a death trap. She curled up, somersaulted out the space where the door had recently been, and landed on her feet in time to devote exactly one eighth of one second to determining the nature of the attack. Assassins, sent by one of the Gentleman's many enemies? Some kind of arrest attempt by this city's law-enforcement community? Something even stranger?

She filtered out the screams of the terrified and the thrill-seeking stares of the curious and even the awestruck smiles of the entertained.

In an instant she had succeeded in reducing the situation to the tactically relevant.

Four young men. One already down, thanks to the flying door. Another reloading a pair of automatics, approaching the limo from behind. One at the driver's-side door, wrestling with Ivan for control of the Glock. Another on the sidewalk on the opposite side of the car, firing wildly over the top of the limo.

Superficially, the attack might have been mistaken for being well organized. Four shooters attacking the limo from four sides, at angles that avoided taking each other. But the attack on Ivan's window had taken place a couple of seconds too early, the attack on the rear window a couple of seconds too late, and the attack from the limo's right was already revealing itself as pathetically sloppy. It attempted to manage in sheer number of rounds expended what simple good marksmanship and a single bullet might have accomplished far less riskily. There wasn't a single one of the attackers who betrayed any professional experience whatsoever.

Her mind still racing so quickly that the three remaining attackers might not have been aware of any pause for tactical analysis, Pity arrived at an aghast, dumbfounded hypothesis that explained everything.

Namely:

They were idiots.

Simple, common, everyday, sloppy, criminal idiots.

Carjackers. They'd gotten wind of the old guy making all the major jewel buys and decided to take him down. They'd followed him to Yeganeh's and waited outside, in the hopes of a quick smash and grab.

Their success in following Pity when she happened to be carrying millions in jewelry testified to the surface effectiveness of their plan. This, however, was more than amply offset by their apparent belief that the unimposing Pity would be an easy target.

All that Pity understood in one-eighth of one second.

Then she moved. Another shot whizzed by over her head, shattering the window of another diamond merchant across the street. She leaped to the side of the young man she'd bowled over with the car door. The door lay beside him on the street, considerably dented by her kick. She used a toe to flip it upward into her waiting hands, then whirled and flung it, frisbee-like, over the top of the limousine, to take out the idiot firing at her from that vantage point. It hit him in the face and immediately removed him from the equation.

Even as she did that, Ivan managed to clear his own weapon long enough to gut-shoot the young man who had been wrestling for its control. That young man stumbled backward, his arms and legs flailing. Pity glanced at Ivan to see if he was all right, and saw at once that he was not. He might have had enough strength to win the battle for the Glock, but at least one of the wild rounds fired through the rear window had found its home in him. He didn't have much of a jaw left . . . and from the way he was starting to slump, not much of a future, either.

Pity whirled toward the last of the four assailants, the one whose bullets had claimed Ivan. That young man, the skinniest and most red-eyed of the lot, had clearly needed pharamaceutical aid to get him through what had probably been intended as a cakewalk shoot-and-grab. He was still approaching at a gallop, firing madly. Though he was too committed to the attack, he also possessed the look of a foe who sees the general trend of battle and desperately wants a graceful way to back down.

It cost Pity a heartbeat's effort to leap to his side, seize him by both wrists, force him to drop his guns, dislocate both his arms, then spin him around and slam him face-first into the roof of the limousine with a force that must have left him with a mouthful of loose teeth.

As he slid to the pavement, Pity heard shouts behind her. She whirled, and spotted a slightly-built young uniformed cop, of the sort that cultivates a handlebar moustache to avoid the look of a teenager playing dress up. The cop levelled his service revolver, not at the would-be robbers, but at Pity, as he ordered her to freeze. He even used her name, thus establishing that he paid attention to departmental briefings. The street behind him was filled with horrified pedestrians torn between the need to see the show and the common sense urge to hit the deck before more bullets flew. At least six people in earshot, eager to demonstrate their own level-headedness in a crisis, were already shouting helpful advice to call 911.

Pity calculated the odds of crossing the distance between herself and the cop before he managed to fire. He wouldn't hesitate to fire, of course. She was, after all, a known member of a prominent paranormal terrorist group, and any sudden moves on her part would have to be taken as an attack. But even assuming extraordinary reflexes and perfect aim, his chances of taking her down were minimal. She could have him flat on his back, and if desired, dead, even before his trigger finger could receive firing orders from his brain.

Her conditioning required her to give the option serious consideration.

Maybe it was her awareness that he was just an innocent doing his job that stayed her hand. Maybe the impulse that spared him came from that small part of herself that the Gentleman had never been able to reach. Maybe she was just restoring the Mission to its proper place in her list of priorities. Either way, she fired herself like an arrow from a bow, not at the hapless cop, but into the back seat of the limousine. Hurtling through the interior in an eyeblink and flying out the shattered window on the opposite side without being eviscerated by the shards of razor-sharp glass still intact in the door, she now carried with her the Gentleman's suitcase, which she was required to value more than her own life. By that time the Darkness she'd harbored for most of her existence was already fanning out to swallow everything within a one-block radius, rendering both the witnesses, and any would-be pursuers, effectively blind.

All around her, lost in the sudden blackness, civilians and other onlookers shrieked in terror. She heard a few scattered voices appealing for calm, but there weren't many of them, and most of those weren't very persuasive.

Five seconds and there'd be a full-fledged panic. Probably fatalities to go with it. The Gentleman might have liked that. But Pity always lived up to her name on those occasions when she was permitted enough personal discretion to do so. She lifted the darkness after only two seconds. By then she was four stories up and still climbing, the special adhesive abilities of her hands and feet providing a purchase that even Spider-Man himself might have envied.

Down below in the street, some of the onlookers were already pointing at her. It was a sign that maybe she should have let the darkness cover them a little bit longer. She didn't allow the recriminations to concern her. She just flipped herself over the rooftop overhang, landed on her feet up above, hesitated just long enough to register a set of distant sirens, and began racing uptown over the rooftops.

She needed to find a subway entrance. If she could find a subway entrance she could make her way back to the townhouse underground. It would mean not bringing the jewels to the Gentleman's vault as ordered, but at least the jewels themselves would be safe.

In terms of the Gentleman's wrath, that was a major difference.

She would be punished, but not as cruelly as she could be.

As she leaped a crosstown street to land on the roof of another building on the other side, less than two minutes had passed since the carjackers had attacked.

Pity had no way of knowing this, of course, but it was at this point, across town at the *Daily Bugle* building, that Peter

SECRET OF THE SINISTER SIX

Parker was being briefed by Editor in Chief Joe Robertson. He would be leaping out a lower floor window as Spider-Man in less than ninety seconds. She would have plenty to occupy her before he showed up. But their confrontation was now inevitable.

Pity was six blocks uptown, following an unpredictable zigzag route across the rooftops that slowed her progress but prevented any of the authorities from getting a fix on her destination, by the time the sirens began to close in all around her. New York's Finest, tried vainly to box her in by dispatching squad cars from several directions at once. This did not particularly concern her. The cars were stuck at ground level, and limited by the streets themselves to grid-like patterns of movement; it took them far longer to get into position than it took her to alter course and render their best manuevers irrelevant. She would by necessity slow down as soon as she entered a neighborhood with taller buildings, but they actually presented an advantage in that they gave her places to hide and more options for movement if the pursuit succeeded impossibly in forcing her inside.

That would also not be a disaster. A sufficiently tall building was a lot like a small town stretched out vertically; it provided a perfect battleground in that it presented thousands of opportunities for concealment and almost as many places to confront the enemy on her own terms. A single undistinguished New York street cop had demonstrated the principle quite effectively during a terrorist crisis in Los Angeles just a few years ago. Spider-Man had done much the same with the *Daily Bugle* building one week ago. Pity wasn't worried about her chances if it came to that. But it wasn't the most efficient way of managing an escape. She reserved the option for use as a last resort.

Seven blocks uptown she experienced serious opposition for the first time, as a hail of bullets drew a line across the blacktop expanse in her path.

It had not been meant to hit her. She darted out of their way anyway, somersaulting to the top of a rooftop utility shed to face the NYPD helicopter that had just swooped down to place her within sharpshooting range.

The copter must have been already in the air and close enough for an intercept order. It was another stroke of awful luck. Regardless, the NYPD sniper in the open hatchway three stories above her had her in his sights.

"Attention!" an amplified voice blared. "The young woman on the rooftop! We know who you are and have been authorized to use all force necessary to stop you! Lie face-down on the roof and you will not be harmed!"

To Pity, the sniper's position was like any other open doorway within leaping distance.

At her bidding, the day vanished, replaced by one moment of perfect darkness.

When light returned, only one second later, Pity stood beside the astonished sniper in the helicopter's hatchway. She yanked the rifle from his hands with a force that fractured his trigger finger, and rammed the butt into his belly. The impact snapped the harness that held him in place and sent him hurtling to the rear of the cabin. He hit the bulkhead with a thud, and slid to the floor, moaning. Pity snapped his rifle in two over her knee, retrieved the Gentleman's suitcase from the open compartment where she'd just stashed it, and turned her attention to the pilot.

In that, she turned out to be a fraction of a second too late, because the pilot had already decided that his own survival depended on jettisoning her at any cost.

She was out the hatch before she realized that he had

banked hard to the left. She did not scream or release the Gentleman's suitcase. She just flipped in mid-air and seized the landing ski with her free hand. Even as the jolt of the sudden stop reverberated down her spine, the broken rifle tumbled past her, closely followed by the semi-conscious sniper himself, who was just awake enough to display vague concern at his impending three-story fall toward the nearest solid surface.

Without letting go of the landing ski she swung out, hooked her legs around his midsection, and seized him with a grip that cracked two of his ribs.

The pilot must have realized the depth of his tactical error then, because the chopper immediately levelled out and hovered. The pilot shouted something Pity could not make out over the rotors, but which were probably words to this effect: "Charlie! Charlie! Ohmigod I dropped Charlie—"

The chopper began to descend.

Two stories above the rooftop.

Then one.

Pity released the landing ski and dropped. She somersaulted on the way down, positioning her injured captive above her so she could take the brunt of the impact on her own back. She tossed him away with a kick; he rolled two or three times before coming to rest against a filthy expanse of graffiti-laden brick.

The chopper above her stopped descending, its pilot instead electing to hover in place as he scanned the rooftop for the two broken bodies he expected to find.

Pity grimaced. Enough was enough, already.

The helicopter vanished, replaced by a sphere of solid darkness floating in mid-air.

She banished the darkness, and allowed the helicopter to appear again.

Pity strobed the lights three or four times before the slow-thinking chopper pilot finally understood her message. She could render him blind at a moment's notice. She could do this above Manhattan, the greatest aerial obstacle course in the world. If she willed it, he wouldn't be able to see his instruments, or the view out the windshield, or the great glass edifices looming on all sides. She could leave him helpless to avoid the kind of collision capable of turning his mighty flying machine into a ball of roiling flame and shattered metal, plunging like a bomb onto streets clogged with screaming innocents.

She would do it, if he forced her. Her conditioning guaranteed it.

She was Pity. Nobody knew what she was like inside because she had always been what somebody else demanded her to be. Nobody knew the kind of things she would or wouldn't do if ever allowed a choice.

But she was still giving him a chance she'd never known. The opportunity to fly away. And the next time she banished the darkness, he took that chance. The chopper turned and retreated, gaining altitude as quickly as it could.

That was the last helicopter they'd send after her.

Sparing one glance at the injured sniper—he was wide-awake now, and staring at her—she grabbed the now severely-scuffed suitcase, spun around once to regain her bearings, then sprinted toward the edge of the roof. One easy leap later she was over the cross street and on the rooftop of the opposite four-story building. The sirens still sounded in the streets below, but they might have been worlds away. They couldn't stop her. Nothing could stop her from returning to the Gentleman's side.

Nothing, that is . . . except just possibly the familiar figure in the red-and-blue bodysuit who chose that moment to drop into her path.

For Spider-Man, who had broken several personal speed records just getting here, the chopper's intervention had proven a godsend. Not only had it delayed Pity the few precious seconds he needed to catch up with her, but it had also prompted her to unwittingly signal her position in a manner so clear that he would have had to be blind himself to miss her. He had spotted the first fleeting use of her darkness-inducing powers when he was still five crosstown blocks away. He had arrived in time to witness the last of her successful bid to force the chopper's retreat.

He couldn't reconcile the "shooting" Robertson had reported with her apparent avoidance of killing, nor could he understand why the newest member of the Sinister Six suddenly seemed to be working a solo act.

He only knew this was his first chance to get some real answers.

Using his web-shooters to spin a net in her path, he said, "Hey, hasty, hasty, hasty! Where are you off to in such a rush, when you and I have so much to talk about?"

Pity said nothing. Of course.

She just dropped the suitcase, leaped over his net, landed beside Spider-Man, and aimed a deadly roundhouse kick to his jaw.

Spider-Man deflected the kick with a forearm, whirled, and aimed a disabling punch at her solar plexus, which she deflected just as easily.

Their arms and legs became blurs as they pummelled each other with more punches and kicks, none of which landed solidly enough to put either Pity or Spider-Man down. Vicious as the attacks seemed, they were just exploratory actions, on the part of combatants who knew they were too evenly matched to risk a poorly-planned offensive.

Less than a minute into the battle, Spider-Man retreated twenty feet in a single leap. "We don't have to do this!" he shouted. "I saw the way you saved that sniper! And I saw the way you drove off that chopper without resorting to deadly force! It underlined something I've known about you since we fought on the *Daily Bugle* roof—that you don't really want to be doing this! This is not the kind of person you are!"

Pity's response was as smooth as a raindrop flowing down a windowpane. She spun and roundhouse-kicked a chimney, shattering it and assaulting the wall-crawler with a hailstorm of brick shrapnel. In a blur of movement, he managed to dodge the deadlier missiles, but what got through hit hard enough to tear right through his costume and, in some places, his skin. He ignored the pain and leaped at her, all his concentration devoted to finding some words capable of reaching her. As he grabbed her by the wrists and drove her back toward the web-net he'd spun before, he cried: "You don't have to let that old man control you like this! Whatever hold he has on you—you can still fight him! I'll help you!"

Pity drove a knee into his belly, knocking the breath out of him and loosening his grip on her wrists. Wrenching free, she did not take advantage of the opportunity to press her attack. Instead, she backed off, feinted a kick that he easily dodged, and curled into a defensive crouch.

They circled each other warily: two of the most dangerous combatants in the world sensing in each other dangers that went beyond strength, beyond speed, and beyond cunning.

This was personal.

Spider-Man knew it. And he could tell she knew it too.

But just how much did she know? How much of what he saw in her eyes was based on things the Gentleman had told her? And how much was just reaction to the sympathy Spider-Man offered? He couldn't tell. But he had to press the advantage: "Please. I can't tell you why I'm taking such a personal interest in this—but I do want to help you. You just have to trust me. Please."

She might have hesitated. Maybe.

Then the darkness erupted. It swallowed the rooftop and everything on it, Spider-Man included. In the fraction of a second he needed to recover, his spider-sense screamed. He dove for safety just in time to evade the worst of the deadly blow aimed at his head. It grazed his jaw lightly, which was just bad enough to feel like the strongest jab ever thrown by the world's strongest heavyweight boxer. While still in mid-dive, and still reeling too badly to enjoy full guidance by his spider-sense, he gave everything he had to a single blind kick, and felt absolutely no sense of triumph when he succeeded in batting Pity aside.

The darkness receded like tendrils of india ink intent on returning to their temporary home in the jar.

Pity stood twenty feet away, the leather suitcase clutched in her right hand. She did not move at first, but instead faced Spider-Man across the gulf that separated them, her eyes a well of unknown thoughts.

Spider-Man said: "Please. Trust me."

The moment lasted forever.

And then Pity turned tail and bolted, racing along the three-foot-high brick barrier that marked the edge of the rooftop.

Spider-Man went after her.

He was aware of the shouts rising from street level where onlookers must have been gathering for several minutes now. There was always a crowd hoping to see something cool whenever he had one of his fight scenes in public. He could hear some cheering him on, and others cheering Pity. There must have been dozens, all in all. He didn't care. His heart was pounding, even though the mere exertion of the fight wouldn't have even left him winded.

He didn't want to fight her.

Not if she was really his—

—or even if she wasn't—

Pity whirled and aimed a kick at his midsection. He backed up, dodging it. She advanced on him, furious now, hurling one kick after another, driving him back.

Cheers from down below.

Why not? They were probably *Bugle* readers.

More punches and kicks on the edge of a four-story drop. More appeals to her alleged longing for freedom from the Gentleman. More blank stares easy to misinterpret as wistful reaction. The battle between them stretched out like an epic poem, the stanzas marked by momentary shifts in the balance of power between combatants. Neither Pity nor Spider-Man made any real progress in defeating the other. It was an endless, interminable status quo that may have encompassed as many as three hundred attacks and defenses in the space of a minute. If anybody was ahead on points it was Pity, since she held her own despite a noticable handica; the one hand dedicated to guarding the Gentleman's suitcase from harm.

And then Spider-Man experienced that familiar, blessed moment of calm epiphany, common to so many of his battles when he suddenly knew exactly what he needed to do.

In this case, he feinted, dodged, and grabbed the briefcase himself. "Give me that!"

SECRET OF THE SINISTER SIX

Pity clutched the corner of the briefcase with her other hand.

Spider-Man tightened his other grip. "No way, lady! If this is important to that old fossil—I am not letting him have it!"

They struggled.

It didn't last long.

They were two of the most powerful human beings on the face of the planet, and they were playing tug-of-war with a creation of leather, cardboard, steel ribbing, and cloth.

The inevitable happened.

The briefcase ripped in half.

Spider-Man stumbled backward one way, holding one half; Pity stumbled backward the other way, holding what was left. It spoke well of their mutual senses of balance that neither of them tumbled off the edge of the roof. The jewels purchased from Sabi Yeganeh, on the other hand, did not enjoy the benefit of any personal input into the degree of their capitulation to the dictates of gravity. They fanned out into the open air, a sparkling rainbow of color capturing the indifferent light of the winter sun. And then they fell. Some clattered on the roof, but most descended like precious manna into the hands of the onlookers below, who needed only a second to register the value of the gifts tumbling from the sky before they fell to their knees, clutching and grabbing and fighting for fistfuls of treasure. The few police officers on the scene waded into the crowd attempting to stop the feeding frenzy—but even as they pulled some of the greedier folks from the mob, others content with smaller jackpots were already fleeing down the street, giggling with acquisitive glee.

In other circumstances Spider-Man could have beaten

most of those jewels to the street and used his webbing to contain the crowd so nobody got away with booty ... but he was too busy defending himself from Pity, who had just become a whirlwind of rage. One look at her eyes and he knew that she wished she was capable of cursing him out loud. It was the kind of anger that only comes from fear and despair and self-loathing, and it gave her next flurry of punches and kicks a fury that rendered them several orders of magnitude more deadly than anything she had ever demonstrated before. He blocked two dozen punches before an unbearably savage kick landed in his kidney, doubling him over with pain. The next blow hurled him against what was left of the shattered chimney and left him moaning, unable to defend himself against whatever she chose to do next.

"I'm sorry," he said, meaning it. It was not an apology for trying to stop her, or even for losing her treasure. It was regret for the price they both knew her master would exact from her. "You ... can't go back to the Gentleman ... now. Surrender ... I want to help ... "

In her wan eyes he thought he detected a glimmer of tears.

Then the darkness descended like a curtain, shrouding the rooftop and everything on it.

It only lasted for a heartbeat or two.

But when the light shone again, and Spider-Man was once again on his feet, Pity was gone—no doubt well on her way to finding out just how enraged the Gentleman was going to be.

The webslinger did not curse often. He was too glib for that. He had far more clever ways of expressing himself.

But today, there was only reaction that occurred to him.

"Damn ... "

CHAPTER SIX

The slap was witnessed by men who had long since forfeited their right to moral indignation—who had in fact spent their own afternoon committing atrocities against innocents.

But it still echoed through the room like a thunderclap.

"You worthless, incompetent trash!" the Gentleman cried, the second time he backhanded Pity across the jaw. "Do you have any idea how much you've cost me?"

Everybody gathered in the living room of the townhouse (a group that, in addition to Pity and the Gentleman, also included the recently-returned Dillon, Beck, Toomes and Octavius) understood that Pity could have dodged the blows. To a young woman capable of trading lightning-fast, super strong punches with Spider-Man, the slaps of an old man must have seemed to move at the speed of a slow walk and arrive with the force of a spring rain. The blows couldn't have hurt. Not physically. But from the way Pity shuddered at each moment of impact, the pain ripped into her soul.

"I've been easy on you so far!" the Gentleman raged. "I've allowed you comforts! Privileges! Well, no more! From this moment on, until you have earned back everything you've just cost me, you will live a life of brutal deprivation unlike any even you have ever known! Do you hear me? Do you?"

When she failed to answer (a foregone conclusion, of course), the Gentleman snarled and drew back his hand for another blow.

Every once in a while time itself seems to stop dead, reducing the world to a snapshot of itself. In that instant, Pity stood cringing before this old man she could have ripped in half. Dillon stood paralyzed with sympathetic pain, unaware of the lightning that sparked between his fingers. Beck took a single step, his usually grim features twisted in an expression of less righteous anger than aesthetic disgust. And Octavius cocked his head as he gauged the best way to play this situation to his advantage. In that instant, the cultured demeanor the Gentleman had utilized to put a civilized face on a career of mercantile savagery slipped, revealing his true nature. He was not a dispassionate investor in chaos. It was not just a business for him. He was a creature driven by a hatred so deep and all-encompassing that no financial setback or personal grudge could have possibly given birth to all of it.

He would have sowed his chaos whether it made him money or not.

He took pleasure in it.

It was what he was.

The gathered members of the Sinister Six all recognized him in that instant.

And because even monsters can be horrified by other monsters, Max Dillon (himself a criminal, terrorist, and mass murderer) raised a hand glowing with enough energy to incinerate the abomination where he stood.

The Gentleman might have died, then.

He didn't, only because by then another hand had already intervened.

Toomes shouted: "Leave her alone!"

If the Gentleman experienced any discomfort from the Vulture's bonecrushing grip around his wrist, he did not show it. "Take your hand off of me."

"I intend to," Toomes said, his voice commanding the room. "As long as you understand that my partners and I will stop you from ever abusing this poor girl again."

The Gentleman might have been expected to respond with anger, defiance, and even fear. Nobody among them expected incredulous, superior laughter. "Compassion, Adrian? I saw on TV how you murdered a young woman the same age today. Dropped her from a thousand feet up, I hear. How can you possibly perform an act like that and still object to a mere matter of corporal punishment?"

Toomes was less than devastated. "The people I killed today were nothing to me. I will lose no sleep over them. But Pity is one of us now. And the Sinister Six," he said, casting a contemptuous glare at Octavius, in a clear reference to past grudges, "with a few... notable exceptions, *usually* look after their own."

Octavius, who might have been expected to take umbrage at this, merely kept his own council as he gauged every aspect of the new group dynamic that was starting to form.

Beck, who had removed his fishbowl helmet but still wore the rest of his elaborate costume, glided across the room without seeming to take a step. His flu, if flu it was, had drawn gray circles beneath his eyes, and there was an uncertainty in the way he moved, but nobody would have ever mistaken him for anything but a dangerous man. He addressed the Gentleman, his demeanor outwardly calm but bearing a dangerous undercurrent of contempt. "I am not, by life preference, as constitutionally solicitous toward the ladies as Adrian. But I'm afraid I'm with him on this, old man. Your treatment of our new partner has been getting on all of our nerves. We say . . . enough."

The Gentleman acknowledged that with an unconcerned nod, then seemed to notice the crackling form of Max Dillon for the first time. "And you, my friend? Among all these other chivalrous defenders why has your own voice been conspicuously absent? After all, you're the one who's fallen in love with her."

Both Beck and Toomes seemed startled by this. Octavius merely nodded with the superior grin of a keen observer who had suspected all along. Pity, who had endured the struggle for her future with blank, expressionless eyes, did not react at all. Dillon, outraged to have the secret trumpeted before the others, snarled and marched across the room, a cascade of sizzling energy erupting from his eyes. "You say another word about that, you unbelievable slime, and I will charbroil you so fast your head will spin!"

"A fine, if illiterately mixed, metaphor," the Gentleman sniffed. "And really, Max, you have precious little ground for pretensions of moral superiority, since you are also the one who bartered his participation in this little enterprise for future—shall we say, 'ownership'—of his coveted lady fair."

This was a second thunderbolt, affecting everybody in the room except for Pity and the Gentleman. Toomes reacted with outright dismay: "Max! You didn't—"

Dillon found himself appealing to one disapproving face after another. "Oh, come on! It's not like that!"

The Gentleman raised an eyebrow. "Isn't it?"

"He's twisting it around!" Dillon cried, with the desperation of a man unmasked. "I wasn't going to . . . like, give her orders to like me or anything! I just wanted to . . . you know . . . get her away from him! Anything after that would have been up to her! Come on, guys! You know me!"

The moment of silence stretched.

The Gentleman sniffed. "Indeed. And that is the very rub, Max. They know you as well as they know themselves. And they know all too well the fine line that, for men of your criminal persuasion, separates dearly coveting something . . . from using all the power in your possession to possess it." His smile was understanding, even compassionate, but as deadly as the gaping maw of the great white. "What about you, Max? Think of all the foul depths you've plumbed in the last few years . . . all the casual brutalities that have become as natural to your existence as the very air you breathe. Could you have ever believed you were capable of such crimes? Can you honestly be certain that once I do hand you total command over our little obedient flower that all the decisions you make for her from that moment on will reflect what she really wants, and not what you would personally prefer her to want? Can you look us all in the eyes and swear that you would not indulge your hungers by taking, shall we say . . . indecent liberties?"

Dillon's voice was filled with torment and self-justification. "I only want her to be happy."

"I'm certain that's what you tell yourself. Just as I am certain that you've already formulated vivid fantasies about what that happiness entails."

"You can't—"

"Please." The Gentleman glanced at Toomes, who still held him by the wrist after all this time, and spoke again, this time in a considerably milder, but still imperious tone. "You may release me now, Adrian. I promise to turn the agenda back to our . . . mutual interests."

Toomes released the Gentleman with obvious distaste. "You are a very revolting man, sir."

"I thought I was talented at mind games," Beck concurred. "But you—"

"I have had many decades to perfect my interpersonal skills. But I thank you for the compliment, Mr. Beck. —A brandy, my dear." As Pity scurried off to fetch the drink, the Gentleman's eyes scanned the room. "Where is our Russian comrade? Smerdyakov?"

"He didn't want to come back with us," Beck said. "He mentioned that he had some personal business to attend to."

The Gentleman looked distinctively unhappy. "Indeed. He will not be pleased when his absence costs him the million-dollar bonus I will be providing each of you at the end of this meeting."

Beck said, "You still owe us five million apiece at the end of the operation—"

"Yes, yes. These bonuses are in addition to that. Something to keep you interested, and provide compensation for bearing with an old man's whims for so long." He glanced at Octavius. "Have you found a safe place to hide the Oltion Generator?"

Octavius said, "It's somewhere in the Manhattan underground. I am not telling you where."

"That is fine. I know you still believe I intend to betray you somehow. But as long as you can put your tentacles on the device when we need it, then I am honestly not interested in where you choose to stow it in the meantime."

Toomes said, "Are we going to find out what this is all about now?"

"Most of it," the Gentleman said. "What I reveal now shall provide you all a clear picture of the goal we have been seeking all this time. As I stated before, I intend to retain one major component of the plan that I shall have to complete myself, as a way of ensuring my own indispensability. But aside from that, what I reveal now should be enough to persuade you that my grandiose promises have not been understatements."

"We're listening," Beck said. "And it had better be good."

"Indeed," Toomes muttered. "At this point I think we're all looking for a reason to be disappointed in you."

The Gentleman chuckled. "If you think it's 'Good', in the dictionary sense of the term, then you haven't been paying attentions. It's downright Evil. I—" He smiled as Pity returned with his brandy. "Ah. Thank you, my dear. It doesn't excuse your earlier incompetence, of course, but it will serve to calm an old man's frazzled nerves."

"Your plan!" Octavius snarled. "I am tired of waiting!"

"One moment more," the Gentleman said, as he took a sip. "Ahhhh. Marvelous." He placed the goblet on the mantelplace, and faced each of his minions in turn: "It is a very brilliant plan, if I do say so myself. I wish I could also report that it was entirely original. but I'm afraid it is not. Although the specifics have been updated in light of current technology, and the strategy is all my personal invention, the essential philosophy behind our operation comes courtesy of my late business associate Auric, who rather explosively departed this veil of tears several years ago. Auric was the one who reminded me that the gross physical manifestations of wealth—gold, jewelry, and precious art, for instance—are not, in and of themselves, valuable at all. It's our perception of that value, and the world's willingness to agree upon that perception, that transforms such things from inanimate baubles to the machinery capable of moving the world." He puffed on his cigar, and said, "We, my friends, are going to attack that perception itself."

While the Gentleman was revealing the next part of his plan, a grim Peter Parker sat on his couch watching the coverage of the Rand-Meachum massacre on the local evening news.

Forty-three people, most of them security forces or lab personnel, had died during the Sinister Six attack. There were also dozens of wounded, some of whom were not expected to survive. The footage of the bloody and maimed being carried out on stretchers, while the unhurt but traumatized stumbled around in shock, made the scene look like a quick tour of hell. Daniel Rand, the company's CEO, appeared via satellite to deplore the carnage and promise the company's full support in obtaining all the wounded the medical attention they required. Connie Chung offered the not-very-startling opinion that the technology the Sinister Six had stolen, whatever it was, spelled bad news if those monsters had wanted it.

Over a commercial break, Peter Parker mumbled: "It figures. Two battles going on simultaneously, and I show up at the wrong one. Forty-three dead..."

A much-recovered Mary Jane, who had been paying more attention to her husband than the TV screen, sighed: "We've been through this before, Tiger. You can't take responsibility for everything that happens. Especially if it was something that happened miles away, that you had no way of knowing about. It was totally out of your control."

"It wasn't out of my control, Red. If I'd been any more on the ball last week I might have been able to catch them before they did this."

"This song is getting old," Mary Jane said, with open irritation. "I lived through the last couple of weeks too, remember? Between the people you saved at Brick Johnson's funeral and the people you saved at that Broadway play and the people you saved on my movie set and the people you saved at the Brooklyn Bridge and the people you saved at the *Daily Bugle*, among other places, we're well into four figures, already. Honestly, Tiger—I don't want to make light of what happened to all those poor folks at Rand-Meachum, but don't you think it's time you started to give yourself a little credit for all the good you've done?"

"It won't bring them back," Peter said.

"No, it won't. And neither will continuing to torture yourself. If you must dwell on this—and I've been married to you long enough to know that you will—please remember that these are the kind of crimes the Sinister Six would have been committing every day of their lives, without interruption, if you hadn't always been there to stop them. You keep this from being worse." She studied him for a few moments, and said: "But of course you knew all that already, didn't you?"

He nodded. "Uh huh."

"It's just hard to make your heart listen to your head."

He squeezed her hand. "Yeah."

"Tough. This time, make your head speak louder."

The commercial break over, the newscasts turned to a related story, a recap of the violent events in the Diamond District. That incident was minor by contrast. There had been only one fatality on the scene, the limousine driver shot by the would-be carjackers. There had, however, been several injuries, including the carjackers themselves, who were all in serious-to-critical condition, and a young bicycle messenger who was expected to recover after collecting a stray bullet in the thigh. The SWAT sniper who'd fallen from the helicopter had broken several ribs and two of his fingers, but he was also expected to enjoy a full recovery. He was, in fact, vocal (if visibly confused) about how he owed his life to the actions of the young woman he'd been trying to cut down. The public feeding frenzy over the spilled jewels had also led to some bruises and contusions, not to mention one bite, but nothing life-threatening. In light of the far more serious carnage at Rand-Meachum, and the discovery that the jewels now appeared to have been purchased legitimately with real money, the on-air reporter wondered whether Pity's actions could possibly be excused as self-defense.

NYPD's Detective Briscoe, giving the cameras a soundbite, rejected that notion. "This woman's partners killed dozens of people today. They endangered hundreds more only a week ago. It's up to the DA, of course, but as far as I'm concerned she's a full accessory to everything they've done."

The reporter asked about the restraint she'd showed by saving the sniper.

"Restraint," Briscoe repeated, rolling his eyes. "Two of the carjackers have fractured skulls. The one she hit with the car door has brain swelling. There was definitely some element of self-defense involved here, but she still defended herself with excessive force. I'm not sure you could hand her any medals for restraint."

The news then segued to an update on the status of the jewels spilled onto the street at the climax of Pity's battle with Spider-Man. Police officers on the scene had acted quickly enough to break up the onlooker feeding frenzy, but an estimated forty percent of the jewels were still missing and not expected to be recovered. A lot of people would be visiting pawnshops tonight. The Czarina's Necklace, which was among the recovered items, had entered the custody of the NYPD Evidence Lockup.

As the newscast moved on to coverage of the major blizzard set to hit Manhattan within the next twenty-four hours, Peter turned off the TV with a touch of the remote.

After a while he said: "I forgot to tell you before. I contacted Doug Deeley, the SAFE guy, by phone after I heard about Rand-Meachum. He told me that Colonel Morgan's going to be holding one of his infamous midnight meetings up in the helicarrier—that they're working a lead on what the Gentleman might be up to. I promised to be there. He'll be giving me a lift from the Manhattan-side tower of the Brooklyn Bridge, a quarter to midnight. I don't know how long it's going to run."

"You ought to get some sleep before you go," Mary Jane said. "A midnight meeting, with who knows what on your plate tomorrow..."

He shrugged. "Maybe. If I can sleep. Are you going to be okay with me being out of touch for a couple of days?"

"I'll worry. You know that. I always worry. But I know it's important."

"I really hate leaving you alone," he said. "Every time."

"I'm okay with it as long as the reunions are sweet," she said.

"I know. But still."

"Well, maybe this time I'll go stay with Jill Stacy in Manhattan for a couple of days. After all, I'm still involved in setting up my acting workshop at ESU, and the way the weather's turning, it'll sure help with the commute." She studied him closely, and said: "But we're still not talking about what's really bothering you, are we? This Pity business?"

"Of course. But not for the reason you think." He sighed and took both of her hands in his. "Where to start, where to start..." Then, resigned: "She's not my sister, Red."

That was exactly the opposite of what she'd expected him to say. "She's not?"

"Nope. At least I'm ninety percent sure she's not."

She wondered why she felt more disappointment than relief. "How?"

"I could say it was because we've been fooled by frauds

and fakes before—and because Mysterio and the Chameleon were involved in some of them—but those have only taught me a certain healthy skepticism. I still kept an open mind until I could get a closer look at her. What I saw today persuaded me that even if I do have a sister I don't know about, it's almost certainly not her."

"Why not?" Mary Jane asked.

"Genetics." At her blank look, Peter elaborated: "Look, I'm a dead ringer for my father. I also look a little bit like my mother, mostly around my eyes—and I can see echoes of Uncle Ben in my shaving mirror every morning. And that's not unique to this family.—Kraven the Hunter Senior and Junior look just like each other. So did Norman and Harry, and little Normie, Osborne. It's a little bit harder to see the resemblance between J. Jonah Jameson and his son John, or for that matter between you and your sister—but it's there to see. You can find it if you look. I might not always pick up on the features if I don't know beforehand, but I can almost always see the resemblance if I've been clued in. Sometimes, when I find out about a family connection I didn't know about, I think, 'Oh Boy, why didn't I see that before?'"

Mary Jane nodded. She knew the feeling. "And Pity?"

"I paid extra-close attention to her during our fight today. I watched her face when I wasn't being forced to watch her hands and feet. And I've been running over my mental snapshots all afternoon."

"No resemblance?"

"None at all," he said, with absolute certainty. "I can't pinpoint a single facial feature that resembles my Mom or Dad or myself at all. Not even if I employ wishful thinking. And when you consider that the only real reason we ever pegged this woman as my missing sister in the first place was the Gentleman's claim to have arranged the deaths of her parents as well as mine—"

Mary Jane colored. "You're right. It's awfully circumstantial."

"Nothing wrong with circumstantial," Peter said. "Most criminal trials hinge on circumstantial. And nothing wrong with coincidental either—our lives are lousy with it. But this is worse. It's thin. Especially since—now that I think of it—the Gentleman has been such a major dirtbag for so many years that he must have arranged the deaths of lots and lots of people. Not just my Mom and Dad. Lots of Moms and Dads. They weren't all related."

She squeezed his hands. "And it doesn't bother you that you can't be sure?"

"Sure it does. And I'm still going to continue doing everything I can to find out for sure. But the thing is . . . what really makes the wondering easier to bear . . . is knowing that it doesn't really matter either way. Not where it's important."

"It's not?"

"Uh uh. Because even if she isn't my sister . . . she is."

Mary Jane thought about that for a while, then softened. "Oh, Peter. You're right. If that monster orphaned both of you—"

"—then our actual blood relationship doesn't matter," Peter said. "Even if we don't have the same mother and father, she and I are still brother and sister by circumstance. We were both hurt by him. She suffered more, of course—I mean, thanks to Uncle Ben and Aunt May I still had a relatively normal childhood until the radioactive spider showed up. But we still have that murdering old creep in common, and that's a link between us. And besides . . . " He hesitated.

"There's also this. I just spent a week thinking that she might be my sister. And even though I'm now pretty sure she's not, I still intend to be her brother. I don't want to fight her. I don't want to hurt her. And I certainly don't want to think she's really as bad as the rest of them."

Mary Jane didn't either, if only because there were already more than enough people as bad as Octavius and company. She said, "I thought you'd already established that she was acting against her will."

"That's what the Gentleman says, anyway. And I don't know how true it is. The guy hasn't struck me as being the most trustworthy person in the whole wide world. But it feels true. I look at her and I see a poor soul who's been chained inside her own head for so long that she can barely even remember what freedom is like." He shuddered. "It doesn't make her any less dangerous, or any more an accessory in the eyes of the law. If the brainwashing defense didn't work for Patty Hearst . . ."

"Then no jury's going to want to listen to it in her case, either," Mary Jane nodded. "Not after everybody her teammates killed. And not after what happened today. Brainwashed or not, she's definitely in for a rough time when you catch her."

Peter said, "That's true." He hesitated again, long enough for Mary Jane to realize that he had not yet arrived at whatever may have been really bothering him. As bad as all his other concerns may have been, whatever he still held inside was as weighty as everything else still put together. Concerned, she gave him time to put it all into words. And then it came out in a rush: "You know—I keep hoping that what I sense about her is true. I keep thinking about the way she didn't kill any of those carjackers (at least not outright), and the way she saved the cop who fell out of that helicopter . . .

even the way she held back when she had me helpless. She seems to have the . . . potential . . . for something better."

"It's been known to happen," Mary Jane said.

"I know. Hawkeye, Quicksilver, the Scarlet Witch, the Black Widow, Hobie Brown, the Falcon, and the Sandman—they all started life on the wrong side. But even that's not the part that really bothers me. Assuming she's as mind-controlled as she seems. Assuming that she's been under the Gentleman's thumb for as long as he says. Assuming that I somehow pull off a major miracle and not only defeat the Sinister Six, but break her conditioning and free her from the living hell she must have been enduring all these years. Assuming *all that*—consider everything she's been through and everything that's been done to her. Consider the kind of effect that can have on a mind that's known that and nothing else for as long as she can remember."

Mary Jane said: "All right. I'm considering it. It's horrible. What's your point?"

His eyes welled with torment and self-doubt. "How do I know that what I'm freeing isn't even worse?"

It was the bottom line, and she saw in his expression just how deeply it had been troubling him.

She wrapped her arms around his shoulders and hugged him tight. "Peter . . . I've known several Parkers in my life. You. Your Aunt. Ben Reilly. You were all the finest people I've ever known. From what I know of your parents, they were in the same class. If she is your sister, then she has to have some of that innate decency still flowing through her veins. And if she's not . . . then maybe she has it anyway. Either-or, maybe it was enough to sustain her, to help her hold on to her soul, throughout whatever that piece of garbage did to her."

He whispered: "And what if she really is as twisted as they've made her? Or worse?"

She kissed him. "Then at least her crimes will be her own, instead of somebody else's. You'll be taking away her excuse—and giving her every reason to grab hold of something better. You owe that much, at least . . . to the woman who might as well be your sister."

Late that night.

The Macchiavelli Club. A midtown establishment dedicated to the pursuits of entrepreneurs of a certain grand and criminal vision.

The Gentleman sat in his easy chair in the Club drawing room, in an almost perfect darkness dispelled only by the glowing tip of his last cigar of the day. It was a rare strain of tobacco imported from the far east; his one-time business asoociate, Casper Gutman, had introduced him to its pleasures. The Gentleman had loved it so much that he'd bought out every grower with access to the strain, simply so he could take it off the market and enjoy its superb qualities for himself. After all, it was not enough to prosper, and enjoy life; to truly triumph, he felt, one must also ensure that one's inferiors lose.

That applied to cornering the market on one's pleasures.

And it applied to making a point of never playing fair with one's associates.

While planning this operation, the Gentleman had never expected to respect the various members of the Sinister Six. They were laughable. They considered themselves master criminals when they were in actuality common thugs, with the aesthetic sophistication and attention spans of common chimpanzees. They qualified as human, by his lights, in a manner that most of the citizens of this fat and decadent country absolutely did not—i.e, they did not shamble through the days and nights of their lives staring slackjawed at the lives their births had provided them. Like the Gentleman himself they seized their destinies with their own hands. But they were still short-sighted and fumble-fingered and utterly without the vision they needed to sculpt that clay properly. They weren't idiots—except for Dillon, of course—but next to him, they might as well be. He'd entered this association with them already prepared to keep that in perspective.

He had not been prepared for just how distastefully common they actually were.

Omitting the two he'd worked with before (his slave Pity, and his impudent serving-boy Smerdyakov, both of whom were only of use as cannon fodder) they had all been disappointments to him. Toomes was a wretched failure of a man who had lived his entire life without acquiring even one scintilla of sophistication. His eleventh-hour acquisition of power, long after a truly formidable individual would have found some other way to forge empires, had simply permitted him to become a failure on an even greater scale. Beck was an effete degenerate fop whose failed movie-director dreams translated to pretensions of thwarted greatness in an already totally worthless art form. Dillon was, of course, Dillon: an idiot. Nothing else needed to be said about him. And Octavius, the only one among them who the Gentleman had expected to be a worthwhile opponent, was, for all his cunning and vision, just another seething, resentful fat boy who had never grown up.

It didn't make any of them less dangerous. But it did remove some of the glory from the last-minute betrayal he planned.

Smiling, the Gentleman picked up the wolf's-head walking stick that rested against the side of his easy chair. He depressed a hidden latch at the base of the wolf's skull. The wolf's-head flipped back, revealing a pair of buttons connected to the electronics concealed within the staff itself.

The red button was a failsafe against Octavius, the only Sinister Six member that the Gentleman could not confidently dominate by force of superior personality alone. He expected that madman, with his attitudes against authority, to come after him before long. In such an event this failsafe, connected to certain subtle modifications the Gentleman had ordered made to the Doctor's tentacle assembly, would cause said tentacles to turn back upon the very man who wore them, hammering him with enough force to shatter concrete. The betrayal would no doubt ensure Octavius a very messy death. The Gentleman looked forward to that. Indeed, given the several occasions when the Doctor had presumed to threaten him, he intended to press that button no matter what the contingency.

But not as much as he looked forward to pressing the blue button.

That button was the other half of the reason he'd come to this filthy city.

It was connected to a very nasty explosive device he'd arranged for Pity to hide in the residence of Peter and Mary Jane Parker.

The Gentleman hadn't bothered to tell Pity why he'd provided her such orders. As he hadn't shared his knowledge of Spider-Man's identity with her, the apparently unmotivated vendetta against an unremarkable civilian couple must have confused her. But he'd given her such orders before. She belonged to him. She did not need to understand. She only needed to Do.

Once this adventure was over and done with the Gentleman would arrange for renewed surveillance on the Parker home. It would not be long before he was able to isolate a moment when Spider-Man was out fighting his ridiculous battles, and the Grade-Z Actress was alone at home.

Then he would press the blue button, reducing the house to a crater and the woman to ash.

After that (he chuckled) hunting down the no doubt grief-maddened webslinger would practically qualify as a mercy killing . . .

CHAPTER SEVEN

It doesn't make any kind of logical sense. But even in top-secret paramilitary organizations known for conducting the kind of precisely-timed operations that always begin with the ceremonial synchronization of watches, administrative staff meetings still have a habit of running up to half an hour late.

There is a wide variety of possible explanations for this, ranging from the necessity of pulling people off critical assignments in other locales, to the arrival of last-minute intelligence capable of altering everything on the agenda.
It may also be that staff meetings are staff meetings wherever they're held, and require a certain amount of annoying lateness just to qualify as examples of their particular species.

Whatever the reason, SAFE was no exception. Twenty minutes before the midnight meeting on the pending Gentleman/Sinister Six crisis, the organization's commander, Colonel Sean Morgan, sent word that he and his crisis analyst, the quadriplegic Vince Palminetti, would both be arriving late, with fresh updated information regarding this latest danger about to confront the beleaguered city of New York. The meeting itself was still expected to convene on time, with the various participants ordered to work from the data already on-hand, even though everybody knew that Morgan's mysterious updates might trash conclusions made before his arrival.

New York Police Commissioner Wilson Ramos did not take to this news at all well. Like the top cops of other major cities, he worked long hours as a matter of course; but unlike some he knew, he absolutely insisted on regular sleep to keep him reasonably alert and competent. The whole concept of a midnight meeting had struck him as ridiculous from the start; the further delay made it seem even more arbitrary and foolish. As two SAFE agents escorted him to the conference room, he grumbled, "Why did you people even bother to invite me? You Feds always seize full control of these things anyway."

Special Agent Joshua Ballard, one of two who had given Ramos the aircar lift from One Police Plaza, said, "You must be mistaking us for the FBI, sir. Colonel Morgan doesn't want any interagency rivalries here. He wants the NYPD kept in the loop."

"Not for decision-making," Ramos muttered. "For equal distribution of blame when things go wrong."

"I'm sure that was a factor, sir." This from Ballard's companion, the perky midwesterner Matt Gunderson.

"And why couldn't we have held this meeting somewhere in Manhattan? Did we have to meet in a floating aircraft carrier, for God's sake? What's the deal with this place? Couldn't you just have an office building like ordinary people?"

Ballard bore the look of a man who found dealing with this Commissioner a lot like dealing with any of his three ex-wives. "Office buildings cannot be deployed in situations that require mobility. And we do have state-of-the-art facilities in this complex."

"Let's introduce you to the guys and gals," Gunderson chirped, "and see if we can change your opinion of us."

Ballard and Gunderson opened the door to a conference room dominated by a long table ringed by straight-backed chairs. There were already five people present, none of them sitting. They included a skinny blonde man wearing a sweater vest and bowtie over a white button-down shirt and gray slacks, a bemused-looking male agent in SAFE's trademark skintight battle armor, an even-more bemused short Asian woman in the same uniform, and a grim, haggard, red-eyed woman in a shapeless gray sweatsuit. The wild card here was clearly the parchment-skinned, white-haired old man in the corduroy suit jacket and loose-fitting black slacks. Though he looked too frail to stand he still remained on his feet as he addressed the others, all of whom honored him with their most rapt attention. They all turned as Ballard escorted Ramos into the room.

"Sorry to interrupt, people," Ballard said. "You are now being joined by the New York City Police Commissioner, Mr. Wilson Ramos. Mr. Ramos, you are now joining Dr. Troy Saberstein, SAFE's stress counsellor and advisor on tactical psychology—"

The skinny blonde man nodded. "Hello."

"—the fellow next to him, Agent Clyde Fury—"

The bemused-looking man nodded. "An honor, sir."

"—one of our newer recruits, Special Agent Shirlene Annanayo—"

The Asian woman nodded. "Sir."

"—And, umm, the woman next to her, who I'm afraid I don't recognize—"

It took the grim, haggard woman in the sweatshirt a second to realize she was being addressed. She looked up and spoke in the kind of voice that established she was in no mood for social niceties. "Dr. Cynthia Monella. Civilian Expert Witness. And tired of sitting around waiting for you people to do something."

"Um, right. You won't have to wait much longer, I promise.—And the elderly guy, there, is Dr. George Williams, retired from both the Treasury Department and Interpol, who has been acknowledged as the world's leading authority on the international criminal Gustav Fiers, who we've come to know as the Gentleman."

Williams wiped his bifocals with a soft cloth. "A pleasure, Mr. Ramos. I do hope that between SAFE and your own people we can put all of these monsters away before they inflict any more damage on this fair city."

Ramos had pressing questions for all of them, but the old man intrigued him the most: clearly over ninety, and clearly having difficulty standing, he still projected a formidable will capable of dominating any room. "Just how do you get to be an expert on somebody like the Gentleman?"

"The hard way," Williams said softly. "I've been hunting him for sixty years."

Ramos, who had never been known for his sense of tact, hesitated two full seconds before expressing his next thought: "You'll forgive me, sir, if I don't consider that all that glowing a job recommendation."

Ballard and the other SAFE agents in the room scowled at this, offended by the slap in the face of a man they had all come to respect, but Williams himself nodded. "You have a very good point, sir. I would have liked to catch him in Casablanca in 1942. And several times afterward."

"You ever suppose that maybe you simply weren't doing all that good a job?"

The scowls grew deeper; Ramos was not making any friends in this room. But Williams continued to take no offense. "All the time. But I also take comfort in the knowledge that I was still the only man who persisted in gathering intelligence on this murderous fiend for the more than two decades that the rest of the world preferred to believe him dead. At least now, with the resources of these dedicated young people, the cooperation of your police force, and the good will of providence, I trust that we now have a greater chance of bringing him to justice than ever before.—Indeed, the two incidents today, tragic as they were, provide us with a great number of promising new areas for inquiry. No doubt we'll have a chance to discuss our thoughts on the matter once this meeting convenes."

Ballard's communicator went off. He checked it, and said: "That's Deeley. He's here checking in our special guest. He'll be officiating until Morgan and Palminetti show up with their updates. I'll go meet him. Take care of each other until I get back."

"You got it," Fury said. He grabbed a plate off a nearby counter and extended it toward Ramos. "Cookie?"

Ramos stared at the dish covered with moist chocolate chip confectionery. "You have got to be kidding me."

"Not at all," said Fury. "I'm a gourmet cook. Specialize in soups, but I also do some baking, now and then. Try one."

"They're gooood," Agent Annanayo confirmed.

"Ya, you betcha," Gunderson confirmed, with eye-rolling melodrama.

Ramos stared at all three of them. "What kind of secret agents are you?"

"No kind," said Fury. "Strictly speaking, there are major differences between secret agents, spies, intelligence analysts, and strategic action specialists. SAFE specializes in strategic action for emergencies, not espionage. Which gives me a lot of time, between missions, to cook." He grinned. "Don't act so surprised, sir. Firemen tend to be good cooks, too."

Ramos remembered the agent's name. "Fury. You're not related to—"

"Nope. Never even met the man. Someday, if I get enough commendations, I hope to live long enough to hear somebody else ask him if he's related to me."

Ramos took a seat by the others. More agents came in, most of them clad in SAFE's trademark battle armor: an intense young woman who introduced herself as Agent Donna Piazza, an inappropriately-grinning male agent named Walt Evans; a muscular grey-suited man who introduced himself as SAFE's FBI liason Martin Walsh; and four or five others whose names Ramos failed to catch. Then Ballard returned with a tall black man named Doug Deeley, who Ramos had encountered several times in the immediate aftermath of citywide paranormal crises. Deeley's very job description, as SAFE's liaison to New York's extensive super heroic community, virtually guaranteed that Ramos would never like him. Ramos didn't like either super heroes or feds, because he didn't like anybody not in the NYPD or the municipal court system who attempted to take an active role in protecting the public safety within the city of New York.

In light of that, the very next person to enter the room after Deeley was downright intolerable. It was Spider-Man, who hopped in, skittered across the ceiling, and settled in on a webline he spun above the center of the conference table. "Hello, bunkies! Sorry I'm late, but you have no idea how hard it is to catch a taxi this time of night!"

Amid the general hellos (some guarded, some warm) Ramos had to raise his voice to make himself heard. "Mr. Deeley, I would like to lodge a formal protest against this... individual... being here. He has no official capacity."

Spider-Man's hooded head swivelled to face him. "You never saw me drink a Big Gulp, cuddles. I have a tremendous official capacity."

The grins on the faces of several of the agents present didn't improve the commissioner's mood. "I must insist that you ask this individual to leave."

Deeley shook his head. "I'm sorry, sir, but Spider-Man's here today because of his years of experience defeating the various members of the Sinister Six. He knows more about them than anybody else alive, and his presence here has been sanctioned at the very highest level."

"I'm not sure that I can be a party to any operation that encourages his involvement."

"Understood," Deeley said, with considerable sympathy. "We were all looking forward to your involvement, but we'll understand if you prefer to leave."

Ramos could not believe the depth of the insult; given the choice between himself or Spider-Man, SAFE was actually going to select an anonymous, undeputized vigilante outlaw. He almost stood up and marched out of there in a huff... but then he considered the very real threat facing his city, and knew he could not afford to leave. Glaring at the wallcrawler and then at Deeley, he said: "No, I'll stay. But I want my objections on the record."

"From the sound of things," Spider-Man noted, "you want them on the broken record."

"That's enough, wallcrawler," said Deeley. He turned to Ramos. "Done."

Spider-Man shook his head ruefully. "Geez. Some people.

—Hey, Gunderson! Any chance of getting a cup of coffee around here?"

"Coming right atcha," said Gunderson, who whistled as he turned toward the percolator.

Though boiling over the webslinger's involvement, Ramos found himself even more taken aback by this detail; he had somehow never imagined a super hero doing anything as mundane as drinking coffee. Considering the lives they led, the forces they commanded, it was downright terrifying to think of any of them also being permitted anywhere near caffeine. He shook his head to rid himself of the image, and muttered: "Can we just get on with this, please?"

"Another minute, sir." Deeley placed his hand to his right ear, and listened to an update on his communicator. He nodded, murmured something inaudible in response, then cleared his throat and took up position at the wall of video display monitors that dominated the end of the room. "All right, people. Listen up. I have just been informed that Colonel Morgan and Dr. Palminetti are going to be a few more minutes. Under the circumstances, I agree with the commissioner; we should get started. I trust we all know each other, for the most part, so I'll limit the introductions to a young woman who just joined SAFE under unusual and tragic circumstances a few hours ago; she's here to brief us on the nature of the technology stolen from the Rand-Meachum research facility earlier today. Doctor Cynthia Monella."

The grim looking woman in the shapeless warm-up suit stood up. She looked beat, her hair limp, her eyes bloodshot and rimmed with dark circles. There was a peculiar list to her posture that suggested either physical pain or the effects of painkilling drugs. Even so, she displayed the seething, furious dignity of a woman capable of being formidable when she wanted to be. She closed her eyes, then took a deep breath to compose herself: "The most important thing to understand about what the Sinister Six killed so many of my friends to steal today... is that it's of no possible use to them."

Spider-Man, now sipping his coffee from a perch midway up one of the walls, started. "You were at Rand-Meachum?"

Monella spoke with devastating self-control: "Yes. I was. I just barely made it to an emergency stairwell after watching my lab partner get incinerated before my eyes. You want to make an issue of that?"

If Spider-Man had any reaction to the naked pain in Monella's eyes, it was hidden by the lines of his all-concealing mask. Several of the SAFE agents present winced in empathy, while others averted their eyes rather than meet hers. Ramos, who hadn't ever been talented at dealing with the survivors of tragedies, even during his days at a street cop when he'd needed that skill regularly, merely grimaced. It fell to Troy Saberstein, the crisis counsellor, to put the general consensus into words: "We all have issues with that, Doctor. You're obviously a tough woman, and a brave one, and I know we need to hear what you have to say, but you're also displaying several of the symptoms of shock—"

Monella glared at him. "You're right. I'm in shock. I plan to fall to pieces as soon as I have the luxury, and I promise you I'll be inconsolable for weeks. You can coddle me then. But right now those maniacs are still out there, thinking about how many people they can kill next, and I happen to be your only expert witness. So do you want to hold my hand or do you want to listen?"

Spider-Man broke the general silence in a soft voice utterly at odds with the nails-on-a-blackboard wisecracking persona Ramos had heard disparaged from so many sources in the NYPD. "I'm sorry for what you went through, Doctor. And I'm sorry I wasn't there to help your friends and co-workers. But I'm ready to listen."

Monella regarded him for a full five seconds. "I appreciate that." She closed her eyes again, this time only briefly, then continued: "All right. I don't need to tell you horror stories about all the killings I witnessed. That won't help us. We all know that killings mean nothing to them. It may have been senseless by our standards, but it was a kind of senselessness that we have to expect from people like them. What doesn't make sense by any standard—is what they went to all that trouble to steal. The Oltion Field Generator."

George Williams coughed. "We were told it was a multi-million dollar piece of equipment."

"That it is. But also a useless one, in and of itself. You've got to understand . . . " She closed her eyes again, hesitated, and started again: "All right. From the very beginning. As I told your Colonel Morgan, several hours ago, Gold and Askegren were developing a process for the real-time animation of plasticized liquid adamantium."

Spider-Man, who was among things a closet scientific genius, seemed to be just about the only person present who followed that. "Oh, no."

Ramos, annoyed that the wall-crawler understood something he did not, said: "What does that mean?"

Monella, looking tired, turned her attention to the commissioner. "It's complicated, but I'll give you a layman's overview. As you probably know, primary adamantium is next to indestructible. It's the most damage-resistant alloy in the history of manufacture. Some grades can stand up to ground-zero nuclear explosions without even retaining heat. That makes it invaluable as armor and as shielding; it has even been used in robotics, now and then."

"Ultron," Deeley said.

Several faces around the room darkened at the mention of the genocidal robot dedicated to the annihilation of all life on Earth, one of the worst monsters ever to threaten a world increasingly beset by monsters. Monella nodded. "Yes. He's a perfect, if rather unfortunate, example. However, the alloy's very invulnerability is also one of its greatest limitations, in that it cannot be forged or shaped at any point after its initial manufacture. Anything you choose to construct with it—tanks, shields, building materials, murderous robots, what have you—must be molded at an earlier stage, before the resin process that renders the stuff so invulnerable. That prevents adamantium-based technology from being used in situations that require adaptability, such as those occasions when you need to retrofit something, or those emergencies when you absolutely, positively, have to cut through the plate. Abbott and Costello—I mean, Gold and Askegren—had worked out a different way to handle the problem."

George Williams said, "I follow. What was their great innovation?"

"Essentially," Monella said, facing all the others at the briefing table in turn, "they had discovered a way to sustain adamantium as a stable room-temperature liquid for long periods after its manufacture, and to control its minute-by-minute shape via the use of coded digital signals transmitted into a network of thousands of implanted microscopic receivers. Whenever their process was activated they were able to forge a large quantity of liquid adamantium into totally indestructible, freestanding, three-dimensional objects that enjoyed a full range of motion without the need for external power sources or internal moving parts.

Machines constructed from such a base would be able to perform any number of dangerous functions without ever wearing out—and then to change their shape on command into anything else they might be required to become."

Clyde Fury looked dizzy. "Indestructible shape-changing robots."

Matt Gunderson glowered. "Ya, the world always needs more of those."

Donna Piazza said, "Like in *Terminator 2*."

Monella acknowledged that last remark with a nod. "A movie Gold and Askegren talked about a lot, onsite. I think it may have been what originally gave them the idea. They were very talented fanboys. They're not alone in that, among scientists these days; after all, Stephen Hawking's a dedicated trekkie. But you're all getting the wrong idea. Rand-Meachum didn't want another Ultron. They made sure that these liquid machines wouldn't be robots, at least not in the sense of possessing any genuine intelligence. These machines would be linked up to remote terminals, and totally controlled by the moment-to-moment instructions of their operators. They would just be . . . adaptable, that's all."

George Williams shook his head in the manner of an old man once again reminded that technology had advanced far faster than any human being could have hoped or guessed. "It still sounds terrifying on the battlefield."

"It would have significant military applications, that's true. The Department of Defense has sunk billions into subsidizing Rand-Meachum's program. But if the process could be rendered practical it would also revolutionize manufacturing all over the world. We could enter a new age, with tremendous growth in manufacturing, housing, transportation—"

"And adamantium tentacles," Joshua Ballard said.

Spider-Man shook his head. "I'm way ahead of you there,

bunkie. Octavius is already almost impossible to stop. If he can equip himself with tentacles capable of instantaneous shape-changing—"

"But he can't," Monella said, with an insistence that shut down the buzz that had been beginning to build among the meeting participants. "Which is precisely why none of this makes any sense. There's no reason to steal the Process. Not yet. The technology is still in its very early infancy; nobody's made it practical yet, and it'll be years before anybody does. Right now, it takes—" A shadow crossed over her face. "Sorry. Took. It took hundreds of support personnel thousands of man-hours just to maintain an animated shape for thirty seconds at a time, and each time we did, the energy involved was so immense that the micro-receivers burned out and needed to be manufactured again by scratch. Gold and Askegren, being nerds, used it to make little animated figures of Claudia Shiffer or Pamela Lee or Mary Jane Watson-Parker that 'lived' only a few seconds before losing cohesion. Sometimes they did the Silver Surfer or even," indicating Spider-Man, "yourself. They liked pretty women and super heroes both."

"They probably loved the Black Widow," Spider-Man said.

"Yeah, they had a whole file on her. But given the current state of the art, there's absolutely no way even a genius like Octavius could take advantage of the Process—not unless he could also figure out a way to build a four-story building filled with support personnel, billions of dollars worth of proprietary technology, *and* use the process to construct something capable of paying back all that investment in only a few seconds of life. That makes no sense at all."

"Maybe he didn't know," Donna Piazza suggested. "Maybe he thought the Oltion thingie was all the Process needed."

"He's Doctor Octopus," Spider-Man said. "He isn't that incompetent. He doesn't enter situations like that unless he knows exactly what he's looking for."

"He would certainly recognize the Generator," Monella said. "It isn't all that startling a piece of equipment; it has no practical function other than creating a very powerful electromagnetic field within a very small enclosed space. The Oltion bombardment is useful for for making the adamantium . . . suggestible, for lack of a better word. But that's still a very specialized use. It has nothing to do with the plasticizing process, or with any of our control paradigms. It's just a spare part. Octavius, with his scientific background, would have to know that."

Ballard said, "Maybe he didn't know what it was until he got there. If the Gentleman sent them in without fully understanding—"

George Williams responded with an old man's laugh, born from many years of disappointment and bitter experience. "Don't ever accuse Gustav Fiers of not understanding anything. His intelligence network is downright frightening."

"But he's pretty old now," Ballard persisted. "And, you said, not nearly as rich or influential as he once was. If he's been AWOL for twenty years, then maybe he's not what he used to be—"

"Please!" Williams spat, his voice dripping with scorn. "Don't give me the senility argument. He's already proven himself capable of gathering, and commanding, the Sinister Six. These are not the acts of a doddering fool. I promise you, he knows exactly what he's doing."

"That's the impression I got, too," Spider-Man said. "He wouldn't go to those extremes just to find a spare part he couldn't use."

"From what I've heard about him today, I agree," Monella

said. "But a useless spare part is still all he got. It doesn't even have its own power supply. And it isn't exactly the kind of thing you can plug into a wall socket; the energy requirement alone is enough to light up most shopping malls."

Spider-Man chuckled. "Powering it is the least of his problems. He has Electro on his payroll."

Monella closed her eyes again, obviously reliving a terrible moment. "Point taken. But again—why?"

"And what, exactly, does that have to do with the Day of Terror they declared against Spidey last week?" Matt Gunderson asked. "We know the Gentleman was involved with that, too, and yet it looked like just another bunch of super-powered malcontents on the vengeance trail."

"Except for the switch Electro and Mysterio pulled at the Brooklyn Bridge," Deeley said.

There was a pause while everybody considered that. At one point during the insane Day of Terror, a man claiming to be Electro had taken hundreds of hostages at the Brooklyn Bridge. He had held the bridge for a couple of hours, until Spider-Man finally showed up to clean his clock . . . at which point he had turned out to be Mysterio in disguise. It had clearly been a diversion to hide whatever the real Electro was doing elsewhere, and it had worked perfectly, in the sense that Electro's concurrent activities were still a total mystery.

"We've spent a lot of time discussing that little trick of theirs," Clyde Fury admitted. "I agree that there's got to be a connection. But we don't have the data to guess what they were really doing. It's like the theft of this Oltion thingie—just another big, confusing puzzle piece."

"I can only repeat," Monella said, "the Generator was only a small part of the Process."

"So maybe we're being distracted by the Process," Troy

Saberstein said. "Maybe they weren't interested in the Process at all. Maybe they just wanted the Generator for some other purpose."

"Our thoughts exactly." The new voice was soft, papery, and accompanied by hissing from a mechanical respirator; it came from Dr. Vincent Palminetti, SAFE's quadriplegic strategic analyst, who now wheeled into the room on his motorized chair. Palminetti was painfully thin (almost emaciated) with wispy brown hair that was just beginning to turn gray in spots; he did not possess enough mobility to nod, but he gave the impression of affirmation as he rolled to an unoccupied position at the table. "Ladies. Gentlemen. Commissioner. Hero."

Marching in directly behind him was the leader of SAFE, Colonel Sean Morgan, a crewcut blonde man with steely gray eyes and a posture that seemed to be all ninety-degree angles. He, too, snapped out acknowledgements and hellos as he strode toward the head of the table, but they were strictly professional hellos. His very presence made all the assembled agents sit up a little straighter and set their mouths a little grimmer. Not that it had been an especially light-hearted meeting before his arrival, but Morgan just happened to have that kind of effect on his underlings. He was not only the kind of commander who brooked no nonsense, but also the kind who maintained impossibly high standards of just what constituted nonsense in the first place.

Just before he relieved Deeley, he murmured a few words to the aged Dr. Williams, who smiled warmly in response. Several of the assembled SAFE agents glanced at each other, silently debating the agency rumors that pegged this old man as a one-time mentor of Morgan's. Certainly, Morgan seemed to treat Williams with a gentle solicitousness he provided nobody else, not even Palminetti, whose professional standing with Morgan had always risen and fallen with the accuracy of his most recent analyses.

They all wanted to know why. They might not have been secret agents or spies under Clyde Fury's lexicon, but they still possessed a professional hatred for unrevealed secrets.

Not that Morgan was going to provide them any more time for speculation. "Thanks for starting the meeting, people. I'm pleased to see that you've already engaged Dr. Monella. She's a valuable resource, both scientifically and militarily, and given the special capabilities of the manace we're facing, her technical assistance will come in handy indeed. For the record, since her military and scientific qualifications are impeccable, and the catastrophe that befell her previous place of employment has freed her to accept a consultant position with this agency, she is to be considered an agent in good standing for the duration of this crisis. I hope she'll be remaining with SAFE for some time to come."

He nodded at Monella, who nodded back. Troy Saberstein, who was supposed to be in charge of certifying agents psychologically fit for duty, looked unhappy but unwilling to interrupt.

Morgan continued: "As for Dr. Palminetti and myself, we regret our lateness, but we needed to conduct some highly classified inquiries suggested by the information Dr. Monella provided us about the nature of Rand-Meachum's Process. Now that she's brought you up to speed, I'm afraid to say that the news is not good."

"At this point," Spider-Man muttered, "I'd be very surprised if it was.—You have something, Colonel?"

"We do," Morgan said. He turned toward Dr. Palminetti. "Vincent? This is yours."

"Thank you." Palminetti's eyes flickered toward Dr.

Monella. "This birthing chamber, as you call it, the place where this Process of Rand-Meachum's was conducted—didn't you say that it was heavily shielded?"

"Of course. Several layers of lead and treated ceramics, reinforced by sophisticated energy fields. The rest of the building needed to be protected."

"From what?" Palminetti said. "What would happen if you ever activated the Generator without shielding?"

"We couldn't. The safety protocols—"

"Yes, I understand. I am certain that Rand-Meachum was very responsible, and had many backup systems. But if you were totally without concerns for the safety of anybody around you . . . and you built the system without safety protocols and without shielding . . . and you found a way to run the Oltion Field Generator as a single unit, let's say somewhere in the middle of Manhattan . . . what, precisely, would happen then?"

Monella hesitated, then winced with sudden understanding. "My God."

Matt Gunderson's eyes went very round. "Oh my."

Spider-Man saw it too. "Damn. How blind could we be?"

The participants seated around the conference table were now about equally divided between those who Got It and those who Did Not. Spider-Man, Dr. Monella, George Williams, Martin Walsh, Shirlene Annanayo, and Clyde Fury Got It; Joshua Ballard, Troy Saberstein, Wilson Ramos, Walt Evans, and Donna Piazza were among those who Did Not. Ramos, desperate to catch up, cried out: "What? What What What *What?*"

Monella looked dazed. "The chamber was shielded to contain the EMP—the electromagnetic pulse. Run that Generator somewhere without shielding, just at its normal settings, and you'll completely scramble every electronic system and electronic recording medium within twenty blocks. Run it at full power, at let's say the capacity possessed by this Electro murderer, and you can probably expand that effect to more than twenty miles."

Ramos Got It, then. "That's enough to blanket the whole city. And more."

Everybody Got It, now. The gasps and mutters of appalled fascination sounded around the table like little explosions, circling the room in waves.

Spider-Man, now dangling over the center of the table on a webline, put their shared horror into words. "That's why he bought the Wyeth painting. That's why he bought the jewels. He's probably been converting cash into other forms of wealth all over the city. If he can use that thing to set off an EMP in Manhattan, one of the financial capitols of the world, he'd wipe out all the electronic records of all the banks. There'd be a worldwide financial crisis, raising the value of all those gold and jewels and other negotiable valuables by god alone knows how much."

"Conservatively," Palminetti said, "A factor of ten. Probably more."

Martin Walsh said, "The bastard plays for high stakes."

George Williams shook his head. "He always did. The bigger the stakes, the more he likes it. Especially if he can simultaneously destroy lives."

"All for a little money," Matt Gunderson murmured.

"More than money," Williams said. "The sheer satisfaction."

"That's why he was willing to risk working with a bunch of loose cannons like the Sinister Six," Spider-Man said. "He could have hired some more manageable bunch of mercenaries easily—but there's only one way he can easily feed that thing the juice he needs—and that's by using Electro."

He secretly knew there was more to it than that: the Gentleman was also in town to take vengeance on the only son of Richard and Mary Parker, and it made a certain sick kind of sense to use that son's long-term enemies as part of that vengeance. After a moment, he said, "But even an Electromagnetic Pulse wouldn't be enough, would it, Colonel? Don't most electronic records have backups on paper?"

"Not most," Colonel Morgan said, "but many. I knew the Gentleman would think of that, too. Which is why, as soon as we realized what was going on here, I immediately made a call to the Naval Base on Governor's Island, just south of Manhattan. Remember, that wasn't far from the switch Mysterio pulled last week, when he took all those hostages on the Brooklyn Bridge . . . "

"We discussed that already," Deeley said. "We agreed that since he was disguised as Electro the whole time, he must have been trying to hide whatever Electro was doing elsewhere."

"Not only Electro," Morgan said. "Pity, too. With all the other members of the Sinister Six taking hostages during their Day of Terror, those two remained conspicuously absent until the final showdown at the *Bugle* building."

"I noticed that," Spider-Man said.

"We all noticed that," said Clyde Fury.

"Everybody noticed that. Even those two idiot disk jockeys who covered the whole crisis kept wondering if the Sinister Six knew how to count. But it now seems that Mysterio's electric light show was a ploy to confuse the systems that would have otherwise picked up Electro's presence on Governor's Island. The security people at the naval facility there noticed electrical anomalies in their readings, but assumed that stray voltage from the bridge was the cause. As a result, they didn't set off any alarms when Pity and

Electro used their powers and that key moment of distraction to slip into a certain highly guarded vault there and walk away with something capable of destroying any financial records that an electromagnetic pulse would leave behind."

"Something capable of destroying paper?" Spider-Man asked.

"Not paper," Morgan said. "Ink."

Dismay rippled around the table.

"It's a Catalyst," Palminetti said. "The weapons research lab at Los Alamos Laboratories developed it by accident in 1983. The Federal Government keeps it on hand in the event international hostilities would ever require us to cripple the economy of an enemy power. It takes the form of a highly unstable gas that, exposed to atmospheric nitrogen, expands with explosive speed to become a new compound that bleaches all inks and dyes in its path. The new compound is itself unstable and breaks down in about five hours, but by then the harm is done. The one liter stored at Governor's Island, released in an airburst over Manhattan, would be enough to turn every single vital document within forty miles to blank paper. That includes every contract, every treasury note, every stock certificate, every medical file, every birth and death certificate, every trial transcript . . . and every single monetary note exposed to the open air. Photographs,and photocopies produced by heat impression would survive, of course . . . and all bills larger than twenties would still be identifiable by the metal strip woven into the fabric . . . but that wouldn't provide much consolation. It would still cause chaos. And used in conjunction with a simultaneous Electromagnetic Pulse . . . " He trailed off, unable to phrase the chaos he envisioned.

The faces around the table seemed pale and sickened.

"There'd be rioting in the streets," Donna Piazza whispered.

Spider-Man grimaced beneath his mask. "Oh, much more than that."

"The webslinger's right," Palminetti said. "Imagine: In Manhattan alone, no hospital would be able to treat its patients, no pharmacy would be able to fill prescriptions, no family would be able to obtain vital food and services. The police would be deaf and blind, with no provable knowledge of any investigations either past or in progress. All jail and prison records would be blanked—there would be no way to distinguish nonviolent offenders from hardened murderers from people yet to be tried who would have been judged Not Guilty in a court of law. Millions of people would be wiped out instantly—there'd be no money, no life savings, nothing but a city filled with paupers, many of whom are armed. There'd be warfare on a block-by-block basis as citizens struggled to defend homes they could no longer prove they owned from people who would now need only superior numbers and superior firepower to take them away. There'd be madness and murder and suicide and a total breakdown of every societal structure; the deaths from that alone would probably run into the seven figures."

"And that's just what we lose by taking away all records," Sean Morgan said. "If you factor in the collateral damage done by the EMP, which would destroy the phone system, cripple 911, eliminate the medical infrastructure, give hundreds of thousands of people cancers and radiation poisoning, kill every vehicle with electronic ignition (including every ambulance and every fire engine) at the same time dozens of powerless jumbo jets packed with people started to fall from the sky everywhere in range..."

Palminetti said, "The fires would devastate entire neighborhoods. More deaths. More homeless. More suicide. And that's just what would happen to Manhattan."

"Nationwide," Sean Morgan said, "and internationally, that would only be the beginning of it. Spider-Man called it a worldwide financial crisis, but he's understating it. It would be a worldwide financial collapse. Corporations would fall. The dollar would fail. Millions of people would be rendered penniless. Racial tensions would be brought to the boiling point. There'd be civil wars and revolutions all over the world—and I, personally, would be very surprised if some of them didn't go nuclear. Either way, the aftermath would condemn much of humanity to a living hell... but the worse things got, the more the Gentleman's cache of wealth would appreciate in value."

"He would consider that a fair exchange," George Williams said.

In the heartbeat that followed, the gathered representatives of SAFE, the FBI, the Treasury Department, the NYPD, and New York's super hero community met each other's eyes, sharing the weight that had just fallen upon all them. They had all dealt with madness and terrorism before; they had all held lives in their hands. Some had even played for global stakes. But few had expected this super-villain grudge match to escalate quite as critically as this.

When Spider-Man broke the silence, he was, uncharacteristically, at a loss for words. "My God... Colonel... I knew he called himself an investor in chaos, but... "

"There is no but," George Williams said. "He's a monster."

"They all are," said Cynthia Monella, remembering.

At the other end of the room, the floor screeched at the sound of a chair violently pushed away from the table. It was the Police Commissioner, Wilson Ramos, whose raging eyes and beet-red complexion signalled the onset of an imminent explosion. "And you ... knew ... about this stuff, Morgan? You not only knew it existed, but let them store it in my city? Were you insane?"

Joshua Ballard said: "That doesn't help, sir—"

Ramos whirled at him. "After what we've just heard, you're about to lecture me on my attitude? What's wrong with you? What kind of irresponsible mind would allow that Catalyst within a hundred miles of an inhabited area, let alone anywhere near the financial capitol of the world? It's Depraved Indifference, is what it is! I should—"

"Commissioner," Sean Morgan said. He did not raise his voice, but the quiet power it contained still halted Ramos in mid-sentence; he was one leader of men, silencing another with a simple word. He said: "You're right. Keeping the Catalyst here was irresponsible to the point of lunacy. And I know that because I spent the last three years of my life arguing for the Catalyst to be destroyed. I would have wrecked my career by going public if I'd been willing to start a panic as bad as anything we've just described. Maybe I should have done it anyway. Maybe heads should roll for this when we're done. Mine can be one of them, if you want. But blame isn't relevant now. The situation is. We have to deal with the crisis as it exists."

"And that's easy for you to say!" Ramos said. "Because it still doesn't tell me how many other nightmare weapons are still being stored in my city!"

"No, sir," Morgan said. "It doesn't." It was an open admission that there were others, and the room hoarded its collective breath as its ramifications of that one sank in.

Spider-Man said: "The Commissioner's right about this, Colonel. This isn't over."

"I'd be disappointed with both of you if it was."

At the head of the table, George Williams stood. "Excuse

me," he said. He looked pale and gaunt, even by his standards; the terrible revelations of the meeting seemed to have aged him a decade he couldn't afford. But his soft, sandpapery voice still commanded the room, and his burning, obsessed eyes galvanized the will of everybody here in turn. He said: "I am aware that there will be repercussions here. I know that it's tempting to fight among ourselves. But before we go down that path, I want to stress one important thing. Gustav Fiers is the enemy here. Gustav Fiers is the one who wants to use this terrible combination of weapons. Gustav Fiers would do so even if there were no profit involved; he would do it just to feed his ego. He would see it as his life's greatest accomplishment. And this time he's allied himself with other monsters with the power to make it happen." He let the words sink in, and astonished them all with a hungry smile, broad enough to make wrinkles ripple like water across both cheeks. "But this time he's also made the mistake that will destroy him."

He waited for somebody to ask.

Joshua Ballard, sensing the need, provided it: "What's that?"

"He has finally raised the stakes so high that the world can no longer afford to let him escape . . . "

The meeting went on for a number of hours after that, with the various participants coordinating the response for the crisis that could now be expected to start at any time. Two hours in, when Sean Morgan ordered a fifteen minute break, few of them actually took a break; they just broke up into smaller groups, discussing the crisis with the same degree of urgency.

Spider-Man, caffeine fiend extraordinare, now on his fourth cup of coffee since midnight, caught up with Troy

Saberstein by an observation port overlooking the brilliant Manhattan Skyline. The corridor where Saberstein had gone to decompress was dimly lit, which allowed the multicolored lights of the city to cast colorful constellations on the counsellor's face.

Spider-Man, dangling from the ceiling, used a webline to lower a coffee cup for Saberstein. The man took it without comment.

"You all right?" the webslinger asked.

Saberstein didn't turn from the view. "My specialty has always been dealing with the aftereffects of stress. I'm not really used to dealing with a life-or-death crisis while it's happening."

"It's not something you ever get used to," Spider-Man said. "It's something you deal with. Sorry if I put you on the spot by drafting you."

"No problem, wall-crawler. At this point, you couldn't drag me away."

"How did you get hooked up with SAFE, anyway? Post-traumatic stress counsellors don't seem to be the kind of idea that comes out of the head of somebody like Sean Morgan."

"It wasn't," Saberstein said. "I was forced on him." He didn't say that he'd been forced on Morgan personally, after the tragic car accident that had claimed Morgan's son... and that Morgan hadn't taken his input very well. He just sipped his coffee, and offered a belated, "Thanks."

After a moment, Spider-Man hopped down to the floor to stand at Saberstein's side. "Have you given any thought to that other matter we discussed?"

Saberstein faced the lights of Manhattan. "Pity."

"Yes. Her."

"You still think she's being controlled? Just because this Gentleman character said so?"

"No," Spider-Man said. "Not just because of him."

"Just a feeling, huh?"

"I've learned to trust my life to them."

"Maybe you're supposed to, in this case." Saberstein turned and faced the webslinger directly, his soft eyes burning with urgency. "Think about it, Webslinger. Her name's Pity. Why would they call her that? It doesn't seem to have anything to do with these darkness-casting powers of hers. Maybe it refers to something else. Maybe it's a reference to the way people react to her. Maybe your inability to treat her as an enemy is the main power she has over you."

Spider-Man, who had considered the possibility himself, winced beneath his mask. "I don't think so."

"You wouldn't," Saberstein continued. "The Gentleman told you enough to make you feel sorry for her, and everything you've seen in her demeanor since then has made you feel sorrier. If it's any consolation, you're not alone—we've interviewed every civilian known to have been in contact with her since her arrival in New York, and they all said the same thing: that she seemed a little pathetic, more a victim than a victimizer. Even the *Daily Bugle* hostages expressed sympathy for her. Even J. Jonah Jameson said so, and as you know, he's never been a man overflowing with sympathy. Maybe it's her special power."

Spider-Man thought of the NYPD sniper. "I saw her save a life today."

"A life she was responsible for endangering in the first place. And there's something else. This darkness power of hers: the way light and infrared and sonic imaging systems won't penetrate it. At first Palminetti said he thought it might be connected to the Darkforce used by your vigilante friends Cloak and the Shroud—but since she can keep her partners from being affected, he now thinks it's psionically generated. Which means that she might have other psionic powers, too. She could just as easily be influencing your mind, forcing you to feel sorry for her so you're totally off-balance in a fight."

There were several seconds of silence as Spider-Man digested that. Then he shook his head. "I don't know. Maybe you're right. But even though this wouldn't be the first time I'd had my head played with—and even if she does give off empathy vibes, which I think makes sense—I'm still convinced that she's in this against her will."

"You are?"

"Yes. I can't be sure . . . but it's still what I think."

Saberstein nodded. "Despite everything I've said . . . me, too."

"Really? After all that?"

"Really. After all that. I'm willing to trust your judgment. But I want you to know that your judgment might have been compromised."

"Assuming I am right . . . can I turn her?"

"I don't know." Saberstein took another sip of his coffee, made a face, and tossed the almost completely-full cup into a combination ashtray and waste basket. "But one thing's for sure. If what the Gentleman told you is true, he's been conditioning her since she was a child. He has made himself the center of her universe. She probably hates him, but that doesn't matter; she still judges herself only by how well she serves him, and has no other frame of reference. That's not a spell you'll be able to break by snapping your fingers or talking nice to her."

Spider-Man listened intently. "How, then?"

"Not by fighting her. Oh, I know you'll have to, given the stakes here, but . . . if she's really been conditioned into obedience, then that conditioning would tend to reinforce itself at the moments of greatest opposition. Anything you could do to stand against the Gentleman will make you an enemy, and trying to free her from the Gentleman would definitely have to be part of that."

"Then what's the alternative?"

"Anything that puts the two of you on the same side. I don't have the slightest clue what that could be in this situation, but if you make yourself an ally, even for a minute, you might weaken the conditioning enough to give yourself a chance at getting through to her." Saberstein flashed a grim smile. "Of course, we both know the major problem with that . . . "

"Yeah," Spider-Man said. "Managing it before she kills me . . . "

At that very moment, another in the growing fraternity of people who wanted to kill Spider-Man grimaced at the stench beneath the city streets.

Dr. Otto Octavius was not a fastidious man by nature certainly not in any moral sense, and absolutely not in any manner that would have interfered with the pursuit of his ambitions. He knew that, sometimes, a man just had to get his hands dirty . . . even if he had appendages far stronger and far less sensitive than hands.

But he didn't have to enjoy it.

Right now he was in an steam tunnel somewhere beneath the city streets. It was a junction of several such passages, more than large enough to stash the Oltion Field Generator until it was time for that formidable device to be used. It was also nice and close to the site where all hell was set to break loose early tomorrow morning. Even with the aid of his marvelous mechanical arms, it had taken Octavius almost two hours to move the device from its previous hiding place in one of his many subterranean boltholes to this site more convenient for tomorrow morning's deployment. It had been manual labor of the most degrading sort, but there was no helping it—he was, after all, the only member of the Sinister Six whose powers included the sheer physical strength required to carry such a heavy object around.

But still, the stench . . . ! The filth . . . !

His lips curled.

The time would come when he dominated the world and never had to deal with such unpleasantness ever again. When it would be the vast, inferior mass of humanity damned to forever suffer such indignities on his behalf.

Octavius imagined how miserable they would be. And how happy he would be, to rise so untouched over the common muck.

His sneer turned into a wistful smile.

He did not like people much.

He supposed he would get the chance to kill a large number of them tomorrow.

But the battle that represented the next step in his long climb toward the realization of his devoutly-wished ambitions was was still hours away . . . meaning that he now had time to perform a personal errand of his very own. It would require a quick trip out to Long Island and back, just to verify certain intelligence that his agents had recently brought to his attention, but the journey would be more than worth it. For events were now reaching their conclusion—and he intended on teaching the Gentleman his folly in presuming to command Dr. Octopus.

He hurried off, already imagining his revenge on the foolish old man.

The steam tunnels beneath midtown echoed with laughter far colder than the frigid winter night above.

CHAPTER EIGHT

10 A.M., the next day.

Manhattan now stood poised at the brink of two disastrous storms.

One had just buried much of the upper midwest beneath four feet of snow. Now, preparing to assault the Big Apple, it announced its presence with a brutal cold snap that made the air a colossal knife slicing the bare skin of anybody unlucky enough to face it from the wrong side of central heating. The day struggling to show itself through the clouds was a weak, crippled thing, pregnant with shadows and bereft of anything approaching warmth. The winds whistling in from Staten Island already sounded angry. They were not yet ready to erupt in a fury, but it was impossible to listen to them without knowing that the assault would arrive soon.

But as terrible as that storm was going to be it paled before the other one, which bore enough destructive potential to drive a stake through the city's heart.

That one arrived, appropriately enough, in the form of a

man who had modelled himself on a classic symbol of approaching death.

The Vulture flew a slow, unhurried oval five hundred feet over the water just south of Manhattan. He had not been spotted until dawn; for all anybody knew, he had been flying that oval course for hours. It was a wide orbit that took him all the way from Port Liberty on the Jersey side to Castle Clinton in Manhattan. It completely enclosed Liberty Island and the famous lady who stands upon it, and bisected Ellis Island where so many hopeful immigrants took their first steps toward an uncertain future. He didn't seem in any particular hurry to see the rest of New York's sights. He just flew from New Jersey to Manhattan and back again, barely stirring his great green wings as he completed one circuit after another.

He had to be aware he was being watched. His route provided a free show for two states and three boroughs. There had to be thousands of eyes already watching his every move, with reactions ranging from confusion to wonder to dread. But he betrayed no awareness of them. He flew his endless ellipses like a man who had no need of destinations. He was like his namesake in that he could afford to be patient.

The first SAFE aircars arrived at the scene by 10:15.

Even as the earliest of the combatants gathered in the sky south of Manhattan, a grimacing man in Yankees earmuffs, black jeans, and a purple goose down jacket stepped out upon the observation deck of the Empire State Building.

The deck was inundated with slush. The wind wailed like an anguished beast, even now in the last few minutes before the storm. Visiting this place now, today, with this damned persistent flu that made his head seemed inflated to four times its normal size, required stupidity, masochism, or dread determination. Were it not for the riches at stake, Quentin Beck would have cocooned himself at home with a pot of tea and a complete collection of F.W. Murnau films on DVD.

But the inevitability of the oncoming storm was so clear in this place among the clouds, that Quentin Beck, aka Mysterio, could feel it with a certainty as primal as his obsession with old movies.

The weather was so rotten that he'd imagined he would be alone up here. But the observation deck of the Empire State Building is a famous site, and as such a magnet for crowds during any season. The place was packed with families, teenagers, tourists speaking Japanese and French and German and Midwestern English, taking snapshots before a skyline threatened by angry gray clouds. As he wandered among them, sometimes smiling, other times reverting to his more natural hostile scowl, Beck revelled in the banality of their reactions to the spectacular view: from their arguments over where to find Avengers Mansion, to their cooing over the gargoyles on the Chrysler Building. He heard several people making stupid remarks about how much they'd hate to fall from such a height, and each time his lips twitched at a pleasant fantasy of how easy it would be to show them the privilege. But each time he moved on, knowing that the time was not yet his.

It was pleasant to be here. This was, after all, the site of so many of his dearest memories. It was the place where the giant stop-motion gorilla had battled biplanes, the place where two different sets of lovers (decades apart) had arranged their last-chance rendezvouses, the place that had survived a (badly simulated) siege by giant mutant grasshoppers, the place that (inexplicably moved to the center of

Fifth Avenue) fell beneath the destructive powers of an alien invader on an imaginary July 2nd.

And besides, it was very much possible that the real Spider-Man might actually die here today.

Beck strolled around the observation platform, circling aimlessly in unintentional imitation of his colleague the Vulture. He listened a little to two tourists, a tall Texan preacher and a spiky-haired Irishman in nearly opaque shades, as they went on and on about their love for the city down below. He moved on, then smiled and said "Sure!" when a bright young couple asked him to take their picture. It was their honeymoon, they said. He wished them luck. They would need it, of course, for even if they did get out of the city in time to escape what was about to happen, the nasty little added images he'd just surreptitiously added to the snapshots would probably cast a pall over their sweet little relationship for years. He moved on, used a pair of coin-op binoculars to check out the situation brewing down South, and then, smiling, slipped what looked like a wad of gum at the scope's base.

So far, so good.

He fought off a spasm of dizziness and waited for things to start happening.

All around him, the first snowflakes started to fall.

Elsewhere in Manhattan, Mary Jane Watson-Parker sneezed.

She was bloody miserable. She had hoped she was getting better—had in fact seemed to be getting better—but the viral misery which had laid her low a couple of days earlier had come back with a vengeance.

"Ecch," she sniffed, dabbing her nose with a soft tissue as she watched trailer trash demolish a talk show set on the fortunately muted TV set. "Dice visit, huh?"

Jill Stacy, who had provided Mary Jane with a couch to sleep on after their girl's night out went unexpectedly late, grimaced as she brought a pot of tea from the kitchen. She was a fairly new friend to the Parker family, as she'd only moved to New York within the past couple of months, but her guileless charm and soon won over the discomfort both Peter and Mary Jane had felt at the appearance of somebody who so closely resembled her late cousin Gwen. It still was discomfiting. Only her hair color, jet black where Gwen's had been platinum blonde, prevented her very presence from prompting worries that somebody was performing tasteless experiments with clones again. As Jill poured the tea for Mary Jane, she said, "Well, there goes that theory."

"Whad theory?"

Jill poured some for herself. "The healthy girl theory."

"I'b subbode to be a healthy girl?"

"I think you are a healthy girl," Jill said, as she plopped beside MJ. "But I meant healthy by comparison. Next to your hubbie, I mean."

"I'b always a healthy girl next to my hubbie."

Jill elbowed her. "No, seriously. My cousin Gwen used to say that Pete was always getting colds and flus and sprained backs and such. She said that his aunt used to treat him like he was ready to keel over at any moment. Hard to believe, the way he looks—but the boy was prone. Me, I always thought he married a healthy girl to compensate. Never really imagined you getting sick while he was out running around healthy as a cat."

Mary Jane thought of all the times she had needed to nurse Peter past the wounds suffered in the heat of battle. "Dis must be my code for the year."

"Ha."

"You're gonna get sick yourself now."

"If so, then you'll owe me one. —Any answer at home yet?"

Mary Jane had just tried the number in Forest Hills. No answer. She hated knowing what that probably meant. "No. Lebt a message."

Jill grumped. "Ah, well, maybe we can . . ."

That's when the trailer trash vanished from the TV screen, replaced by the words SPECIAL BULLETIN and, a second later, shaky footage of the Vulture circling over the waters south of Manhattan. A graphic in the upper right corner of the screen read: SINISTER SIX RETURN?

Jill Stacy dropped her own cup to the floor. "Oh, no . . ."

Mary Jane, who had suffered through many such bulletins, but for different reasons, thought the same thing.

By 10: 45 A.M., an entire fleet of SAFE aircars was deployed in hovering positions around the Vulture's flight path.

There were a couple dozen of them, all told: gleaming, manuverable, and deceptively unaerodynamic cruisers that had been compared to floating bathtubs. Manned by two to three kevlar-clad agents apiece, the heavily-armed vehicles presented no enclosed cabin for its operators; that would have interfered with manual weapons activity. The necessary protection from high-velocity winds and extreme weather conditions was provided by an invisible ionic field that blanketed each vehicle—an in-factory feature that was going to prove invaluable if (okay, when) today's crisis escalated into aerial combat in subfreezing temperatures. That didn't prevent the pilots of SAFE, let alone the representatives of the NYPD, the FBI, and the United States Department of the Treasury, from feeling the winter's chill anyway. The air just looked cold, that's all.

Colonel Sean Morgan, surveying the deployment from

his position in the lead aircar, looked even colder as he followed the Vulture's flight with a pair of high-powered liquid-crystal binoculars. "That is the Vulture, right? Not one of Mysterio's illusions?"

"We've checked all our sensors to fifteen decimal places. That's him."

Morgan's faith in the sensors had been severely burned during the Day of Terror. "You're sure."

"Yes, sir."

"Positive," Morgan said, with extra urgency.

"And we have him completely contained?"

"If it's just him," said Vince Palminetti. The quadriplegic crisis analyst was piloting, courtesy of a personally-designed cyberlink that jacked him into the aircar's guidance and weapons systems. When linked, the aircar felt more organically part of him than his arms and legs ever did; maneuvering, he flew with the sheer exuberance of an eagle recently released from a cage. That didn't stop him from grimacing as he checked the aircar's sensors for a third and then a fourth time. "I wouldn't want to bet five dollars on the chances of this being just him."

"It wouldn't be," Morgan said. "He's baiting a hook out there."

"He looks like he's willing to fish until somebody bites."

"He wants our involvement, then."

"He wants our first move," Palminetti said. "Oh, he'll act if we don't—but he's definitely providing this invitation for a reason."

Morgan didn't like it. He had tasted more than his share of manipulation during the Day of Terror, when Mysterio's stunt at the Brooklyn Bridge had tricked his people into keeping their distance for hours. He grimaced, wishing that he shared the cigar habit cultivated by certain other paramilitary leaders of his acquaintance. He frankly hated the things, but given his current mood he could certainly sympathize with the urge to bite something. He said: "Web-slinger in place?"

"Deeley relayed a message from him five minutes ago. The wall-crawler is on land, and standing by. He's been informed of the Vulture's position and has elected to continue covering midtown."

"NYPD on-line?"

"Dispatchers connected city-wide, waiting for the flag to go up."

Sean Morgan took a deep breath, and felt that final inaudible click that came with deciding on full tactical commitment. "All right. Pass the word that the surprise package is going to have to be a flyer with massive offensive capability, which among these hostiles almost certainly means Electro. Give them time to check shields and counter-measures. Tell them that if we are going to be forced to start this, we're absolutely going to be the ones to stop it. We move in five—flagship first."

The aircar occupied by Morgan and Palminetti was the flagship.

Palminetti, approving, said, "Yes, sir."

SAFE agent Donna Piazza, piloting one of the other aircars, peered worriedly at her passenger, the grim-faced George Williams. It was the latest in a series of worried looks. As a veteran of several SAFE wars she knew how strenuous they could be, and it bothered her to spend this battle watching over an old man as frail as Williams. She half-expected the guy to have a heart attack during the first banking turn. But Colonel Morgan had insisted on permitting the ancient and retired treasury agent a seat, front-row center; She wished she knew what kind of past the two must have shared to account for that little regulations breach. Either way, the old man's presence made her uncomfortable.

Williams, watching the Vulture through a pocket telescope of the sort sold at souvenir shoppes throughout the city, said: "I'm not going to break, you know."

"Excuse me, Dr. Williams?"

"Don't be worried about me. I've lasted this long tracking this monster. And I'll last however long it takes to bring him to heel."

The venom in Williams' voice, which as always seemed to pump up every time the subject of Gustav Fiers aka the Gentleman entered the conversation, made her hesitate. "Just how personal is this for you, Doctor?"

"Is that what you think?" Williams asked, as he squinted through his telescope. "That it has to be personal? That only a debt can explain why I'm still after him at my age? That I can't be an old man too proud and stubborn to let go of a duty he failed decades ago?"

Donna considered that for several seconds, then went for broke. "Yes, sir. That's exactly what I think. I think you hate him."

Williams chuckled, the sound containing more bitter knowledge than mirth. "Smart woman."

11 A.M.

The aircars hovering in a circular formation paralleling the Vulture's flight path all had their weaponry fixed on the flying man. It was enough firepower to reduce a city block to a cinder, but the chances of any of that being fired were slim to nil, since SAFE's tacticians were smart enough to realize the main reason firing squads don't line up in circles. The initiation of hostilities took a more subtle form than that, with the aircar piloted by Vince Palminetti and commanded by Sean Morgan breaking away from the outer line and spiraling inward on a path designed to intersect the Vulture.

Morgan didn't actually expect to catch the Vulture that easily, any more than a champion fencer expects to strike a hit on the first jab. This was an exercise in prompting a response.

He got it three seconds from contact, when Lady Liberty's torch seemed to fire off a comet. It was a streak of pure light that arced two hundred meters into the air in the course of a heartbeat, exploded, and then plummeted toward them, shooting off sparks.

Something rocked the aircar, filling the air with ozone. As Palminetti compensated, the Vulture banked and plummeted toward the water himself, cackling madly. The aircar plummeted too as it followed Toomes toward the water; a streak of white-hot something shot by on the port side, missing the aircar and Toomes but vaporizing thousands of gallons of river water in an explosion of white-hot steam.

A thin, reedy voice somewhere behind them shouted arrogant threats. Morgan noted the tenor of the curses, but didn't bother to listen to the actual words. It didn't matter what the maniac was saying. In situations like this, maniacs just conjugated different metaphors for bloody murder. Knowing whether the bad guy was threatening to blow his head off, or make him die screaming, or stomp him underfoot like a bug, or simply introduce him to a whole new world of pain, helped only if, like Spider-Man, you spent your battles hoping to sling snappy rejoinders. Morgan had never been one for snappy rejoinders. To him, taking the bad guys down was about as eloquent a rejoinder as anybody could possibly hope for.

"You called it," Palminetti noted, levelling off to pursue

the Vulture at five meters over the gray-brown waters. "That's Electro, all right!"

"I think I got that," said Morgan, as he fired a SAFE plasma blaster at the glowing sociopath behind them.

"Should we engage the countermeasure?"

"This early in the game? He'll see it coming a mile off. Stay on the bird-man, and tell Teams Lincoln and Jefferson the Sparkplug's theirs . . ."

Max Dillon, aka Electro, was a star in the shape of a man. The energy he commanded was enough to incinerate entire city blocks, and attempts to take him down with cruddy government plasma blasters was pathetic. He simply flew through the incoming fire, allowing the plasma to explode in little bursts of light as they encountered the interference field that radiated from his body in all directions. There was no danger of them getting anywhere near him; they were as useless as bullets or tranks or gas or any other weapons the authorities were likely to try. That's why he was Electro. That's why he was unstoppable.

That's why it was so annoying that wimps like Spider-Man and Daredevil and Captain America and Wolverine kept taking him down anyway.

That's why they were all high on his long list of people he intended to incinerate.

Another plasma burst exploded before him, temporarily obscuring his vision. Skimming the water, enjoying how the river an arm's length below him turned to superheated steam at his passage, he flew through the the haze only to find the aircar he'd been chasing suddenly gone. The Vulture was still visible up ahead, a green bird of prey busily evading the two separate aircars converging on him, but the aircar that had been chasing him, the aircar Electro had been chasing in turn, was nowhere to be seen. Electro suffered a heartbeat of confusion before he heard the whoosh of air directly above him and realized that the spy-creeps had taken advantage of his momentary blindness to stymie him with a simple aerial u-turn. They were probably doubling back again and charging him from behind.

It was the kind of dirty rotten cheat the webslinger had been getting away with for years.

Electro whirled in mid-air, and saw the aircar bearing down on him. He caught a glimpse of its two passengers: one thin man attached to his console with a knot of wires and cables, one grim-faced military type aiming a plasma blaster his way.

Oh, come on! You don't expect me to be that easy, do you?

Grinning, Electro fired a lightning barrage powerful enough to incinerate them both.

Colonel Sean Morgan had been involved in SAFE air battles before, and he was accustomed to sudden violent manuevers, but the ninety-degree vertical turn almost realigned all the vertebrae in his back.

The sky turned a brilliant shade of white, and the ionic field maintaining cockpit climate control flared with interference.

"What . . . the . . . hell . . . " he grated.

"He had us zeroed-in!" Palminetti shouted. "We needed to use our undercarriage for shielding!"

It was not a decision Morgan would have made. He would have maintained course, even at the cost of his own life, on the theory that the impact from a speeding aircar would have done Electro serious damage. But he was not about to argue with Palminetti's logic. He shouted: "Loop around again! Don't let up for a minute!"

Shouted words crackled over the commlink, "Evans here! I've got Electro! I've got—" Crackling, followed by a wave of unearthly heat, and then nothing.

Another voice, "Evans is down! Evans is down! Believed dead! Pulse affecting systems!"

More crackling. Visibility dropped to zero as the aircar passed through a cloud of superheated steam from evaporated river water. The vehicle's ionic field shielded Morgan and Palminetti from the extreme heat, but not from the mingled sounds of explosions, of shouting, and of metal tearing itself to pieces from violent impact with the river. Then they were hit by the shockwave, and the aircar tumbled as helplessly as a playing card caught in the wind. The steam around them thinned just long enough for Morgan to catch a glimpse of a boiling riverscape, at what seemed entirely the wrong angle.

"Another one like that and we'll eat dirt!" Palminetti shouted.

Morgan agreed. "Everybody get some altitude! We need to get another fix on Dillon!"

The aircars detailed to take down the Vulture seemed to be having an easier time of it.

There were currently four of them pacing the man. They were all far faster and more manueverable than he, and they had little difficulty hemming him in, the only real problem being his ability to change course at an eyeblink. Twice, he slipped through little holes in their net. Twice, they quickly surrounded him again, covering him on all four sides. After his third escape attempt, the Vulture seemed content to let them cage him, reacting not at all even as another pair of aircars completed the midair cage by taking up new positions both fore and aft.

"This is boring," Joshua Ballard said. "Like catching a canary with a net."

His co-pilot, agent Shirlene Annanayo, said, "Don't underestimate him."

"What underestimate? He's tough fighting guys in spandex, but we've got mach-speed capability. He's outgunned. I say we take him out and help out with the spark plug."

Clyde Fury, following the conversation over comlink, said, "Net, guys?"

"Net."

The aircar immediately above the Vulture released a weighted titanium net from a compartment in its underbelly.

What happened next occurred so quickly that the SAFE postmortems required twelve hours of analysis just to identify it. The Vulture spun in mid-air and slashed at the plummeting net with both of his metallic wings, turning them to steel confetti. Then he stopped dead, inviting the aircar behind him to join in a mid-air collision.

It was an insane thing to do. The aircar would have survived such a collision. The Vulture would have been reduced to a scarlet blot on its fusillage.

Donna Piazza, who was piloting that rear aircar, had scruples that prevented her from simply running him down. She slammed the attitude controls, flipping the vehicle ninety degrees and rocketing past the Vulture with inches to spare. She caught a glimpse of his aged, hate-filled face as they passed by. They were so close that she could have reached out and touched him had she wanted, but they were also moving so fast that the contact would have shattered every bone in her arm.

She didn't have enough time to be grateful she'd missed him.

Because she hadn't.

There was a crunch, and a thud, and a screech, and a chorus of shouting voices on the comm. For a heartbeat Donna dreaded turning around, certain that she'd see a charnel-house stain across the aft section. The Vulture might have deserved such an end, but she wouldn't have wanted to be part of it. Then she heard his cackle, right behind her.

He'd boarded the car.

Electro stood one hundred meters above the water at the center of a glowing ball of energy, roaring with laughter as the idiots came after him, one aircar at a time.

They were fun. There were so many ways to take them out.

That salt-and-pepper team strafing him from above? A gesture, and the electrical impulses inside their brains went kablooey, giving them both the equivalent of grand mal epileptic seizures. Their aircar spiraled off, completely out of control, doing loop-the-loops that wouldn't end until the pilots recovered or the vehicle disintegrated on impact with something solid.

That scowling woman in the next aircar to attack, the one firing an endless series of plasma blasts she knew to be useless just to draw his fire away from the two guys doing unintentional aerial acrobatics? Another gesture, and he fried all the electronics in her guidance system, sending her aircar to a fiery death in the Hudson.

The aircar that almost succeeded in ramming him from behind, that would have shattered every bone in his body on impact? That one deserved overkill. That one deserved a lightning storm of pure rage, one so intense that the car came apart in mid-air, releasing pilots who emitted high-pitched screams as they tumbled into the deadly, freezing waters below.

It was just like playing a video game. One he was good at. Go figure. Too bad Pity wasn't here to see it.

His sneer softened into something almost wistful as he entertained a momentary fantasy of being her hero. He imagined her throwing herself into his arms, smothering him with kisses, and gushing in a soft, whispery voice that she had never seen anybody so brave. Okay, granted it couldn't happen that way. She couldn't talk. But the spirit of it, the flavor of it, was still an attainable dream. She could love him. He could make her happy, whether she wanted to be or not.

Only that would have to wait until later, when they fought together.

Right now, with the opposition concentrating all its fire on him, and bouquets of plasma-burst explosions affecting him through even his nimbus of electrical energy, it was time to begin Phase B.

He dropped, led half a dozen pursuing aircars on a jaw-rattling chase two hundred meters across the junction of two rivers, and fired a perfectly aimed bolt of lightning at a certain silvery buoy that was still bobbing precisely where his good friend Mysterio had placed it.

Exactly as planned, the world exploded—

Even before she turned to confront the Vulture, Donna Piazza knew she was in for the fight of her life.

She knew what had happened even before she able to confirm it with her own eyes. She had passed so close to the Vulture that he had been able to strike the rear of her aircar with both of his great metal wings. He had hooked the fuselage, grabbed hold, somehow braced himself against a sudden acceleration that should have broken his neck, slammed against the vehicle, and then somehow survived the impact with both his bones and his malevolence intact. As only made sense for a guy who regularly engaged in super-fast battles with Spider-Man, his recovery was nigh-instantaneous. By the time Donna turned around, he was already scrambling into the cockpit, leering with imminent triumph.

"Congratulations, my dear. You will be the first of your army to precede the hated Spider-Man into the land of the dead!"

Donna spared a brief glance for her elderly passenger. The white-faced George Williams, still strapped into his seat, had managed to turn his head enough to see what was happening. He looked more appalled than frightened, more aghast at the Vulture's rudeness than aware of his own imminent danger. Perhaps out of reflex, perhaps out of belief that even a pathetic weapon was better than no weapon at all, he had pulled his cane from the cargo net where it had been stored.

His presence did turn out to have some practical value, as it lent Donna another second out of danger. The Vulture spent that second scowling at the sight of Dr. Williams, registering his age, wondering just what somebody of his own generation could possibly be doing here.

Donna used that second to pull her plasma blaster. A lucky shot —

"No!" Dr. Williams shouted.

Given the Vulture's speed, it was a miracle that Donna had a chance to fire her weapon at all. She did not have the chance to aim it properly. Even as she drew it from her shoulder holster, the Vulture was already slashing his right wing against her wrist. It was a lot like being slammed with an aluminum baseball bat filed to a razor's edge. The pain was red-hot. The two pieces of her blaster somersaulted into empty space, trailing streaks of coruscating energy. Donna fell back against the controls, stumbled as the deck of the aircar tilted beneath her feet, and flinched as the Vulture's wing descended again, this cleaving her pilot's seat in twain. It was such a powerful blow that the Vulture's wing not only bisected the seat but also imbedded itself in the deck, a development that ratcheted the perpetual annoyance on his face to an even higher level.

It would take the Vulture, with his power, less than a second to pull his wing free, but Donna took advantage of that second by bracing herself against the control panel and sweeping the heel of her left boot against his jaw.

It was a powerful kick from a trained martial artist, and it connected even more solidly than Donna could have hoped. It would have killed most people.

But the Vulture regularly shrugged off kicks in the face from a guy capable of smashing through brick walls.

"Nice try, my dear." He leered as he raised both wings for a slashing guillotine strike that would reduce her to three vertical slices. "But it's your own fault for underestimating the elderly!"

"Never a good thing to do," agreed Dr. George Williams, as he pressed the tip of his cane against the Vulture's chest.

The explosion was a small one by the usual scale of such things. It certainly failed to match any of the billowing cataclysms that marked Electro's half of the battle. It was just a burst of heat and light, with a bang only as loud as the average cannon. But as the tip of Dr. Williams's cane disintegrated and flame rippled across the Vulture's chest, it seemed just about right. The villain stumbled backward, tripped over the edge of the cockpit, and tumbled out into open space. The aircar's velocity reduced him to a tacky streak of green diminishing in the distance.

Donna gaped.

Dr. Williams smiled at her. "I love the classified ads in the back of *Modern Maturity*. You find such marvelous merchandise. You'd better grab the controls, young lady—I don't know how to pilot this thing, and we're in danger of crashing into the river."

Donna grabbed the conn just in time to feel the slightest of bumps as their aircar skimmed the whitecaps. Feelings of relief didn't even occur to her. The Vulture's body armor was impervious to most small arms fire, which meant that he was almost certainly still in the picture . . . along with five others just as deadly.

And then the world exploded.

The flames burst forth like magic. They rose from the water itself, in sheets of white-hot fury ten to twenty feet high, spreading in straight lines along a perimeter that stretched from within fifty yards of Port Liberty on the Jersey Side to an equivalent distance from Castle Clinton in Manhattan. Every fifty meters or so they were punctuated by larger explosions that spread the flames further, dozens of them, closing the circle, trapping everything inside them in an earthly approximation of hell.

Electro, who had lit the fuse, was so jazzed by the sight that he fired off a shower of sparklers just for emphasis.

Mysterio had devised the plan, and implemented it with a little design help from Dr. Octopus. It involved a couple of hundred miniature buoys packed with incendiary bombs and enough compressed accelerant gas to set the river ablaze. The gas that now blanketed the air surrounding Liberty Island was breathable enough, but extremely conducive to fire. Unchecked, it would produce a holocaust capable of laying waste to everything in its path. Unchecked, the wall of flame would have the destructive potential of a baby nuke. Given time to ignite buildings on land, it had the power to devastate large sections of Manhattan, New Jersey, Staten Island, and, if everything went well, even Brooklyn. It would not be quite as fast as a nuke, because it wasn't meant to be. Indeed, Mysterio, who had called this his Peshtigo Option (a reference to another wall of flame that had once levelled the city of Peshtigo, Wisconsin, killing thousands), had labored for hours diluting the chemical mixture enough to create a disaster that would take its time.

After all, the last thing the Sinister Six needed here was a disaster that would be over quickly.

This one was just a distraction.

Electro wished he could stick around long enough to see the flames engulf Liberty Island. It would be neat to see the Statue of Liberty melt like a jungle gym at Hiroshima. He especially wanted to see it because he had been part of the gang the time Octopus and a bunch of his cronies had used an antigravity beam to steal the statue whole. The beating they'd all received at the hands of the wall-crawler on that occasion had been nobody's idea of a trip to a theme park.

Laughing, he rose into a sky both white with falling snow and black from rising smoke.

Sean Morgan and Vince Palminetti, flying high above the disaster, saw the comet in the shape of a man rise from the sea of flames. A couple of aircars were already diverting course to engage Electro, but Morgan knew they wouldn't manage more than a holding action—not with the monster ready for them. He would be able to move on to more chaos within minutes. As for the Vulture, he was already on his way into Manhattan. Morgan could have ordered his people into pursuit, but that particular maniac was so far down the priority list that he didn't even consider it.

"Three units down," Palminetti said. "Four confirmed

deaths, two more agents missing somewhere in that holocaust down there."

Morgan grimaced. "How many units do we have watching the rest of Manhattan?"

"Another twenty supplementing NYPD and a strike team at ground team level. We had the aircars running patrol grid Alpha, in case the Six—"

"Bring all aerial units here, and deploy anything still hangared at the Carrier! Load all flame retardant equipment! Containing this is priority one!"

Palminetti complied, after first giving Morgan a look that confirmed the grimmest of sitreps. They both knew that committing all available resources to this disaster left SAFE in check and the NYPD ill-equipped to deal with the likes of the Sinister Six. It was the equivalent of leaving Manhattan unguarded, and potentially abandoning the world to the hellish future desirable only to Gustav Fiers. With luck, SAFE would be able to contain the blaze in time to make a difference. If not—

—well, if not—

—then, as of now, everything depended on just one man.

11:13 A.M.

The intersection of Fifth Avenue and 33rd Street.

The streets of Manhattan never stop, even during catastrophes, even when the air itself turns as bitter as a slap. If anything, the first few flakes of snow just beginning to tumble from the slate-gray sky hurried the freezing pedestrians along. They all felt the deluge about to fall, and they were all still possessed by errands that wouldn't wait for anything save the end of civilization. The hundreds traveling past this world-famous site may have been aware of the deadly battle taking place in the waters downtown, but they also knew that this was nothing new for Manhattan, longtime stomping ground of heroes, villains, Atlantean invaders, and, yes, fifty-foot white guys wearing purple Ws on their heads.

That didn't stop them from screaming or recoiling when the bus flipped over, or the street exploded in a shower of asphalt and rubble.

That didn't stop them from knowing the crisis had come home when Dr. Octopus emerged from the freshly cratered pavement.

Dressed in an unseasonal double-breasted white suit that couldn't have done much to spare him today's monstrous cold, Dr. Otto Octavius bobbed along atop two of his long snaky tentacles. The other two, who emerged from the crater a second later, came up carrying a great bell-shaped machine that none of the onlookers recognized, but which in his possession could not spell good news. Somebody shouted that it was a bomb, that Octavius was going to blow up the Empire State Building. Octavius, a specialist in miniaturization who would have been ashamed to need a bomb the size of the Oltion Field Generator to accomplish such a mundane purpose, hesitated for just one heartbeat as he considered flattening the cretin for his temerity.

For a second he remained in the center of the street, basking in the shouts of appalled recognition that battened his ego from all directions. Then he craned his fat neck and peered up at the towering structure that, drab statistics to the contrary, some sentimental people will always consider the tallest building in the world. His lips curled in the expression that for him could be either smile or sneer. Then the two tentacles that carried him sprung into action, propelling him not only the rest of the way across the street but also two stories off the ground in one mighty leap. Clutching at cornices and ledges, they anchored him on the climb once accomplished by a fabled giant gorilla, while his remaining two tentacles dragged the Oltion Generator along with him, floor by floor by floor.

If the weight proved a strain even for his enhanced strength, it didn't affect the determination on his broad, scowling face. Nor did it prove any impediment to the long rant about his own genius with which he narrated every single foot of his climb. If anything, it only slowed him down a little, rendering his ascent ominous and deliberate rather than meteoric. Even so, he expected to reach the observation deck within minutes.

The city would pay for mistreating him, then.

The city, and the world.

Everybody.

It was amazing how many people deserved to die for thwarting his will.

He might have laughed insanely at this juncture. It was the done thing.

But the moment wasn't complete, though, and he felt the lack until the inevitable happened.

He was just beginning to pass the tenth floor. The leading edge of the storm blew a thick flurry of white powder against his face. Some of it got past his wraparound shades, momentarily blinding him. As the non-mechanical part of him was still woefully vulnerable to such assaults, he gasped from the cold, blinked several times to clear his vision, and noted that his momentary blindness had obscured the moment when the day's missing element was finally provided.

It took the form of a man in a skintight red-and-blue costume, crouching against the wall just one story above.

"Tenth Floor," Spider-Man said. "Hosiery, Electronics, Doomsday Machines. How ya doin', Cuddles?"

CHAPTER NINE

The storm began in earnest now. The flurries that had thus far only punctuated the coldness of the day thickened, joined, and became a united front. The flakes came down in clumps, adding a fresh dusting of white that began to accumulate in drifts almost as soon as it hit the ground. In those parts of the city not directly under siege pedestrians grimaced, lowered their heads, and moved a little faster, unwilling to stay outdoors one second longer than absolutely necessary.

The deluge was beautiful, like all snowstorms. The wind at street level twirled the gusts into dancing sheets. Children and young lovers turned their faces to the sky and luxuriated in the sight of so many constellations of white. More than one playful soul gathered up an early snowball and tossed it into the face of another, daring retaliation. But the storm was young, and already gathering in intensity. The wind that came with it howled down Manhattan's concrete canyons like an invader upset that not everybody in its path had enough sense to see it for the destructive force that it was.

All over Manhattan schools saw the inevitable about to

happen, and began the hard business of closing down for the day. The sanitation department began to call in all its shifts. Anybody with an excuse to go home began to think of going while travel still remained a possibility. Both in and out of the city progress on the roads began to slow, as visibility suffered beneath the falling white.

The only notable super hero or super-villain action other than the day's main event was a minor skirmish in Chelsea involving a petty costumed criminal called the Red Bear, who fled on foot from the tiny art gallery from which he had just stolen the day's grand receipts of less than two hundred dollars. The Red Bear, whose ambitions were greater than his abilities, dreamed of taking on Thor someday. He had a reputation for getting taken down by civilians and beat cops. Today he got all of two blocks before he collided with an old lady and was himself decked in retaliation by a second pedestrian outraged by such rudeness. The pedestrian who defeated him was not a super hero. He was just a retired stunt man and failed actor named Joe. This didn't have much to do with anything. It was a little drama, in a day filled with much larger ones.

11:16 A.M.

The day's first confrontation between Spider-Man and Dr. Octopus, ten stories above Fifth Avenue, was marked by a rare moment of indecision for both.

The catalogue of physical damage Dr. Otto Octavius wanted to wreak upon his longtime foe would have filled some entire libraries. When he saw the hated wallcrawler squatting just one story above him, his dearest wish was to immediately begin the battering and probably plucking of super heroic limbs. But the Doctor couldn't. Ironically, he just didn't have enough limbs for it. He needed at least two tentacles to cling to the building, and he needed at least two more to hold the heavy Oltion Field Generator. He didn't dare let go of the building, he couldn't put down the Generator, and if he did anything to attack he would have only his flesh-and-blood limbs to fight with. That would be worse than a joke. The wallcrawler would tear him to pieces.

"Pookey-pookie pooh!" Spider-Man waved.

There was something strange about the wall-crawler's costume. He was wearing a version of his regular winter costume cut from some different kind of cloth—a darker, metallic fabric that looked like SAFE cloth-and-kevlar. Probably something to give him an edge in the cold. Possibly even something insulated against attacks by Electro.

It wouldn't have protected him from the Doctor's tentacles. If the Doctor were able to use his tentacles.

"Wakka-wakka wakka!" Spider-Man said.

Octavius was tempted to just swing the Generator like a club, flattening the arachnid oaf against the Empire State as thoroughly as any meat tenderized by too big a mallet. Alas, the Generator wouldn't survive the experience either. Taking the bait in a situation like this, getting so caught up with the natural desire to pulverize the "Boy Scout" that you also ended up destroying your own master plan, was the kind of boneheaded move he supposed the Rhino would pull. Octavius was smarter than that.

But that still left him with nothing to do.

"Ah, well," said Spider-Man. "If you're not going to make the first move . . ."

The webslinger leaped off the wall and plummeted fist-first toward him . . .

"Foam the perimeter!" Sean Morgan, riding shotgun on a SAFE aircar riding low over the burning harbor, bellowed at his people as if he had been personally consigned to the flames. "Keep the fire from spreading, and the heart will burn itself out!"

But somewhere over the water, two SAFE agents screamed their last breaths as the aircar dissolved in a fiery airburst.

Electro.

Who wasn't about to cooperate with any attempt to put the fire out.

Spider-Man had never seen Dr. Octopus present such an easy target.

That was the thing about Otto Octavius: a madman, a terrorist pig, a murderer, and a self-absorbed lunatic with a rotten haircut, he really was the kind of guy who could only be improved by being punched as frequently as possible. It was just too bad those tentacles of his did such a good job of protecting him. But right now, with all four of the not-so-good Doctor's tentacles otherwise occupied, the knockout punch almost looked like it was going to be easy.

As easy as figuring the site of the Sinister Six's big play had been.

The Six wanted to set off an electromagnetic pulse in Manhattan. But if they powered the Generator too close to street level they ran the risk of allowing the effect they wanted to be contained, at least in part, by by all the surrounding buildings. For the best results they needed to get themselves a rooftop, the higher the better. It was also obvious that moving an object as large as the Oltion Generator into place would be a time-consuming and highly visible operation. There would have to be an even more visible distraction taking place elsewhere.

The good people of SAFE had spent more than an hour

last night just arguing over which tall building the Six was likely to choose. The Empire State Building had been mentioned as a possibility, but few had believed it. It had been considered too neat, and too theatrical even for a team with Mysterio among its members. Favorite candidates had included the Chrysler Building, the Metlife Building, and Citicorp Center.

Spider-Man plummeted toward the a target between the Doctor's upper and lower chins, already calculating how much power to put into the punch. He tried to estimate just how many impact pounds per square inch it would take to stun Octavius into dropping the Device while simultaneously taking care to make it an experience the very mortal Octavius was likely to survive without permanent impairment. Half a second from impact he knew that he had Octavius sussed. He felt absolutely no warning from his spider-sense, no sense that Octavius was going to be able to defend himself in time, no telltale tingle that would have indicated interference from one of the Doctor's partners in global terrorism.

He had time to think that this was too easy. Something was going to go wrong.

Then, and only then, did the tingle flare at the back of his neck.

Then, and only then, did some idiot turn off the lights...

The flinching Octavius missed the moment when the the world turned dark directly above him. He did, however, hear the familiar sound of two bodies slamming against each other with a force that knocked the breath out of both.

He opened his eyes and saw that Spider-Man had vanished.

No. Not vanished. The fool was somewhere behind him

now, shouting the usual inane quips that always characterized him in battle.

Octavius followed the sound of the arachnid's voice, and saw two tiny figures peppering each other with kicks and punches on the roof of an eight-story building across the street. One, hopping from place to place in streaks of mingled red and blue, was Spider-Man. The other, landing a solid kick to the wallcrawler's jaw even now, was Pity. The bug's words, which never stopped, were too obscured by the growing wind to hear, but the punches carried like miniature thunderclaps.

Good.

Octavius truly doubted a mere woman could ever defeat Spider-Man when his own much more capable efforts had failed. No woman was Dr. Octopus's equal. But he had every faith in Pity's ability to keep the pest busy while he did what had to be done.

The snow had intensified, its conditions now approaching whiteout.

Octavius, who hated the cold, nevertheless resumed his climb into the face of the storm, shepherding the Oltion Generator toward its world-shattering future.

At that very moment, Adrian Toomes, alias the Vulture, fled the holocaust he and his colleagues had ignited south of Manhattan.

As usual in his life, he was irritated. He had been within a heartbeat of killing that lady SAFE agent when that old man in the passenger seat decided to interfere. He couldn't blame the old man; as a member of that generation himself Toomes actually admired the gumption of oldsters who remained active in their twilight years. It was, in fact, one of the few things he liked about the Gentleman. But he resented having his own whims stymied that way. He would have looped around and made another attempt, but he had other insects to fry.

A blast of especially brutal heat buffeted him from behind, searing his skin and lending an unwanted degree of lift to his wings. For just a moment he cried out, thinking that he'd finally been delivered to the hellfire that so many of his victims had predicted for him for so many years. He struggled to regain control, spun, breathed smoke, zigzagged to avoid a SAFE aircar that for a fraction of a second seemed about to strike him head-on . . .

. . . and then found himself surrounded, not by heat, but by sweet comforting cold.

The sounds of exploding aircars and crashing lightning receded. The site of his next contribution to today's finely-tuned operation still waited for him, far uptown.

Entering Manhattan airspace just over Gateway Plaza, relishing the sounds of open warfare as it receded in his wake, the Vulture sneered with anticipation as he made way for the true battle.

He had to hurry.

He wanted to get to the webslinger before the others did.

He wanted a piece while there was still some left to carve.

Pity, hell. Had the name not already been taken, she should have been called Fury.

Having succeeded in diverting Spider-Man from what should have been his number-one priority, she was now easily kicking his butt the width and breadth of an office building across the steet from the Empire State.

She fought with a ferocity and a rage that surprised even

Spider-Man, who had last confronted her just yesterday, and who encountered other paranormal martial artists on an almost daily basis. This was a revved-up Pity, a Pity on overdrive, a Pity operating on a level that almost dwarfed anything he'd seen before. It was all Spider-Man could do to block the punches and kicks as they came, to back up only one step at a time while she continued to advance, the hatred and despair warring on her scarred gamin face.

"This still about the jewels?" he said, avoiding a blow that would have staved his skull in. "Because . . ."

She showed teeth and leaped straight up. He matched her leap, clutching her upper arms with both hands, fighting to keep them pinned to her sides so she couldn't strike him again.

". . . I thought I said . . ."

She bent both her arms at the elbows, delivering a pair of truncated punches. Both possessed enough force to turn his next words breathless and filled with pain.

". . . I felt just *awful* about that . . ."

Still airborne, Pity wrenched her arms free and went for him, throwing one strike that failed and one that connected all too well. Still airborne, Spider-Man deflected the next blow with a force that wrenched from her a gasp of pain.

". . . I know how you ladies are about your shopping . . ."

The two of them flipped in mid-air, spinning five, six, seven times while exchanging ten times as many crippling blows.

". . . I didn't want to, like, cramp your style or . . ."

The tip of her left boot slammed hard into the soft underside of Spider-Man's jaw. Cut off in mid-quip, he gasped, tumbled, seized her by the right ankle, felt a flurry of punches hammering his ribs in the time before their crash-landing on the roof.

They were both off-balance. They both hit hard.

Normal human beings would have required hospitalization.

These two both rolled away almost as soon as they landed and rose on shaky legs, facing each other from twenty feet away.

Spider-Man, who had taken the worst of the brief battle, faced her through wary eyes. He wouldn't have needed spider-sense, or years of experience dealing with dangerous people, to know that she was deadly. He could tell it just by the way she stood, the way every muscle in her body seemed like a piston under tremendous pressure. And then there was the look on her face: the despair and fear and hatred and even shame that warred beneath the surface like demons battling for even the briefest moment of supremacy. She was a woman lost, a woman in pain, a woman being torn to pieces by all the forces inside her.

For a moment he imagined the Gentleman's laughing face superimposed over her own, and he felt his anger burning deep inside him. He knew what Fiers had done to his parents . . . and was sworn to make him pay for that. He knew the other deaths Fiers had caused . . . and was sworn to make him pay for that. He knew what Fiers planned to do to the city of New York . . . and was sworn to make him pay for that. But what Fiers had done to this woman . . . whether she was Carla May Mendelsohn or not . . . whether she was Peter Parker's sister or not . . . was all by itself an act as evil as anything Spider-Man had ever seen. It was an assault that had kept this woman in hell, at war with herself For years on end. The kind of evil capable of inflicting that amount of damage on another human being, and then bragging about it, was so hateful that it was capable of stunning even a man with Spider-Man's life experience.

The shock of her sudden attack had caused him to fall back on the standup comic persona he so often adopted during his battles.

Now he cursed himself for his stupidity.

He had to win more than just a fight. He had to win a soul.

Humor wouldn't accomplish that.

And with the Oltion Field Generator well on its way to ignition atop the Empire State... he had only minutes left to try.

He said: "Wait—"

It was the only thing he had the chance to say before Pity's fingers wrapped tight around his throat.

Just south of Manhattan, a platoon of SAFE aircars flew low over the burning harbor, dropping chemical retardant on the flames. The dive would have been a demanding one at the best of times. Today, it was complicated even further by the turbulence caused by the interface between the intense high temperatures at the waterline and the equally intense blizzard higher above. With next to zero visibility due to the oily clouds of black smoke and the whiteout weather conditions, navigation was already next to impossible. Surviving it when an insane human dynamo circled the holocaust firing explosive lightning bolts at any aircar that wandered into range rendered even impossibility itself a tragic understatement. But it still had to be done. Two aircars shuttled back and forth between Liberty Island and the Jersey Shore, evacuating the few tourists adventurous enough to try visiting the great copper lady on the coldest day of the year. Six others escorted the squads attacking the flames, taking the bulk of the fire that was directed at them by Electro. The number of SAFE casualties had been last reported at seven dead.

The eighth was Agent Donna Piazza.

Tasked with the assignment of helping to provide escort for the forces attacking the fire, she was in the act of radioing for permission to fly her passenger George Williams to safety when one of Electro's explosive lightning bolts burst just under their line of flight. Their aircar shuddered, bucked, then began to spiral toward the river. Donna seized the controls and tried to pull up. She plummeted into a wall of billowing smoke, levelled off, screamed as the air around her abruptly turned hot enough to sear her skin through the aircar's ionic temperature-maintenance shield, then woo-hooed as the blackness all around her suddenly gave way to an unobstructed view of blizzarding sky. It was a small miracle of virtuoso piloting that left her heart pounding at the near brush with death, but when she glanced at George Williams to see how he'd weathered the strain she saw that he was still seated calmly beside her, wearing the same look of grim determination as before.

She might have said something about that.

But then there was another explosion, just ahead, this one taking the shape of a man lit up brighter than the sun. While it didn't drive the aircar into another spin it did shatter the inertial restraints on Donna's pilot seat. She found herself airborn, felt a fleeting sense of cold, rebounded hard against the deck, and in one terrible slow motion tumble she was stumbling over the aircar rim into open space.

She held on long enough to see Colonel Morgan's pet old man rise from his seat and, despite bucking turbulence that would have thrown a much younger man, lurch toward her with extended cane. "Hold on!" Williams shouted, his hoarse voice somehow audible over all the mingled din of wind and engines and explosions and shouting sociopathic villains. "You'll be all right!"

For a moment, she really did think that the old man was going to save her life again, for the second time in five minutes.

But then the aircar bucked again, and her grip failed. She groped for the extended cane but missed it by inches. Her last view of life was of the stricken old man peering over the aircar rim.

She cried out just before the sea of blackness engulfed her.

An aghast Dr. George Williams tightened his grip on the side of the SAFE aircar as he watched the brave young lady disappear into the smoke and flames. He wanted to cry out, but just closed his eyes and turned away, adding hers to a long list of other lives cut short in decades past.

When he opened his eyes again, Electro was just a bright streak of light, who had done all the damage he could do here and was now racing to join his partners in Manhattan.

Williams briefly considered hating the man, but he had no room for more hate.

It was Gustav Fiers who had set these events in motion. Gustav Fiers who had sacrificed so many lives to his single-minded quest for profit. Gustav Fiers whose entire life was a history written in blood.

Dr. George Williams, who had spent the past sixty years of his life tracking down the monster, could only pledge that today's atrocities would be the monster's last.

Now soaring over Chase Manhattan Plaza, grimacing from the cold, the Vulture could just barely make out the taller spire of the Empire State Building many blocks ahead. This far out, there was no sign of any battle going on there.

But he knew one was happening.

He looked forward to paying back a thousand old humiliations in blood.

Pinned to the rooftop by a raging Pity, Spider-Man seized her by both wrirsts and focused all his strength on prying her hands from his neck. But her grip was solid, as tight as any he had ever felt. Her fingertips bit hard into his windpipe, closing off his breath, isolating him from a world filled with life-giving air. It was all he could do to hold back some of her strength, to keep her from tightening her grip even more and squeezing with a force that would have reduced his neck vertebrae to powder.

It hurt.

But not as much as the sight of her face.

The average super-villain having him at this kind of momentary disadvantage would have been crowing with rage or bloodlust or even triumph. They all tended to be strong-willed people, proud of the choices they had made. But Pity seemed to be hurting almost as much as Spider-Man. Her lips curled in a grimace, her eyes burning with more horror than determination, her chin trembling in the manner of a child who had just been scared by a loud noise. She seemed tormented by what her own hands were doing. He couldn't believe it, but her eyes were even bubbling over with tears. Her vision must have been blurring as much as his.

It could have freed him to throw everything into a single fatal blow.

Instead, he released his grip on her wrists and pressed the flats of his palms against the sides of her jaw. Her eyes widened slightly. With her assassin's training, she probably believed he was about to twist her head sharply to the right, thus breaking her neck. He could have. He certainly had enough strength. She tried to pull her face free, but the natural adhesive qualities of his hands held it fast.

She tightened her grip on his neck.

In her mind it had to be a contest over whose neck broke first.

Spider-Man curled his hands, applied just the right degree of pressure against the underside of her jaw—

—two quick squeezes in rapid succession, far below the threshold of damage—

—a pair of matching thwip sounds, on either side of her face—

—a pair of slimy, sticky web-balls, splattering her at point-blank range—

—no worse than snowballs, really, just more viscerally revolting—

—something to give her a scare—

—she couldn't be human and not recoil—

—the Gentleman couldn't have robbed her of that much—

—her face contorted—

—the grip on his neck loosened a few paltry pounds per square inch—

—he arched his back and flipped himself off the roof—

—breaking free of her, tossing her free with a shove, twirling four times in mid-air before landing in a crouch against the next building.

Pity stood. The two web-balls Spider-Man had fired at her hung on her respective cheeks like fuzzy warts; they looked really stupid, and if she had been any other opponent he would have immediately cracked wise about them. But this was Pity—and he found himself more concerned about the glistening twin tear-tracks that had just sprouted on her cheeks, retracing the scars that the Gentleman had left there an unknown number of years ago.

He tried again: "Listen to me! We don't have to fight—"

Unnatural darkness radiated from her hands, swallowing everything within a fifty yard radius.

The battle resumed.

The crowd of tourists on the Observation Deck of the Empire State Building had thinned, mostly because the scenic appeal of the earliest phases of the blizzard was history. With conditions approaching whiteout, Manhattan was no longer a thriving metropolis in the process of being transformed into a winter wonderland, but a dim array of gray monoliths disappearing behind the storm. Visibility was now limited to a few scant blocks in every direction. The world-famous view from a height would soon be just another blank white screen, bereft of any projectionist possessed by the tools to make it magic. As a result most of the tourists had already headed down. The handful who remained were here only to take a few last pictures and buy a few last souvenirs before surrendering to the inevitable.

Quentin Beck was not surprised when security guards in blue descended en masse from the central gift shoppe to corral even those few. They cited the horrid weather as the major reason for their safety concerns, but no doubt the imminent arrival of Dr. Octavius had a lot more to do with it. As Beck watched a pair of Mutt-and-Jeff security guards escort the last group, a posse of Norwegian college students in backpacks, through the glass doors into the gift shop, he wondered if he should do something to interfere with their escape. After all, he deeply loathed performing without an audience. It would be so fun to have them screaming and begging when dear old Electro arrived to set off the EMP. But then he decided not. Even if Octavius didn't just toss them over the balcony in a fit of pique at their frenzied yammering, the effort involved in guarding them was more than Beck felt up to right now. He had such a beastly headache he just wanted to play his scripted role, wreak worldwide havoc, and curl up at home with a hot toddy and some Harryhausen films on DVD.

He was so busy thinking about which Sinbad film to play that he failed to register the security guard's approach until that chubby-cheeked fool was right on top of him. "Sir? Are you all right?"

Beck looked up. "Ennh?"

The guard resembled the old silent-movie comedian Roscoe "Fatty" Arbuckle, whose entire *oeuvre*, lost films and all, Beck possessed in one of his many safehouses. Baby-faced and innocent-eyed, the fool's attempt to wield the voice of authority would have been laughable for anybody who had been in and out of as many prisons as Beck. He said: "We're evacuating the Deck, sir. Can you come with me, please?"

Beck regarded him with curiosity. "First can you tell me why you asked if I was all right?"

"You don't look good, sir. I think you need a doctor..."

Beck, who had better things to do than to deal with the condescending empathy of a security guard capable of over-reacting to mere flu symptoms, flashed a sneer filled with tobacco-stained teeth. "It's fortunate, then, that there's already one on the way."

The guard said, "What?"

Beck jabbed the remote control in his coat pocket.

The explosives he'd set at many places around the Observation Deck went off all at once, with great bursts of concussive light that filled the already stormy air with ozone haze. A huge section of the suicide-barrier fencing all but disintegrated, tumbling over the edge in shrapnel-sized fragments. A set of nearby coin-operated binoculars tore free of its bolts and slammed against the opposite wall, leaving a crater before it fell to pieces. The glass windows of the Gift Shop disintegrated and tumbled to the floor in a white shower momentarily indistinguishable from the blizzard itself.

The guard went for his sidearm.

He moved so slowly, though. At least as far as Quentin Beck was concerned. To a man who had conditioned himself with sufficient speed to spar with Spider-Man, the guard's clumsy attempt to draw was more than just slow-motion. It was a series of still photographs, studied at leisure, and easy to intercept. Beck neutralized the poor bit player almost at leisure, first disarming him with a jab to a certain nexus of nerve endings just below the elbow, then robbing him of the will to fight with a punch to a sensitive place just below the ribs, then stealing even his consciousness with a club to to the back of the neck.

Glowing red smoke swallowed Quentin Beck, then dissipated, revealing Mysterio: the sparkling green bodysuit, the flowing purple cape, the awesome bubble of a helmet that revealed but a suggestion of the master showman who lurked beneath.

Beck much preferred this guise to his real face. Nobody was going to say Mysterio looked pale. Nobody was going to say Mysterio looked drawn. Nobody was going to say that Mysterio had just popped a cold sweat. Nobody was going to say Mysterio was a wannabe or a never-was. They would just look at Mysterio and see what he was: the greatest showman in the history of the world, about to conduct his greatest performance with the aid of his customary supporting players.

He considered the Sinister Six naught but his loyal troupe in this. It didn't matter who wrote the script, or even who directed; it mattered only who starred. And while this may have been an ensemble piece, there was absolutely no doubt, at least not to Quentin Beck's trained critical eye, who out of today's players approached his role with the most grace and elan. It was so obvious it was sad. He wished the media critics of the *Bugle* or the *Times* could be persuaded to review his appearances as something other than crime news. If they would only just forget the various illegalities and brutalities, and come to appreciate his actions as manifestations of brilliant performance art, he would be the toast of the town. He, and not Octavius, would always be granted top billing in all subsequent press coverage.

He stepped over the unconscious guard and moved to the Fifth Avenue side of the building, awaiting his rendezvous with Octavius.

Despite the weather, despite his flu, despite even his perpetual annoyance at not being able to kill Spider-Man yet, he was ebullient. After all, he would soon be a very wealthy man. When the EMP fried all of Manhattan's electronic financial records, the millions in cash he and his colleagues had been paid by the Gentleman would appreciate in value by a factor of ten.

All that lovely cash. That lovely, lovely, lovely cash.

Who would have guessed that, for all his other faults, the Gentleman really was the type to keep his end of the bargain?

CHAPTER TEN

The nondescript black van screeched around the corner of Fifth Avenue and 33rd Street, pulling to a stop half on and half off the curb. As the few pedestrians still on the street recoiled, its side doors clanged open, and a heavily-armed interagency assault team composed of equal parts S.H.I.E.L.D., NYPD SWAT, FBI Tactical, and SAFE burst out, fanning out around the van as their tactical leader for this phase of the operation, FBI Special Agent Martin Walsh, took point.

Walsh, cocooned in the padded kevlar armor his agency always provided for paranormal combat, took exactly five seconds to peer up the great wall of the Empire State's Fifth Avenue face. He hoped to see Spider-Man or Pity or Doctor Octopus or any of the other combatants from this position, but he wasn't surprised he couldn't. With visibility fading as the blizzard intensified, the building faded into nothingness less than twenty stories up. He could hear something, distorted both by howling wind and the acoustics of Manhattan's concrete canyons: the distant sound of thunderclaps any modern law-enforcement officer was trained to recognize as the sound of paranormals in frenzied hand-to-hand combat. But though the most recent reports had Spider-Man engaging Dr. Octopus on the building's face, there was no telling whether that battle was ongoing, or whether the situation had altered in any significant way. For all he knew, these particular thunderclaps could be some other paranormal battle entirely, taking place miles away and totally unrelated to the Sinister Six crisis—Nova taking on Nitro, or some such silliness. This was midtown Manhattan, home of such things, after all.

Matt Gunderson, listening intently into his earpiece, said: "Agent Walsh? We just got a heads'-up from Deeley, downtown. Electro and the Vulture are both converging on this position and are expected here within minutes."

Walsh grunted: "When can we expect air support?" Morgan's team was going to be essential for taking down the biggest gun, Electro, and was probably the best shot for taking down Dr. Octopus as well.

"Right now Morgan's devoting all our aerial resources to containing the river fire. He says he'll send help as soon as he can, but right now it's up to Spider-Man and—for what it's worth—us."

Walsh could have done without that "for what it's worth," even if the best-equipped law-enforcement personnel had never been able to do much against the likes of the Six. But, like Morgan, he'd be damned if he'd let the wall-crawler fight this battle alone when he had so much as one warm body to contribute. "All right, people, listen up. We're entering an unknown field. Bogies can be anywhere—and they're all tougher than we are. You are to split up into teams of two, make your ascent as quickly as possible, and locate those Bogies. Do not, repeat, do not engage unless you're in imminent danger, or you see civilians in imminent danger. And even then resist direct contact unless you know for a fact that you can put them down clean. We are here for tactical support, not to make ourselves heroes. Is that clear?"

"Yes, sir!" his people responded.

He noticed the slightest hesitation from the new SAFE recruit, Dr. Cynthia Monella, and damned Morgan's folly in deciding to permit a recently traumatized newcomer to take a central role in the operation. But he didn't have time to buck that particular decision right now.

"Excellent." He addressed the female agent at his side. "Starling, you're with me. The rest of you, fan out."

11:32 A.M.
It had been just another Manhattan rooftop. Now, shrouded in psionically-generated darkness, it was the battleground between two combatants with more power than any human being had any right to possess. Their punches and kicks sounded like duelling thunderclaps.

Despite his keen awareness of the battle's stakes, Spider-Man could not fight his determination to reclaim Pity's soul. He kept working on it even as he dodged a succession of potentially deadly blows. "You know what he wants to do, don't you? The suffering he wants to cause? You don't want to be a part of that! I can tell you don't!"

He acted more sure than he was, since any feelings she might have had on the subject remained hidden behind a cold assassin's mask. But he kept it up anyway, foregoing several easy openings in order to get her with words instead.

"You're not as trapped as you think you are!" he cried, as he somersaulted over one of her roundhouse swings. "You're never trapped! Whatever he's made you do in the past . . . you can stop him by saying you're not going to take any more!"

Was he getting to her? He couldn't tell. That controlled expression of hers was almost as opaque as his own full-face hood. It slipped now and then, but only enough to confirm that there was a soul in there, never enough to confirm what kind of soul it was, or whether it was capable of being stirred by chances at redemption.

But he still felt, in his gut, that she didn't have to be an enemy. That she was sickened by everything the Gentleman made her do. That she secretly wished he could find her a way out.

Was that a genuine gut instinct on his part? Or was Counsellor Saberstein right about it being some kind of psionically implanted smokescreen instead?

The doubt slowed him long enough for Pity to make a serious frontal assault. This time, instead of hurling a punch or kick that his spider-sense would give him a fair shot of evading, she simply darted forward and grabbed him by the wrists, yanking both upward before he had a chance to react. It was an attempt to hurl him into the air, but Spider-Man had the soles of his feet planted firmly against the roof, and refused to let himself be moved. The moment of inertia threw Pity off balance. She showed teeth and tried to hurl him backwards instead, but he remained planted. What's more, he tensed both arms with all the strength he had, and drove them toward her, not only keeping Pity from pressing her attack, but forcing her, for the moment, to use all of her own considerable strength to hold him back.

The two combatants, who had been leaping and darting and dodging each other's feints and parries faster than the normal human eye could follow, now for the moment found themselves standing stock still and face to face, as the duel of strength prevented either from pushing the other aside.

"If you . . . switch sides . . . I know people in SAFE . . .

willing to give their opinion... that you acted under duress... and I'm... friends... with the best lawyer in Manhattan... who will sweat blood to help me prove it..."

Was that fear that just flickered on Pity's face?

He remembered what Saberstein had said, that she would be conditioned to regard any attempt to help her as a threat. She would show increasingly more resistance the more such attempts seemed likely to succeed. Was he getting to her?

He didn't need to wonder. It was as clear as the eyes on her face.

He was getting to her. Not enough, but some.

Pity relaxed her arms without warning. Had he fallen for it, his own exertion would have allowed her to flip him over her back. He didn't fall for it, but instead compensated without even thinking. Spider-sense hadn't warned him. He'd just known. The feint forced her back no more than a single step before both Spider-Man and Pity recovered, leaving them in perfect check again.

She went to trip his ankle.

The kick in the shin hurt, but not any more than he could take. He pressed on: "And something else! Even if they don't believe you—even if you have to go to prison for your involvement—I need you to know this! I'll still do everything I can to help! I won't abandon you!"

It was probably the most honest, most heartfelt pledge of personal commitment anybody had ever spoken to her. Spider-Man meant every word of it. The air was so electric between them that she had to know he was telling the truth. Maybe, in another second, it would have been enough to break the Gentleman's hold.

But he didn't have that second.

He felt the painful tingling at the base of his neck that

warned him of something deadly approaching at full speed. He knew that if he remained where he was he would die. And he cartwheeled to the right, both breaking Pity's grip and getting out of the way of a swift, terrible something that cleaved the air where he'd been.

By the time he landed on his feet, Pity was lost to him again. She just stood, impassive, looking not at him but at a gnarled bird of prey in human form, who had just tried to slice Spider-Man in half with his razor-sharp metal wings. Now circling three stories above, the Vulture looked like he'd just returned from a war. His costume was grimy with soot, and at the center of his chest with a burn mark, but the man himself looked as fresh as he ever did, which was to say he looked withered and ancient but still empowered by the sheer force of his hate.

"Wonderful," Spider-Man muttered. "Another county heard from."

The Vulture, circling, shouted down at Pity: "We need you elsewhere, dear!"

Spider-Man glared up at the bird-suited man. "I need you elsewhere too, pookums, but you're not likely to oblige!"

The Vulture ignored him and continued to address Pity. "I just saw a team of heavily-armed men, evidently SAFE agents, enter the Empire State. I could go after them myself, but they're probably spread out already, and close quarters aren't my element. If you take care of them, I'll be more than happy to eviscerate the insect."

Arachnid, Spider-Man thought automatically. *I keep telling you people.*

Then Pity nodded, and a more serious thought gripped him: *No, I almost had her.*

He lunged forward, desperate to intercept her.

But the Vulture swooped down to intercept him...

giving Pity more than ample time to disappear into the storm.

11:34 A.M.

The Van Wyck Expressway is one of Long Island's busiest and frequently most clogged arteries—an "express" only at certain times of the day, and even then only when the stars are in alignment. Plagued by heavy airport traffic, often torn up by construction, and extremely vulnerable to poor weather conditions, it has long been the habitat of sweaty-faced, muttering drivers helpless to do anything but count the scant minutes remaining between them and their departure at John F. Kennedy International Airport.

Alas for the Gentleman, who now fumed in the back seat of his stretch limo cursing the gods for damning his glorious enterprise, the stars were not in alignment today. Construction of the new monorail system had shut the already-burdened roadway down to one lane for much of its length. Rush hour had extended to accomodate Manhattan commuters who didn't decide until they saw the first few flakes of snow that this was not the best possible day to put in a whole day of work at the office. There was an accident involving a van, a station wagon, and, of all things, a portable ferris wheel that had fallen off the truck carrying it back to the rent-a-ride warehouse. The road had become a parking lot. Then the storm slammed into Long Island as suddenly and as ruthlessly as it had slammed the doomed city just north of here. LaGuardia was down to one runway, and would be shutting even that one down within the hour. Kennedy was expected to quickly follow suit. And though the Gentleman intended to use neither, the road was still packed bumper-to-bumper with fools hoping against all odds to make their flights to other American cities just as filthy and fatuous as this one.

The Gentleman, studying their slope-browed faces from behind tinted glass, raged: Where do you intend to go? To warmer climes? Ha! Your warmer climes are culturally inert rabbit warrens! To distant cities? Ha! Your cities are colonies of the damned! To two-week vacations you use to distract yourselves from the emptiness of your national character? Ha! You could just drug yourselves into a mass stupor, like always! If any of you had evolved past the ability to count to ten on your fingers, you would clear this thoroughfare to make way for a man worth all of you—a man who unlike you actually has someplace to go.

The SUV to his immediate left responded by speeding up to prevent the limousine from entering its lane.

I hope you keep your life savings in Manhattan, you troglodyte!

The grimfaced cigar smoker behind the wheel of the SUV, a man defined by jowls and nothing else, must have sensed the hostility coming from his immediate right. He cast his vacant expression at the limo, furrowed his idiot eyebrows, and mouthed something foul that led the Gentleman to take down his license plate for the benefit of future paid assassins.

"It will get better once we pass Kennedy," the limo driver said.

His name was Serge. That was another annoyance. Serge. The Gentleman had expected to use Smerdyakov's man, Ivan. Alas, Ivan was unfortunately deceased, a victim of the carjackers whose interference had led to the loss of the Czarina's necklace and other valuables. The Gentleman had been forced to hire this Serge character from a certain Manhattan agency that specialized in chauffeurs for the criminal element. Serge evidently knew the rules of the road, but he was so much a product of this country's perverted egalitarianism that he honestly believed the Gentleman would be interested in something a mere servant had to say. The Gentleman responded with the cold silence the remark deserved.

True, he wasn't on as strict a timetable as the rest of these sheep. It was his jet, and he could take off anytime he wanted. He could even take off if both airports closed. He had the jet hangared at a private facility further east, and was sufficiently confident in the improvements he'd paid for and his own brilliance as a pilot to take off even in conditions much worse than these.

But the delay still vexed him. He had so wanted to be in the air already, unleashing the Catalyst over Manhattan. There would have been a certain elegance involved in conducting that aspect of the operation as close to the activation of the Electromagnetic Pulse as possible. There wouldn't even have been any special risk involved in doing that; the shielding he'd had installed to his jet's systems was the same that protected Air Force One. He supposed it wouldn't make all that much of a difference if he performed his own role an hour or so after the Sinister Six performed theirs, but he was used to having his wants and needs fulfilled on demand, and having to crawl behind these half-human pigs flying off to theme parks and other ephemera was more of a personal insult than he was willing to take.

He stewed.

The view beyond the windshield was a white haze, only partially dispelled by the constant efforts of the limo's windshield wipers.

He stewed some more.

Then he brightened.

He knew what he could do.

He could blow up the third-rate actress now.

He raised an eyebrow at the deliciousness of the thought.

Certainly, he'd intended to do it later, but desperate times required desperate measures. Blowing up Mrs. Spider-Man would be fun, it would be satisfying, and it would provide a marvelous distraction from all this tedium and aggravation. A single push of a button, and boom—say goodbye to one more rattrap in Forest Hills. Indeed, since this very road was passing through Queens, and since the bomb was powerful enough to take not only the Parker domicile but also much of the surrounding block as well, he might even be lucky enough to hear the distant explosion itself.

He flipped back the wolf's head, ran his thumb over the smooth white button, and leered, thinking of the elder Parkers and their effrontery in shutting down Operation Croesus. He could almost imagine them as unseen, unheard phantoms, damned to follow and witness all of the manifold successes he had enjoyed since their elimination—wailing at him in helplessness and despair as he taught them that his vengeance was not yet done. How delicious that would be!

—but if the third-rate actress wasn't home—

—if she was somewhere else, shopping, or visiting friends—

—there would at least be satisfaction in destroying the Parker home—

No.

He curled his lips, and flipped the wolf's-head closed, shielding the button once again.

It would wait.

After all, he had nothing but time.

Curled up on Jill Stacy's couch, watching local TV coverage of SAFE's battle with Electro and the Vulture, Mary Jane

Watson-Parker could only shake her head in weary recognition. She had watched some scenes many times before, an uncomfortable number of them close up and personal. She had in fact survived two such situations in the past two weeks. But she never got used to it.

This particular coverage was hosted by Jay Sein and Cosmo the K, local radio personalities who specialized in providing New Yorkers with coverage of Manhattans's regular paranormal crises. Their jocular treatment of life-and-death battles was hard enough to take on the radio. Their dark glasses and primary-color wardrobes, designed to mimic domino masks and super hero costumes, rendered them downright offense.

"A major move by the Six," Sein noted, with brutal obviousness. "Setting the river on fire checks the authorities and leaves them free to do whatever it is they came here to do."

"Which, offhand," Cosmo the K said, "seems to be wrecking stuff."

"Giving the people what they want," said Sein. "That's some ultimate weapon, huh? Setting the river on fire?"

"Not much of one, Jay. It's been known to happen all by itself in Cleveland. Meanwhile, we have word that two more members of the Six, Pity and Doctor Octopus, have been spotted at the Empire State Building, where there's evidently some kind of major action underway. There are also unconfirmed reports of Spider-Man at the scene, though details are sketchy due to weather conditions."

"A rematch made in heaven," Sein said, "after his stunning defeat of the Six one week ago. We should discourage anybody who wishes to travel to midtown to watch the show. Even if visibility wasn't poor due to the weather, a front-seat view won't be anything to brag about if a building falls on your head."

"That would hurt," Cosmo the K agreed.

Tuning out the inane banter as beneath her notice, trying not to think of the danger Peter faced at this very moment, Mary Jane turned to Jill Stacy to see what she thought, and found her friend frozen. Jill had the look of a woman paralyzed by the sight of bodies being pulled from a car wreck. Her eyes were wide, her chin was trembling, and her hands clutched one of her throw pillows with such desperation that it might have been the only solid object in the whole world. At first, Mary Jane mistook it as mere fright at the disaster in progress, but it was more. It was memory. Jill had been very close to Gwen, who had died at the hands of a man just as insane as the Six.

Mary Jane said, "Jill?"

Jill's face was agonized. "Him."

"Who?

"Spider-Man. The one who killed Gwen."

Mary Jane recoiled. "He didn't kill Gwen. The Green Goblin killed Gwen."

"That's what they say. But Spider-Man was there too. He had something to do with it."

"Yes, he did," Mary Jane said. "He tried to stop it."

Jill's face contorted in pain. "How do you know for sure?"

There was no answer Mary Jane could afford to give to that. She did know for sure. She had known for sure for years. But she'd been given an inside view. It hurt, sometimes, to know that the inside view was denied the vast majority of people. To them, Spider-Man was just another colorful costumed figure bouncing around inside orgies of mass destruction, as much to blame for such carnage as the maniacs he fought. They didn't know what it had cost him. What it continued to cost him. The ultimate sacrifice it might still someday cost him. They didn't know that he did it, not out of recklessness, but out of a sense of responsibility that sometimes overshadowed all else.

Mary Jane wished there was a way to explain her faith in the webslinger without explaining how she knew. But there wasn't.

That was her part of the burden.

So she said nothing, and continued to watch the updates about the river fire and Doc Ock's attack on the Empire State Building. Switching channels to get rid of the DJs, and perhaps to get some better updates, she saw the Dan Rather report that the SAFE firefighters were losing . . . and, only a few minutes later, the Trish Tilby report that Spider-Man had been killed . . .

11: 37 A.M.
Dr. Octopus had never been one of Mysterio's favorite people. He was a good guy to have around when you wanted to plan a gigantic crime or work out a way to kill a pesky super hero, but the guy had a major attitude problem, even by the standards of people in the super-villain profession. Mysterio was aware that was saying a lot. He was also aware that it was just one of those things that needed to be dealt with if you wanted to accomplish anything.

Even so, Ock was being even more of a pain than usual today.

The Doctor had managed to drag the Oltion Field Generator all the way to the observation deck atop the Empire State, and had used his uncanny strength to twist the steel bars of the suicide barriers into supports to lash it in place. Mysterio had in the meantime occupied himself checking the connections between the device and its power source, a circular plate that needed only one focused blast from Electro in order to start the device at hundreds of times its usual intensity.

Mysterio, his vision blurring from the fly or whatever the hell it was, performed his half of the job efficiently, with only minor delays. He considered adding Octavius to his List, but no... there was such a thing as not going completely crazy. Instead, he shouted loudly enough to be heard over the wind: "Back off! These aren't perfect conditions, you know!"

"They're never perfect," Octavius shouted back, "when I have to contend with fools!"

"Max will be here as soon as he can!"

"I wasn't talking about Max!"

And so on. A real charmer, Octavius, even by the standards of this profession. It would be enough to give Mysterio a headache even if he didn't have one already.

It was just too bad that Manhattan was wracked by a blizzard and not by a lightning storm. In one of those, they wouldn't have had to wait for Electro at all. The elements would have provided them with all the juice they required. Even better, Mysterio thought, such conditions would have provided a wonderful homage to the Frankenstein films directed by James Whale... one of the only auteurs Mysterio actually credited as deserving his respect and reputation. Whale had been an inspiration to Quentin Beck, both personally and professionally. He would have said this to Octavius, but he thought better of it. The Doctor never reacted well to hearing the word genius applied to people other than himself, even if those people happened to work in other fields. So Mysterio just did his work and mused quietly on what a great movie this would make.

Meanwhile, supported by his tentacles, the Doctor's pudgy form took the equivalent of one step back from his handiwork. Though not dressed for the cold, he seemed unbothered by the blasts of freezing wind that lashed him so high above the street, nor did he seem bothered by the icy sheen that seemed to have rendered his thick glasses a virtual blindfold. After a moment, he grimaced. It may have been his version of a smile, but it resembled the look of a man who'd just been sucker-punched in the belly. "It will have to do!" he shouted. "I have other places to be!"

Mysterio fought off a fresh wave of dizziness. "If you're going after the wall-crawler, I'll join you!"

The laugh that came from Octavius was as soft as a death-rattle, and about as charming; it managed audibility despite the power of the storm. "I promise you, Beck... the wallcrawler's the last thing on my mind right now! If you want him, he's all yours!"

Octavius didn't stick around long enough to tell Mysterio what he meant. He just sank from sight. His tentacles, freed now from their previous heavy burden, were able to carry him down the Fifth Avenue face several orders of magnitude faster than they'd been able to carry him and that burden to the summit. That, and the damage the blizzard had done to visibility at this altitude, gave his departure the air of a magical disappearance. Even Mysterio, master of such things, felt a moment of odd discomfort when he reached the edge and saw that the Doctor was already well out of sight.

"I'll be damned," Mysterio murmured.

It was a more or less accurate appraisal, but that's not how he meant it. Doctor Octopus with a hidden agenda was not good news for anybody, not even his teammates. The thought was so unnerving that for just one moment, less than a heartbeat, really, Mysterio, the man who had killed time and time again, who was already this morning a party to threatening Manhattan with fiery holocaust and was now fully prepared to set off an EMP capable of reducing the city to chaos... found himself hoping that Spider-Man would be able to stop Octavius before that madman did something really crazy. But then the thought passed. He remembered the plan. And he turned back from the edge to continue preparing the Generator for Electro's arrival . . .

The fleet of SAFE aircars flew low over the blazing river, dumping sheets of flame-retardant foam. The fumes from the blaze, already black and oily, only grew thicker in response. The flames themselves danced just as high and burned just as hot, inconvenienced not at all. Although SAFE containment efforts had shielded Liberty Island and kept the heart of the fire from spreading to south Manhattan, that wasn't going to make much of a difference. Reports had parts of Pier A and Battery Park already smoldering from radiant heat.

Palminetti, tracking the efforts, shouted: "We're losing her! The foam we have left won't do the job!"

"Then it's time to get creative!" Morgan said. "Link me with the helicarrier!"

The last few seconds before Dr. Octavius retreated from the observation deck.

One of the newest additions to the skyline above Time's Square was a giant three-dimensional billboard advertising the current Broadway hit *Submarine!* The show, now in hiatus while the production searched for a new theatre capable of housing it while repairs were made to the previous venue recently destroyed by Mysterio, was nevertheless well on its way to becoming a New York institution, and therefore deserved advertising as completely tasteless as the show itself. Hence the billboard, a gigantic sculpture of lead actor Morrison Cord's head, looking noble and determined beneath the brim of a navy dress cap. It looked so very noble and determined that not five minutes passed, at any time of day, when somebody down below demonstrated New York attitude by facing down that stare with an equally defiant: "What the hell do you think you're looking at?" People who passed it more frequently—like the city's large population of cab drivers—reported other reactions. Some were downright unnerved, and at least one person had run screaming from the impression that he was being watched.

Thanks to the weather, not many people saw that sign get what it deserved.

The two costumed figures, locked together in a tangle of walloping arms and legs, smashed into its forehead hard enough to make a great gaping crater right between its eyes. For a moment, the head rocked from side to side, as if in denial of the battle taking place within. Then the top of the head exploded, and two figures burst forth, like children born from the head of an ancient god.

One was Spider-Man; the other the Vulture.

They had fought entire wars in the last couple of minutes. It had been a knock-down, drag-out slugfest that had carried them all the way from 5th Avenue and 33rd Street to Broadway and 42nd. The high winds and worsening visibility had made it a sloppy battle for both aerial combatants, their usual total mastery of the high-altitude battleground reduced to a lurching clumsiness as deadly to both as they were to each other.

The Vulture landed on his back on the giant hat brim, sliding backwards on a snowdrift, bracing himself just in time to avoid rolling over the edge. He saw Spider-Man leap toward him, and attempted to knock him out of the sky with a wild kick. Spider-Man leaped over that attack, flipped, changed trajectory in mid-air when a defensive slash from the Vulture's left wing threatened to cut him in half, and sailed all the way past the Vulture and over the edge. One pair of thwips later, the plunging Spider-Man had landed a pair of web-lines on the Vulture's shoulders. The second his weight pulled both lines taut, the Vulture was yanked right off the hat brim and into open space.

For one terrifying moment, the old man found himself surrounded by total whiteout, unable to distinguish up from down, deadly brick wall from open air. Then he corkscrewed, oriented himself, and sought higher altitude. When in doubt, that's what he always did. That was his element. The insect hitching a ride on those web-lines could wait.

He heard the hated voice of Spider-Man, just behind him. "When will it be enough, Vulchy?"

Higher; higher; let the self-righteous nuisance waste his breath on witticisms. "What?"

"When will you finally have enough money? I've been keeping track, you know! The police haven't found even a fraction of what you've stolen over the years! You must have plenty still stashed away, more than an old guy like you could possibly spend in the time you have left! Do you really need more so badly you're willing to keep hurting people to get it?"

The Vulture executed a hard right and slashed at the wallcrawler, like a puppy trying to catch the tip of its own tail. The very act yanked the weblines, and the wallcrawler at the end of them, out of harm's way. "What would you suggest I do with my life then, fool? Sink into a chaise lounge and spend my retirement watching sunsets in the tropics?"

Spider-Man's response was aghast. "You consider terrorism just a way to keep yourself busy in your golden years?"

"Why not?" The Vulture, who had at one point nearly driven himself further around the bend with the inactivity he found in a planned retirement community, flipped over again. This time the weblines hanging down his back looped over his shoulders, allowing him to shred them with a quick slash of his wings.

This gave him no satisfaction at all, since there was no longer any annoying crimefighter hanging from them.

No. Spider-Man landed on the Vulture's back. His powerful hands ripped at the padded material of the old man's costume, searching for the insulated power pack that gave the suit its juice. It was a move that had won several of their previous battles for him, and which had been known to backfire when the Vulture electrified the housing. Today, it was just a waste of time. Toomes had discarded the bulky old power pack in favor of a more integrated assembly that threaded throughout his entire suit.

Now, while the wallcrawler wasted his time in search of a nonexistent power pack, all Toomes had to do was find a handy brick wall to scrape against.

He veered toward a building face.

The trespasser on the Vulture's back abruptly leaped off, disappearing into the storm.

The Vulture corrected course. "Is that the best you can do, cretin? Flee?"

Spider-Man's hated voice mocked him, from somewhere impossibly close: "You've seen the best I can do many times, Toomie—at least as long as you still remained conscious! But I'm not going to let you distract me any more today! Not when I have more important people to fight!"

More impor—

The Vulture forgot that this whole fight was entirely an exercise in keeping Spider-Man away from the Empire State Building, and exploded with affronted rage. "*You dare insult me—*"

A scarlet fist shut the old man up in mid-rant. "Yeah, yeah, yeah! Like I'm ever *not* insulting you!"

The Vulture reeled from the impact, lashing out with the edge of one razor-tipped wing. An open-palmed slap, exploding out of nowhere, almost knocked him out of the sky. A second later he gagged as a great wet gob of something burst against his face. He thought it was a ball of congealed web fluid, but then he swallowed some that had gotten into his mouth and realized it was something far more insulting than that. Slush.

Another punch impacted the Vulture's ribs, knocking the breath out of him, leaving dark spots at the corners of his vision. The Vulture gasped, fighting off unconsciousness, knowing that he needed just one moment to recover before he could re-dedicate himself to slicing the wallcrawler in half.

But it was not a moment the wallcrawler intended him to have. The next few words were accompanied by almost as many triphammer punches: "You're a real bad egg, Vulchy—but you're low priority today, so I'm going to give you a chance you don't deserve! Stay away from me while I keep your maniac teammates from doing something stupid, and I'll put off knocking you silly 'til later! Get in my way before then and I'll put you down so hard they'll have to paste your feathers on a body cast!"

"Y-you . . . d-dare . . ."

The Vulture would have said more, but that's when Spider-Man grabbed him by the shoulders and flung him, as easily as a skipped stone, across a snow-shrouded rooftop. The Vulture bounced once, twice, three times. Each landing would have been enough to cripple a normal man. The final impact, against a brick retaining wall, was harder than the old man would have expected it to be. The Vulture, who had experienced this moment before, and who recognized it as the last heartbeat before another humiliating defeat, flinched and held both winged arms before his face in an attempt to ward off the inevitable *coup-de-grâce*, expecting it to come at any moment.

It didn't.

Several seconds of panting terror passed without incident before the Vulture realized that the worst had been postponed. He lowered his arms, scowled, and saw that he was alone. The arachnid had gone to rejoin the fight at the Empire State.

A sane man would have realized that he was lucky to have gotten off so easily.

A reasonable man would have decided that the web-slinger was right and that it was time to flee to his ill-deserved retirement.

A rational man would have seen no point in pressing his luck.

But the Vulture was none of these.

He wiped blood from his lips, swore to know the pleasure of snapping Spider-Man's neck, and took to the air again.

A few short minutes later.

The object of this latest in a long line of sworn oaths of vengeance was eating up the long blocks between Times Square and the Empire State Building with every ounce of speed available to him, barely even bothering with the casting of weblines as he hurled himself on a zigzag course from one building face to another. He moved with a hundred times the speed and dexterity of the greatest gymnast ever to win Olympic Gold, and he never made a misstep as he negotiated concrete canyons beset by clumps of snow the size of silver dollars ... but there was still a desperation to his manner that exposed him as a man who knew he was moving too slowly and too late.

How much time had he wasted dealing with Pity and the Vulture? Was the Generator in place yet?

He tapped his SAFE throat-mike as he took most of a snow-shrouded block in two great leaps. "Morgan! Deeley! Anybody! Talk to me!"

Colonel Morgan's voice came in, even more harried and grim than usual. His crisis analyst Palminetti was audible, shouting in the background. "We're a bit busy here, Spider-Man! What's the sit-rep?"

"The sit-rep here stinks on ice, Colonel! I got badly detoured from the Big Monkey Jungle Gym and I'm still on my way back there! If you can give me an ETA on some reinforcements I'm not too proud to ask for them!"

"Deeley!" Morgan cried. "You getting this?"

Doug Deeley's voice came in, explosions and jet noises audible in the background. "I'm getting it, Colonel!"

"Then brief the hero! I've got my hands full!"

Spider-Man hopped another rooftop and saw the gray shape of the Empire State looming up ahead. The storm reduced it to just a silhouette, bereft of meaningful detail, but he could just barely make out a fuzzy patch on the side of the building . . .

Deeley's voice came in: "We've inserted a squad, Spider-Man! Last report I received they were still making their way upstairs! But you're going to have to wait a little longer for aircar support! We need every unit we have just trying to keep lower Manhattan from going up in flames!"

The fuzzy patch disappeared behind another faceful of snow, but not before Spider-Man saw that it looked like a great big Daddy Longlegs moving swiftly across the face of the building. The momentary confusion he felt upon spotting his old enemy there—*Gee, hasn't Ock reached the top yet?*—abated almost immediately with the realization that

Ockie wasn't climbing up anymore, but rather coming back down.

That didn't make sense. Wouldn't Octavius, with his technical expertise, prefer to stay with his magic machine as long as possible? If only to protect it in case SAFE or Spider-Man showed up intent on smashing it? For one terrible moment Spider-Man's heart sank as the darkest of all possible explanations occurred to him: Ockie doesn't need to stay there any more, he's already set it off. I'm too late.

Then Deeley broke in again, prompting the realization that the SAFE communicators would have been as fried by the EMP as any other electronics. As long as they continued to broadcast signals, there was still time. Spider-Man's sense of relief was so strong he missed what Deeley actually said. "What?"

"—on his way—" The rest eaten by static.

The EMP? Spider-Man tapped his mike again. "Deeley! Come in! Dee—"

Only an observer with perceptions as unnaturally fast as his own would have been able to spot the moment when he stiffened with realization.

He changed course too quickly, corkscrewing in mid-air as his spider-sense permitted him to evade the worst of the gathering danger. It was a near thing. The glass face of the office building he'd been about to light upon buckled, glowed, and exploded outward in a shower of pebbled lexar. Spider-Man's mid-air contortions, as the blast wave engulfed him, were violent enough to resemble an uncontrollable seizure on the part of a body trying to tear itself apart, and not the more accomplished gyration of a paranormal swift enough to dodge shrapnel.

He wasn't entirely successful at that. By the time the blast wave had passed him, a stretch of costume across his shoulder blades flapped in a bloody tatter. There was no pain yet, but he knew there would be if he survived this next few minutes.

The good news was that the static on his SAFE communicator was not the legacy of a city-wide Electromagnetic Pulse. The bad news—

(as he plunged toward the street forty stories below)

—not quite the worst possible news, given today's stakes, but definitely the *bad* news—

(a man-shaped star flared into existence directly above him, radiating arcs of electricity in all directions)

—the *bad* news, which just might spell game, set and match—

(a man-shaped star cackling with his usual idiot braggadacio that he'd been looking forward to this moment for years)

—was that Electro was here.

CHAPTER ELEVEN

"This just in!" Cosmo the K cried. "One of our competitors just broadcast an eyewitness report that Electro murdered Spider-Man at an Italian restaurant in midtown!"

Jay Sein, sounding dubious, repeated, "An Italian restaurant?"

"An Italian restaurant! One of the waiters just called in to say he saw it personally!"

Dead air. Then, from Jay, "I thought it was supposed to be mob guys who went that way. Super heroes die defusing doomsday machines."

"Maybe there's a doomsday machine at this Italian restaurant."

"Maybe," said Jay. "We will have full details on that situation as soon as they come in. Meanwhile, recent reports have the river fire continuing to rage south of Manhattan, and we have no word, repeat no word, on attempts to contact the Avengers, the New Warriors or the Fantastic Four. There's no telling what this one's all about, but it looks like this one's going down to the wire . . . "

* * *

Several minutes earlier.

The multi-agency operation to secure the Empire State Building almost seemed a waste of time, given how long it was going to the various representatives of SAFE, the FBI, and the NYPD to reach the crisis zone at the Observation Deck. The Six had killed the Elevators, which, given the likelihood of booby traps set by Mysterio, the team couldn't have risked taking anyway. That left the several stairwells, which though not an insurmountable physical challenge for men and women capable of passing the entry exams for SAFE tactical, was nevertheless a frustratingly slow route given how frequently the situation kept changing outside. On the plus side, the overwhelming majority of the businesses which maintained offices here had closed due to the monstrous weather, leaving the building with only a small fraction of its usual daytime population, and reducing the number of encounters with civilians who had to be ordered to take cover.

SAFE agent Matt Gunderson, leading fresh transfer Cynthia Monella up on the stairwells at a full-speed run, had no illusions about any personal opportunities to play hero. Considering the forces that were at play here, even crack SAFE troops weren't going to be able to provide much more than tactical support. He also knew that if there was any contribution he could make, he was darn tooting going to make it.

He did think darn tooting, and not any harsher phrase, courtesy of his upbringing by a Minnesotan lady sheriff who had always frowned on language more explicit than that. He was sometimes kidded by fellow SAFE agents who found his speech patterns a little gee-whiz, but he had never turned his vocabulary any bluer in order to fit in. After all, his Mom was tough enough to take on kidnappers and murderers, and she never said anything worse than "Oh, my." Following in her footsteps, he could say "darn tooting" and mean it as sincerely as another man would have meant an oath that curdled milk. It was just the kind of guy he was, darn it.

The walls around them rumbled as if from some distant explosion. Training drove Gunderson's back against the wall while he waited for the sound to fade; he glanced at Monella to make sure she had done the same, and was gratified to see her in place. Homebred Brainerd gallantry made him ask: "You okay?"

Grim-faced and covered with sweat from the climb, Monella still showed enough guts for another hundred stories. "Don't worry about me."

"Is that a yes, I'm okay?"

"Yes." She wiped sweat from her brow. "That wasn't the EMP, in case you're wondering."

"I wasn't." His earpiece was still broadcasting all-clear from the other teams.

"An EMP generated by this device would be silent."

Gunderson knew that too, but had no problem with the reminder. He waved Monella silent as he listened to an update from one of the other teams. "It's nothing from inside the Empire State, and it's not part of the mess below the Battery. Walsh places it at about four blocks uptown. He—" There was another rumble, just as distant, but like the first strong enough to vibrate the walls. He swallowed. "Oh my. That sounds like a war."

Monella's grimace was a testament to the power of painful memory. "Like a war I've heard before.—That's Electro, blowing up things."

"But the Six would need him here, to power the Generator..."

"Yeah—but he's an idiot, and he must be taking on our

pet hero. Which means we might be able to wreck the Generator before he gets to it." Another rumble, this one (encouragingly enough) more distant. Monella shuddered, pushed herself away from the wall, and faced the stairs with an urgency that was practically longing. She clearly respected the chain of command enough to wait for the senior Gunderson's authorization before moving on. But when the next rumble came, she just as clearly tensed with the need to press on, to stop this, to earn back a little of what the Sinister Six had taken.

Gunderson, admiring her gumption (another of his mother's favorite words), smiled as he gestured toward the next flight up. He and Monella hit the steps at a hard run, their SAFE-issue ion blasters cocked and ready. Maybe, he thought, they could make a difference in his battle after all.

But that was before they encountered a whirlwind.

11:43 A.M.
The world outside the limousine was a sea of snow, piling up on the glass almost as quickly as the straining windshield wipers could sweep it away. Other cars were visible only as the glowing globs of red that represented their brake lights. The only forward progress came in sudden, spastic jerks of one car-length or less.

The Gentleman had hoped that abandoning the Van Wyck in favor of Long Island's intricate web of side streets would result in faster progress—but, alas, the subhumans who travelled this roadway were not completely brainless, and a large number had concocted the same plan. The exit lane was clogged with such brilliant refugees. The Gentleman, despairing of his ability to deal with these subhuman idiots, feared that the escape would be a poor one, and that the side streets would be similarly overpopulated with specious American fools who had no idea where they were going and therefore insisted on flouting as many traffic laws as possible just fighting their way back to territories they recognized.

The Gentleman rapped the back of the driver's seat with the head of his wolf's-head cane. "May I remind you that we're operating on a strict timetable here?"

"I'm sorry," said Serge, squinting at the snow-shrouded world up ahead. Red lights flashed, somewhere in that impassable muck. "That's an ambulance up there. Somebody must have had an accident or something. We're going to have to wait for the police to wave us through."

"Can't you do something?"

"They don't normally consult me," said Serge. His tone was nothing if not professional, but it was impossible to avoid the insolence in the words themselves.

The Gentleman's eyes narrowed. He didn't allow proletarians of Serge's ilk to speak to him in such a manner, even if the point itself was well-taken. Later, when he was past this obstacle, and the situation was less dire, he would have to place the slope-browed fool on his long list of individuals who deserved to be taught a lesson for their effrontery. "And when we get past this?"

"Most people will be getting off the road," Serge said. "We can probably get to the airfield within forty minutes. Getting off the ground then will be entirely up to you."

More insolence. Showing teeth now, the Gentleman fingered his wolf's-head cane, wondering if Serge had any progeny still in infancy. Pursuing a fresh vendetta until they reached adulthood would be an excellent way to keep himself in good spirits for the next few decades. He might even arrange for them to have super hero origins like the pathetic Parker, just to ensure that the game remained interesting.

But that was a thought for the future. Right now, the last phase of the plan still lay ahead. And it needed to be performed quickly, before the madmen he had left behind figured out just how brutally they had been betrayed.

He whispered a single word: "Hurry."

"Yes, sir," said Serge.

Also 11:44 A.M.

Mysterio, whose costume had taken on an all-white coloration to better hide him behind the waves of plummeting snow, stood guard over the Oltion Field Generator as the city rocked with the sound of nearby explosions. Visibility was so poor that he couldn't discern the explosions themselves except as bursts of distant light, but they were clearly the signature of his old teammate Max, blasting Spider-Man back and forth across the city. Mysterio would have bet a small fortune that Electro was taking his time about it, too, too busy enjoying himself to remember the main point of today's festivities.

Max had always been easy to distract that way.

Mysterio said something he had said about Electro any number of times in the past. "That idiot!"

Still 11:44.

Spider-Man's latest leap carried him four stories straight up, but the updraft from Electro's latest explosion rose even faster. He hurtled skyward atop a pillar of super-heated air. The web-shield he had spun to protect himself from the worst of the scorching heat flared, glowed, and then vanished in a puff of ash and steam. Spider-Man tumbled past the zone of unbearable heat, and found himself savoring a brief taste of the day's true cold before he had to spin another shield to take the brunt of another explosion. This one was close, real close. It was white-hot and deafening. It felt like a coming attraction for the end of the world. The concussion wave sent Spider-Man hurtling backward, slamming him into a rooftop just as a crackling sphere of ball lightning vaporized an air vent arm lengths away.

The glowing man floated above him on an arc of pure crackling energy. "Tired, Spider-Creep? You sure look it! Me, I can keep this up all day!"

Leapfrogging past another series of lightning-bolts that reduced the rooftop behind him to a cratered ruin, Spider-Man didn't doubt it. This was easily the worst trouble he'd been in all week.

The thing was, the days when it had been possible to take Electro down with a well-aimed bucket of water were over and gone. Max Dillon was something much more, since his last power-up. He could bat Spider-Man back and forth across the city like a wiffle ball, secure in the knowledge that the webslinger wouldn't be able to counter him with the fancy footwork or insulated-glove haymaker that had, once upon a time, often reduced the last seconds of their bouts to comical anticlimax. These days, Electro was a force of nature. He was a creature of cataclysmic power on the level of a Magneto, held in check only by an attention span about as limited as Homer Simpson's and a level of ambition about as grandiose as any other third-rate thug's. That didn't make fighting him any less suicidal. But along with the limited protection afforded him by the special insulated costume provided him by SAFE, it gave Spider-Man the only advantages he had. Frankly, they didn't seem to be enough today. Spider-Man would have been killed a dozen times over already, were it not for Electro's insistence on having his not-so-little fun.

If only the guy would stop crackling.

It would feel so good, after all this *mishagos*, to take him out with a common, everyday sock to the jaw.

"You know what I think I'll do?" Electro shouted, his voice amplified by the forces within. "I think I'll keep you hopping from building to building 'til the whole city's rubble! It'll be fun to see who lasts longer—you or the architecture!"

"Kinda repetitious, don'tcha think?" Spider-Man snagged a distant cornice with a webline and sailed around the next intersection. "Even Super Mario gets to the next level sometime!"

Electro pursued him in a streak of light. "You'll know the second it gets old to me, bug-man! Because you'll be dead!"

Spider-Man tsked. "Now, that's the kind of flawless logic that makes life with you such a joy! You ever think of running for office?"

The webslinger released his webline, dropped four stories, rebounded off a stalled bus, then ricocheted from one side of the street to the other in a dizzying series of zigzag leaps that carried him from street level to forty stories up in a manner of seconds. That was how he had to fight Electro nowadays, by staying on the move, and fleeing as fast as he could until some kind of opportunity presented himself. Unfortunately, today, with the concrete canyons of Manhattan turned to wind tunnels under assault by waves of lashing snow, it didn't seem like that was going to be anywhere near enough. The very elements that were taking such a toll on Spider-Man couldn't even touch the will of a man whose power made him his own native heat source.

As long as I keep him away from the Empire State, Spider-Man thought.

If I can keep him busy with me, then maybe SAFE has a chance.

Given how easy it had always been to play with Electro's head, it was a reasonable thing to hope for.

Given how powerful this new version of Electro was . . . and how quickly he moved, even by Spider-Man's standards . . . it qualified as the blindest wishful thinking imaginable.

Because even as he climbed for the sky . . . Electro was once again above him.

"You don't get it, do you?" the human dynamo raved. "This ain't like the old days anymore, webslinger! You can't outrun me, outfight me, or even outthink me! I'm a class act now—and I'm gonna teach you so you never forget!"

"Uh huh! Is this one of those things I'm supposed to remember after I'm dead?"

As Spider-Man descended toward streets turned white with gathering snow, he made for a certain sewer grate that had provided him an emergency escape route more than once in the past. If he could break through that, take this fight underground, and trick Electro into burying himself in a cave-in of some kind, he might—repeat, might—be able to not only live through the next few minutes, but also get back to the Empire State in time to make a difference. It wasn't a great plan, but he didn't have time for great plans. He didn't even have time to worry about Pity, or worry about where Doc Ock had been rushing to. He just had to act.

Two stories above a street filled with huddled figures in tightly-fitting coats, he suddenly knew that he had run out of time.

He would never get near that grate today.

The source of the danger that pursued him had just moved. It was no longer above him or behind him or some great distance away from him. It was here.

He had just enough time to cry out before the explosion blew him out of the sky.

Still 11:44 A.M.

Beneath the East River, and continuing to accelerate.

SPIDER-MAN

The gleaming adamantium skimmer racing toward Long Island at seventy miles per hour was the size of a Minivan and the speed of a Ferrari. It used the city's ancient subway lines, following a complicated series of protocols that prevented violent confrontations with any of the city's more conventional subterranean vehicles. Twice it seemed trapped behind poky commuter trains travelling at a comparative crawl. Twice it folded up into a box just large enough to accomodate a prone man, leaped off the tracks, and rocketed along the top of the train just ahead, raising sparks along the roofs of each car as it leapfrogged what the city was arrogant enough to call rapid transit. Each time it sailed off the lead car, descended with perfect accuracy toward the tracks, and re-engaged, picking up even more speed as it continued down the tunnel.

Most passengers locked inside such an insane vehicle would have been screaming with terror and vertigo as it careened along the tracks wracking up enough G's to pin them to their acceleration couch.

Doctor Otto Octavius, who had cobbled together this little toy several years earlier during his Master Planner phase, barely noticed. He saw the journey as nothing more than the sum total of course/speed vectors. As for the skimmer itself, it was but a minor achievement of his genius, one that he normally had little use for. Under most circumstances his magnificent tentacles were more than capable of taking him anywhere he deigned to go. But even they couldn't carry him overland at more than fifty miles an hour . . . and today he needed to reach a certain private airfield somewhat faster than that. His timetable being too tight to take chances, he had just last night retrieved the vehicle from one of several armories he maintained beneath the city streets.

Cocooned in his tentacles, facing a control panel that

reduced the pre-programmed journey to a mere measurement of distance traveled, he thought of nothing but revenge. Not revenge against Spider-Man—which, though an achievement still worth fighting for, remained rather low priority at the moment. Revenge against another, who had so recently had the temerity to treat the great Octavius like a fool.

Octavius knew no crime more worthy of an agonizing death.

Still 11:44 A.M.

The whirlwind that greeted Agents Gunderson and Monella was a flash of white innocence trailing darkness like a banner.

Pity dropped down from one of the upper flights, sweeping her right leg in a kick that missed Cynthia Monella by inches and instead dug a deep gouge in the wall of the stairwell.

Monella, registering only a black-and-white blur, fired her ion blaster, knowing even as she did that she was only human and therefore far too slow to get the drop on a combatant capable of trading punches with Spider-Man. The white blur moved in some way too fast to perceive, and the broken, sputtering remains of the blaster smashed to pieces on the opposite wall.

Monella dropped, feeling a burst of cold wind as something moved impossibly fast over her back. Whatever it was missed her and hit Gunderson. Gunderson made the sound all men make when struck hard in the diaphragm. His ion burst cratered the opposite wall. Gunderson grunted again as he hit the floor of the next landing down. Monella went for a spare blaster strapped to her left leg, then cried out in pain as something moving too fast to follow deflected her hand. She scrambled backwards, and reached for the same holster with her other hand, only to be deflected by another slap.

She knew then that she had no chance to win.

Not against a foe whose assaults came faster than a normal human being could think.

One half-flight below, Matt Gunderson cried out: "Monella! Look out!"

Like that helped.

The whirlwind passed over Monella again, once again trailing darkness behind it. Monella caught a quick glimpse of Pity's leg, and did the only thing she possibly could under the circumstances. She grabbed for the girl's ankle.

It was a desperate gesture, which should have been futile as well. After all, the briefing had reported Pity's reflexes as being in the same league as Spider-Man's. The grab should have been deflected as easily as Pity deflected Monella's attempts to draw her spare weapon.

It wasn't.

Monella's fingers closed around Pity's right ankle. She twisted, hard, in an attempt to knock the paranormal assassin off balance. Miracle of miracles, that worked too. Pity tumbled and fell, landing as flat on the landing as Monella had a moment before. Monella, unable to believe that taking out a Sixer could possibly be this easy, but unwilling to surrender even with this most fleeting of chances, hurled herself forward, landing on Pity's back. The body pinned beneath her felt small, even girlish, her costume both wet from the snowstorm outside and so silky it felt like tissue paper next to the stony muscle of the flesh beneath.

Feeling the power in that back, Monella knew again that the fight was going her way too easily. Pity should have been able to tear her to pieces. Something was wrong.

Gunderson gave more useless advice as he raced up the stairs. "Hold on!"

Monella wrapped an arm around Pity's neck and pulled the smaller woman's head back. She caught her first glimpse of Pity's face as she did so. Although Pity hadn't been part of the slaughter at Rand-Meachum, Monella had seen enough photographs and video footage at the briefing to expect the youth, the impression of wounded innocence, or even the big brown war-orphan eyes set off by the vertical scars on each cheek. But she was still stunned by the forces at war on that face. This wasn't the look of a ruthless killer, or even the terrorized slave Spider-Man had insisted her to be. It was a convulsing mask, twitching and grimacing as it was stretched to the breaking point by some kind of subsurface conflict.

Gunderson knelt beside them and reached for his belt. "If we can lock on the power-dampeners, we'll—"

Monella felt her prisoner tense. "—no—"

They had never had a chance.

Pity erupted. Her limbs spasmed and her spine arched as she propelled herself off the floor in what felt like a violent act of will. Monella, thrown clear, slammed into Gunderson and rolled with him into a tangled unsighty heap. Pity, strobing waves of light and darkness that gave the stairwell the feel of a flickering silent movie, landed on her feet and glanced at the two SAFE agents, her expression blank but for regret.

Then she moved toward them.

Gunderson went for his throat mike, to summon aid. Pity, moving like a streak of light, had him by the wrist before he even got close. Gunderson winced at the force of her grip, then watched with the most stoic expression possible as she drew back her other arm for a blow destined to kill him instantly.

Monella, like her senior partner, braced herself for a quick kill. It was inevitable. Flashing back to the moment of Judi Goodman's death, Monella felt not fear but a terrible, helpless rage.

The stairwell went pitch-black.

Less than a heartbeat later, it filled with light again. Both Gunderson and Monella stared at empty air where Pity had been, almost unwilling to believe that they were both still breathing.

"She almost killed us," Gunderson said.

"She could have," Monella said. It would have been easy... as easy as the slaughter at Rand-Meachum. She saw the vague outline of an explanation, didn't want to accept it, but was finally forced to murmur an epiphany that still made no sense to her. "I think... she was trying not to."

11:49 A.M.
Nathaniel Bumppo, professional work-at-home envelope stuffer, had been provided that name by a father who doted on the novels of James Fenimore Cooper, and who imagined that such a monicker would influence his newborn son toward an athletic love of the great outdoors.

It didn't take.

Mr. Bumppo had not developed into a rugged outdoorsman, but into a worshipper of fast food. His day was a neverending journey from pizza to french fries to burritos and back again, all consumed in vast quantities, all applied directly from stomach to arteries, producing a body shape best defined by the number of times he had needed 911 assistance to pry him loose from bathtubs and narrow doorways. He was, in short, a pair of parentheses stuffed with lard. He didn't get into midtown much. He usually stayed in his little apartment in lower Manhattan, subsisting on disability checks, his envelope-stuffing business, and his neighborhood's vast array of fast-food home delivery services—an existence that others might have thought of as constrained, but which was positively joyous for a man like himself, whose brain's pleasure center was almost entirely wired to his taste buds. And it must be said that he shared this joy whenever possible. The fellow residents of his apartment building always appreciated the warm hellos and kindly conversation he was always there to provide.

Travel, especially in stormy weather, presented special hardships for Mr. Bumppo, but there were errands he needed to run in midtown, and he had gotten his hands on some coupons for All-You-Can-Eat Lasagna at Vito's Pasta Trough, so why the hell not? He could sit at his center table (being unable to fit in one of the scandalously tiny booths) and test the boundaries of "All-You-Can-Eat" while the view through Vito's giant picture window provided him with a panoramic vista of Mother Nature assaulting the city in all her fury. It was like, you know, being warm and cozy in a huge inside-out snowglobe that catered.

He even had company, of a sort. There was another man, at least as large as himself, taking similar advantage of Vito at another table, while pretending to listen to his skinny girlfriend's rants on liberal politics. This other man wore a red flannel shirt and a green hat with earflaps. He ate almost as incessantly as Mr. Bumppo, and came up for air only to say, "Yes, Myrna," whenever his girlfriend paused to breathe between jeremiads on the Male-Capitalist-Reactionary-Racist-Colonialist Power Structure. The other man occasionally winked at Mr. Bumppo, sharing with him the awareness that it was the food that mattered, with all else reduced to soundtrack music.

Mr. Bumppo, who had sat down to his expansive meal at

about 10:30 A.M., and who found each heaping dish of steaming pasta even more splendiforous than the one before, had virtually no complaints at all—with the possible exception of the ambience, since the massive booming noises which had been tearing down the avenue for the last seven minutes or so were completely drowning out the Dean Martin jukebox song about the moon hitting your eye like a big pizza pie.

He was just being delivered another huge slab of lasagna dripping with meat sauce when the picture window imploded in a shower of broken glass. A figure in red-and-blue spandex, smoking at the edges, hurtled through at what looked like terminal velocity, skipped across four of Vito's fancy formica tables, and landed, hard, atop Mr. Bumppo's plastic-flower placesetting. The impact looked pretty painful, but it was still a flawless landing in that the figure in spandex didn't disturb anything on Mr. Bummpo's plate. The figure was sopping wet from snowfall and glittery with the remains of broken glass. A three-bulb traffic signal, complete with length of shattered power line, lay on the table beside him, having somehow joined him on his hurtling journey to this impasse. Mr. Bummpo, who barely heard the horrified shouts of the man in the green flannel hat and his marxist-fanatic girlfriend, peered down at the man who had just so violently joined him for lunch, took particular note of the web-patterned stocking mask with its two teardrop-shaped eyeholes, and found to his consternation that he even recognized the guy from frequent perusals of the New York *Daily Bugle*.

"Spider-Man?" he ventured.

"Oh boy," the super hero on the table moaned. "This isn't happening."

The restaurant's lights flickered ominously, and snow

swirled through the remains of the shattered window. Lightning arced in the streets outside, burning so bright that it cast purple afterimages on Mr. Bumppo's retinas. A high-pitched, arrogant voice, amplified to the volume of thunder, wafted through the opening, easily overpowering the howl of the wind: "What's the matter, bug-man? Don't you like that? Don't you have some kind of snappy comeback to show me how clever you are?"

Spider-Man didn't leap off the table and fling himself back onto the street in search of another righteous whupping. He just remained flat on his back, shook his head to clear whatever dizziness the impact must have inflicted, turned toward the still-frozen Mr. Bumppo, and murmured: "Play along with me, willya, sir? This next move is going to make super hero history."

"Uh," Mr. Bumppo said, ". . . sure, I guess . . ."

With the speed of thought itself, Spider-Man seized Mr. Bumppo's plate of meat lasagna and upended it onto his own chest. Warm savory sauce, hot enough to steam before the restaurant's precipitous drop in temperature, and positively smoking now, streamed down his costumed ribs in rivulets of messy high-calorie goodness that pooled in puddles along his arms. The lasagna itself fell flat against his spidery chest emblem, to form a glistening mound that even close up looked like flesh ripped into a horrific wound. Spider-Man completed the illusion with a single ragged shard of glass, plucked off the table and impaled on the impromptu pasta-sculpture like a dagger that had just pierced his heart.

The insane, unnaturally-amplified voice in the street outside cried out: "No answer, Spider-Man? Then here I come!"

A crackling ball of energy in the shape of a crewcut man levitated through the shattered window, surrounded on all sides by arcs of electricity and the puffs of steam that represented snowfall turning to steam from his very presence. Glowing like a star, laughing maniacally as his eyes spat out sparks, he exuded power in its most terrible form: the potential for pure destruction, guided by a will mad enough to use it. His costume, a green bodysuit with a chest emblem of matched lightning bolts, was downright banal in the face of the madness that burned in his eyes. Mr. Bumppo recognized him, too, also from repeated exposures to the *Daily Bugle*. It was Electro, the Human Power Battery.

The marxist girlfriend of the man in the green flannel cap made high-pitched squeaking noises. The waiters cowered. Somebody shrieked in the kitchen: a waiter shouting to some radio station that he had just witnessed the death of Spider-Man. The man in the green flannel cap, unperturbed, merely sucked tomato sauce off his fingers.

Electro cried out: "Where's the wall-crawler? *Where?*"

Mr. Bummpo was astonished to find himself able to speak: "H-he's dead."

Electro's gaze flickered toward the table where Mr. Bumppo sat. He floated over to his side of the room on a cushion of pure crackling light, and peered down at the still-dripping, still-steaming form of his supine foe. Exultant victory warred with what had to be most bitter disappointment on his callow, wolfen face. He reached out, clearly tempted to prod the corpse to make sure it was real. But revulsion, propriety, or perverse respect for the dead made him pull back. He looked up, and stared Mr. Bumppo in the eyes. "You witnessed this," he said. "Remember it was me who got him. Not Beck, not Toomes, not even Octavius. Me. Max Dillon. Electro. I was the one who got him. Make sure the newspapers get it right."

Mr. Bumppo was aware that his hair was standing on

end, though whether from fear or his proximity to this human energy source remained open to debate. "Sure."

"Tell them his death was an offering for the woman I love. Her name is Pity. Stress that part. I want to read it in tomorrow's *Bugle*."

Mr. Bummpo felt hilarity building at the back of his throat. "Okay.

Electro threw his head back and laughed long and hard, holding on to his hilarity even as his arc of lightning carried him back across the now-freezing restaurant and out the shattered window. He cried out as he went: *"Do you hear that, world? After all these years of humiliation, I was the one who got him! And I'm the one who'll set off the disaster he tried to stop!"*

His laughter was sweeping an exultant, audible long after he sailed up into the storm, and out of sight.

Mr. Bummpo blinked many times as the glow faded. He fought back a burp, glanced down at the sauce-covered wall-crawler, and made what he supposed was eye contact with the guy, though the hero's opaque lenses made that impossible to tell. There seemed no possible reaction to the experience of watching a super hero successfully defeat a villain using Italian food. He had never heard of such a thing, and firmly believed that he would never see its like again. After what seemed a million years, populated by the whimper of whipped waiters, the soft sobs of the mock-revolutionary named Myrna, the tinny voice of an over-the-counter television already passing on the inaccurate report of the web-slinger's death, and the self-satisfied noises of the man in the green cap, Mr. Bummpo somehow managed a comment anyway: "That guy was an idiot."

"He gets that a lot," Spider-Man allowed. He rolled off the table, landed on his feet, scraped the worst of the culinary goo off his chest with one gloved hand, and said: "Now it's my turn to remind him exactly why.—Sorry for disturbing your lunch, folks."

Spider-Man seized the traffic light by its cord and leaped from the shattered restaurant in two giant bounds.

Mr. Bumppo sat there blinking as the restaurant grew cold.

It had been, he decided, an interesting morning.

Just the sort of thing a man needed to work up an appetite.

11:50 A.M.

Mysterio, who was not feeling well at all, whose face inside his opaque-bubble helmet was clammy with sweat, nevertheless maintained a defiant stance as a dark patch in the storm grew close and resolved itself into the form of the Vulture. The old man looked almost as bad as Mysterio felt, even for him, his cadaverous, old-man face granted an unsightly sheen from all the falling snow that had melted against his skin.

"What's taking so long?" he demanded.

"I . . . don't know," Mysterio said, hoping that the Vulture wouldn't notice the less-than-than impressive strength in his voice. "Still waiting for Max. I think he was fightig Spider-Man."

"And you didn't do anything to help?"

"I'm protecting the Generator." It was a handy excuse, when right now it was all Mysterio could do to stand.

The Vulture would have scowled if it wasn't his usual facial expression regardless. "I'll go find him before he blows it for all of us. If Spider-Man shows up, leave a piece of him for me."

"I'll do that," Mysterio said, a weak and uninspired comeback indeed from a self-proclaimed genius who normally took pride in the dialogue he wrote for himself. He still made it sound like a grim vow, powered by confidence; being the master of showmanship, he could do no less.

The Vulture, grimacing, disappeared into the storm.

11:52 A.M.

Electro was flying high in more ways than one.

Looking down on Manhattan, performing loop-de-loops of sheer exuberance as he inflated his false impression of Spider-Man's death into unqualified success in his ongoing campaign to woo Pity, he exulted in the beauty of the blizzard that whipped him on all sides and the gloriousness of the city below. Firing lightning bolts in all directions just to share his happiness with the world, ranting that he had just accomplished what Ock and Venom and The Green Goblin and Doctor Doom had never been able to do, and at the same time rehearsing the witty romantic badinage that would burble from his suave lips as he squired the lovely Pity hither and yon, he embodied not just his usual sociopathy but also the truism that love makes fools of us all, especially for those of us who already happen to be far from the swiftest bulbs in the marquee.

A man who didn't function as his own personal heating system might have raced to the Empire State at top speed, less out of urgency to complete the plan than a pressing need to get this nonsense over with. To Electro, who made the air around him toasty-cozy, who evaporated the snow before it touched him, and whose mood would have been enough to warm him in any case, the windswept veils of snow that lashed him on all sides were not aspects of a Mother Nature enraged. They were just the caresses of a world intent on providing this moment with as much lyrical beauty as possible.

His loopy flight path and gratuitous fireworks were, in short, the maniacal super-villain equivalent of Gene Kelly performing "Singin' In the Rain."

He was, in fact, so very far gone in his romantic fantasies that as he flew low enough to take in the sight of streets blanketed by whiteness, the words "winter wonderland" passed though his mind with no ironic intent.

But he wasn't gone enough to forget that he still had something to do today.

The Empire State loomed up ahead.

In a few short seconds, he could do what needed to be done, and win Pity once and for all.

11:55 A.M.

With the latest in a long series of leaps from building to building, Spider-Man alighted on the 33rd Street Side of the Empire State Building. He landed twenty-three stories up, and hit the wall running. Running was the accurate term here. He didn't speed-crawl, which was usual method of climbing buildings in a hurry, but rather ran perpendicular to the building face as he ran on two legs.

This was a good measure of his desperation. The soles of his feet were more than capable of clinging to walls without any help from his equally adhesive palms, but he still liked to use all four limbs when possible. The improved grip was always a plus this high above the pavement, especially with the world so densely populated by maniacs itching for a chance to pry him loose. Given today's blizzard conditions, using both hands and feet would have been an especially good idea. But speed-crawling was just a hair slower than an all-out run . . . and his spider-sense was even now screaming at him that these were fractions of a second he just couldn't afford.

As he ran, he was unable to see anything more than ten stories above him, but he didn't need to. Every sense in his body screamed that the moment was here and the time was now.

It was happening.

He could follow a certain nexus of bright light hundreds of feet above him: it was diffused by the storm, but it couldn't be anything but Electro, coming to set off the Pulse. Even given Electro's tendency to rant first before he did anything important (a character trait he shared with many of his colleagues, that had long served Spider-Man and his fellow heroes well), that nexus of light was still too far away. Spider-Man was going to get there too late.

Maybe only a few seconds too late. Maybe less.

But too late nevertheless.

Forty seconds earlier. 11:54 A.M.

Mysterio, whose headache had just been joined by an overwhelming nausea, nevertheless almost jumped up and down with relief when the glowing form of Electro finally emerged from the storm. He shouted: "Max! Was that you fighting Spider-Man?"

Electro pointed at the sky and emitted a shower of sparks from his fingertip. "Yup. It was also me killing him."

"What!?!"

"You heard me!" Electro cried, so proud of himself that he performed a little jig on his platform of coruscating energy.

"Did you see the body? You can't be sure unless you saw the body!" Mysterio had not only learned this rule from bitter personal experience, but learned to exploit it for his own benefit.

"Yup. No mistaking it, either. I made a hole in that creep's chest so big that his guts poured out." Another shower of celebratory sparks, each as bright as a miniature sun.

Mysterio didn't know whether to be delighted or enraged: delighted that the wisecracking hooded thorn in his side was finally gone, or enraged that it had to be Electro of all people who finally managed it. It disturbed him, in the end, to feel only a great, draining emptiness (though whether that was because of his current depleted condition or an actual, unexpected feeling of grief remained beyond him). He decided to belay judgment until he could be sure it wasn't just Max being stupid again, and refocused himself on the task at hand. "Max—"

"I can't wait to tell Ock and wipe that superior grin off his face! Or Pity, for that matter! I did it for her, after all! Do you know she—"

Mysterio, who may have been the only member of the Six constitutionally immune to the appeal of their waifish distaff member, set off one of his costume's many sound-effects generators before Electro could go off on another tangent. The blizzard a thousand feet above Manhattan suddenly filled with the thunderous sound of stampeding elephants. Mysterio's amplified voice rolling deep and resonant over the din: "NEVER MIND! JUST ZAP THE GENERATOR SO WE CAN GET OUT OF HERE!"

Electro glared at the Generator as if annoyed by the reminder that it was still there, and extended both arms toward a certain power-absorption interface that Octavius had installed. "Yeah," he said. "Why not? After all, I already took care of the fun part..."

11:55 A.M.

Spider-Man was still racing up the building face.

A patch of storm just above him darkened and resolved almost immediately into the shape of a gigantic bird of prey.

It was the Vulture in full power dive, coming for him, his perpetual snaggle-toothed grimace twisted into the leer of a monster who believed that vengeance was finally his.

Spider-Man didn't blame the old coot for thinking that. It was a textbook attack that normally would have peeled the wallcrawler right off the side of the building.

Today it was pathetic.

Spider-Man didn't even break stride. He still had the traffic light with its long length of power line. He swung it around his shoulders in a parody of a cowboy's lariat and hurled it at the attacking old man, striking him right in his ugly slit of a mouth.

Still diving, but thrown off-balance by the pain, the Vulture might have flown away to recover. He might have lashed out with his razor-sharp wings. He might have cried out yet another version of the usual threat about dropping the webslinger's mangled body from a height. But he didn't have enough time to do any of this. He was too busy reeling beneath a blitzkrieg of punches from an angry red-and-blue blur, so many in less than a heartbeat that it scarcely seemed possible. The first blow deflected the Vulture's power dive so effortlessly that the aghast old man was not only halted but actually propelled upward. The second and third and fourth and fifth pummelled his ribs and his shoulders and his jaw faster than any possible attempt to defend them. The next slammed him hard against the Empire State, destroying something vital in his flight suit. The ones after that were so unrelenting they shamed the worst of the storm. They all happened in less than two seconds. They happened so quickly, in fact, that the Vulture was both defeated and hurtling through a glass window, into the showroom of a fashion importer, before his reeling brain even registered that he'd been struck the first time.

SPIDER-MAN

Spider-Man, who hadn't even lost step, who was still racing at top speed toward the bright lights up above, was not encouraged in the least.

He could feel it.

This was the moment.

The Generator was being fired up now.

And he'd been right about not getting there in time.

11:55 A.M.

Electro's hands disappeared in twin spheres of expanding light, building up the potential for the blast less than fifteen seconds away. He could just zap it now, of course; he certainly had enough juice. But Octavius and the Gentleman had both stressed to him that the riches to be won here increased in direct proportion to the damage done by the Electromagnetic Pulse—and Electro was determined to give them everything they'd asked for and more. Not just enough to blanket the city. Maybe enough to take out the whole State.

Ten seconds now. Nine. Eight.

Then he lost patience, thought what the hell, and fired.

CHAPTER TWELVE

Two seconds earlier, Sean Morgan had shouted: *"Now!"*

The three dozen SAFE aircars in position over the Empire State, just now dispatched from the other crisis south of Manhattan, all opened their bomb bay doors at once, releasing what initially might have looked like clouds of free-floating metallic hornets. The flimsy objects seemed as helpless before the wind as all the other flakes of snow in this blizzard. For a fraction of a second they seemed about to disperse in a manner that followed the chaotic pattern of the storm, but then they all seemed to listen to the dictates of one guiding mind and changed direction, moving against the prevailing direction of the wind to surround the glowing man who hovered just off the world's most popular observation deck.

They engulfed Electro just as he thought, *What the hell,* and fired.

The supercharged air around Electro acquired the brilliance of the sun as the hundreds of thousands of shards of metallic chaff, divided equally between those carrying positive and negative charges, diffused his blast. A hundred windows on that side of the building blasted inward in explosions of pebbled glass. The building face pitted and cratered. An explosion on the observation deck walkway hurled Mysterio through the plate glass window to the gift shop. The Oltion Field Generator roared with energy, blanking digital clocks and wiping hard drives throughout the top fifteen stories of the Empire State before it died, deprived of the energy source it needed to run.

That happened when the clumps of positively and negatively charged chaff, attracted to each other by the force of their opposite polarities, converged on the man-shaped nexus of energy at their center.

Electro, terrified, unable to understand what was happening, tried to evade them. But they followed. He tried to blast them out of the sky. But there were too many of them, and they were ruled by the very laws of nature that powered him. The chaff attacked him on all sides, pelting his chest and his back and his legs and his face, covering him in layers, even cutting off his attempt to scream as one ragged wad the size of a baseball plugged his open mouth.

His glow flared. Then faded. The titan so recently exulting in triumph became just a figure entombed in copper and silver. His light went out. He started to fall.

Only one of Electro's eyes was entirely covered. The other could still make out a pinprick of sky through a gap in the chaff. That eye saw a spinning kaleidoscope of images as he tumbled head-over-heels toward the earth: first a panorama of shattered windows, then a gray sky scarred with streaks of snow, then a vertiginous drop toward a ground too far away to see, then the shattered windows again. The kaleidoscope sped up, and the images turned to blurs, as gravity pulled him faster and faster toward terminal velocity.

SECRET OF THE SINISTER SIX

It occurred to him that he could try switching his own polarity. He could do it fast enough to repel the chaff with explosive force. The shrapnel might take down whoever had done this to him. It could work. Whatever. He had to do something fast, or he was a dead man. And he didn't want to be a dead man. He had so much to live for, with a goddess like Pity in his life. A family. Children. World domination.

He might have managed an escape, too.

But then he spotted something through his one unobstructed eye. Something approaching him in arc of red and blue primary colors. Something that had no reason to be here, because it should have died.

It was denial more than fear of death that made the man once known only as Max Dillon try, unsuccessfully, to scream.

The sole of Spider-Man's left boot filled his field of vision, like a red flag signaling yet another in a long series of defeats.

11:56 A.M.

Palminetti exulted. "It worked! The webslinger's a genius!"

A rare grin passed across Colonel Sean Morgan's face. Were he a man more generous with praise, he might have expressed agreement. After all, it had been Spider-Man himself who, at the briefing that followed last week's Day of Terror, proposed a certain audacious way of countering Electro. It had been a surprising idea, given the webslinger's usual methods, the kind of suggestion Morgan would have expected a bright physics student to make. Spider-Man had said it was something he'd always wanted to do, and that he lacked only SAFE's resources to make it work.

From the look of things, it had worked perfectly. Even

better than the unconventional method Morgan had finally used to put out the worst of the river fire.

Morgan made a mental note to compliment Spider-Man on his inventiveness, knowing even as he did that it was a reminder he was soon destined to forget. This battle was too far from being over. His momentary smile faded as he barked into the horn: "All right, people! *Move!* We don't want to have to do this again today!"

The two figures tumbled from eighty stories up, pursued by a glitter-trail of errant chaff. Spider-Man, riding the cruelly-entombed Electro like a lumberjack riding a fallen log down-river, used his feet to spin the villain's prone form like that log as he used both webshooters to cement the chaff in place. He not only managed this while falling twenty stories toward certain death in the middle of one of the worst storms the city had ever known, but he also performed a serviceable voice-impression of a certain old-lady beautician once beloved by his late Aunt May: "Don't be so prissy, Mrs. Laningham, dollink! Once this mudpack comes off I promise you you'll be gorgeous!"

So what if it was a personal joke. The unconscious Electro wouldn't have appreciated anything more accessible.

It was only after Dillon was securely trussed that Spider-Man took the time to save their mutual hides. He tucked the unmoving Dillon under one arm, fired a webline at a cornice stone below, and braced himself as the line drew taut, transforming the angle of their mutual descent into an arc. He needed four more weblines to slow what had become terminal velocity into the kind of building-to-building trajectory that rated as mere gymnastics. Within less than a minute he dropped down to the roof of a five-story building just up the block from the Empire State, which housed one of the many

Manhattan gray-market electronics emporiums that claim a GOING OUT OF BUSINESS SALE lasting longer than some Presidential Administrations. The several inches of snow on the roof reminded Spider-Man of the cold he'd almost blocked out throughout the worst of the battle. He dropped Electro to the roof and tapped his SAFE throat-mike. "Spider-Man here! You really believe in cutting things close, don't you, Colonel?"

Palminetti's voice sounded almost jovial as it rang in Spider-Man's ear. "The Colonel's busy mopping up the area, webslinger! But I will say that from the look of things, so do you!"

"Yeah, well," said Spider-Man, who was caught without a quip. He shivered. "I have Electro down here! What's on up there?"

"We've dispatched our people in the Empire State to secure Mysterio and the Vulture! No sign of the others at present, but we'll keep you posted!"

"And the situation in the river? What's up there?"

"That one was pretty hairy for a few minutes, but the Colonel came up with a pip of a way to deal with it. The blaze is still burning but is now rated under control. I'll fill you in on the details once we've found . . ."

Spider-Man, alerted to imminent danger by a sensation like burning wires at the base of his neck, cut him off in mid-sentence. "Sorry! Can't talk now! Have a situation here!" He tapped the throat-mike again, ending the connection, then whirled, surveying the snow-shrouded rooftop to locate the source of the threat. He knew only that it wasn't Electro. As far as danger went, that thoroughly-cocooned individual still registered as a big fat zero. That meant one of the others, but which one? Ock? Mysterio?

A wave of darkness crept over the parapet and flowed

across the rooftop, replacing its pristine white blanket with an even purer layer of all-encompassing black. It surrounded Spider-Man and his prisoner in a heartbeat, shutting off the rest of the world. Spider-Man's heart sank.

Oh. Her.

Next round.

The Vulture found himself in one of those special states of battered semi-consciousness familiar to those whose lifestyles include frequent pummeling by super heroes. He was aware where he was, and how he'd gotten here. He even possessed enough cognitive ability to give careful consideration to possibly getting up sometime soon. But the leap between considering that probably a good idea, and the will it would have required to actually go ahead and do it, was for the moment farther than he was willing to go.

He lay flat on his back on a metal desk in a lady's apparel showroom rendered freezing by the shattering of the window he had just been hurled through. The shrapnel flung across the room by that implosion had also shattered the glass door on the opposite end of the room, creating a crossdraft. The winds that passed through the darkened space carried with them not one blizzard, but two—the meteorological one from the embattled world outside, and its more bureaucratic cousin, which was composed not of snow but of the hundreds of loose papers that whirled above him in great fluttering circles. The Vulture, watching the latter with the mild interest of a sleepy TV watcher at 3 AM, found himself contemplating the remote odds of the wind dying down at the precise moment that would have allowed all those sheets of densely-typed documentation to settle back into a single neat stack, correctly-numbered and in their original order.

SECRET OF THE SINISTER SIX

He might have gotten lost in that image.

The sound of running footsteps from somewhere down the hallway made him blink, wince, and swing his legs over the side of the desk so he could sit up. The ache in his ribs as he did so only deepened his perpetual scowl. Remembering the ease with which Spider-Man had disposed of him not once but twice today made that scowl even nastier. It was the kind of humiliation the Vulture knew he would have to carry with him a long time. Even if the EMP went ahead as scheduled, the humiliation of that moment would remain intolerable... and the Vulture, groggy as he was, found himself brimming with renewed hatred.

He would attack again. He would rip out the webslinger's spine. He would drop the still-twitching corpse from a height. He would stalk and eviscerate anybody foolish enough to attend the webslinger's funeral, and he would return to desecrate the grave on the anniversary. He would teach the whole world the folly of disrespecting the Vulture.

But first, just to get his dignity back, he would kill whoever that was approaching in the corridor outside.

An invoice, borne aloft by the cross-draft winds, slapped him in the face, blindfolding him. He felt a moment's panic as he mistook the obstruction for a web-blindfold. Then he ripped it free, and saw the lady SAFE agent framed in the shattered window panel of the showroom door.

Matt Gunderson arrived at the door a fraction of a second after Cynthia Monella did, and witnessed the sheer perfection of her shot.

SAFE blaster fire hit the unprepared Vulture mid-chest, hurling him off the desk and into a cork bulletin board on the opposite wall. He hit hard enough to crater that wall, and hung there for a second, his eyes aghast, his armored chest smoking from the energy-weapon's impact. Then he peeled loose and tumbled to the floor, landing face-down in a pile of laminated loose-leaf catalogues. Both Gunderson and Monella hurried into the room, blasters levelled at the back of the old man's head in case he somehow proved resilient enough to get up again. That was far from an unreasonable fear where members of the Sinister Six were concerned.

Monella levelled her weapon at the Vulture's head. "Did his armor hold?"

Gunderson knelt to touch the base of the old man's neck. He half-expected to be torn in half when the Vulture, like any horror-movie monster, proved strong enough to mount yet another attack just as he seemed downed for good... but no. The Vulture didn't move. Nor would he. His pulse was the steady, but weak beat of a combatant who had been thoroughly beaten. "Oh, my."

"He's dead?"

"No. He's alive. But he'll probably be in the hospital a while. From the looks of the bruising on his face, you hit him hard just as he couldn't take any more."

Monella's aim didn't waver. "Good."

For one terrible moment Gunderson thought that SAFE's newest recruit, traumatized as she was by what had happened at Rand-Meachum, would take it upon herself to pull the trigger again, this time as the Vulture's executioner. She may have wanted to. But she didn't. She just stood guard, like a professional.

That freed Gunderson to spare one last look at the old man in the bird suit. It was strange. The same figure so helpless now had been, earlier, willing to endanger a city, and wreck the lives of millions, just to enhance riches of his own. And this man was not an aberration... but one of many, so numerous that they banded together in groups. Gunderson could only shake his head and murmur, "All this for a little money...."

Pity didn't pursue her usual modus operandi by blanketing the entire rooftop in darkness. Perhaps it took too much effort to keep the effect going for long, or perhaps she was too torn up inside to concentrate on what she was doing. Perhaps she was just so angry at the ruination of her master's plans that she wanted Spider-Man defeated in the light. Whatever the explanation, the darkness she summoned now was an amorphous, liquid thing, that swirled around the roof in smoky eddies and currents. Parts billowed up like clouds of dust. Parts ebbed and flowed like waves of ink. Parts seemed diffuse, diluted, less like blackness than a bleak twilight gray. There were even a few sparks of bright light, though they flickered and died almost as soon as they were born. The effect was the same. As she leaped from the worst of the darkness, and aimed a kick at Spider-Man's face, the air surrounding her was so saturated with fuzzy black spots that she might have been under attack by swarms of gnats.

Spider-Man leaped over the kick and gave her a gentle bop on the top of the head as he passed overhead. It was more a nudge than an attempt to take her out; he knew from experience just how much it took to take her out. "So don't you think you've seen enough of New York for one morning? What with the weather and all?"

Her punches were vicious, machinelike, inhumanly fast, capable of seriously injuring him if they connected—but not quite as rich in the reluctant killing instinct that had characterized her earlier attacks.

He danced around the roof, carrying the battle to the next building. When she followed him, leaving the trussed

Electro behind, Spider-Man hopped backward one or two steps at time, allowing her to throw her punches but staying sufficiently far away to avoid the deadly impact. The blackness that swarmed around them both, at approximately waist-height, pitched and rolled like any other sea churned by a battle among titans.

"You came close!" he said. "But if you ever talk to your boss again, you should tell him that he shouldn't have hired Electro!"

A punch whirred past Spider-Man's ear, shattering a rooftop utility shack.

Spider-Man curled into a ball, dodged, came up twenty feet away, and said: "No, I'm serious! I mean it! I'm not just making fun of him for being stupid!"

Not listening at all, Pity kicked the shack again; an entire brick wall disintegrated and peppered him at high speed. They should have cut him to ribbons, but even before they got near him, he had spun a web-shield modeled on Captain America's. Shrapnel impaled itself in the spongy goo as he said: "I'm talking about something I've known about him for a long time! Something he doesn't even know about himself!"

Blackness descended upon him like a fist intent on crushing him into silence. He leaped clear and met Pity in mid-air. They spun a dozen times, grappling for any advantage as he parried her attempts to gain a stranglehold.

"Something that explains why a guy who can blow up entire city blocks keeps losing no matter how hard he tries!"

Just before they tumbled back into a world of swirling-darkness she got past his protective hands and closed her fingers around his neck. She was more than capable of exerting enough pressure to snap his neck. His own fingers, wrapped just as tightly around her wrists, prevented her from managing such a firm grip. They hit the rooftop beneath her shroud of darkness, grunting from the bone-crushing impact not cushioned nearly enough by the accumulation of snow. Spider-Man managed to keep talking even as she drove her knee into his belly with a force that might have paralyzed anybody else: "You see, I know what kind of life he lived before he became this way—because he told me! The way he ran away from his dreams! Put a lid on his ambitions! Refused any chance to make something better of himself! It made him a failure—ruined his career—drove his wife away! Made him so bitter that by the time he got his powers there was nothing left to him but hate! But even that didn't help his real problem!"

Pity had him pinned now, and was pelting him with enough blows to populate entire heavyweight championship bouts. Spider-Man rolled his head to avoid a punch that cratered the rooftop beneath him and flipped her over his shoulders with the basest twitch. "Don't you see? Even before he became Electro—he just didn't want to win! He did whatever he could to keep that from happening! And now that he is Electro—he still doesn't want to win! He keeps screwing up because he's afraid of having to deal with whatever comes next!"

She didn't answer. Of course.

Spider-Man felt a moment's reprieve when standing up left him head-and-shoulders over a layer of churning darkness. It was thoroughly diffused now, as distinguished by strips of relative light as it was by strips of relative black. What remained was a pattern writhing and twisting like a pit filled with asps.

Pity rose from the writhing darkness, her face blank, her eyes burning with a rage that might have been meant for him and might have been meant for the torment her life had become.

"Which is the same reason I think you can't win! Because you don't want what comes next, either! Fiers never took that from you!"

She only leaped at him again, her hands twisted into claws, her mouth agape in a soundless cry.

Mysterio lay in the ruins of the Empire State Gift Shoppe, surrounded by broken glass, fluttering postcards, and the assorted knickknackery of Tourist Central: snowglobes, stuffed animals in I Love New York t-shirts, plastic replicas of the Statue of Liberty with thermometers in them, and a life-size cardboard cutout of a talented lady dancer who had been foolish enough to devote the best years of her career to a musical which required her to put on tiger stripes and pretend she was a cat. A cash register, blasted off its counter by one of Electro's runaway lightning bolts, now lay on its side a few inches from Mysterio's helmeted head, its cash drawer spilling enough pennies to pay for perhaps one of the rock-hard salty pretzels being warmed to cancerous perfection beneath the heat lamp at the nearby snack counter.

He knew something had gone wrong, of course. He had no idea what, but he had experienced moments like this often enough to recognize them. He supposed it was the webslinger again. He hated supposing that, but knew it could have been worse; after all, he had once been defeated by a band of super-powered children, none of whom had been over twelve. After an experience like that, getting your head handed to you by Spider-Man yet another time, in a career where that seemed to happen every few months, qualified as business as usual. He loathed the experience and felt it twist his soul even more than it was already twisted, but knew that he could handle it. After all, he had before.

But he wasn't a defeatist, either. If there was any way to

wrest an advantage from this particular setback, he was going to take it. Maybe he could even find some way to set off the Oltion Field Generator himself.

He pressed both gauntleted palms against the litter and pushed himself off the ground, just barely managing to stand, only to be wracked by another wave of bottomless nausea. This was the worst attack yet, and it was accompanied by a spasm of coughing that left black spots dancing at the corners of his vision. A concussion, maybe? Then why was he feeling this way all day?

Voices.

Two SAFE agents in kevlar burst through the door to the emergency stairwell. One was a burly man with close-cropped white hair, the other a shorter and thinner companion with a thinning blonde fringe. They emerged from the stairwell, their blasters drawn. In a second they would have him.

But he was Mysterio... and he'd spent his morning wandering about with the rest of the tourists, planting his little devices throughout this shrine to Big Apple kitsch.

One stray impulse from the cybernetic sensors in his helmet, and the devices kicked in.

All of them.

The Incredible Hulk burst through the elevator door, bellowing in rage. A beanie baby display melted into the floor as the gates to hell opened up in the wall behind it. A gigantic gorilla fist reached in through the shattered window and grasped at empty air. A tiny Galactus hurled cosmic energy from the souvenir model of the Baxter Building. A cartoon rabbit hopped down from above and fired a persuasively real AK-47. Two space rogues in orange jumpsuits leaped out of the rest room and began slapping each other in a fit of pique. An ex-football player best known for a protracted murder trial popped up behind the pretzels and claimed innocence. A yellow submarine floated by to the accompaniment of trumpets. The room filled with smoke; the air echoed with the warring cries of elephants, pterodactyls, and Zulu warriors. It became a moonscape, scientifically accurate in every detail, up to and including the gibbous earth hanging in the sky behind it, with the one exception of a small suburban house on an acre of verdant green lawn. Then that faded away, replaced by hypnotic spirals and dizzying Escherian landscapes.

It was enough brilliant special effects work to keep Spider-Man busy for ten minutes. Mysterio, expecting the wallcrawler's arrival, had intended to use it to do just that. He blew it all now, in a matter of seconds, just to confuse the two SAFE agents long enough to eliminate them. But though he heard them shouting in disorientation, he was unable to gain any advantage out of it. Because his head was pounding so hard he could barely stand.

Mysterio directed his cybnernetics to turn the illusions off, and sank to his knees as the two frazzled SAFE agents inched toward him, their blasters leveled at his head. He pressed the hidden release that popped the helmet off, breathed deeply as the stale air inside was replaced by the cold but fresh air of the greater world outside, and craned his neck so he could face his captors. They were nobodies, he decided, and found some comfort in that. After all, if Spider-Man also regarded these battles as a matter of pride, perhaps he'd find source for humiliation in the awareness that his all-time greatest enemy had this time been captured by nobody important. It was a victory of sorts, Mysterio thought. It was certainly the only one he could take comfort in today.

The burlier of the two SAFE agents said: "Quentin Beck? You're under arrest."

Mysterio coughed. "I know."

The SAFE agents both seemed suprised to win their victory this easily. They shared glances, then focused on Mysterio again as his coughing became a spasm.

The one with the balding red fringe said: "Are you all right?"

Mysterio just looked up at him and said the only two words that came to mind.

"... help me ..."

Pity's darkness was grainier than ever. It was not the impenetrable field Spider-Man had experienced in their earliest encounters, nor the surreal pattern of warring light and dark she had managed in the first few minutes of this battle, but a thinner, soupier fog punctuated by inexplicable bright spots. It accomplished nothing but making their battleground look like a place filled with smoke. That, combined with the sheets of swirling snow, made eyesight tricky at best, but Spider-Man had senses that more than compensated.

What he wanted was a few minutes of warmth again. Thermal costume or not, grappling around in snow accumulation was turning this fight in a bold new adventure in masochism.

It slowed him down so much that Pity was able to tag him again.

It was a high kick, right from the hip, and it landed in middle of the chest, at precisely the place where the ribs protect the heart. Spider-Man was able to deflect some of its force with a sideways jab to the sole of her ankle, but that only altered the kick's impact point by a scant inch or two. It was still an impact that might have been envied by the average Mack truck blaring down the highway at eighty per. The force of it lifted him right off his feet, and sent him flying thirty feet backward into a brick utility shed. He took the brunt of the crash with the small of his back, but momentum snapped his neck back, slamming the back of his head against the wall.

Spider-Man tumbled to the rooftop, half-buried by a fresh snowdrift, surrounded by a haze of black spots that might have been Pity's doing and might have been unconsciousness coming to claim him.

On the opposite end of the roof Pity hesitated, and began to stride toward him.

The speaker in his ear crackled. Morgan's voice. "Spider-Man? We now have Vulture and Mysterio, confirmed in custody and on their way to holding cells. You said you have Electro . . . ?"

Spider-Man wished he had the time to tap his throat-mike—not to give Morgan a sit-rep (and oh lord, how he hated that abbreviation), but to tell that man to just once in his life shut up.

Pity was still coming . . . and from her stance, she wasn't coming to tell him, oh, sorry, didn't mean that, hope we can be friends. She was coming to administer the *coup-de-grâce*.

He didn't have the luxury of trying to get through to her anymore.

He was going to have to put her down hard. If he could.

He forced himself to his feet, and staggered a single step forward.

Pity immediately halted her advance. She bent into a battle crouch, arms held out before her, eyes wary and watching for his moment of fatal weakness.

Either that . . . or using what free will she had, to offer him another try?

Spider-Man took another step, brandishing web-shooters, not firing yet, aware that she'd dodged his webbing in the past. She stepped back again, circling. Darkness danced around her in spirals.

He thought back to his conversation with Troy Saberstien.

What had the crisis counsellor said?

... if she's really been conditioned into obedience, then that conditioning would tend to reinforce itself at the moments of greatest opposition. Anything you could do to stand against the Gentleman will make you an enemy, and trying to free her from the Gentleman would definitely have to be part of that.

Spider-Man had asked: Then what's the alternative?

Anything that puts the two of you on the same side. I don't have the slightest clue what that could be, in this situation, but if you make yourself an ally, even for a minute, you might weaken the conditioning enough to give yourself a chance at getting through to her.

And he knew. Fresh strength filled his limbs as he drove himself forward. "Aren't you worried about your boss?"

She immediately looked stricken. It was like he'd stabbed with an actual blade instead of mere words. Her expression turned questioning, urgent.

She still went for him, hurling a punch that should have snapped his neck.

He dodged it easily, landed behind her, kept taunting her even as she whirled and went for him again and again and again. "Think! Who should have wanted to stick around, to provide his technical expertise in case something went wrong with the Generator?"

Wind whistled from the speed of her next punch.

"And who should have wanted to stay in the neighborhood, if for no other reason than to tear me limb from limb? And who instead made himself conspicuous by leaving as soon as he could? Ock, that's who! Where do you think he's going?"

Frantic now, Pity peppered the air between them with punches, none of which connected. They were driven more by emotion than training, and Spider-Man easily deflected or dodged every single one of them. The real battle, now, was being fought with words ... and Spider-Man barely let up on those long enough to take a breath.

"He must be after something a lot more important to him than terrorizing New York and trying to kill me—and the only thing he's ever found more important than those two hobbies is control! Being in charge! He hasn't liked not being in charge of the Six this time ... has he?"

Pity's eyes filled with terror. She turned her back on Spider-Man and began to run, hopping from this rooftop to the next one over. Spider-Man covered the same distance with a single leap, then continued to pace her as she fled south at a clip that ate up entire blocks in seconds. The darkness trailed behind her like a swarm of ninja hornets.

"I can see you know I'm right! The question is—what are you going to do about it? Are you going to try to handle it yourself, knowing that Ock has such a huge head start—or are you going to tell me where your boss went so I can get SAFE's entire air force there first? Be honest and decide the best way to save that old bastard's life!"

That got her. She braked against the gravel of the rooftop where she was, stood silently with head bowed, her hands curled into resentful fists.

He said, "Please! Let me help you!"

Something went out of her, all at once.

Either that... or something else came back to life.

She turned to face him.

Pity stood there, a figure all in white, framed by a raging blizzard that seemed for this one moment to exist only that she could stand in perfect isolation at its center. Her puffy black hair was spotty with melting snowflakes. Her breath was a series of white clouds bursting from her lips in puffs. Despite the globs of webbing dissolving on her cheeks, the pain in her eyes remained her most prominent feature. It had been deposited there by years of torment at the hands of a man who allowed her no freedom and no joy, and there was so much of it that some would always be left, even if she died a hundred years from now, as an old woman lucky enough to have experienced nothing but perfect happiness for all her remaining days. There was nothing Spider-Man could do to lessen that. But there was something else there now, something that hadn't been there before. Something Spider-Man saw only because he had aching to see it... a dim spark, that if properly nurtured could still grow to an open flame.

She studied his mask, as if its inexpressive design could possibly communicate as well as eye contact. And then she nodded.

Wishful thinking allowed him to interpret that expression as a smile.

He tapped his throat mike. "Morgan?"

The Colonel's voice came in, harried and urgent. "Where were you, webslinger? You've been out of contact for a while! We were worried about you!"

"Yeah, well... I shoulda written sooner. Listen, I have Electro wrapped up on a rooftop a few blocks north of my current position." He gave the address. "And here's a new wrinkle: I have Pity standing here beside me."

"Standing there? You mean, free?"

"Yes," Spider-Man said, wishing he dared to believe it. "She has information she's anxious for us to hear . . ."

CHAPTER THIRTEEN

12:18 P.M.

The Zachary Mosely Corporate Air Center sits on a small patch of land in Lynbrook, Long Island, just south of the Valley Stream State Park. A private airfield, leased to a consortium of businesses which mostly use it to fly their executives to and from other small airfields up and down the eastern seaboard, it doesn't feature any of the services or amenities available at the giant JFK Airport just a few miles to its west. There is no ticketed travel, and therefore no need for terminals. Nor is there any customs office, since none of the small planes hangared here are rated for Trans-Atlantic flight. It's rare indeed to find a jet, even a small one, on the field. On the other hand, it's even rarer to find a flight delayed because of overcrowded runways. To busy execs who want the convenience of a Long Island takeoff without having to deal with big-airport delays, Mosely's facilities are ideal.

To international investors in chaos who wish a speedy departure at the moment of greatest departure, they're even better.

The Gentleman had flown his private jet into LaGuardia about three weeks earlier, enduring the usual customs rigamorole in an effort to render his entry into this corrupt barbarian nation as legitimate as possible. He did not, of course, intend to leave this country in the same condition when he left, so he had wasted no time moving his jet to a hangar at Mosely as soon as possible. The fee for renting a private hangar, with no prior contract and no advance reservation, had been something in the upper obscene, but it was well worth the investment. After all, the Federal presence at Mosely was considerably lighter than at the major airports... and the chances that a last-minute dragnet would think to include this particular facility were minimal.

Not that this stopped the oafish uniform at the front gate from making a fuss. Warm as toast in his little hut, seemingly unmindful of the low station his subhuman ambitions had driven him to, the jowly, red-faced, slit-eyed excuse for a human being squinted through the meter of driving snow that separated the window of his gatehouse from the front window of the limousine. "Sorry, sir! These facilities closed an hour ago! Everything's grounded within fifty miles of here!"

The driver, Serge, turned around and said: "You heard that, sir?"

The Gentleman gave his rent-a-lackey the kind of look capable of melting glass at fifty paces. "Of course I heard that. Just because I'm old doesn't mean I'm also deaf." He leaned forward and flashed his most charming smile at the idiot in the guardhouse. "Don't worry, my dear man. I'm not insane enough to think we could actually take off in this beastly mess. I'm only here to retrieve some documents from my plane in hangar E. It shouldn't take more than a few minutes."

"I'm sorry, sir, but the facilities are supposed to be closed to all business for the duration of the snow emergency."

Was there no end to this country's inane indignities? Keeping his temper with a supreme act of will, the Gentleman forced more continental charm into his smile. "I think you'll find that I called ahead. The hangar's registered to a Mr. D.W. Jaxon?" (This the name of a cargo pilot who had worked for him briefly in the late 1940s.)

"Lemme check," the guard said, disappearing into his hut.

The Gentleman sank back into his seat, shaking his head in sincere disbelief. Lemme, indeed. What kind of civilization allowed the free use of a bastardization like lemme? What kind of society allowed these undereducated, underdeveloped buffoons to fling them in the face of their obvious betters? The same society that permitted its teenage girls to misuse the word "like"? It was horrifying.

Truly, the inhabitants of this infernal cesspool deserved everything that was about to happen to them . . .

Ten minutes later:

Colonel Sean Morgan had a reputation for being stern. He achieved results by being angry, and sometimes by being explosive. He wasn't often downright livid, but he was now. Standing on that snowtossed Manhattan rooftop, facing down the agency's current super hero ally *du jour* while a dozen of his agents watched from their hovering aircars, he seemed about to bust a vein.

"Are you out of your mind?"

Most of the SAFE aircar fleet was either still dealing with the remains of the river fire, or had returned there to help with the cleanup. The few hovering here were occupied with people who Spider-Man was now relieved to find still alive and unhurt. All the cars here had underbellies sooty from smoke. Joshua Ballard and Doug Deeley occupied one. A grim-faced Clyde Fury stood with the old man, Dr. Williams, in another. Agents Walsh and Starling of the FBI, freshly plucked from their canvas of the Empire State Building, were in a third piloted by a soot-faced, openly weeping Shirlene Annanayo. Vince Palminetti, strapped into his command chair, sat in Sean Morgan's flagship. A female pilot Spider-Man didn't recognize had Cynthia Monella and Matt Gunderson. Another pilot Spider-Man didn't know had Troy Saberstein (who looked game enough but green at the gills, as if he didn't take well to aircar travel). Having already heard that there'd been fatalities, including Walt Evans and Donna Piazza, Spider-Man couldn't help being distracted by the need to remember the names and faces of every other SAFE agent he'd encountered in this past week. Who was missing? Anybody he'd known?

Not giving him a moment, Morgan continued: "I have nine good agents dead, a city that almost went up in smoke, more than forty other corpses still being buried from Rand-Meachum, and you want to let her change sides?"

Spider-Man's mask made him incapable of facial expressions, but he still tilted his head in a manner that made him seem sheepish. "Yeah."

"She belongs in a prison cell, and you know it!"

"Or a psychiatric facility," Spider-Man said. "And maybe that's where she'll end up, after this business is done. But until then, we can use her help."

"And what am I supposed to say to the families of all those people?"

Spider-Man spread his arms before him, palms up, in a gesture meant to communicate both empathy and helplessness in the face of tragedy. "I don't know. Maybe that this was the only way to save some lives."

"Sean?" This came from Doctor George Williams, who had been helped down from the aircar which had rushed him from the cleanup south of Manhattan. He hobbled over with terrible urgency, leaning on his cane, his weathered face grimacing from the effort. Williams was not dressed for the weather at all; he was in fact wearing the same thin and outdated casual wear he'd worn when briefing SAFE about the Gentleman's career, after the Day of Terror. The cold must have cut right through to his skin. Nor did he bear it well. He was an old man, and the shock of leaving the aircar's climate-controlled environment, to enter the rooftop beset by the worst blizzard Manhattan had seen since the disastrous storm of 1888, drew his wrinkled skin tight against his cheeks. But nobody stopped him as he dragged himself across the rooftop and tapped the Colonel with the tip of his cane. "You're a principled man, Sean. I've always admired that about you. But this is not the time or the place for principle."

It was frightening how quickly Colonel Morgan lost all of his air of command in the presence of this one old man. "It's freezing out here, Doctor. You really shouldn't . . . "

"Yes. I should." Though he was shivering, the old man's voice rose just enough to suggest an unlimited fury. "I would crawl across broken glass for a chance to spit in that monster's eye. And so should you."

Morgan made one more attempt: "Doctor—"

Williams cut him off. "You know I'm right. If this young lady can help us, for whatever reason, we don't have the right to refuse her."

Vince Palminetti, amplifying his voice from his immobile command chair on Sean Morgan's personal aircar, added the coup de grace: "He still has the Catalyst, Colonel."

Anybody who didn't know Morgan might have considered his blink a mere reflex rather than the gesture of a man at war with himself. When he opened his eyes again, his jaw, a t-square at the best of times, had tightened impossibly another notch. He muttered a heartfelt, "Damn." Then he decided. "All right, everybody. Load up. We still have a big job left to do today. Wallcrawler, you and that—that whatever she is—are with me."

"I want Saberstien with us too," said Spider-Man. The crisis counsellor could prove helpful, dealing with Pity's unstable loyalties.

The T-square jaw ratcheted still tighter, a natural reaction given the Colonel's antipathy toward the counsellor's input. "Fine. Let's just get in the air."

Ten minutes earlier:

The guard emerged from his hut, a hearty sniff demonstrating the heights of the martyrdom he saw himself damned to by actually being forced to work in this weather. This time he carried a clipboard. "D.W. Jaxon. Yeah, there's a note here. Unimpeded access to your hangar in all conditions. As long as you know that the runways aren't clear and the tower isn't allowing anything out."

"I understand." The Gentleman was the picture of old-world elegance, but his teeth grated.

He deigned to participate in the signing of the clipboard, another American ritual that had always baffled him. Who looked at those things? But with the mindless formalities observed, the last obstacle between himself and the destruction of this poor excuse for a civilization was pushed aside. The guard returned to his hut, performed the necessary mumbo-jumbo there, and lifted the gate so the limousine could pass through unimpeded.

As Serge steered the vehicle along the access road,

their headlights lit up the snow pelting the windshield, giving it an unearthly glow that completely obscured anything beyond. "You might need to guide me, sir. Where's Hangar E?"

The Gentleman lifted his front of his cane over the front seat and gestured toward a low, squat shape in the distance. "Do you see that? It is Hangar A. Registered to Baintronics."

Serge took a right toward the low squat shape. "Yes?"

"Beyond it is Hangar B. Registered to the Brand Corporation. Drive past that and you will find Hangar C, registered to Blum Database Associates. Do I really need to elaborate on this quite simple, and I would think, absurdly obvious pattern? Or was command of your own alphabet not part of the training you received for this humiliating, menial career of yours?"

"I got it," said Serge.

The Gentleman might have added several additional notes to his patrician sarcastic aria, but his heart wasn't in it; he was too busy looking forward to his joyful reunion with all his worldly goods. The treasures stashed away in the cargo hold of his jet—precious gems, priceless antiques, the finest cultural and artistic heirlooms available at any price—represented almost everything he had left in the world. At only a couple of hundred million worth, it wasn't much by the standards of the fortune he had commanded at the height of his success, but it was, given his reduced circumstances in these past few years, a fine testament to his skill at appraising the proper value he received for his buying dollar. He had all but exhausted the last of his considerable fortune obtaining it—necessary, since any untouched reserves of conventional currency would soon be as useless as this brainless oaf of a chauffeur. He looked forward to the moment when the value of that hoard was multiplied by a factor of ten, while so many unworthy others wailed in unexpected poverty.

"Here's Hangar E," said Serge, a helpful announcement indeed considering that the limo had just pulled to a stop before the rear of a large building with the legend HANGAR E. "Need some help inside, or do you want me to wait here for you?"

The Gentleman considered that as he fingered a small revolver in his jacket pocket. Part of him, the sensible part, advised him to let this poor, mindless peon go. The oaf would soon suffer enough in the chaos this society would become. And it had been so long since he had murdered a human being himself, instead of arranging for underlings or associates to do it—more than seventy years, in fact, since the last occasion had been his participation in one of Al Capone's lovely baseball bat parties. He was out of practice. Nevertheless, this worm's incompetence had led to unconscionable delays at a time when the Gentleman could ill afford them ... and the dullness of his intellect was offensive to the Gentleman's sensibilities as well. Allowing him to live would be a travesty. It made more sense, the Gentleman thought, to simply indulge himself in this one pleasure now, and worry about targeting the rest of the man's family later.

So he smiled. "Come inside. You can have some nice hot coffee while I get what I need from my plane."

The murder being contemplated on Long Island was already ten minutes old before the SAFE fleet could take off.

Pity had summoned darkness in the shape of an arrow, pointed Southeast. Now, as Palminetti led Morgan's fleet in that vague direction, following the arrow which still seemed to fly no more than an arm's-length before them, she became an island unto herself at the rear of the aircar. She stood, silent and impassive, facing the angry streaks of white that buffeted the intangible ionic shield without penetrating to touch the grim-faced passengers that field protected.

The city itself was far below, entirely swallowed up by the storm, but Pity still behaved as if she could see it, and the people imprisoned within its vertical walls. She knew the other SAFE aircars had to be following, too, but they were also next to invisible in the storm. Every few seconds she saw a shadow that could possibly be one of them, but there was no way to be sure. She supposed it didn't matter.

It did not escape her attention that, but for Palminetti, whose fixed position in his command seat kept him facing forward, all of the men in the aircar were watching her back. She was also aware that they watched from different perspectives... all understandable, all miles away from the loathesome puppy-dog attentions of the psychopath Max Dillon. Colonel Morgan had his hand on the handle of his blaster, and was prepared to cut her down at the first suspicious move. The soft one, Saberstein, studied her through the eyes of a scientist, looking for the key that would enable him to figure her out. Trying to figure her out. And Spider-Man...

... Spider-Man...

... Pity knew what Spider-Man said he wanted, but she feared there was no part of her capable of giving him the trust she would have to provide in return.

She was still the Gentleman's.

And she would protect his interests until death came to claim her.

Still fixed in position facing the control panel, Palminetti said, "It's official, you know. This the worst blizzard to hit this town since March of 1888. That one was one of the city's all-time worst disasters, you know."

Spider-Man, leaning over his shoulder, murmured: "Let's hope this one isn't."

"I'm afraid it already is, Spider-Man. Before you factor in the snow."

Spider-Man knew the other man was referring to the death toll south of the island, and the property damage caused by Electro during the battle of the Empire State Building. "Yeah, well . . . let's hope we stop it here."

"Amen," said Palminetti.

"How did you people stop the fire, anyway? Last I heard over my headset, it was out of control."

"It was," Palminetti said. "But Colonel Morgan rethought the problem. You ever put out a fire by stomping on it?"

"Not in these socks. But when I'm wearing shoes . . . sure."

"Well, Colonel Morgan has the city's biggest shoe at his disposal. It's called the Helicarrier, and it's designed to take even greater heat extremes. He ordered it to come down for a series of water landings in the burning areas. At four city blocks long, that's an awful lot of smothering power, even for a chemical fire. And every time the helicarrier took off again the displaced water rushing back in to refill the trough drowned much of what was left. There was enough foam left to contain the perimeter. The blaze was still burning when we had part of the fleet redeploy to help you with Electro, but it's under control now, and should be completely out by the time we get back . . . assuming, of course, that we somehow manage that little trick too." Palminetti's eyes flickered. "You want to know the odds against us?"

Spider-Man knew that Palminetti's probability estimates

were always uncomfortably close to the mark. "No, thanks. There's somebody else I have to talk to."

Seven minutes earlier:

The dying man fell slowly to the floor, his chest a bubbling open wound. He managed to stay on his knees for several long seconds as he stared up at the man who had taken his life away.

The Gentleman contemplated the writhing figure for several seconds, the most obscene of all possible smiles playing about the edges of fine aristocratic lips. That was a lesson he'd enjoyed teaching, all right. The fool hadn't entertained even the ghost of a suspicion that his life was entering its final moments. He had just accompanied his murderer into the cavernous Hangar E, so relieved to be in out of the storm that he had lost all other powers of observation or self-preservation and thus missed the sight of a deadly weapon being leveled against him.

Now look at him. He was a perforated sack of skin and flesh, spilling the last of his life blood upon the concrete floor. And look especially at his eyes, which were wild, bereft, and uncomprehending.

Few things in this life could possibly be so delicious.

He considered putting the wretch out of his misery with a killing shot to the brain, but no. Better to leave him here, drifting in and out of consciousness, for the half hour it might take for him to die. Better to leave him contemplating his foolishness.

He knelt before the dying man, murmured a few scornful words to accompany him on his journey to the hell he deserved, and—just to add insult to injury—rolled him over on his side, to gain access to the wallet in his back pocket. Unbelievably, the fool clutched for it, as if regaining control of the riches within could possibly buy back his stupidity of the last few minutes. But fighting him off was pathetically easy. There was already almost no strength left in those arms. Taking the billfold, and emptying it of all all cash and credit cards, was the work of a moment. Tossing the empty sack of leather on the chest of the soon to be emptied sack of flesh took no longer.

It was a small gesture, he supposed. Perhaps even a foolish one, given the far greater stakes in play today. But he had always believed that destroying a man meant leaving him with nothing, not even pocket change.

"So long," he grinned.

The dying man did not have the breath to curse him.

The Gentleman rose, crossed the hangar, and retrieved the wolf's-head cane that rested against the tool locker. He tapped it against the concrete floor twice, enjoying the sound. It was a good, strong sound, almost a parody of the gunshot that had so recently split the air.

He did not rely on it as all as he climbed up the gangplank of his specially modified Bettelhine Transtar. It was an elegantly designed vehicle in that it was supposed to be anything but. To most eyes it would have been the clunkiest airborne bus: an antiquated four-engine cargo plane big enough to accomodate seventy passengers in cramped proletarian misery. Even the airport inspectors who had seen the interior noted only that the number of standard airline seats, all up front, had been reduced to a sparse twenty, with bulk of the passenger section taken up by a private lounge appointed in elegant old-world charm. They saw what they were intended to see: the toy of a foolish old rich man.

But even with this beauty's camouflaged jet engines revealed, few would have expected it to possess anything in the way of speed or manueverability. Most professional pilots, asked to take it up on a day like this, would have turned a shade that might have rendered them invisible against the snow. But then most professional pilots wouldn't have recognized it as a military vehicle, with enough lift to take off in monsoons and enough agility to take on most modern fighters in aerial combat. This plane could take heavily-armed platoons, and their materiel, into hot zones on the front line, then take off again and strafe the enemy with machine-gun fire. Already a little antiquated by today's standards, it had nevertheless proved invaluable in many last-minute escapes from cities being reduced to flames and rubble in the last moments of profitable wars. The Gentleman hadn't imagined that the weather on the day of his escape from New York would have been quite so beastly as this, but he had imagined a need for the most versatile flying machine available, and had thus selected this beauty as his chosen means of escape.

Good thing, too, the old man thought, as he doffed his coat and gloves in the coat closet behind the cockpit. It was just his luck to be forced to make his getaway during the storm of the century.

He went to the cargo hold, first, to make sure that everything was in order. The gold, the jewels, the fine works of art, the illegal furs that represented the last of their species, even the bottle of fine champagne from a vintage valuable well beyond its merits, were all safe and tightly secured. More importantly, the Cannister sat positioned in its chute, directly above the bomb bay doors. The Gentleman had equipped it with an explosive device that would incinerate it in a ball of flame high above Manhattan. It would have burst open anyway upon hitting its first solid object, but an airburst would initiate its catalyst effects both faster and more efficiently. Come to think of it, the storm was also going to be exceedingly helpful in that regard; perhaps it was not a potential problem so much as an opportunity making itself known.

The thought made the old man clap his hands in glee. This was going to be fun. Every second of it, starting with the protests of the Tower the second he took his steed on the runway. That is, it was possible for them to protest at all: it was entirely possible that the coming EMP in Manhattan would have shut them down by that point.

Fortunately, the Transtar was insulated against such problems.

He climbed back up the stairs and returned to the cockpit, taking his place behind the pilot's seat. He strapped in, grinned, and pressed the transmitter he had programmed earlier. The hangar doors began to slide open, as the Transtar rolled forward.

As Spider-Man returned to the rear of the SAFE aircar, he passed both a glowering Sean Morgan and an urgent Troy Saberstein. Morgan's face showed nothing but its usual grim determination; Saberstein's far gentler features showed a version of the same thing. The stress counsellor grabbed Spider-Man by the wrist, then indicated Pity with a nod. He mouthed a word: "Now."

The wall-crawler nodded back to show that he understood. If Pity was a victim of mind control, as advertised, then this was a critical time for her. The way Spider-Man handled himself, in the next few minutes, was going to have an immense effect on which way she went. Right now, she was up for grabs.

Morgan, who had been apprised of the mind control theory, read their silent exchange and let them both know, with an equally silent look, that he didn't like it at all. That was no surprise. Morgan showed even less sympathy for criminals than he did for people on his own side. Given that most of the bad guys he encountered were murderous international terrorists of one kind or another, he even had a point. Spider-Man, whose own bad guys tended to re-appear in New York about as frequently as the yadda-yadda episode of Seinfeld appeared on cable television, had even less of a reason to believe in the possibility of redemption and rehabilitation—but it was as much a part of his philosophy as his credo about great power and great responsibility. He had to believe Pity had a chance. Especially because of who she might be.

So he moved past Morgan and Saberstein and stopped beside Pity, joining her in her contemplation of the angry white streaks that turned the view beyond the ion-field into angry representations of chaos.

He didn't wait for her to look at him. He knew, without trying, that she wouldn't. But he spoke softly anyway, confident that she would hear him.

"Pity..."

It was a false start. He began again.

"There's an old couple I used to know. Retired, on pensions, just scraping along, neither one of them in the best of health. Nobody would have blamed them, at their age, for not wanting to be bothered with somebody else's problems. But there came a day...a terrible day...when they found out a child needed them. They gave up their lives to him. They made sure that he was fed, and clothed, and educated, and always—always—shown that he was loved. They were good people. I wish you could have known them, and not the old man you knew instead. You shouldn't have had—what you had."

Her face was still blank, but at least she regarded him now.

Spider-Man swallowed so hard it hurt, studying her calm face in profile, knowing that he'd already persuaded himself that she wasn't his sister... but for this moment, at least, changing his mind, deciding that she was. He lowered his voice a notch and said: "I told you I took this personally. I can't tell you exactly why. Not now, at least. But if you can just take one step away from what he made of you, and trust me... I promise you that I'll meet you more than halfway. I'll work with you so you can find the kind of person you should have been allowed to be. As for the law... well, I told you I know the best attorney in New York. I promise you he'll make sure the jury knows what was done to you. I promise you we'll get you help. And whatever happens... believe me... like I said before... I promise I won't abandon you."

Still no reaction. She appeared unhappy, as always. He couldn't tell whether she felt moved, or instead regarded his words with the utmost, hopeless scorn.

He thought of the psionic abilities Saberstein had postulated, and felt a sad sinking sensation in his stomach. Of course. If Saberstein was right, then this was nothing new for her; she was well used to receiving facile sympathy from total strangers. She was also used to it meaning nothing.

He leaned in close and said, "Listen to me, dammit."

He had put just enough urgency in his voice to startle her. She glanced at him, not quite flinching, but wary nevertheless.

He said, "This isn't your power making me jump through hoops. I mean what I'm saying. I will not abandon you."

If that got through to her at all, he couldn't tell.

Nor did he have time to push the matter, because that's when Palminetti said, "We're over Kennedy Airport."

Morgan said, "He intends to take off from here? Under these conditions?"

"Apparently not, Colonel. At least not from here. Look." The arrow curved off to the east, now. "She's directing us along the shore."

"She's leading us away from him," Morgan said, with the black satisfaction of a man who had suspected it all along. "He could be anywhere, releasing the Catalyst—"

Spider-Man, studying Pity's face, said, "No. No, Colonel, I think that's wrong." He turned away from her. "If she's new in New York, she doesn't know the area by heart. And take it from someone who commutes at forty stories every day—in conditions like these—even folks who know every brick still use landmarks for navigation. Kennedy Airport would qualify. I'll bet she's looking for something near Kennedy, but harder to find from the air. Is that right?"

Pity gave an imperceptible nod.

"Terrific," Morgan said. He then defied all caricatures about men being afraid to ask for directions: "Quick! Palminetti! Get into the database and tell me what's east along the shore from Kennedy airport!"

Camouflaged by the storm, running with all its cabin lights off to avoid being spotted by the Tower, the Transtar taxied into position.

Although the blizzard had closed the storm to both incoming and outgoing traffic, the runway lights still glowed bright as far as the limited visibility allowed them to be seen at all: after all, there was no telling what planes stuck in these conditions might need to come in for an emergency landing. There had been little thought, of course, to any planes that might want to make emergency takeoffs.

The normal takeoff would have taken the Transtar south, over the ocean. That would have been all right for today's purposes too, but for the subsequent necessity to turn around for the low pass over Manhattan. That would provide the authorities with several additional minutes to scramble pursuit and/or interference. No, it was better to take off overland, head straight to the target zone, expedite the release of the Catalyst, and then flee to some nice tropical place where a wealthy man could ride out the financial chaos soon to swallow the whole of western civilization.

Snow accumulation on the runway seemed to be several inches deep. The air up ahead looked like it was being churned by angry Gods. Any ordinary pilot taking an ordinary plane up in these conditions would have to be insane. The smiling old man in the pilot's seat had faith in his abilities and in his equipment.

He would do this.

One more second, and in he would be positioned for takeoff.

But then the Transtar shook so violently that only the safety straps prevented the Gentleman from being thrown from from his seat. For one terrible heartbeat he thought this a runway collision. Some other plane, coming in for an emergency landing, must have smashed into him broadsides. Another nanosecond and the jet, his riches, the Catalyst, and all his plans for the future would be vaporized by a fireball of superheated gas.

When he survived to take another breath, he knew it had to be something else. Something smaller. An automobile, perhaps? What the Americans, in their tiresome vernacular, called a fender bender?

The Transtar shook again, lifted a few centimeters off the tarmac, and fell down again, shaking the entire cabin. Somewhere, something breakable shattered. The fusillage groaned like an ancient reptile sinking into the noxious pit at La Brea. The old man gasped, tried to taxi out of the way out of whatever was doing this, heard the engines protesting with loud moans as something held the powerful vehicle in place.

Understanding came a fraction of a second before the view through the windshield confirmed the worst.

"No!"

A serpentine ribbon of unbreakable adamantium curled into position less than a meter from where he sat helpless to stop it. It was followed by a familiar sneering face, beneath soupbowl bangs now half-white from snow accumulation.

The old man whispered the newcomer's name: "Octavius!"

This was going to be very, very bad.

CHAPTER FOURTEEN

Several hours earlier.

The Old Soldier returned home both battered and weary after a battle fought on the far side of the world. It had been a hard fight against hard people, in an arena where the value of human life was not an ideal to be cherished but a price to be paid. He had won, if you could dignify walking away with such a name, but he had needed to compromise himself in fresh ways in order to emerge as the last man standing. Sometimes he could live with that. Other times, it left a hollow where his heart was.

He returned home an hour before dawn, to a country landscape buried beneath a light dusting of snow. He knew, less from any weather report than from his own personal instinct for such things, that more snow was coming sometime after dawn. That might have cheered him, at other times. He had always felt most at home in winter. Indeed, he was so inured to cold that he greeted the freezing temperatures, not with a bulky winter coat of the sort necessary for folks less talented at holding on to body heat, but with a battered old leather windbreaker, more appropriate to early spring than one of the coldest days of the year. On a normal night, the raking wind, cutting through its flimsy material as if it didn't exist, would have struck him as the touch of an old friend. But on this particular night he had just returned from a battleground even colder, blanketed by a snow that by the end of the fight was not pristine virgin white but instead a filthy free-flowing scarlet, marking the last resting place of both vicious killers and also the innocents he had failed to save. Tonight, for once, the Old Soldier craved warmth. Comfort. He was a man who never showed his age, but who nevertheless felt old; a man who did not bruise easily, but who was nevertheless bruised; a man who did not tire easily, but who was tired; a man no stranger to darkness all his life, but who just this once craved a little light, a little smile, and a little reason to feel hope.

The Old Soldier returned to a darkened house resonant with the distant snoring of friends who had watched his back in other wars. They, at least, were enjoying a few uncharacteristic hours of peace. They did not hear him come in, and he did not try to wake them. He just moved from the foyer to the study, dropping his canvas duffle on the oriental rug before collapsing, exhausted, on the couch. He noticed that the fireplace was heaped with fresh wood. He considered starting a fire before the others got up, perhaps even surprising them with one of his rare offers to cook breakfast, but apathy got the better of him, and he just sank a little deeper into the cushions.

He might have drifted off into uneasy dreams if his keen eyes hadn't spotted the yellow post-it note on the coffee table. He might have ignored it too if he wasn't so pathologically conscientious. A low growl stirred deep in his throat as he sat up, took the note, registered that it was for him, muttered something definitely not nice when he saw that it was several days old, and bared his teeth when he identified the phone number written there as one that required immediate response. This particular sequence of digits belonged to an old contact of his who regularly provided him with hard data regarding several of the developing situations in which he took an active interest. Ignoring such a message was foolish at best and downright suicidal at worst.

Feeling older than ever, the Old Soldier shuffled off to an elegantly appointed library in the rear of the house. It was dark in there, but he did not bother to turn on the lights. The cavernous space, which stretched four stories to a wrought-iron skylight, suited him as much dark as it suited the others well-lit. Books, ranging from valuable first editions to popular paperback novels, surrounded him by the tens of thousands on all sides. The Old Soldier, nobody's idea of a voluminous reader, sometimes wished he had more time to explore this treasurehouse the way it deserved to be explored, but knew that with his lifestyle such moments were fleeting and often interrupted by more pressing concerns.

The Old Soldier moved across the carpeted floor to a huge antique desk beneath a tinted window. He sank into a chair that dwarfed him, glanced with wry amusement at the book left open on the desk blotter—a rare 1937 edition of the Frederic Prokosch adventure novel, *Seven Who Fled*, which had been based in part on his own travels in the far east. He wondered if his friends would believe that, decided it was an experiment best left untried. He then took a customized cellular phone from the top drawer, ran the latest encryption and anti-trace software to avoid unauthorized listeners, and dialed, not the dummy number on the post-it, but the genuine number he was meant to call back instead.

The phone rang exactly once. A voice distorted by electronic filters to sound exactly like a friendly announcer said: "Hello! Welcome to Movie-Fone! If you know the name of the movie you want to see, press or say One!"

The Old Soldier growled a word considerably ruder than, "One."

It wasn't the most dignified sign and countersign ever devised, but the Old Soldier preferred it to the traditional "The Rooster-Crows-At-Midnight" stuff.

"Yeah," his informant said, now speaking in his own accent: a mix of Ivy League and Brooklyn. "Took you long enough to call back. Where the hell were you, last couple of weeks?"

"Out of town," said the Old Soldier. "Way out of town."

"Where?"

"No place you'd like."

"Ha. My fault for asking. No place you frequent is anyplace I'd like."

The Old Soldier could have taken that as an insult, but it happened to be literally true, so he let it pass. Words couldn't harm him. And sticks and stones couldn't break his bones, either, as far as that went . . . so he supposed he had nothing to complain about. He grimaced anyway as he pulled a cigarillo from his shirt pocket. "Anyway. You answered on the first ring, so I figure you're up."

"Up's an understatement. This is a white-knuckle all-nighter."

"Yeah?"

"Yeah. This is big. It's connected to two of your hot buttons, and going down any second now. I may have to cut out in a hurry."

"Then tell me already. What's the hit?"

"It's not one hit. It's two. Two separate hits. It's easy to miss the connection between them unless you take a closer look—"

"Just talk. If there's a connection, I'll see it."

His informant took a deep breath. "First and least. From our mutual friends in the NSA. There have been some inquiries regarding your old colleagues. The Parkers."

The Old Soldier sat up straighter. "Richard and Mary Parker?"

"The same. Didn't look like much at first. A *Daily Bugle* reporter named Ben Urich pulled some strings to get copies of their personal files, then asked some questions about their activities in Prague."

"*Daily Bugle?*" The Old Soldier curled his lip at the thought of several of its more aggravating editorials. In his estimation, the rag rivalled the *Weekly World News* for yellow journalism. "Hey, doesn't their kid work there?"

"Exactly. As a photographer. Which is why I say this part of it is probably nothing. As far as I can tell, the bulk of Urich's inquiries have nothing to do with the infiltration against the Croesus operation, but focus instead on whether the Parkers ever had a baby girl named Carla May Mendelsohn. The way I analyze it, Urich's probably just being a pal, helping the kid find out if he has a long-lost sister or not. It's kind of sad, really. Almost makes me want to call up the kid and let him know."

"Yeah," the Old Soldier said. His eyes narrowed. "What else?"

"This major operation we have going down in Manhattan? It's connected to the main man behind Croesus—your old pal, Gustav Fiers."

The Old Soldier's heart thumped. "You gotta be kidding me."

"I wouldn't kid about that. It's him, all right—as nasty as

ever. And keeping up with the times in that he's finally gotten around to providing himself with a code-name. He's calling himself the Gentleman now."

His informant gave him a quick rundown of the past few weeks, covering the Sinister Six's Day of Terror, the assault on Rand-Meachum, and Spider-Man's involvement in an inter-agency operation to stop the destruction of the world economy.

The Old Soldier barely heard it. He was too busy thinking of a certain torture chamber in the hold of a certain yacht where he'd spent several days taking a tour of hell until the Parkers had come to rescue him. He had suffered greater torments in other places at other times, but not often, and he had watched other dirtbags escape without paying for their crimes but couldn't think of more than four or five whose getaways had rankled him more than this one. After years of no word, he had almost resigned himself to the belief that the old bastard must have passed away peacefully in his sleep. Under the circumstances, he wasn't sure that word of the old man's continued health qualified as good news or bad. He started to say something creative about his plans for the old man's heart, then had another thought. A disturbing one. "Aw, hell. Wait a minute. This ain't good. You mentioned the Parker kid?"

"The photographer? What about him?"

"Never mind," the Old Soldier said. "I'll be in touch."

"B-but . . . Fiers! Our situation! Don't you want to—"

"You have a big team on that already," said the Old Soldier, who was not beyond regretting a lost opportunity to go after an enemy he'd wanted for years. "Right now, I have somewhere else I've got to be!"

He hung up the phone and ran from the room.

* * *

The Gentleman had killed more men by guile and deceit than a prolific serial killer could in a lifetime, but he was not Octavius—nor was he the kind of powerhouse capable of surviving ten seconds of the Doctor's wrath. He needed an edge.

So he unstrapped himself and bolted from the cockpit, stopping at the coat closet where he'd stashed both the coat and the handgun it harbored. It was the only item of clothing in that coat closet, but he fumbled anyway as he groped through its pockets, first selecting the wrong one, then upon finding the correct pocket getting tangled up with a cloth handkerchief that insisted on interfering with his access to the weapon he needed. Even after he got his fingers around the grip, he couldn't seem to pull it from the pocket itself. The unbearable sound of metal sliding against metal, which seemed to fill the world all around him, was enough to rob him of all his strength and all his coordination. Because he knew Octavius. He knew what the man was capable of. And he knew that the handgun could not possibly be enough.

Just as he managed to pull the handgun from the coat pocket he stumbled, and knocked over the useless wolf's-head cane which he'd stowed against the wall. It fell against his knees and fell with a thud into the carpeting. He almost kicked it. Stupid old thing! What the hell use are you now?

Then he felt a draft of cold air, and he knew that he was dead.

He whirled anyway, raising the handgun, hoping for the lucky shot that would permit a stray round to get past the indestructible tentacles to a home in the Doctor's brain. Cold pincers closed around that wrist before he could even see the target. They applied not quite enough pressure to break his arm. He yowled and released the gun, which fell but did not strike the carpet. Another pair of pincers caught it before it had fallen half a meter, twirling it with as much verve as any Hollywood cowboy.

Octavius stood in the open hatchway, his grimace bearing as much fury as the storm that raged behind him. His soup-bowl bangs lay matted against his skull. His dark glasses had fogged from the passage from the storm into the warmer temperatures of the Gentleman's jet. His white suit sat wrinkled and sodden on his frame, but he was anything but comical, anything but diminished. As he stepped into the interior of the plane, pulling his tentacles in after him and using his flesh-and-blood arms to close the hatch against the elements, he was impossible to mistake as anything but a monster. Even so, his grin, as he deployed his two free tentacles to seize the squirming Gentleman by both ankles, was almost jolly. "If you think it's cold out there, you should have been at the Empire State Building. Penguins would have cried. If there's any consolation at all in the webslinger still being alive after all these years, it's in thinking how uncomfortable he must be in that glorified underwear!"

The Gentleman exploded. "Octavius! Listen to me! I—"

The tentacle holding the gun snaked around the old man's midsection, squeezing just tightly enough to cut off the air that would have permitted the sentence to continue. All the tentacles retracted, pulling the Gentleman close, allowing Octavius to taunt him from across a gulf of inches. "No," the Doctor said. "You may be allowed speech again, at some point in the limited time remaining to you, but for now I think I'll impose the disciplinary measure you placed on that unfortunate ward of yours. You are commanded to silence, except in response to direct questions. Any unauthorized words from you will result in a painful, perhaps even crippling, injury. You may nod if you understand."

The old man's eyes glistened with fear and frustration as he managed the nod.

"That's better." Octavius released the Gentleman's wrist and ankles, instead tightening the grip his remaining tentacle had around the old man's waist. Depositing the gun in his jacket pocket for safekeeping, he ambled along the row of seats and down the stairwell leading to the plane's cargo hold, his tentacles trailing the helpless, grimacing figure as he went. "You see, you made a serious mistake, you old fool. Well, actually you made a number of mistakes, which I'll be more than happy to explain to you at length, but chief among them was the fatal assumption that I was as great an idiot as my colleagues. You thought I wouldn't see your betrayal coming, or read the telltales that you, in your clumsy arrogance, provided me."

The Gentleman's eyes were mute pleas.

Octavius smiled at him as he inspected the array of treasures bundled up in the cargo hold, and the mechanism for delivering the cannister into the chute to the bomb-bay doors. His inspection was cursory, given the time pressures, but enough to determine that all was in order. "The first telltale was the way you made such a big deal about paying us in cash. That in itself might have been easy to miss. After all, we would have required cash anyway. It's a cash business, after all. But there was something about the way you kept emphasizing the word "cash," italicizing it, even—to one with ears capable of hearing the difference—mocking it. Mocking us. Add that to the way you went to so much trouble to change your own cash to other forms of wealth—typified by that shopping expedition Pity bungled—why would you take such measures if you felt that all your cash was still going to be valuable? Consider also the way you glossed over the cannister you had Pity and Electro steal: this cannister. You said you had some purpose for it that benefitted our plan. And that may have been enough for the others, but was also enough to alert me that it had to the instrument of your betrayal."

Back up the stairs, the Gentleman's helpless form bobbed along like a pet at the end of a leash. Octavius moved toward the cockpit, where he knelt prior to using one of his tentacles to pop the cover off a circuitry panel.

"But there has never been any chance of you getting away with it. I've been tracking your every movement, both by myself and with agents, since the beginnings of our association. I've known about this jet, and your stash of valuables, for almost a week. It has been fascinating to inventory the steady accumulation, and delightful to know that all of it will soon be mine. It's been equally fascinating to bleed off and test a minute sample of your catalyst, in order to determine its properties—which were just about what I'd inferred, given your mocking attitude toward cash."

The pincers pulled out a circuitry board, smashed it, then tossed it into a corner; another tentacle pulled down an overhead first aid kit, ripping off its lid to reveal, among the bandages and antiseptics, a circuit board that might have been its twin.

"My most recent stop was just last night, after taking the Oltion device to its staging point beneath the Empire State. I came out to this airport, and made a few special adjustments to your electronics, to make sure that you would not be able to take off without me in the event the webslinger or his cronies delayed this delightful meeting of ours. But those—"

Octavius inserted the replacement circuit board in the position vacated by the first.

"—are easy to fix. See? All done."

The old man imprisoned by the adamantium tentacle looked around wildly, searching for something, anything, that might rescue him from destruction. Octavius, regarding this, laughed the cruellest laugh at all. "Ahhh. You are searching for your cane. You are thinking of the fail safe beneath that ridiculous wolf's-head handle. The red button that would set my tentacles against me."

The Gentleman's eyes widened with shock until Octavius closed them with an open-handed slap.

"Oh. Please," Octavius sneered. "You're surprised I know? That, I find downright insulting. You actually believed I would have no idea that you'd made such adjustments to my cybernetics, that I would just blunder along considering myself untouchable while you rested secure in the ability to trump me at any moment."

Octavius chuckled.

"That, my elderly friend, was your most ignorant mistake. You imagined my tentacles to be mere unfeeling machines, as much without life as your limousine or your jet or any other dead weaponry. But you heard me tell you of my psychic link to these beauties! You heard me say I'm connected to them—that I know them as intimately as I feel the flesh I was born with! I felt your little improvements, your little alien presences, as soon as the tentacles were returned to me! I was able to remove them the second I was first out of your sight!"

For a moment, just a moment, an errant doubt crossed the Doctor's face.

"Of course, I still don't know what the other button does, and I'm not about to push it until I have the leisure to beat it out of you properly. But right now I don't care. Right now I'm going to give you your only chance of surviving until your natural death of old age. You may speak."

The Gentleman's voice was very frightened and very small, in the manner of a child well used to being tormented by bullies. "W-what do you want?"

"That's good. But call me sir."

"W-what do you want . . . " The old man nearly choked on the taste of the next word, but managed it. ". . . Sir?"

"Right now, since I do not know how to fly this vehicle, you will do what you were going to do anyway. You will take off, exactly as planned. You will release the Catalyst over Manhattan, exactly as planned. You will destroy the world economy, exactly as planned." The coiled tentacles gave the Gentleman a painful squeeze. "You will do all of this knowing that I will have your neck in my grip every moment . . . and that it will now be I claiming the full proceeds of our partnership. If you do everything I say, without fail, then you will be permitted to live on, as my wretched manservant, darning my socks and cooking my meals in the palace where I'll live in comfort as I arrange for the next phase in my conquest of the world."

Octavius didn't ask for the Gentleman's agreement. There was no point in asking. He just uncoiled his tentacles and let the trembling, ancient figure slip from his grip and onto the floor. He stood there, grinning the grin of the playground bully, as the Gentleman rose to his feet, considered saying something, remembered with painful clarity the cruel Doctor's warning about the consequences of unbidden speech, and moved on shaky legs to the pilot's seat. The Gentleman's hands shook so hard by now that buckling the straps was almost beyond him.

"Are we in position for take off?" Octavius asked.

Did Octavius really not know? Or was it the groundwork for a trap?

The old man made his decision in a moment. "N-no. We

have to taxi to the other end of the runway. In these conditions, we have to take off to the south. Over the water ... th-then turn around for the assault on Manhattan ... "

"Get to it, then."

The Gentleman resumed his taxi. The jet moved slowly up the length of the runway, taking at a crawl the distance that he had planned only minutes before to travel at takeoff speeds. The view beyond the windshield was pure white-out; this plane could take off in that muck, but for the old man feeling the weight of adamantium pincers at the base of his neck, it was a stark reminder that he had no allies, no rescuers, no master plan still at work: just this weak delaying tactic that might or might not provide him with the opportunity he needed to come up with an idea.

Octavius kept up his rant as they went, delivering many happy variations on the theme of his own unparalleled greatness and the foolishness of anybody stupid enough to oppose him. The words were familiar, of course; they would have to be, since Octavius shouted many like them even when he thought he was alone. But they had never felt so true to the schemer at the wheel, as they did now when he was denied even the right to speak up in his own defense.

The great, liberating brainstorm did not come. The Transtar reached the end of the runway. It turned in a half-circle and faced the road it had just travelled: one that seemed no more promising now than it had a second before. The radio, with volume set to zero, flared as the desperate controllers in the Tower tried to ask the suicidal moron in the Transtar just what the hell he thought he was doing.

The pincers tightened just enough to establish that if Octavius wanted they could tighten still more and snap the unwilling pilot's neck. "No more delays. Take off. Now."

No choice.

The Transstar began speeding down the runway, turning the chaotic windswept snow into streaks of brilliant light. The plane rumbled and roared with the pent-up energy of a bird eager for the skies.

And then a black slab rose from the tarmac up ahead, swallowing the earth, swallowing the runway, swallowing even the running lights of the jet. It extended for what seemed to be miles in every direction, like a coming attraction for the darkness at the end of the world.

It was too late to stop. Just as the jet's wheels left the ground, the old man quailed at the solid wall up ahead and forgot the silence that had been demanded of him: "W-we're going to crash!"

"No, we're not," Octavius said. His voice was jaunty, his tone delighted. "It's just that little tart of yours, coming to the rescue too late.—I wonder if that's means the wall-crawler's dead?"

CHAPTER FIFTEEN

Bucking tradition, the good guys did not arrive in the nick of time.

Although SAFE's forces had already been at the airfield for several minutes by this point, they were by all meaningful standards too late. Deploying some personnel to speak to the skeleton staff of controllers in the tower, others to interface with airfield security, and still others to search the hangars, the support buildings, and the large number of small aircraft which had been parked outside in the storm, they did everything right but nevertheless failed to see what they'd come to find.

It wasn't their fault, really. The limited visibility, and the considerable odds against any airplane actually attempting to take off in this weather, had delayed their discovery of the lone jet taxiing for a takeoff on a runway already rated closed because of snow conditions. Given another sixty seconds to play with, they may have had time to make the connection.

But by the time the wall-crawler's spider-sense warned

him of imminent danger, and SAFE's receivers picked up the Tower warning any other traffic in the area of an unauthorized takeoff in progress, the Transtar was already rocketing down the runway at full speed.

Colonel Morgan's aircar, which was supervising the search from the air, came the closest to providing some kind of adequate response. Palminetti flew into the jet's path, hoping to discourage a takeoff. Pity cast a zone of darkness rising six stories from the tarmac. Morgan drew his blaster and fired at the oncoming plane. Saberstein yowled and gripped the nearest solid object for protection. Spider-Man tensed, readying a hopeless last-minute leap which might have smeared him as flat as a highway bug caught on a SUV windshield.

It was all for naught. The jet took off, passing so close over the aircar that the smaller vehicle spun in its slipstream. The inertial dampeners which normally provided both passengers and crew with some protection against turbulence and acceleration kept those aboard from being flung to the four winds, but not by much. Saberstein slipped and collided with Morgan, who slammed against a bulkhead and almost tumbled over the side. Pity grabbed the Colonel's arm and pulled him back inside the aircar. Spider-Man was forced to leap over her to grab Saberstein.

By the time Palminetti was able to bring the aircar under control, the jet was several miles south.

Spider-Man released Saberstein, who fell, gasping, to the aircar deck. "Well. That was interesting. Something tells me that wasn't a special charter to Club Med Jamaica."

Saberstein quailed. "R-remind me not to do that again."

Colonel Morgan tore himself loose of Pity's grip, cast her the kind of appraising glance that pretended it was possible to understand her, then rushed to Palminetti's side. "Give me good news, Vince."

The quadriplegic crisis analyst, immobile in his command seat, had survived the turbulence with more equanimity than any of his able-bodied colleagues. He looked green, but there was no sign of any discomfort in his voice: "I'm not sure I have any."

"Give me what you have."

"All right. We have at best a two percent chance that's not our boy."

"Who else could it be?" Spider-Man wondered.

"Any number of people, webhead. Drug dealers fleeing an imagined bust. Smugglers carrying contraband. Even a garden variety idiot behind the wheel, taking off out of sheer misplaced machismo—airline horror stories are full of them. But the coincidence would be pretty unlikely. It's almost certainly him."

"Almost certainly's not good enough," Morgan said.

"It's as good as we're likely to get, Colonel. I don't see him answering a demand to identify himself."

Morgan wiped blood from the lips from the back of his hand. "All right. So what else is wrong?"

"Our maximum airspeed," Palminetti said. "It's not quite up to his. If we could find some way to intercept, I might be able to match velocities long enough to enable a midair transfer—but catching up with him is not a possibility."

"Can we field a shootdown solution?"

Palminetti spoke with the haste of a man who dared not allow himself a pause for breath. "We have missiles, sure—but if that is the right plane, a crash would release the Catalyst over much of Long Island."

"Better than over Manhattan."

"Still a disaster," said Palminetti. "Especially if it's not the right plane."

The still-hyperventilating Saberstein pulled himself to his

knees, wiped his brow, and managed a hoarse: "Have you noticed it's headed the wrong way for an attack on Manhattan?"

The moment of silence that followed was a measure of how disoriented the tumbling of the aircar had left them; they normally might have been expected to pick that up first thing. Morgan spared Saberstein a glance, then turned back to Palminetti. "Talk to me."

Palminetti checked his instruments. "They're banking. Sharp turn to the west. Not as sharp as they could; they must be taking it easy because of the weather. They'll be headed north in a minute—and flying right past us again."

"With luck not into us," Saberstein said.

Morgan ignored him. "Can we intercept?"

"Plotting their course . . ." Palminetti seemed to do it in his head. "All right. If we hustle, ninety seconds. I'll just have to compensate for the slipstream."

"Go for it," Morgan said.

As Palminetti laid in a course, and the aircar veered off to the west to make one of the most important rendezvouses in SAFE history, Morgan turned to the super hero among his passenger list. "Spider-Man. Can you make it to the jet?"

"I can't give you exact odds like Palminetti would. I left my calculator in my other tights."

"Tough. With these stakes I can't make do with just doing your best. If you can't assure me with absolute certainty that you'll make it over, we'll have to try for a shootdown. Or worse, a ramming. No time to argue. Can you make the transfer?"

Spider-Man didn't hesitate. "Yes, Colonel. I can."

They had both forgotten about Pity, who chose that moment to advance to Spider-Man's side and thump herself on the chest. Her beseeching eyes presented as eloquent an argument as any possible words. But both Morgan and Spider-Man took this offer about as well as they would have taken a meal of hot sand—Morgan because he still couldn't afford to trust her, Spider-Man because he didn't trust the odds of keeping her from harm.

Palminetti said, "Sixty seconds."

Morgan said, "No way. She's a Federal Prisoner and she just wants to get back to the Gentleman so she can take his orders again."

Pity thumped her chest again, this time twice, her eyes imploring.

"You may be right, Colonel. Unfortunately, I don't think she and I can fight it out now. There's not enough time for one of us to win. If she wants to come—I'll have to let her."

The running lights of the fugitive jet were already visible through the storm.

Palminetti said, "Thirty seconds."

The aircar started to shake.

Morgan moved a fraction of an inch closer to the web-slinger. "And when she turns on you, out there? Are you prepared to save Manhattan by any means necessary?"

Spider-Man knew what the SAFE leader was really asking: whether he could kill Pity in self-defense. He also noted that Morgan had said "when," not "if."

Provided more time, he might have given Morgan the answer that question deserved. He might have said that though he'd given in to rage, even murderous rage, once or twice (that he had, in fact, been driven so close to the edge by outrageous provocations that only luck and conscience had prevented him from ridding the world of people like Octavius, Norman Osborn, and a certain two-bit burglar with his own hands), he had never been able to rationalize murder as an option. Not under any circumstances. He had always fought for life, because he passionately believed in life even for those who would have taken his without a second thought.

He might have said all that, if he'd had the time.

But the runaway jet was almost upon them. It was going to pass less than twenty feet above their heads. Palminetti was already giving the aircar the burst of speed to match velocities for the few seconds Spider-Man and Pity would need to transfer from one vehicle to another. Any further talk, and the opportunity would be gone.

"Matching velocities," Palminetti said. "Ten seconds, maybe less."

Spider-Man curled an arm around Pity's waist and said the only thing he had time to say: "Can't chat, Colonel! You know how it is when you have a plane to catch!"

They leaped together, just as a wall of silvery metal passed directly above them.

For the three men remaining aboard the aircar, the departure of the two paranormals was like a hammer's blow. Spider-Man and Pity pushed off with so much force that the recoil made their own vehicle drop thirty feet; the temporary loss of control, combined with the struggle to counteract the turbulence surrounding the jet, almost sent the aircar into another tailspin.

This time Saberstein was able to fight off the temptation to yelp. He just held on with as much strength as his fingers could summon as the runaway jet disappeared into the howling storm, now carrying a pair of fragile stowaways on its undercarriage.

By then his ears were ringing so much he almost didn't pick out the lower roar of Colonel Sean Morgan's voice, shouting at him.

"What!?!" Saberstein cried back.

The first few words of Morgan's question disappeared behind the ringing in Saberstein's ears, but he caught the rest of it. ". . . on your observations, do you think she'll turn on him?"

Saberstein wanted to believe that Spider-Man had gotten through to her, but was forced to give the honest answer. "It can go either way, Colonel! Depends on what they find up there!"

"And who!" Palminetti said.

Morgan whirled. "What?"

"Just got word from one of the ground teams. We have a new development. . . ."

It was one thing to cling to the side of a building in inclement weather.

It was another to hold on to the underbelly of a massive runaway jet well on its way to breaking the sound barrier during the storm of the century. This was not an experience Spider-Man would have recommended to anybody, even J. Jonah Jameson.

The wind battered him and Pity like a succession of punches, making both their costumes and the flesh beneath them ripple like pondwater. Worst of all was the snow itself. They were fortunate enough not to have to contend with hail, which at this velocity would have ripped through their flesh like machine-gun fire. But the snow was itself half-frozen and hard as grit, which made the experience a lot like like being sandblasted.

Making headway against that wind was next to impossible. Making headway while a woman who had tried to kill him less than an hour ago brought up the rear was impossible times ten. Spider-Man's fear for that woman's safety complicated things still further: he kept wanting to turn around to make sure that she was still holding on.

She was in his league. Better than him in some ways. He had to remember that and can the protective brother act for now.

He grabbed the wing, and held on as a wind-shear dropped the jet twenty meters and left his legs flapping in the slipstream like banners. Another dip and he was almost torn free. Pity, pulling herself up onto the same wing, seemed to suffer no such difficulty. Spider-Man scrambled forward, planted the adhesive soles of his feet against the wing surface, and resisted the temptation to freeze in place out of craving for some imagined relative safety.

(Trade secret: sometimes this stuff was scary.)

The wind chill factor ripped at his body heat. Now, from the way his uniform was flapping, he found himself in imminent danger of having his pants peeled off by the storm. He grimaced. Please, not that. Being Spider-Man hadn't been the most dignified hobby in the world, but that would have been a new low.

Pity turned toward him, her short-cropped hair whipping her face like a thousand demons. Her eyes were mere slits shut against the wind. Her scarred cheeks were landscapes rippling from the acceleration. She mouthed something, but Spider-Man couldn't tell whether she was talking or just making lip movements.

For one nervous instant he remembered that she might be his sister, and that whether she was or not, they were both about to face the man who had stolen so much from them both. It occurred to him that if he were another man, he might have craved payback for what that monster had taken; maybe, if circumstances had been different, he would have had time to give that urge free reign. Right now, simple payback no longer entered into his thinking at all. The Gentleman had killed his parents. And others. The Gentleman had wreaked hell with his life. And others. The Gentleman owed him answers. And more. But all of that could be settled later. It was what the Gentleman wanted to do now that kept him going today.

Hmmm. I wear tights and I play super hero.

But maybe that's a sign of growing up.

He scrambled forward, closer to the main body of the jet. A line of brightly-lit passenger windows gave the air around them an eerie flickering glow. He popped his head up and saw neither William Shatner nor John Lithgow peering out at him in terror, but instead a double row of ordinary seats, all unoccupied. Better yet, this section of fusilage bore the seams of an emergency exit.

They weren't high enough to worry about explosive decompression, but pressure equalization was still going to make the air blow out out of there with a velocity they most assuredly did not need. He pressed his fingertips against the fusilage on either side of that door, and tapped both palms to shoot weblines at point-blank range. These he spun out to lengths of five feet apiece, grabbing one while directing Pity to grab the other. She held on tight and waited.

He ripped the door loose.

The wind from the jet's interior tore the door from his hands and hurled it away into the sky before he could stop it: another potential burr in his conscience, if it happened to land on anybody's head. The jet lurched and dipped, almost but not quite bucking the two uninvited passengers into open space. Spider-Man's face and chest stung as dozens of tiny objects, from pens and pencils to loose pillows, hurtled from the plane and pelted him before disappearing into the storm. Pity grabbed him, adding her strength to his as they both leaped into the plane's interior.

The wind was still deafening inside, but at least Spider-Man could hear himself think. At least, he could hear himself mutter, "That does it. Next time I book tickets with a reputable agency!"

Pity was already on the ceiling and racing toward the cockpit. Spider-Man took the center aisle in two leaps. It wasn't a failure to feel that telltale jolt from his spider-sense, but he still didn't have time for caution.

The cockpit door flew off its hinges with a force that sent it barrelling down the center aisle. Spider-Man hopped over it before it could flatten him, heard it smash with shattering force against something aft. The jet dipped again, for the moment making everything weightless. Four angry tentacles shot from the cockpit, tearing one of the seats from its moorings before hurling it at Pity. She batted it aside with a slap of her hand and waited as Dr. Octavius emerged from the cockpit.

The Doctor's gaze flickered from one enemy to the other. "Pity. Spider-Man. Working together now. How cozy."

Spider-Man advanced down the center aisle. "Yeah, well . . . it's a real greeting card moment, all right."

An adamantium tentacle lashed out with the speed of thought, smashing the seat against the bulkhead where Pity had been. By then she was no longer there. She grabbed the indestructible tentacle with both hands and shimmied along its length in a rapid crawl that almost brought her within striking distance of the man it protected. Another tentacle looped around to bat her away. Pity rode out the worst of the blow, surviving an impact capable of turning a brick wall to dust.

Even as Pity slammed into the nearest intact row of seats, Spider-Man dodged another pair of tentacles so intent on tearing him from limb that his several seconds of leaping up and out of their way bore a lot in common with the act of jumping rope. He fired a webline at Ock's glasses, a manuever which had often proven helpful by temporarily blinding the nearsighted Doctor. It didn't work today. Though his webbing splattered the lenses nicely, the fluid just dripped off, leaving the villain's vision as unoccluded as it had been a moment before.

"Have you forgotten, webslinger? The improvements I made in my eyewear?"

Spider-Man dodged another grasping tentacle. "Told you I wasn't impressed with that, Ock! You want to get my attention, you should invest in a pair of more tasteful frames!"

The tentacles were now a quartet of angry snakes, moving so quickly they reduced the cabin to an adamantium-gray blur. Spider-Man was forced further and further aft as the flesh-and-blood Octavius advanced down the center aisle on foot.

"Have you also forgotten the extreme advantage you suffer fighting me in close quarters? You cannot outmanuever me here, Spider-Man! I will smash you as easily as I smashed that silent trollop!"

Spider-Man grabbed two of the tentacles by their tips as they went for his heart. It required all the strength he had just to prevent them from punching through his ribs. He couldn't prevent them from ripping free of his grip and making another attempt.

The problem here was that though Ock's limbs lost some power at full extension, they were still many times stronger than the webslinger had ever been—and the farther he was driven back, the sooner he would have to deal with them at close range.

Pity lurched to her feet and went for Octavius. Bad move. One tentacle, moving independently of the others, batted her aside, and flipped her battered form toward the front of the plane. She smashed hard against the galley shelves. Octavius would have had no difficulty dispatching that same tentacle to finish her off, but he seemed to regard her as, at most, an annoyance: it was Spider-Man, the bane of his criminal career, who he wanted to dismember first.

Misrepresenting the history he and the webslinger shared, Octavius crowed: "I have smashed you a hundred times, Spider-Man! I have crushed you and defeated you and still you keep coming back to bedevil me! Why?"

Evading a blow that tore a gash in the panelling of the jet's private lounge, Spider-Man said: "I thought you were like the airlines, Ockie! I wanted to qualify for frequent smashing miles!"

"I will be happy indeed to experience the last of your witless jests!"

That's when gravity went berserk.

Both Spider-Man and Octavius were hurled off the floor and against the curved ceiling. Spider-Man managed to flip and hit that surface feet-first, while Octavius banged his head and fell back to the floor in a tangle of writhing metallic limbs. Seats smashed to pieces as his tentacles whirled about in random panic. Spider-Man, sensing the Doctor's moment of weakness, hurtled toward the man at the center of the cybernetic nightmare, hoping to get there before Ock recovered enough to protect himself again. But though he managed to strike the fallen villain a glancing blow across the jaw, a tentacle was still able to lash out and send him flying against the same forward galley where Pity had landed a few seconds earlier.

Spider-Man would have hit the wall, but then gravity went berserk again and the floor came up to meet him. Everything and everybody not secured in place tumbled toward the aft section. For one dizzying instant the aircraft seemed almost vertical. Spider-Man's adhesive hands and feet weren't at their best gripping carpet, but they kept him from tumbling down a cabin that had become a vertiginous well. He held on for all he was worth as his face and arms stung from the impact of dozens of plastic cups and ceramic plates that peppered him upon spilling en masse from the battered galley. Just above him, Pity gasped as the plane's change in orientation left her dangling from a wall that had just become the equivalent of a ceiling. Just below him, Octavius cursed as he used his tentacles to brace himself, and cursed again as the same litter that had pelted Spider-Man now reversed direction to hail against his face and upper arms.

When gravity went berserk a third time, the result of the unseen pilot taking the jet into a sudden dive, the same litter pelted all three unwilling passengers on this roller coaster from the opposite direction.

Spider-Man's SAFE communicator crackled again. Palminetti said: "Spider-Man! Your flight has become very erratic! Please advise!"

A tentacle groped for Spider-Man's ankle. He kicked it aside and sent back the response: "You know, you guys have a real knack for coming up with great moments to ask for updates!"

"What's happening?"

"I don't know! The pilot's having some kind of conniption fit!"

"You're over Manhattan now, webhead! Another dive like that and you're going to knock a hole through a building!"

Spider-Man looked "down" and saw Doctor Octopus advancing toward him again, pulling himself forward with two tentacles while groping for the webslinger with a third.

Shouting "Cowabunga!", a word that had accompanied another attack on Octavius one week earlier, Spider-Man let himself drop. He grunted in pain as one of the groping tentacles clipped his side, but felt a dark satisfaction as his plunge delivered a devastating kick to Ock's head.

A tentacle whipped around and seized Spider-Man by the arm, ripping him away from the Doctor's fragile human body. Its pincer clamped onto the webslinger's flesh so tightly that Spider-Man had to give up some skin and muscle in order to tear himself free. Spider-Man leaped to the ceiling, then felt another rush of vertigo as the jet banked to the east, turning the cabin floor on edge again.

"That senile old fool!" Octavius grated. The ghost of a lisp in his speech testified to the damage Spider-Man's last impact must have done to his jaw. "Don't you see what he's doing, arachnid?"

"From the way he's flying, he must have spilled hot coffee in his lap!"

"No!" Octavius cried. "He knows I'm the greater threat to him, and he's hoping these manuevers will throw me off balance long enough to permit his rescue at the hands of you and that idiot girl!"

"Not a bad idea, Ockie! He might have done even better, scheduling something bad for the in-flight movie! I hear ARMAGEDDON sucks!"

Octavius ignored him. "It was my own fault for being generous enough to offer him a chance at life! But he will learn the cost of trying to betray me again—"

As the jet levelled off one more time, Octavius advanced to within a few yards of his longtime enemy. But he didn't press the attack as zealously as he might have had this battle been taking place at sea level. Instead, he used two of his tentacles to anchor himself against the walls, and a third waving in circles before him to guard against another attack. The fourth would have been sufficient to batter Spider-Man to hell and back. But it had another target. As it whipped past Spider-Man, it didn't engage the webslinger's spider-sense at all; it just went straight for the cockpit door and ripped it from its hinges. A familiar voice, the Gentleman's, cried out as Ock's tentacle lanced through the doorway, the nature of that scream switching from terror to agony in mid-breath.

Octavius laughed. "Have I gotten your attention, old man? Turn on the autopilot now! You and I have matters to discuss!"

An outraged Pity hurled herself at Octavius. The tentacle guarding him darted toward her with a force that might have torn a crater in her chest. Spider-Man had less than a heartbeat to decide whether to take advantage of Ock's distraction and go after him, or go instead to Pity's aid. He leaped up and seized the attacking tentacle with both hands, wrestling it away from Pity. He wouldn't have been able to hold it for more or a second or two, with only his own strength to work with, but then Pity took his cue and grabbed the same tentacle from the other side.

Spider-Man and Pity stood together, trembling with effort, dedicating everything they had to holding this one tentacle motionless. The tentacle bucked and twisted. The deadly pincers at its tip clicked open and shut like piranha jaws, waiting for their opportunity to rip life from flesh, denied if only for this moment the mobility they needed to claim that dark pleasure.

Both Spider-Man and Pity realized that this was a wasted tactic. Now that they had the tentacle, there was nothing they could do with it. They both let go simultaneously, allowing the tentacle to withdraw, staring it down as it once

SPIDER-MAN

again became a spinning shield separating them from Octavius.

"I will kill you both in a moment," Octavius told them, as if in apology for the delay. "Right now I have somebody else to attend to."

The tentacle that had invaded the cockpit came out wrapped around a writhing old man.

There was no arrogance in the Gentleman's demeanor now. His face was twisted in agony, his legs were kicking not so much in struggle as in helpless spasm. His hands, clawing at nothing beneath the girdled tentacle, were white and fleshy . . . not an old man's hands at all.

Pity might have been expected to leap to her master's aid, but she didn't. She just stood stock-still, twitching as warring impulses fought for supremacy inside her. She made no move to defend herself when one of Ock's tentacles came for her again. Spider-Man shoved her out of the way, crying out in pain as the sharp edge of one pincer drew a bloody line across his back. The webslinger moved quickly, certain that Octavius would press his advantage with another attack, but no. Evidently, the Doctor was serious about wanting to take care of the Gentleman first.

Given his good reasons for hating Gustav Fiers, Spider-Man almost didn't believe he heard the next words coming from his own mouth. "He's just a helpless old man, Ock! Leave him alone and come for me!"

Octavius laughed. "I don't intend to kill him, Spider-Man! I need his piloting skills! But he still needs reminding who his master is, and he has ears and several fingers he can do without . . . "

Fingers, Spider-Man thought.

Hands . . .

The tentacle that had attacked Pity twice now went for

the immobilized Gentleman. Pity darted forward and placed herself between it and the man who had tortured her all her life, grabbing hold with both arms, managing by sheer force of determination to hold it in place even as the strain of that effort seemed about to tear her apart.

Behind her, the Gentleman watched with eyes gone very wide and very round.

Spider-Man, standing as still as any disinterested spectator, despite the additional two tentacles that now undulated toward him like angry cobras, hooted as the last connection clicked into place. That hand . . .

He whirled, sprayed a webline that miraculously penetrated all of Ock's defenses to slam against the Doctor's forehead, and shouted: "Pity! Let me worry about the old man! He's none of your business! Just use your darkness to blind Ock!"

Confused, Pity took a single stumbling step backward as the tentacle she wrestled forced itself closer and closer to the whimpering old man behind her. Its pincers still snapped hungrily. . . .

Spider-Man somersaulted over and around and above and under Ock's remaining two tentacles, fighting his way to the man who commanded them. "Don't you get it? We worried so much about Laughing Boy here that we completely failed to notice somebody *else* who went AWOL today!" He managed to tag Octavius with a punch not nearly direct enough to matter. "Somebody who's always been much easier to miss in a crowd!"

The words burned like a lit fuse.

Pity got it first. She released the tentacle she'd been wrestling, raced it to the side of the old man it sought, and slapped that imprisoned figure across the face with the flat of one hand.

The Doctor got it too. He began to shout something about the cost of betrayal. But then a sphere of darkness, cast by Pity, materialized over the top half of his head, blinding him much as shots of Spider-Man's webbing had, so many times in the past.

A tentacle slammed Spider-Man against the fusilage.

As for the old man the Doctor held in his coils, who was even now blacking out from the pressure—

—well, he wasn't old at all.

Nor was he the owner of this jet, or the mastermind behind an attack on Manhattan.

He was just, as Spider-Man had figured out, a nobody named Anatoly Smerdyakov. The Chameleon.

Whose face was now nothing more than a smooth white mask.

Several minutes earlier, just after Pity and Spider-Man managed their midair transfer:

The SAFE agents who had fanned out among the support buildings of the airfield, before the jet's getaway, were still continuing their search of the grounds. Few expected to find anything under the circumstances, but there was still no confirmation that either the Gentleman or his Catalyst were aboard that plane.

Dr. George Williams was warming a seat in an aircar hovering outside Hangar E. It galled him to be sidelined like this. He ached to participate in the search himself, but he was an old man, with one leg stiffened by a past stroke; he knew he would only slow down the younger and more able-bodied agents of SAFE. Besides, much as it tormented him to think so, the ground search was probably a waste of time at this point. The real fight was in the air, and it would probably end with his lifelong enemy eluding him once again.

Then the two agents who had rushed to check out Hangar E came running out. One, Agent Annanayo, ran directly to him and said: "Sir! What kind of Doctor are you, exactly?"

Williams blinked. "Economics." He had gotten his doctorate in 1934, before moving on to the United States Treasury.

"Dammit," Annanayo said.

Williams studied her face, uncomprehending. Why would she want to know about his Doctorate?

And then, all of a sudden, he knew.

CHAPTER SIXTEEN

Gustav Fiers, aka the Gentleman, lay sprawled on hard concrete, choking on his own life blood.

It was odd indeed, that taste.

Not just in the sense that it seemed fouler and harsher than the miniscule previous tastes he'd experienced under more routine circumstances like dental appointments and cut fingertips; that had been as coppery as people said. But this was something else. It was thick and sickening, flavored with everything else that had been shattered inside him. Whatever the precise ingredients of that grisly cocktail might have been, it was impossible to taste it without knowing that no other flavor . . . not cognac, not gourmet food, and not a single unobstructed breath . . . would ever pass his lips again.

The surprise was that the taste, like his life, continued to linger.

He had been expecting to die, or at least to pass out, for several minutes now, but some cruel providence, (helped along, perhaps, by the preservative qualities of the freezing temperature inside the hangar), had slowed his bleeding, delayed his death, and tethered him, unwilling, to this world that would never again have cruel pleasures to offer him.

For all his supposed superiority, Fiers did all the mundane things dying people are supposed to do. He denied that this was happening to him. He fantasized that medical authorities might come in time to save him. He raged at the unfairness of it all. He relived his entire rapacious existence, over and over, lingering at the high points. His escapes from the *Titanic*, the *Hindenburg*, the Cocoanut Grove, and the *Andrea Doria*. His childhood joy at sitting in the automobile his father's business associate Professor Fate had used to win the race around the world. His early infatuation with a lady opium smuggler in China. His wry amusement at watching the inept spy ring in which he had just wisely divested all interest fall to pieces at the hands of a nobody ad exec named Thornhill. He recalled his investments in AIM, in HYDRA, in certain Presidential candidates and in corrupt regimes from Rumania to Zaire. He swelled with pride, relived his successes a thousand times... and then found himself back where he had started. Here. Gasping, dying, despairing, marinating in a puddle of his own blood as he tried not to think of how foolishly he'd allowed himself to be betrayed.

One sequence of events insisted on playing itself out again and again. He remembered his annoyance at the chauffeur, Serge. His plan to murder Serge out of annoyance at the man's incompetence. Serge as dull and unsuspecting as any other beef being led up to ramp to the slaughterhouse. Then Serge's face turning soft, rearranging, the previously convincing veneer of flesh turning smooth and plastic and inhuman. Smerdyakov standing revealed, mad triumph shining behind the two narrow slits in his mask. Smerdyakov then changing again, turning into Fiers himself this time: the last step in his own master plan to claim all of this operation's proceeds as his own.

The Gentleman remembered thinking, *But I'm superior* . . .

Then the mask-faced reprobate had gunned him down, relieved him of all the valuables on his person, stolen the wolf's-head cane so crucial to his revenge on the Parker brat, and left him to die like any old man mugged for pennies on the street.

The confusion tormented Fiers more than the pain. How had it happened? How had he not recognized that chauffeur, Serge, as the Chameleon in disguise? Hadn't he always been able to see through that idiot's disguises before? Hadn't it always been easy for him? Hadn't he always been so impressed with his own perspicacity?

Could it be—this part being the most unbearable—that the Chameleon had been planning this for years? Had in fact been deliberately allowing Fiers to see through all those other masks, all those other times, as a way of rendering Fiers too complacent to anticipate the deathblow the Chameleon had always intended to inflict at the moment of greatest possible profit?

The Gentleman tried to find satisfaction in the knowledge that Smerdyakov couldn't know just how valuable a treasure that wolf's-head cane was. But it was small comfort. Because he'd still been beaten. He'd still been humiliated. He'd still been murdered . . . even if he was not quite dead yet.

He barely registered the pair of SAFE agents who found him, examined him, then ran out, calling for a medical assistance. They had no hope to offer him.

He did come back to life, a little, when he saw another

wasted, grim-faced old man standing above him, leaning on a cane of his own. The personification of Death? Or Smerdyakov, come back to torture him some more?

The old man said, "The youngsters have gone to summon paramedics for you. But I don't believe it will do you any good. You're dying."

The Gentleman grimaced with impatience. He knew he was dying. He didn't need the obvious underlined for him. He managed a word: ". . . who . . . ?"

The old man said, "I'm Doctor George Williams. Remember me?"

The Gentleman did, if only vaguely. He had, after all, had so many enemies. This one had been an ambitious young treasury agent, from half a century ago. Fiers had escaped him twice, once in Lakehurst during the *Hindenburg* affair, and later in Casablanca during the much more important incident that involved Captain America and the Invaders. He remembered holding Williams personally responsible for his losses, and swearing to teach the man a lesson for his effrontery.

The Gentleman should have been able to remember what happened next, but his thoughts seemed to be so unclear. . . .

Then it came back to him, in a moment of painful clarity.

The pretty young woman Williams had loved.

The honeymoon night. The bomb in the hotel room.

The congratulatory telegram, timed to arrive immediately after the lovely lady's demise.

It had all been so delicious.

The Gentleman could only be grateful for the opportunity to leave this life on a note of triumph. "Yes . . . I remember you . . . and I still won . . . you still wasted . . . your entire life . . . tracking me down . . . I still . . . lived a . . . long life . . . revelling in my . . . wealth . . ."

Williams tapped the concrete floor with the tip of his cane. "And just how much wealth do you have left now, Gustav?"

For a moment the Gentleman didn't understand the question. Then the full horror of it hit him. He had come to America with his fortune a fraction of what it had once been. It had still been a fortune, but he had spent it all paying the Six and buying his treasures. There had been several thousand dollars in his wallet, but the Chameleon had stolen that, and his ring, and his watch, and his wolf's-head walking stick, and flown away with it. Everything, from pocket change to art treasures, was on its way to Europe.

The Gentleman had nothing left.

"No," he whispered. "No. I will not . . . die a . . . pauper! Not . . . penniless!"

The other old man's lips curled. "Far be it from me to deprive you of something obviously so valuable to you."

He removed an object from his pocket. Something made out of copper.

Something he held up to the light so the Gentleman could recognize it.

A penny.

Then he hobbled to the other end of the hangar, and placed it flat on the filthy concrete.

Then Williams turned, flashing a grin as cruel as the Gentleman's own. He spoke in a whisper, but his voice carried: "If you try hard enough . . . you might be able to reach it before blood loss takes you the rest of the way to hell."

The Gentleman would have screamed, but he had no breath for screaming. He would have protested, but he had no strength for protests. All he had was his will, and his empty pockets.

Williams returned to the storm, and the Gentleman began to crawl.

It was high above Manhattan that the battle reached its final, and most deadly, stage.

Though the Doctor had been blinded by the zone of darkness Pity had materialized around his head, that just rendered him more dangerous by robbing him of his finesse in a small enclosed space. No longer did he hold himself in check to avoid damaging the aircraft. Instead, he was so overcome with rage at his teammate's betrayal and so threatened by the temporary loss of his eyesight that he made one of the worst mistakes of his life.

He didn't release the Chameleon from his grip, as that traitor had not yet paid the price for betraying him. But he did strike blindly, thrashing his tentacles at the darkness before him, hearing from the oofs and grunts of pain the little indications that he had found the enemies who were hiding from him. He grabbed a leaping body, slammed it against the cabin ceiling, felt a rush as another enemy leaped past him without connecting. He couldn't tell which enemy was Spider-Man and which one was Pity, but he didn't care. He struck out, missed, punched a hole in the fusilage, felt the jet lurch from the fresh assault on its structural integrity, then withdrew that tentacle and groped for the enemy still free while still slamming the enemy he had against the ceiling.

He heard a rustle above him and struck out. Metal screamed. He felt the floor of the cabin fall away beneath him.

The darkness vanished just as he looked up and saw a great gaping hole in the cabin above him: the crater left behind when a section of fusilage tore itself free. He registered the dirty gray sky above him, spared a moment for academic speculation about just how long even the Gentleman's customized jet could stay in the air after suffering such damage—then felt the result of the crosswind created between the open hatchway and the hole in the ceiling. As the jet plunged, his feet rose off the cabin floor. The wind caught him and hurled him skyward even as he rushed to save himself.

The last thing he saw inside the plane was Pity, racing to the cockpit to seize the controls. He realized it was Spider-Man and the Chameleon who he held.

Then: open air.

He might have tumbled away and been doomed. But he was Doctor Octopus, and he would not go gently into that good night. Instead, he reacted with the speed of firing neurons, abandoning both Spider-Man and the Chameleon to the raging winds and directing all four tentacles to seek a grip on the jet now receding below him. He almost didn't make it. Another nanosecond and he would have been lost to gravity. But the pincers at the end of one tentacle managed to grasp the edge of the ragged hole in the fusilage, anchoring him to the plane just in time for the jerk of arrested momentum to crack three of his ribs.

The wind, whipping him in the face, was enough to take his breath away. So was the cold. He may have been the next best thing to superhuman, once his tentacles were considered—but as a man he was a very fragile, very vulnerable human being, who could not survive more than a few seconds of this. He moaned, looked down, cried out in rage at the sight of one hated enemy, Spider-Man, clinging to the fusilage with another hated enemy, the Chameleon, clutched under one arm.

Doctor Octopus wondered whether it was more important right now to get back inside or devote the work of one moment to giving those two annoyances what they deserved.

He did not have time to make the decision before it was taken out of his hands.

Spider-Man's midair catch of the Chameleon had been neat enough to impress even him. But his quick leap back to the plane had been a lot like running headfirst into a brick wall.

The exterior of the plane, slick and slippery from the storm, hadn't wanted to cooperate with his adhesive abilities, either. He'd slid almost the entire length of the plane, burdened by the Chameleon's dead weight, before cementing his grip and starting to climb forward again. It took all his strength to manage it against the wind, and he knew it might not be enough. Smerdyakov was already in bad shape from the abuse he'd received from Ock, and wasn't going to be able to take more than a few seconds of these wind-tunnel conditions before shock or hypothermia proved too much for him.

Unfortunately, Octavius remained between them and even relative safety.

Clinging to the edge of the breach by the pincers of a single tentacle, Ock wasn't in all that good shape himself. His other three tentacles whipped about uncontrollably, controlled as much by the wind as by the confusion of a man too disoriented to know which way was up. The flesh-and-blood figure at the center of those flailing metal snakes shouted something that the wind whipped away. It might have been a threat, or even a cry for help, but he too was only human and this was not a place hospitable to the words of real humans.

Maybe Octavius was actually responsible for the trajectory of the single tentacle that seemed about to strike at

Spider-Man. Maybe the threatening move was just a random twitch directed by a mind in too much distress to plan an attack that deliberate. Either way, the blow never struck home. The section of fusilage Octavius clung to chose that moment to tear loose, abandoning him to the howling wind.

Spider-Man ducked, using a hand against the back of the Chameleon's head to make the master of disguise kiss metal. A knot of churning tentacles with a screaming man at their center whipped by only a few inches over their heads. Spider-Man turned his head to follow Ock's unwilling flight and caught a nanosecond glimpse of a terrified man flailing at the center of what looked like a nest of angry snakes. Then Ock slammed into the tail assembly with a painful whang. A section of stabilizer wing snapped loose and followed the writhing eight-limbed man into the storm.

Spider-Man had never been one to wish death on anybody, even the madmen and murderers he fought. Nor could he make himself believe that this was the last he'd see of Doctor Octopus. Instead, he thought, *Maybe I'll have a few months without him this time.*

Or maybe not.

If he lives through that, I hope at least he has the decency to tell me how.

The jet banked. Spider-Man grimaced and crawled forward, defying the wind. When he reached the hole in the fusilage he jumped in, carrying the Chameleon with him. He wasn't surprised to find the violent wind whipping the interior as well; right now, the jet was a high-altitude wind tunnel, staying aloft by sheer momentum.

Palminetti's voice exploded in his ear. "Spider-Man! Our instruments say something just detached from your plane!"

Spider-Man tapped his throat mike as he examined the semi-conscious Chameleon for wounds. The master of disguise seemed all right—battered, bruised, and in deep shock, but definitely alive. "I know all about it, guys. That was Doc Ock and part of our stabilizer!"

"How big a part?" Palminetti demanded.

"Big enough that I'm not gonna bother starting the articles in the in-flight magazines. The rest of the plane's a wreck, too. I have the Chameleon here. The Gentleman is—"

"We know," Palminetti said. "The real Fiers is back at the airport. He died of gunshot wounds two minutes ago."

"Your people?"

"No. We found him that way."

Spider-Man wished he could be surprised by this development. He'd suspected something like that as soon as he'd realized it was the Chameleon, and not the Gentleman, at the controls of the jet. He wished he could feel satisfaction at the death of the man who'd arranged the deaths of his parents, instead of frustration at all the questions that might now remain forever unanswered. But he was not wired that way, and he had other things to worry about right now—among them, the screaming of his spider-sense and what it seemed to say about the jet's sudden serious list to the right. "So what do your doodads have to say about how we're doing?"

"The good news is that whatever just happened broke off the circular course you were flying and gave you a new heading southeast, away from Manhattan. The bad news is that it isn't going to last long. Assuming the damage you've already suffered doesn't make you fall apart in mid-air before you get that far, you'll probably make it as far as the Atlantic.

Spider-Man web-cocooned the Chameleon and strapped him into one of the few seats not smashed by Ock's rampage. "Will it be far enough?"

There was a moment of silence as Palminetti digested the question.

Then the crisis analyst said: "Assuming the storm continues blowing out to sea, keeping the Catalyst away from the mainland before it dissipates . . . and assuming that you still have a pilot capable of keeping that crate in the air as long as possible . . . yes, webslinger. It will be enough. But on the other hand . . . even assuming you survive the crash, or rig some kind of workable parachute, the chances of us getting you out of that chop before you drown or die of hypothermia have got to be less than one in—"

"That," Spider-Man said, "is one I don't wanna know. Keep tracking us. I'll be back in touch in a few minutes."

He tapped the throat mike and fought the bucking floor and turbulent air all the way to the cockpit.

Conditions there were better, but still a long way from good. Pity was at the wheel, her brow furrowed, her neck corded with the effort of keeping the crippled aircraft steady. She spared a nanosecond's glance at Spider-Man, confirming that it was indeed him and not Octavius, before turning her attention back to the impossible task before her. She looked like she knew what she was doing. Spider-Man wondered just how often she'd been required to pilot planes without the voice that would have permitted her contact with the ground, and decided it was a question best left for another time.

The jet bucked again, the cabin behind them resonating with the shriek of tortured metal. Spider-Man winced as the telltale tingling at the base of his neck underscored just how close the jet had just come to breaking apart. Then he sat in the co-pilot's seat, strapped himself in, and just to delay the inevitable, said: "Billy, do you like gladiator movies?"

She didn't react to that at all. Not even with the confusion he expected.

He hesitated. "You know which way we're headed, right?"

Her mouth was a cold hard line.

"Away from Manhattan. Away from your target zone."

She remained silent.

"You know that, and you're making sure that's how it stays."

No answer.

"Why?" he asked, desperate to know.

Again: not a clue.

It was maddening. She seemed to be doing the right thing, for the right reasons, but this could still be nothing but self-preservation on the part of a killer who knew when to cut her losses. He wished he had a telepath here. He couldn't remember the last time he'd so desperately craved a peek inside another person's head. But somehow, there was never an X-Man around when you wanted one.

The view through the windshield was a field of gray streaks.

After a moment, he sighed and gave in to the worst. "Pity . . . the Gentleman is dead."

That hit her. Her look of dark determination remained fixed, but her straight line of a mouth twisted at the edges, becoming a grimace. There was nothing lost or wan about her now, nothing that showed grief. There was just an anger as intense as anything Spider-Man had ever seen—though whether it was directed at himself, or at the man who had tormented her all her life, remained impossible to tell.

Then he saw the ghost of a tear glistening in her eye.

Mourning the Gentleman? Or feeling the grief that all victims of abuse feel, when those who have tormented them for so long die before the words of accusation can be spoken? Had she loved the old man, or did she mourn the same thing Spider-Man mourned—the lost opportunity to confront the old man with his crimes?

Spider-Man wanted to tell her that the Gentleman was not worth her tears. He wanted to tell her that she was free. He wanted to tell her that he hadn't changed his mind about standing by her as she faced the law. He wanted to tell her that the world was a cruel and dangerous place, which sometimes drove people like her to acts that their own better natures would have refused to permit from them. He wanted to say that he knew redemption was possible, because his entire adult life had been about atoning for the act of selfishness that had meant death for his Uncle Ben. He even wanted to tell her that she might have a family she didn't know about. But there was no time. And so he said the only words available to him. "I'm sorry."

That startled her.

He might have gone further, but that's when his damnable ear-receiver buzzed. Palminetti again. "Spider-Man! Come in!"

Spider-Man tapped his throat-mike. "Yeah, yeah, yeah. What?"

"Whoever's piloting that thing—"

"Pity," Spider-Man said.

"—has done a good job maintaining altitude, but you're over the Atlantic now . . . and our best projections say you'll be eating seawater in three minutes. If you have a plan for saving your skins, now's your time to implement."

"Thanks," Spider-Man said.

Colonel Morgan cut in. "We're not giving up on you, Spider-Man. Not SAFE, and not me. Stay alive and we'll find you."

"Staying alive is what I'm best at. But you'll find three of us—myself, Pity, and the Chameleon." He unstrapped himself, and asked Pity: "Any parachutes?"

She shook her head.

"I figured not. So . . . trust me one more time?"

She nodded, set the autopilot, and followed him into the passenger cabin.

The jet came equipped with enough flotation devices for forty passengers. Many of these were under the seats not destroyed by Ock's rampage; Spider-Man removed about two dozen at a dead run, tossing them into a pile at Pity's feet. He also stripped the overhead compartments of as many pillows and cushions as he could find, creating another pile which the windswept Pity regarded with aghast skepticism.

"Don't worry," Spider-Man assured her. "I know how hard a jet goes down. But I'm used to working with the tools I have."

She said nothing.

He began with the cocooned Chameleon, using his webbing to secure a layer of pillows around the unconscious villain's form. He used up an entire cartridge just burying that in a spongy layer of webbing. Five life preservers followed, each of them buried by another layer of webbing; by the time he was done, less than a minute later, the reinforced cocoon looked less like a human being and more like a sphere.

"That's triple-ply," Spider-Man explained, as he began the same procedure with Pity. "It's a weave I've used before—porous enough to admit air, but water-resistant. The good news is that it's kept me alive in freezing water before."

Pity, clutching a belt of seat-cushions around her body, raised an eyebrow.

"I was afraid you'd ask me that. The bad news is that my webbing evaporates in an hour. The flotation devices should keep us above water for a few minutes after that, but if we don't get picked up quickly, the cold won't give either of us time to drown."

She made a falling gesture with one hand.

"That's something else I'm working on. It's gonna be close."

He moved closer, to cover her arms with webbing, but she grabbed him by the wrist. It came as a complete surprise to him; his spider-sense, always wonky around her, hadn't given him any warning at all. Nor was he fooled into mistaking the move for a hostile one; one look at her trembling face and he could tell it wasn't. The presence of such fear, in this woman who had survived so much, surprised him until he looked closer and saw that it wasn't fear, or even strong emotion. It was the stress of fighting herself, of summoning the voice that had been denied her for lifetimes.

She said, "Buh."

It sounded like the first word spoken like a toddler: both thick and unformed.

"B-buh," she tried again, this time almost choking on it. She closed her eyes and forced it out. "Baaaa." The word choked off in mid-vowel. She grimaced in frustration and tried a last time, "Baaaaa ... "

By the time that one choked off too, tears had rolled down her scarred cheeks.

Spider-Man ached for her the same way he ached for any other human being in pain, but the tingling at the base of his neck insisted that they didn't have time for this. He said: "First things first, kiddo. We'll get to that as soon as we're through with this."

She had time to nod once before the the cocoon covered her face.

He wrapped her in a triple-ply web-sphere following the same design as the one he'd made for Smerdyakov, quickly constructed a third sphere with the same number of cushions and flotation devices but with the addition of an opening large enough to admit himself, then connected all three with a series of web-cables and leaped with them through the gaping rip in the fusilage. He gave the leap all the strength he had, carrying them the equivalent of four stories straight up. The combination of turbulence and slipstream put a kink in his trajectory, almost arranging a sequel to Ock's impact with the stablizer. They cleared it, though, and as the jet moved out of his line of vision Spider-Man saw a violent churning oceanscape not nearly as far down as he would have liked. Web-cocoons or not, they were all still heading toward that certain death with a force capable of jellying them on impact.

He leaped to the top of the cocoon he might or might not have time to occupy and began to spin a broad, airtight sheet, anchored to himself and his crazyquilt lifepod with a series of strong cables. Spinning with one hand as he shaped his creation with the other, he only moved faster as it began billowing with trapped air. This one parachute would not be nearly enough.

Another, also anchored to the web-cocoons. This one larger, sloppier, spun with even more haste. More captured air.

An explosion up a couple of miles up ahead. The jet breaking up as it hit the water. All the Gentleman's treasures lost to the flame and shrapnel. The broiling hot gases banishing the winter for a few precious seconds. Hope for a shockwave. More to fill the parachutes. Probably too far away to make a difference.

Keep spinning.

Spider-sense an agonized shriek. Every instinct in his body shouting enough, you've done enough, save yourself while you still have a chance.

Still descending too fast. Another parachute. Steer.

Flames down below. Updraft.

Catch that updraft. Fill the chutes. Gain altitude. Don't come down in the fire. Give the ocean enough time to disperse the oil, swallow the wreckage. Hope the flames continue burning long enough to bring SAFE.

Another web-chute.

Flames behind them.

Still moving too fast. Waves like hungry faces reaching up for them. White churning foam. Seconds. The web-chutes rippling like things desperate to avoid the water.

Something splashing up at him.

Spray. Each drop so cold it struck like a little knife.

Gusts of wind. Lashing snow.

The three web-cocoons shuddering as they grazed the top of a wave. Bouncing upward. Almost flinging Spider-Man into open air. A think, keen wail, mysterious until he identified it as the Chameleon, awake and howling from inside his strange prison.

The realization that his own costume was no longer red and blue, but as white as the snow that fell on all sides.

Bleached by snow?

No. The Catalyst. Released by the crash. Reacting to the dyes in his costume.

Winds, blowing it out to sea?

Civilization saved, or not?

No time to think about it.

Ocean a gaping maw below him.

Below all of them.

Spider-sense. Peaking again. No more time.

If this wasn't enough, nothing would be enough.
Inside the cocoon. Fast.
Web it closed. Fast fast fast.
Spider-sense going insane.
Wishing he had made one big cocoon for all three of them. Hard to accept the Chameleon as roommate, but no other way to know how the others were doing. How they were weathering the crash. If they were alive or dead.
Keep spinning. Close that hole.
Make a cushion.
Spinning.
Click.
Empty web-shooters.
No time to put in another cartridge.
Spider-sense letting him know – here it comes.
Impact.
Breath knocked out of him. A force so powerful it scrambled his senses, robbing him of the ability to distinguish up from down. A sensation of overwhelming cold, leading to the terrible certainty that he hadn't done this well enough—that the cocoon wasn't watertight after all, that the ocean would still come in.
This was it. He wasn't going to make it.
Colonel Morgan's voice, shouting in his ear: "Spider-Man! Do you read?"
Response beyond him.
Tumbling. The sensation of flying. Another impact, almost as bad as the first.
More tumbling.
The Chameleon crying out in pain.
No sound from Pity.
"Spider-Man! We've lost your signal! Come in! Repeat!"
Another impact.

Waves crashing down on them like hammers.

"Spider-Man! Spider-Man!"

Please don't think we're dead. Or think what you want, but try.

Do what you can.

Save us.

Impact again.

More screams. Not the Chameleon's this time. His own.

No more super hero. Not now. Just the same terrified kid who used to run scared from Flash Thompson in high school.

Cold. Alone. Afraid.

Head pounding.

Concussion? Now?

Blacking out.

One last prayer before darkness claimed him.

Mary Jane . . .

Six SAFE aircars, detached from mopup operations in Manhattan and Long Island, flew as low over the churning surface of the Atlantic as they dared, skimming the wavetops as their respective pilots strained their instrumentation for signs of the survivors they all knew they weren't going to find.

Troy Saberstein, who had turned very grim very fast following word of the jet's crash, scanned the water obsessively, seeing nothing but mist, churning whitecaps, and curtains of all-encompassing snow. He was sure that the webslinger was dead, doubly sure that there was something he could have said, some advice he could have given that would have provided Spider-Man a better chance at life. This was nothing new for him; as SAFE's stress counsellor, he had seen many agents he'd worked with fail to come back from missions. But he always felt it like a personal wound, much the same way such losses were taken by Sean Morgan himself.

Vince Palminetti said: "It's been almost an hour, Colonel. The maximum projected survival time immersed in water of this temperature is fifteen minutes."

Sean Morgan, studying the storm-tossed sea through infrared binoculars, cursing with every aircar vapor trail that muddied his vision, said: "For a normal human, maybe."

"For anybody, Sean."

"He's survived extreme conditions before."

"He has to have some limits."

Morgan said, "And I'm not prepared to say this is beyond them. We keep looking."

The Colonel's voice, wound as tight as a noose, betrayed determination and nothing else. Some of the agents of SAFE, who liked to trade jokes about the Colonel being more military hardware than human being, might have mistaken his insistence for the mere perfectionism of a hardbitten commander incapable of seeing casualties as anything worse than a sign of sloppiness in planning. Saberstein, who had seen the grief of a bereaved parent finally catch up with Morgan six weeks after the death of his son, knew better. The man hid it well. But he took death—any death—like a slap in the face.

Palminetti frowned as he completed instructions for a new search pattern, then downloaded them to every other aircar in the rescue operation. "I still need you to understand the odds, Colonel. To believe he's still alive we also have to believe that he successfully bailed out of a crippled jet in blizzard conditions. We have to believe he managed to slow himself down before hitting the water, and that he managed to avoid immersion. Finally, we have to believe it possible to find him, despite visibility approaching zero and a storm system that by this time could have blown him anywhere within a couple of hundred square miles. The chances of him surviving the crash at all are almost nil. The chances of him being able to stay alive this long are also almost nil. And the chances of us being able to find him before he drowns or dies of cold are almost nil as well. That's three infinitesmals, multiplied. Calculate the odds and the number of zeroes after the decimal point exceeds—"

"Please don't give me a figure," Morgan said.

"I just want you to face the possibility that there's nothing to find."

"I've faced it," Morgan said. "But we're still looking. Don't give me odds again."

Palminetti indicated assent with a minimal nod, then returned to his search pattern.

Despite the climate-controlled environment within the aircar's ionic field, Saberstein still shivered like a man exposed to the subzero temperatures outside. He considered leaving Morgan alone in light of the discomfort the Colonel had always felt around him since their counselling sessions, but then joined Morgan at Palminetti's side. "Colonel."

The Colonel stiffened so imperceptibly that only a man who had seen him in full emotional collapse might have noticed it. "Troy."

"You're showing a considerably more than professional concern for the life of a man you claim not to like."

The Colonel looked nauseated. "Is that what you think, Troy?"

"That's what I know, Colonel."

"I don't like him," Colonel Morgan said. "He's disrespectful, infantile, obnoxious, and annoying. He doesn't give straight answers when stupid jokes will do. He doesn't do anything efficiently when a hotdog stunt will do. He doesn't think the rules apply to him. He has an ego the size of a planet and simultaneously a sense of self-esteem so brittle that I have to waste precious energy telling him that not everything bad that happens is automatically his fault. Worst of all, he's an amateur—with no training, no real knowledge of proper procedure, and nobody to answer to." The Colonel took a deep breath, held it, let it out with the reluctance of a man who wished he could have held it until nobody was looking. "He must have gotten his powers as a teenager. Nothing else could explain his appalling lack of maturity."

Saberstein, who agreed with the analysis a hundred percent, said, "And?"

The Colonel stared out at the pitiless storm. "And he does it for no money, no applause, no real gain to speak of, nothing but the conviction that the work needs to be done. He does it and he keeps his idealism doing it and he keeps fighting when any sane man would just lie down and die." Another deep breath. "I'm proud of everybody who works for me, Counsellor . . . including you . . . but I wish I had a hundred more like him."

There were any number of things Saberstein could have said to that, but he couldn't think of any that might have helped. Any reassuring lies he could have offered meant nothing, in the face of the far more eloquent numbers offered by Palminetti.

And then the sky lit up.

It was the kind of radiance that might have preceded the blast wave of a nuclear explosion. It banished every shadow, every patch of darkness, every cold and gray and hopeless aspect of the day . . . and though its sudden blossoming should have blinded the searchers, it did nothing of the kind. It was warmth, and hope: a flash of spring in the middle of an all-encompassing winter.

Then it went away, restoring the world to the furious stormscape that made sense.

Colonel Morgan said, "What the hell was that?"

Palminetti said, "I read no electrical surge anywhere in range. That was psionic."

The light appeared again, filling the world. This time it was beautiful enough to make Saberstein gasp. All thought of giving up hope disappeared as warmth infused him, caressing his skin, giving fresh strength to his bones, bestowing upon him a peace he hadn't known since early childhood. When it faded again, in favor of the storm, Saberstein was not surprised to find his eyes brimming with tears. He wasn't alone, either; even Sean Morgan, the original no-nonsense man, seemed about to break into a giddy smile. "Somebody tell me what that was," Morgan said. "Anybody..."

"Another psionic burst," Palminetti said. His voice, which his disability limited to whispers, seemed hoarse for a different reason, now. "That was almost like...being able to dance. I haven't felt anything like that since..."

"Where's it coming from?" Morgan demanded.

Another burst, the brightest and most wonderful of them all, intoxicated them with its purity. This one almost robbed them of speech... and it might have left them paralyzed with their goofy senses of well-being, if not for the epiphany that struck Saberstein with the force of a thunderclap. He whispered it, "Pity."

Morgan blinked. "Pity? But she never showed any sign of being able to do something like this. We knew she could cast darkness, but..."

He got it.

So did Palminetti, but it was SAFE's counsellor who put their mutual realization into words. "The son of a bitch. He must have figured that light like this was of no use to him. He wanted darkness instead."

Another flash. This one less intrusive than the others. They could still see the storm beyond it, and still recognize it as dangerous. The high winds, the whiteout blizzard, and the thirty-foot swells still represented a deathtrap for anybody caught out there—but even so, they no longer seemed quite as terrible as before. The light brought the hope that had been hiding there all along back into sharp relief.

The idea that any man, even the Gentleman, could feel such light, and see in the young woman blessed to command it only a potential victim and assassin, was downright horrifying. But as long as that light shone, Saberstein still couldn't find it in himself to hate the man. He could only find Fiers an object of—

"Pity," he murmured.

Morgan leaned over Palminetti's shoulder. "Tell me you can track this."

"Well ahead of you," Palminetti said. The screen before him bubbled with figures. "It's about four hundred meters away, Colonel."

"Get there," Morgan said. "Coordinate with the other units. I want every car we have searching that area!"

The light flared again just as the aircar banked to search its apparent source. It remained just as bright even after Saberstein closed his eyes in prayer, even as he imagined the hell suffered by a young woman with this gift inside her, who knew she had this gift inside her, but who had spent a lifetime being denied the chance to use it. He found himself sorry that the Gentleman was dead. He would have wanted to face the man, not to spit in his face as might have seemed appropriate, but to study what might have been an alien form of life only masquerading as human. He doubted it would make such greed and malevolence any easier to understand. He had faced other monsters in his days at SAFE, and it had never brought such understanding before. He supposed that in the end it was no easier than understanding somebody like Spider-Man.

The light faded, flared again, faded out and this time stayed out.

When it didn't come back, Saberstein said: "I hope we didn't just lose her."

"So do I," said Morgan.

"It may take a lot out of her," Palminetti said. "This cold—"

"—even assuming she bailed out without injury—" said Morgan.

"Yes," said Palminetti.

"The endurance it must take to stay afloat in this chop," Morgan said.

"I know," said Palminetti.

The aircar banked again. Circling. None of the three men were willing to speak, for fear of missing a cry too weak to carry beyond the storm.

"Come on," said Saberstein. "Come on..."

Another circle. Saberstein's fists clenched so tightly that his fingernails bit into the flesh of his palm. A million years went by. No sound. More circles.

Then Morgan said: "Did you see that?"

"I saw something, Colonel."

"Circle around. Get a closer look."

Pause.

"Where is it?"

"It was there a second ago. It keeps shifting... wait. There."

"What is that? Seaweed?"

Saberstein joined Morgan at the edge of the aircar.

Whatever they had just found was sudsy with a material that looked like foam, and as fuzzy at the edges as a lollipop dipped in lint. It might have been easy to miss if they hadn't been on the lookout for something, and they might have overlooked it anyway if not for the fortunate swell that lifted it up out of the trough that had hidden it, and the form of one semiconscious man, struggling to bear the weight of another.

The fuzz turned out to be webbing well into the process of decomposition, with indeed only a few minutes of life left to it. It might not have resisted evaporation even this long if the cold hadn't preserved it for the few additional minutes vital to keeping the two men alive.

The one who had been fighting to keep the other from drowning was a delirious Spider-Man, who was both half-drowned and half-frozen. His skin felt cold as ice when they pulled him from the ocean. He had lost all but one of his flotation devices as the webbing dissolved, and had been reduced to treading water. Although he couldn't have had direct exposure to the sea for more than a few minutes, his pulse was fluttery, and his body temperature was hovering somewhere on the wrong side of eighty.

The one he'd been fighting to save was the Chameleon, who had water in both lungs, was unresponsive to all initial attempts to revive him, and who seemed an even unlikelier candidate for survival.

Though SAFE continued its search for another twenty-four hours, there remained no sign of Pity at all.

EPILOGUE

No story ever ends. Life can be messy that way.

For those who survived, there was an aftermath.

The blizzard ended by midnight. The freakish weather maintained its reputation by following the storm with an unseasonal warm front. This did not exactly bring spring back to the citizens of New York, but the temperature did rise several degrees of freezing, and most people flashed smiles as they began to repair the damage that Mother Nature and the Sinister Six had done.

The rumor that the Sinister Six had in fact been seven, with the extra member being a mutant with the ability to summon convenient snowstorms, persisted despite denials by SAFE, the NYPD, and the meteorologists who had been tracking the powerful but entirely natural storm since before its earlier assault on Chicago. It remained a popular conspiracy theory, discussed ad nauseum on the Jay Sein and Cosmo the K show, until the next cataclysm hit town, perhaps all of two weeks later.

Spider-Man and the Chameleon were rushed to the SAFE

helicarrier for medical attention. Spider-Man, whose life signs were borderline at best, remained in critical condition for seventeen hours before stunning the medtechs with a somersault out of his bed. He refused an offer of further medical attention and accepted the offer of an aircar lift back to Manhattan. The Chameleon was transferred to Midtown General's security ward for further treatment.

The United States Coast Guard joined SAFE's search for the missing Pity. She remained among the missing.

Max Dillon, aka Electro, was returned to custody and informed of Pity's apparent death. The sonnet he wrote in memory of his departed lady fair was the subject of several academic conferences in abnormal psychology.

Doctor Otto Octavius, aka Doctor Octopus, showed up alive a few months later, though he typically failed to explain how. His next rampage across Manhattan caused the usual millions in property damage before the (by then) long-recovered Spider-Man put him away again.

Adrian Toomes, aka The Vulture, escaped from prison, knocked over a few armored cars, and was soon back in prison, once again vowing revenge.

Anatoly Smerdyakov, aka the Chameleon, turned up alive a few months after Octavius... but this time, changed in ways that could only be attributed to a major life epiphany. That appearance, in which he declared himself a fraud and his life a failure, climaxed in his apparent suicide in a swan dive off the Brooklyn Bridge. This was just too bad for him, since that day's delivery to his secret maildrop included a letter congratulating him on his brilliance at outsmarting the Gentleman and offering him a membership in the Macchiavelli Club. He would have been thrilled, but he never saw it.

Quentin Beck, aka Mysterio, received routine medical care in prison, where for a time he wrote off his persistent illness as a bad case of flu. When symptoms returned, worse than ever, he requested and received a complete medical workup . . . and was told that he had both lung cancer and an inoperable brain tumor. His vow to go out with his greatest scheme ever resulted in several tragic weeks for another New York vigilante named Daredevil. Like Smerdyakov before him, he ended up as a suicide, having accomplished nothing of any note in his cruel and wasted life.

A front-page publisher's rant in the *Daily Bugle* attacked SAFE for nearly burning down the city during an irresponsible training exercise, and Spider-Man for nearly wrecking the Empire State Building in a malicious act of terrorism. An interior story by Ben Urich got the facts right.

The body of Gustav Fiers, aka the Gentleman, was turned over to the National Security Agency, which performed extensive DNA testing to make sure that it was really him and not some unlucky imposter. When they acertained that the corpse was indeed Mr. Fiers, and legitimately, permanently dead, they turned it over to the city of New York, where he had maintained his last known place of residence. New York could not find any friend or relative willing to claim the deceased villain's body. He was laid to rest, an anonymous pauper, in an unmarked grave in Potter's field.

Dr. George Williams, who had devoted his life to tracking down the Gentleman, survived his long-time enemy by six months. He was buried alongside the bride who had been murdered so long ago, in a ceremony attended by hundreds of friends. Colonel Morgan spoke the respectful eulogy.

Rand-Meachum closed down the facility wrecked by the Sinister Six and re-established the liquid adamantium project in a new complex at a top-secret location in the desert Southwest. Dr. Philip Askegren resumed his research as soon as he recovered from his injuries, but resigned without results less than a year later. Soon after that all funding was cut, and all the data obtained up to that point was sold to Stark-Fujikawa for an undisclosed amount. The breakthrough remained elusive, which was pretty much a good thing, since it meant fewer indestructible shape-changing robots.

Dr. Cynthia Monella remained a field agent of SAFE. Her decisive action in taking out the Vulture did not prevent her from being placed on desk duty until she could be analyzed and judged fit by Troy Saberstein. Their sessions together were loud.

SAFE itself, as led by Colonel Morgan, remained instrumental in dealing with several major crises that threatened New York and life on this planet for many years to come.

Mr. Nathaniel Bumppo, the gourmand who got to see Spider-Man defeat Electro with a clever use of lasagna, returned to his apartment in lower Manhattan, where several months later he got to see the Punisher defeat a crazed Russian assassin with a clever use of sausage pizza.

For almost everybody, that seemed to be all of it.

But there was, still, a little bit more.

After a little side trip to retrieve his civvies from a certain air vent above Lindelmann's Bagelry, Spider-Man changed back to Peter Parker, then picked up Mary Jane at Jill Stacey's apartment so he could share with her the joys of mass transit back to Forest Hills. The journey was marked by many miserable sniffles from Peter and many murmurs of poor baby from Mary Jane. He wanted nothing more than to curl up with a bowl of hot soup, the love of his life, and the stupidest daytime TV he could find.

They didn't speak much about the final battle aboard the Gentleman's plane. Long habit had trained them to minimize discussion of his super heroic activities in public, even when they thought they were alone. It wasn't just to avoid being overheard, though that was definitely a consideration. There was also the fact that some of the things that happened to Peter in his "moonlighting" job weren't very nice, and strained their relationship even without Peter placing that particular subject of conversation on a tight leash. It sometimes meant awkward silences in public, but they always made up for it at home. What they managed at Jill Stacy's apartment was only the shortest of all possible exchanges. She said, "Pity?" He said, "I don't know." Then they hugged, and for a long time rode in pensive silence, sometimes sharing a few sentences about friends or the weather, the real unspoken topic of conversation between them being how good it was to have each other when the day was done.

The 800-pound gorilla topic didn't come up again until they were off the train and a block from home, crunching snow as they strolled arm-in arm through the quiet Forest Hills streets. One moment she was dishing the latest gossip about the messy romance between their friends Flash Thompson and Betty Brant, the next she leaned on his shoulder and said: "Are you going to be all right with this?"

He sighed, and spoke in a voice the texture of sandpaper. "I have to be, Red."

"That's no answer."

He fought off a morose sneeze. "No, it's not. But what can I say? I would have liked to meet Fiers face-to-face again. I would have liked to make him answer for what he did to my parents. I would have liked to find out for sure if Pity really was who we were beginning to think she might be. And I would have liked to get her treatment for what that old creep did to her; it would have been good to see if I was right about her still being capable of something better."

He shook his head. "But the one thing I've learned about this crazy business is that I don't always get to see the happy endings I want."

Mary Jane tweaked his ear. "Except for saving some lives, putting some monsters back in prison, and, oh yeah, averting doomsday yet again. Poor underachiever you."

"Yeah," he said. His wan smile betrayed the hint of an impulse to argue with her, to claim failure yet again . . . and to know that she would allow him none of it. He changed the subject. "You still have any of that mulligatawney soup?"

"From that recipe you got from your secret agent friend?" Clyde Fury had insisted on writing it down for him after the Sinister Six's Day of Terror. "Got some in the fridge. It'll heat right up."

"Good," he said. His hoarse throat made that note of approval sound a lot like something out of the mouth of the Frankenstein Monster; in another mood, he might have milked the effect, saying Soup Good, Fire Bad. But with the Carla May Mendelsohn mystery still hanging over his head, his reservoir of energy for such things was running about as low as it ever did.

They walked beside the front path of Aunt May's venerable old home, avoiding the path itself because their mutual absence during the storm had left it a sheet of glistening ice. (Better sand that before somebody trips, said the voice of the guy wearing Peter's Typical American homeowner hat.) Mary Jane got the door, and they went inside, finding the house a mite dim after all the reflected glare of the snow-covered lawns; home it was, though, and they both looked forward to a long lazy day of hot soup, friendly company, and Brick Johnson movies taped off cable . . . at least until Peter gripped her by the arm, shushing her with a look.

You can't be a part-time super hero's wife without knowing that look. She mouthed, what?

A gravelly voice carried all the way from the kitchen. "Don't bother, kid. I smelled ya comin' a block away."

Peter closed his eyes. "Oh, God. Not him."

Mary Jane could see from her husband's expression that he was still upset at the intrusion, but not frantic about the invasion of their home. "Who?"

"Somebody I know," he said. "It's okay, I think."

"Come on," said the voice in the kitchen. "I've only been waitin' for ya a whole freakin' day."

They approached the threshold of the Parker family kitchen. There, seated at the table reading a Joe Lansdale novel and constructing a miniature Stonehenge of empty beer cans, sat a short, but stocky figure in jeans, cowboy boots, and a checkered red flannel shirt with the sleeves rolled up. The exposed arms were dense with hair and denser with corded muscle. Two other elements of his ensemble, a battered brown flight jacket and a brimmed cowboy hat, rested on the chair beside him. The man himself was rough-hewn and of indeterminate age; from the freshness of his features, it would have been easy to mistake him for a man in his twenties were it not for the considerably greater age implied by the harsh experience that burned in his black slitted eyes. He was a man whose face had always seemed most natural curled into a grimace, but was now, oddly enough, smiling—a friendly grin framed by a pair of muttonchop sideburns cut to match the hair that flared to points at both temples.

Peter knew this guy. He had fought him and fought alongside him. He had seen the way he operated. He was not happy about seeing this man at his kitchen table.

The visitor favored them both with a wave. "Hey, kid. Ma'am."

On most other days, Peter might have exploded. Today he was too tired to show anything but grumpy exasperation. "What the hell are you doing in my kitchen, Logan?"

The visitor placed the latest emptied beer at the end of his aluminum-can Stonehenge, completing the illusion that the Parker kitchen table had just been settled by blue-collar druids. "Drinkin' beer. Readin' a Hap and Leonard novel. Waitin' for you."

"That's no answer!"

"Don't sweat it, bub. I ain't here to cause trouble."

Peter was still reluctant. "I just got back from a major blowout myself. I'm not really in any shape for a titanic team-up right now."

"From the looks of you, I guess not. Naaah, like I said, there's nothing to sweat. I ain't here to draft you into any secret wars. Just wanna talk."

"I didn't think we were exactly on visiting terms," Peter said.

"Which is one reason I'm tryin' so hard to be blasted civilized about this. Come on, I brought my own brews, avoided freakin' the neighbors, an' refrained from fillin' the place with cigar smoke. What else do you want?"

Still reluctant, Peter said, "Just talk?"

"How many times do I gotta say it? This is a friendly visit, for the sharin' of information. An' I promise you, you'll be thankin' me by the time we're done." Logan used a beer to gesture at Mary Jane. "Ya wanna start by introducin' me to the lovely lady?"

Peter remembered the wife shifting uncomfortably at his side. "Oh. Ummm." He didn't believe this. "Mary Jane, this is Logan. First name, last name, all in one."

"Like some of your model friends," Logan supplied.

"Yeah," Peter said, finding that clarification an added note of surrealism he didn't want. "Logan, this is Mary Jane Watson-Parker. My wife."

Logan raised a fresh can in salute. "Charmed."

Mary Jane squeezed Peter's hand a little harder. "And?"

"And . . ." Peter hesitated, then took the plunge. "He's in the business."

His wife was not calmed. "Not the newspaper business, I take it."

"Nope."

"And not," she said, raising her voice just a tad, "the modelling business either, right?"

Logan pulled the tab from the newest can. "Ha. That'd show a serious decline in the standards of beauty, all right."

"My . . . moonlighting business," Peter said, giving the word special emphasis.

"They call me Wolverine," Logan supplied. "I'm one of the X-Men."

Mary Jane's grip on Peter's arm didn't loosen, but her voice sounded a trifle less lost. "I think I've heard those names once or twice. What side is he on, again?"

Peter didn't take his eyes off Logan for a moment. "Usually, the right side . . . even if he gets even less credit for it than I do. But that doesn't mean I approve of him, or that I consider him welcome in our home. He doesn't exactly play by my rules."

Logan didn't seem to take any particular offense at that. "Ain't always your biggest fan myself, kid. (Yer wife's different; I love her movies.) But, like I said already, this is a friendly trip."

Mary Jane, still playing catch-up, said: "And he knows about—"

"Has for a while now," said Peter. "Since the time he met

Spider-Man and Peter Parker on the same day. See, he has a hypersensitive sense of smell that clued him in—"

Logan burst out laughing. It wasn't a sound that Peter had often heard from him, nor one that he had ever imagined. Usually, when fate required them to work together, Logan's demeanor was one of several possible variations on grim: either grim, or savage and grim, or world-weary and grim, or determined and grim, or just plain grim and grim. He wasn't quite as obnoxious about it as his teammate Bishop, with whom Spider-Man had once been stranded for several exceedingly uncomfortable days, but he had never struck Peter as somebody who ever laughed at all, let alone accomplished it with such sheer unguarded ebullience. "Sorry to burst your bubble, kid, but I knew who you were a lot longer than that. Since the very first time we scrapped, in fact. Could hardly miss it.

"You got your Dad's scent."

Peter couldn't have been more surprised if Logan had put on mouse ears and offered to dance the rhumba. "What?"

"You heard me, kid. We knew each other, back in the old Intelligence days."

"You knew my Dad," Peter said, in a tone as flat as paper.

"An' your Mom, of course."

"Are you old enough?" Mary Jane wondered.

"Part of my deal, darlin' . . . I'm a lot older than I look." Back to Peter: "Anyway, they saved my life more than once."

"My parents," Peter said, again without affect, "saved your life."

"Yeah. We didn't work together all the time, you understand—they worked for your guys, an' I worked for Canada—but we partnered on a number of joint operations, including the Croesus infiltration that came within a fingernail of nailin' your buddy Gustav Fiers for good."

"You partnered with my Mom and Dad," Peter said, his voice still spooky with calm.

"Yup. I liked workin' with 'em, too. Wouldn't exactly say we were friends—I wasn't the kind of guy who let himself make friends back then, and still don't make 'em lightly these days—but I liked them. They were good people."

"You're not kidding," Peter said, in the manner of a man confronted by sentences that refused to parse.

"That's right. Fact, I was standin' right next to your Dad in the hospital, that day the Doctor gave him the news that your Mom was pregnant with you." Logan popped yet another pull-tab. "You know, I was the first guy to congratulate him, but I don't think he heard me. I never saw a spy that tough turn to so much mush so fast."

That did it. Peter rolled his eyes and addressed the ceiling. "Wolverine knew my Mom and Dad. Wolverine partnered with my Mom and Dad. Wolverine was the first guy to congratulate my Dad when the Doctor gave him the news that my Mom was pregnant with me. Wolverine's practically my Uncle. That's it, world. I only thought the Beyonder using my bathroom was the last straw. I only thought the talking duck was the last straw. I only thought the Disk Jockey was the last straw. As of this moment, I have just reached my lifetime saturation point."

He might have gone on from there, but that's when Mary Jane gave his shoulder a calming squeeze, said, "Oh, hush," and moved past him. Her smile, as she extended her hand to Logan, was warm and genuine. "It's always a pleasure to meet one of my husband's co-workers—as long as they are, in fact, on the same side; we haven't had much luck with the other kind. Tell me: Do you prefer to be called Logan or Mr. Logan?"

Logan shook her hand. "Logan's fine."

"Then why don't we move this conversation into the living room? We might as well get comfortable while you say whatever it is you've come to say. If you want, I'll even whip you up something to nibble on."

"My wife," Peter said, still eyeing the ceiling in the manner of a man who imagined himself addressing a silent observer on the moon, "just invited Wolverine to have munchies in my Aunt May's living room."

"Never mind him." Mary Jane gave Logan an apologetic shrug. "He's had a rough day."

Logan just shook his head. "Darlin'... you can't spend much time in this business without having a bunch of days like it."

The little gathering repaired to the Parker living room. At Mary Jane's urging, Peter went off to change into fresh clothes that didn't smell of bagels. Logan settled into a battered green recliner that had once been a favorite of Peter's Uncle Ben and began to page through WEBS, a coffee-table book of Peter's Spider-Man photography. Mary Jane, showed him an album containing the recently discovered photos of the elder Parkers, and Logan paged through that a little bit, too, sometimes smiling, sometimes grimacing at the waste. After a bit: "Ain't seen these faces for a while. Brings back old times."

"Good times?" she asked.

"Not always, in that business. I know this Chinese fella calls it a game of deceit and death, an' he's pretty much right about that. But sometimes you deal with folks who still have a sense of honor, an' still try to do the right thing. Folks like the Parkers who still have their souls. That doesn't happen nearly often enough." Logan shook his head. "It's a lot like this business your hubby and I work at, I guess."

"In a lot of ways," Mary Jane said, with feeling.

"It must help him to have somebody like you to support him when he gets home."

"My husband and I support each other, Logan."

"That's what I hear," Logan said. He cocked an appraising eye at her. "Y'know, darlin'... I don't know if the kid ever told you this, but I have a partner named Bishop who shared a few rough days with your hubbie a few months back. Bish says Spidey talked about nothin' else but gettin' home to the missus. Now that we've met, I'm beginnin' to understand why. You're actually able to handle this crap."

"I try," said Mary Jane.

"I get the idea you do more than try. I get the idea you're good at it.—You know, you look a little bit like this other partner of mine, named Jean..."

Peter came back, dressed in loose gray sweatpants, a white pullover, and a dungaree jacket. His hop over the back of the sofa, which placed him at Mary Jane's side, seemed no more deft than that which might have been accomplished by any suburban showoff his age; his recent dunking really had taken a lot out of him.

He sat there a moment, as boggled by Logan's casual demeanor here as he had been in the kitchen. The man he'd encountered so many times when he was Spider-Man was a snarling, ill-tempered, catchphrase-spouting savage, as grim in his outlook on life as the Punisher before his morning coffee. This guy was still rough-edged, still dangerous... and still, Peter had to remind himself, a killer, which Spider-Man had never allowed himself to be... but he was also, in his rough-hewn affability, something hard to recognize in the Wolverine Spider-Man had known. Likeable.

Maybe that explained a lot about why he'd lasted with the X-Men for so long.

Disturbed, Peter said: "So. You knew my parents."

Logan flashed a grin. "Never saw the point in tellin' you before, webhead—figured, the way we usually get along, it woulda just upset you for no reason."

"You're right about that," Peter said. "But I'd appreciate it if you didn't call me Webhead when I'm in civvies."

Logan nodded at that. "Fair enough, kid."

"That," said Peter, "is not much of an improvement."

"Tough," Logan said, with a genial just-kidding wink that Peter never would have expected from him. "Anyhow... kid... in case you're wonderin' why I happened to come today, I just got back from a little dustup outa town, and I found a message from one of my sources in the Intelligence Community. He's one of these spotters I got, here and there, payin' back old favors by givin' me heads-up whenever they hear something about one of my hot topics. Most of 'em mutant issues, of course..."

"Of course," said Peter.

"... but some other things, old business like your Mom and Dad among them. And when he told me that you were havin' your pal Urich askin' questions about what your folks did in Prague... an' about Carla May Mendelsohn in particular... well, between that an' the entirely separate news that you and SAFE were tanglin' with Gustav Fiers, who's been on my unfinished-business list for years, I had a number of good reasons to rush right here. The very least among them, that you deserve some answers."

"I appreciate that." And how. Under the circumstances, Peter could only marvel at the depth of the gratitude he felt for Logan, whose ruthless tactics had always rendered him an uneasy ally at best. Glancing at Mary Jane, to steel himself for the truth, he let the greatest of his questions burst from him like a miniature explosion: "Was she Pity?"

Logan took that with all the aplomb of a man receiving a surprise slap across the face. "You mean, the one who was working with your pals the Six?"

"Yes. Her."

There was a moment of awkward silence, at that one.

And then Logan heaved a deep sigh. "Aw, cripes. Kid. It never even occurred to me that you might be thinkin' that. Is that what you thought, all this time?"

"She was the right age," Peter said. "The Gentleman had her parents killed just like mine. And though there's nothing genetic about my powers, hers mimicked mine in some ways. It seemed to fit. I knew it wasn't necessarily true, that it was probably a stretch, but . . ."

"Stretch ain't the half of it," Logan said. "Kid, I knew you were askin' about Carla May Mendelsohn being your sister . . . and I knew that Fiers came to town with an agent named Pity . . . but I didn't draw that connection at all. Jeez. No wonder you smell so nuts."

"Are you saying she isn't?"

"Yeah, I'm sayin' that," Logan said. "She wasn't Carla May Mendelsohn. An' she wasn't your sister either. You never had a sister."

For Peter, the words were definitive. He could feel in them the weight of truth, as spoken by a man who had been present when the truth was fresh. He remained unsure just how he was supposed to take that truth. He knew it hit him hard, but the roaring in his ears and the flush of warmth rippling down his back could have meant anything from overwhelming relief to equally overwhelming loss. Grateful at the very least for Mary Jane's comforting touch, he managed: "I didn't . . . ?"

"I guess I don't blame you for bein' fooled," Logan said.

"You saw exactly what anybody investigating their activities was supposed to see. What they wanted you to see: a couple of American expatriates raisin' a kid in a quiet neighborhood in Prague. But it wasn't what was really happening."

Mary Jane exhaled a long sigh of understanding. "It was a cover."

"Bingo." Logan favored her with a wink, then turned back to Peter. "See, kid, your problem is, you and Urich only asked half the questions. You found out that your Mom and Dad were living in Prague as the Mendelsohns, but you didn't check on any background the Mendelsohns might have had before your folks took over."

"Which was?"

"They weren't made-up identities. They were real people, a couple of Defense insiders with a baby girl named Carla May. They were goin' for easy money by using their connections to smuggle classified information out of the country. The FBI found out what they were doing only after the whole family, including the poor kid, got wiped out by a drunken driver in Baltimore."

Mary Jane winced. "That's sad."

"Happens all the time, darlin' ... but it doesn't always involve national security. Under normal circumstances they mighta been written off as a couple of little fish who escaped justice ... but then somebody in the CIA noticed that your parents looked a little bit like them. They weren't identical, you understand ... or even clones, which the scuttlebutt says you oughta take as good news. Just folks with similar faces an' body types, who mighta been able to pass for the Mendelsohns among folks who only knew the originals through photographs. 'Specially if the Mendelsohns first got off the merry-go-round for a while."

"Which is why they moved to Prague," Peter said.

"You ain't as dumb as you act sometimes. The suits ordered your folks to spend a year or so livin' somewhere out of the country under the Mendelsohn name. The plan was for your Mom and Dad to turn the local civs into witnesses to the Mendelsohns bein' alive and well. After a while, the identities would earn credibility... an' your folks, still holdin' on to those names, would be able to provide the creeps who buy stolen secrets with any incorrect information your government wanted to feed them."

"It's pretty byzantine," Peter said.

"Says the kid with the secret identity," Logan said.

"And ghoulish," Mary Jane said. "Using a dead family like that."

"It can be a ghoulish business, darlin'. An' don't forget—the family was used that way only after they first sold out their country."

"The baby didn't," Peter said.

"Yeah," Logan agreed.

Mary Jane furrowed her brow in confusion. "But wait—if the real Carla May was dead, then who was the baby girl the Parkers had in Prague? Don't tell me the CIA has undercover infants too!"

"Now, that's an image to conjure with, darlin'. Naaaah, no undercover infants. Just locals willin' to cooperate. In this case, a young mother whose hubby had abandoned her a couple of weeks earlier, leaving her penniless with a kid Carla May's age. The Agency moved her into the flat next door to the Parkers, installed a connecting door so she could spend as much time with the kid as she wanted, sprung for food and board and things for the baby, and paid her big bucks for the privilege of letting the so-called Mendelsohns take the kid out in a stroller once a day. For the baby, it was just all one big happy family. For the Mom, it was an opportunity to make enough money to give the kid a future. An' for the Agency... it was just part of the cover story... at least until they decided to pull the plug and send the Parkers to Paris. Wasn't much later that we met, actually."

Peter objected: "But the photos of my Mom pregnant... and holding the little girl..."

"The pregger pictures are fake. Easy to do. Just stuff to have around the apartment in Prague, to make the cover look real. The ones of your Mom holdin' the kid, well, I guess those were real enough. She woulda spent a lot of time with the girl."

"But she kept the pictures..."

"Why not? Think about it. After a year of pretendin' to be a Mom, she musta felt some attachment for the little tyke. This was a couple of years before you came along, so she probably took it as a dry run for the real thing. Your Dad pretty much felt the same way, I guess, which is why he felt he had to tell me about it, on one of the jobs we worked together. But please... kid... stop thinkin' that Carla May Mendelsohn was your sister. She couldn't have been. An' Pity wasn't your sister either."

"Then who was she?" Peter wondered, ready to punch something out of sheer frustration.

"I dunno. Never heard of her, before this business. I had some time to kill while I was sittin' here on my duff waitin' for you, so I used a secure line I brought with me to get some data on her an' the rest of this Six business from a source I have at SAFE. But that still hasn't helped me much... aside from giving me the idea that she was probably a mutant the X-Men coulda helped. But you say Fiers had her parents killed?"

"That's what he told me. He betrayed her parents to somebody with reason to see them dead. The same way he betrayed mine. From what he said, even the circumstances were similar."

"I can see how that might look like it means somethin'," Logan said, "but ya gotta remember that Fiers did that kind of thing on a regular basis. Maybe hundreds, even thousands of times. The folks he offed outa one grudge or another woulda been enough to fill a stadium. The kids he orphaned doin' it—and made a habit of goin' after once they grew up—coulda been enough to fill a small town. It don't mean they all came from the same family tree. Heck, even if everything he said was true, he mighta told you just 'cause he knew it was likely to screw you up."

"If so," Mary Jane noted, with a gentle hand on Peter's shoulder, "he did an excellent job."

Peter considered the long days of frustration and uncertainty, the moments where he'd doubted his parents, the fights with Pity that had left him wondering if he was fighting his own blood. He also remembered how the Gentleman had gone out of his way to taunt him with Pity's past. Had any of that been part of the Gentleman's plan? How could it be when Mary Jane had found the baby photographs independently? And how could it not be when Fiers had just happened to choose that moment to make his pilgrimage to New York? Could it be that Fiers had somehow arranged for the photos to be found?

His ears still burned with the possibilities when Logan said, "Yeah. Manipulatin' folks an' messing with their heads was what he was best at. I know he almost broke me on the Croesus, before your folks burst in and saved me . . . an' watchin' him get away on that midget sub of his almost broke me again." He rubbed his chin. "Wanted him as much as I've ever wanted any of these creeps, an' if you know my history, kid, you know that's sayin' a lot. Anyhow, when I was alerted to what was about to go down in Manhattan, I thought I was finally gonna get my chance."

Peter knew from past experience that Logan could be relentless when he got the scent. "Why didn't you go for it?"

"For reasons that come back to you an' Fiers," Logan said. "Because Fiers liked to wait for the children of his enemies to grow up, so he could go after them as adults..."

"He told me that."

"An' while I had no way of knowin' whether Fiers knew who you really were..."

"He did," said Peter.

"...his grudge against your folks meant pretty good odds he'd be plannin' an attack on your family sometime before he left town."

Peter blinked. "I thought you said you only came to set me straight about Carla May."

"I didn't say that. I said that tellin' you went down was the least of the reasons. Which is another way of sayin' I had more important ones. Specifically, I had to get here before Fiers sent somebody after your little lady. An' a good thing I did, too, since it took me less than thirty seconds to sniff out the nasty radio-controlled firebomb he had tucked away in the basement."

The blood roared in Peter's ears. He found himself standing, the room spinning in ways capable of giving even an experienced webslinger vertigo. By the time he managed to find his voice, he discovered Mary Jane had leaped to her feet as well.

They both said, *"What!?!"*

Logan's chuckle was soft, amused, and as close to affectionate as anything Peter had ever heard from him. "Oh, you think I just left it there without doin' something about it? Don't worry; I took care of it right away. Snipped the wires and dismantled the components. It's now a soggy, harmless mess soakin' in your upstairs bathtub. I'll dispose of it when I leave."

The stunned Mary Jane plopped back down on the couch, shaking her head in pure information overload. "And you're sure it was Fiers..."

"Can't be sure, hon. But the timing's right; if the scent's any indication, it musta been set sometime this past week."

Mary Jane spent several seconds considering that before rising to her feet, crossing the room, and surprising Logan with a grateful peck on the cheek. "You said we'd appreciate this visit, and you were right. We owe you a lot."

"Skip it," Logan grinned. "Gimme an autographed eight-by-ten glossie for the kids I work with, and we're square."

There was an awkward silence while Mary Jane and Logan waited for Peter to add his own thanks ... but Peter, who had collapsed onto the couch only a second after his wife, was too occupied with another reaction entirely. He looked past Mary Jane, past Logan, past the walls that had been such an integral part of his life ... and finally, past his own shock and exhaustion. He looked straight back to a moment aboard the Gentleman's plane, that he had not had time to consider until now. He said, "Buh. Baaaah."

Mary Jane said, "What?"

"Pity," he murmured.

"What about her?"

Peter's eyes burned with such an unexpected heat he had to blink several times to free them of the tears that threatened to blur his vision. "That's what Pity was trying to tell me on the plane. Before the crash. She almost choked with the effort, but she tried like hell to break through the silence the Gentleman had demanded from her. She said Buh. And then, Baaah." It felt sinful to have been present at such a moment of potential redemption, and missed it, but the truth of it was too overwhelming to deny. "She was trying to say Bomb. Maybe she knew it was my house and maybe she thought it belonged to somebody else . . . maybe she couldn't even say the whole word . . . but she tried. She tried to take a step back."

Mary Jane gave her husband a tight hug. "It probably helped her, at the end."

"Not enough. She deserved more. She deserved everything that monster stole from her all her life." He held Mary Jane tight, taking comfort in her presence, drawing from her the strength that even a Spider-Man needed whenever things seemed too hopeless. "She deserved a chance to be what she could have been."

Logan didn't rise from Uncle Ben's chair. "Yeah. Don't we all.—But I should ask you one last question, kid."

"What?" Peter said.

"How long do ya have to be in this business before ya learn not to believe them dead unless you see the body?"

Peter, who indeed should have learned that lesson by now, was thunderstruck. He gaped at Logan, and then at Mary Jane.

Mary Jane wiped away a tear of her own. "Gee, Tiger. I thought even I had learned that one."

It couldn't be true for everybody. The Gentleman was dead. He'd been identified, pronounced dead, and shipped off to the morgue. The autopsy would leave him in pieces. Even Spider-Man, who'd seen his enemies return from seeming death time and time again, who burned with the terrible certainty that Dr. Octopus would soon turn up alive, unhurt, and more dangerous than ever . . . knew in his heart that the Gentleman had paid the final price. That much was a given.

But was Pity dead?

Peter didn't want her to be dead. He knew she probably was. He certainly couldn't think of any plausible way for her to have survived.

But he also knew that probabilities, and plausibilities, had never been deciding factors in his life. And now that Logan had raised the possiblity, he found himself unable to let go of the gut feeling that she was somewhere on dry land right now: lost, friendless, alone, and terrified by the first moment of (however tentative) free will she'd experienced in a lifetime of cruel control by another.

If so, what would she do now? Would she retreat back to the familiar confines of her mental prison? Would she manage to break the rest of her conditioning? Would she manage to avoid becoming as great a menace on her own, as she'd been when the Gentleman controlled her every move?

And if she ever met Spider-Man again . . . would she be friend or enemy?

Peter didn't know. There was no way to know. In this life, there was no way of knowing anything. Not until it happened . . . and sometimes not even then.

But he knew what he hoped for.

I'm pulling for you, kid.

But even that was not the end of it.

Several nights later, in the hours after midnight, a lone woman stumbled north along the side of a rainswept highway in Maine.

Clad in thin black pants and a flimsy white jacket, she did not look even remotely prepared for the storm. Indeed, her clothes had just soaked up the wet and the cold, hoarding them, keeping them close, treating them like they and not warmth and shelter were the treasures beyond price on a night such as this. Her gait was the slow headlong stumble of a woman who only remained on her feet through stubborn refusal to fall. Her insistence on hugging herself, as she drove herself farther way from whatever she might have left behind, was less the act of a woman who wanted to stay warm than of one who needed that grip in order to keep from falling apart.

She had some things going for her, though. The rain may have been like a wall of needles driven by the most furious of winds, but the warm front that had just swept the Northeast had at least spared her the greater hardships of a blizzard like the one she had survived. She may not have eaten for three days, but she still had a reserve of strength that refused to let her fall. There may not have been any lights on this stretch of road, but she walked in her own little patch of moonlight, that followed her with every step she took. And there may not have been any cars willing to stop for her before, but that was about to change, with the pair of headlights that now appeared over the next rise, and lit her up like a prisoner about to be interrogated.

The beams hit her head on, but she did not squint, nor did she make any move to get out of the road. She just faced those accusing white circles with an equanimity that might have been mistaken for apathy, and waited for them to bring whatever they had to offer.

The white van turned onto the soft shoulder and pulled to a stop. The driver's-side door opened, releasing a muscular young man in his early twenties. He was blonde and athletic, and dressed in blue jeans and a white pullover that soaked up the rain as completely as her own clothes had. He said, "Are you all right? You look like you're freezing out here!"

She allowed her chattering teeth to answer for her.

"Were you in an accident?" he asked.

More eloquent chatters.

SECRET OF THE SINISTER SIX

"Oh boy. Look, I can't leave you out here. You wanna ride with us?"

She considered that all of two seconds, measuring the advantages of comfort against the inconvenience of unanswerable questions, before taking the single step that ended with her collapsing into the blonde man's arms.

The swoon was a real one.

The blonde man lifted her with no trouble at all and took her inside through the set of double doors at the van's rear. The total population inside the carpeted interior turned out to be four people and one Great Dane. Aside from the blonde man, the inhabitants consisted of one other man (a thin guy with terrible posture, a mop of unkempt dark brown hair and a goatee) and two women (one a short-haired brunette in a loose orange sweater, the other a tall and shapely redhead whose fashion sense seemed devoted to purple). The Great Dane made a quizzical whimper as it stared at the drenched newcomer.

"Oh my god!" the redhead cried. "She must be freezing!"

The guy with the goatee said, "She's, like, totally wet! What's she doing out here?"

"That," said the blonde guy, as he grabbed a stack of towels from a box, "seems to be a mystery."

The dog ambled over to give the woman's hand an investigatory sniff. His tail gave one cautious thump as he whined again.

The blonde man handed a towel to the shorter of the two women, who immediately set about helping to dry the newcomer. "We're going to have to get her to some kind of shelter, figure out what's going on here . . ."

"Poor thing," said the redhead, who had just noticed the scars on the freezing woman's cheeks. "She looks like she's been through hell."

SPIDER-MAN

The freezing woman, who had seemed about to drift into unconsciousness, came to life at that moment. Grabbing the redhead's arm by the wrist, she forced hoarse words through chattering teeth. "N-no..."

The redhead winced from the unexpected strength in the grip. "It's okay. We won't hurt you."

"N-no..." The freezing woman closed her eyes, and with what seemed like an extraordinary effort, managed to say something else. "Not that. No... pity... ever again..."

The redhead understood then. "No. No pity."

"Just a lift from friends," the blonde man said, as he reclaimed his place at the wheel.

The freezing woman smiled then. It was impossible, for any of the passengers looking at that face, not to suspect that it was the first smile that face had known for a long time.

A little island of warmth, which was exactly what the freezing woman needed, the van pulled away from the side of the road, and roared off into the night.

And if she ever met Spider-Man again...

THE END?

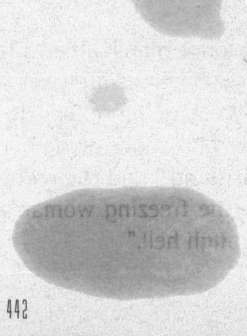